Staying Home
Is a Killer

Sara Rosett

KENSINGTON BOOKS
http://www.kensingtonbooks.com

KENSINGTON BOOKS are published by

Kensington Publishing Corp.
850 Third Avenue
New York, NY 10022

ISBN-13: 978-0-7582-1339-6
ISBN-10: 0-7582-1339-5

First Kensington Hardcover Printing: April 2007
First Kensington Trade Paperback Printing: March 2008

10   9   8   7   6   5   4   3   2   1

Printed in the United States of America

THE MOM ZONE MYSTERIES

by Sara Rosett

MOVING IS MURDER

STAYING HOME IS A KILLER

GETTING AWAY IS DEADLY

Published by Kensington Publishing Corporation

To Edna, Faye, and Marguerite
The three best grandmothers a girl could have.

Frost Fest

February 19–26

Dreams Take Flight

Beat the winter doldrums at the
Vernon, Washington, twelfth annual Frost Fest celebration
This year Frost Fest salutes Vernon's rich aviation history

EXHIBIT: Retrospective of Flight in Vernon
Historic photos and memorabilia capture the role men
and women from Greenly AFB played in aviation from
WWII to the present

ART SHOW: Local artists' work featured in downtown
galleries

STUDENT ART SHOW: Artwork from Vernon public
school students displayed throughout the Sky Mall
and Sky Walk

Free hot chocolate
Discounted ice-skating at Memorial Plaza Pond
Sales at downtown retailers and restaurants

Chapter
One

As soon as I opened the door to the 52nd Air Refueling Squadron I knew something was off. Penny Follette held open the inner door at the top of the incline, her smile radiating like a beacon in the dim light.

Penny didn't radiate. In fact, she was usually unnoticeable. "Penny, are you okay?" I asked.

"I'm fine," Penny said as frigid wind sliced across the back of my neck before the squadron's outer door thudded shut. I lurched up the steep hallway to the squadron. The incline was a safety feature left over from the Cold War. The squadron, located in the old alert facility at Greenly Air Force Base in eastern Washington State, had once housed rotating shifts of aircrews ready to respond to nuclear threats. I guess the steep walkways had been designed to slow down Communists raiding the building. They certainly slowed me down.

And I'm not that fast to begin with since I lug a small arsenal of toys, diapers, wipes, and snack food in a diaper bag, not to mention my twenty-month-old daughter, Livvy.

I squeezed through the inner door, dropped the diaper bag and my purse, a fuchsia Belen Echandia shoulder bag I'd snapped up from eBay, at my feet.

I'll admit it—I'm a bagoholic. I'm addicted to purses. They're my one indulgence. Well, that's not strictly true because I indulge in chocolate, too. But that's it. Only two indulgences. My fuchsia bag provided a nice bright spot on an otherwise dreary day, just like my purses provided the only stylish accent in my typical Mommy ensemble of sweaters, sweatshirts, jeans, and snow boots. I was too tired to coordinate outfits. All I could manage right now were purses with panache. Later, maybe when Livvy went to kindergarten, I'd try to accessorize. I shifted Livvy to my other arm. She wiggled and said, "Pen! Pen!"

"Are you sure you're okay?" I asked again.

Penny was practically glowing. She pushed her dull brown braid over her shoulder and reached for Livvy. "Hello there, little Livvy," she murmured. Even in the dim hall, in her droopy gray sweater and sagging broom-stick skirt, Penny looked luminous. "I'm wonderful." Her smile's wattage edged up another notch. "The most amazing thing has happened. I'm dying to tell you." She sighed, "But I can't. I promised."

She handed Livvy back. Her petite size forced her to look up at me as she grinned mischievously. "I'll call you this afternoon and tell you."

"Okay," I said slowly. In the year and a half that I'd known her, I'd never seen Penny look mischievous. And I'd gotten to know her pretty well since Penny and her husband, Will, another pilot in the same squadron as my husband, lived down the street from me. She was one of my most dependable babysitters for Livvy.

She slung her scuffed backpack off her shoulder and pulled a small gold bag out of a webbed side pocket. A crossword puzzle book fell from the pocket to the floor.

"Here. Won't be eating these anymore." She shoved the gold bag at me, then picked up the book and put it away. "You take them. Then I won't be tempted." The curly font on the bag read *Chocolate Covered Espresso Beans*.

I tried to give them back. "I don't even like coffee. You love coffee." My hands were full enough with Livvy squirming, but I knew better than to set her down. She'd motor away around a corner and I'd have to chase her down.

Penny continued to paw around in her bag. "I don't want them. Throw them away if you don't like them."

"I'll drop them off at Mitch's office. Someone will eat them."

Penny paused in her search of her backpack. "There is one thing I need to talk to you about." Her face still glowed, but her brown eyes were serious. "The thing last year." She hesitated, tucked a strand of wiry hair back into her braid. "Well. You figured it out."

I'd been embroiled in a search for a murderer in the squadron. "I didn't really . . ." I said.

"Yes, you did. You knew something was wrong and didn't let it go. I think I need someone to—"

The outer set of doors clanged open. Icy air gusted up the incline and snaked through the cracks under the inner doors. We shifted to make room. Penny stood on tiptoe to catch a glimpse of the flight crew laboring up the incline. Livvy went still in my arms, her attention on the heavy tread and voices that echoed up the vaultlike incline. Penny's face shuttered. She zipped her backpack, heaved it up on her shoulder.

I blinked at her abrupt change. Penny was back in her usual lurk mode, fading into the wallpaper. Captain Zeke Peters, the pilot, led the crew. His tall figure filled the doorway as he said, "Come on. I've got to be out of here in an hour."

The next guy, Staff Sergeant Rory Tyler, strolled through the door. "She's not going to leave without you," he said. His round glasses reflected the light from the hallway, and I couldn't see his expression as he held the door open for the last crew member.

Zeke smiled at us and strode down the hall, saying over his shoulder, "Yeah, but you don't have to ride all the way to Seattle with her if you're late, so get a move on."

First Lieutenant Aaron Reed, the copilot, didn't look at us, just ducked his head with his thin blond hair as he stowed his hat in the ankle pocket of his flight suit, then hurried to catch up with the other two men as they continued down the hall. Their heavy flight bags and pub briefcases bumped against their legs, giving them an exaggerated swagger.

As she watched the departing men, I caught a change in Penny's expression that I couldn't identify, a flicker of fear or anger in her eyes? "Are you sure you're okay?" I'd never seen Penny's mood zigzag. Her emotions were usually as straightforward as a ruler.

"I'm fine." Penny pulled her gaze back to me. "Later? Can we get together?"

"Sure. I'm going to lunch with Mitch, but I'll be home this afternoon." With Mitch scheduled to leave in two weeks for a forty-five-day deployment to the "sandbox," the nickname for the desert, we were trying to spend as much time together as we could. "What have you been doing today?" I asked.

"I've been over at the Mansion interviewing General Bedford for an article about Frost Fest." The Mansion, a large antebellum-style building complete with portico, held the wing commander's office and various base VIPs.

"You're interviewing the wing commander about Frost Fest? Is he on a committee or something?"

"No. It's a human interest story. Bedford's dad was stationed here in the sixties and flew B-52s. Interesting angle, from military brat to wing commander."

"What does that have to do with Frost Fest?" I was still confused.

"Every year the organizing committee tries to showcase some aspect of Vernon. Last year it was the River. This year it's the base. The theme is 'Dreams Take Flight' and there's going to be an exhibit about Greenly along with an art show with local artists. I'm putting together a press kit with human interest write-ups for the media."

Maybe her volunteer job was the source of her sudden animation? "So you like being on the committee?"

"It's fine. Volunteer work to keep me in touch." She shrugged. Obviously not the source of her excitement, from her bland response. "Still no openings at the universities," she continued. "What can I say? Middle Eastern art archivists are not in high demand." With Penny's fade-away personality it was easy to forget she held a doctorate in ancient Middle Eastern art. "At least it gives me something to put on my resume."

"And you're teaching art appreciation, too."

"Just continuing ed, though." Her mouth quirked down. "Not very impressive."

"Teaching is teaching," I insisted, trying to encourage her. We'd been over the woes of being a trailing spouse. Wonderful designation, trailing spouse. Makes spouses sound like we have a chronic disease that causes lethargy, but it meant we were trying to get a job at the new duty station. It was even harder for Penny because her skills were so specialized.

"Oh!" Her lips twitched up and her energy level zoomed up again. "I meant to tell you. Guess who showed up last week at my class? You'll never guess. Clarissa Bedford."

"The wing commander's wife?" I transferred Livvy to my other arm and leaned in closer. "Ms. *Cosmo*? Why?"

I'd met Mrs. Bedford during a spouse orientation flight, a flight that lets the spouses go on a local sortie to see an AR, an air refueling. It was hard to think of her as Mrs. Bedford, since that name brought to mind a middle-aged matron. Clarissa Bedford was anything but matronly.

When she arrived for the orientation flight she'd glanced around, said a vague hello to everyone in the vicinity, and then commandeered one of the airline seats. She'd tossed her brown curls over her shoulder and spent the rest of the time flicking through a *Cosmo*, red nails flashing each time she turned a glossy page. I couldn't imagine her being interested in art appreciation.

"I'm not sure. She added late." The wing commander's recent marriage to a woman twenty years younger than him had generated plenty of speculation.

"She called me the other day," I said. "She wants me to organize her closets." I run a part-time organizing business, Everything In Its Place, in any spare moment I happen to catch between changing diapers.

Penny said, "Wow. You'll know all the dirt on her. Keep me updated. Well, I'm off to call my insurance company again. They have almost as much red tape as the Air Force."

"What happened?"

"Didn't I tell you?" Penny leaned on the bar to open the door. "Last week, someone broke into my car, stole my radio and a handful of change out of the cup holder."

"That's awful. Where did it happen?"

"On our street. At least they didn't look in the trunk and find my backpack. I'd hate to lose my notes and my camera. I'll call you. Maybe stop by this afternoon."

"That would be great." Penny lived off base in our neighborhood along with practically every other member of the squadron. Thanks to the remodeling going on in base housing, our neighborhood of Windemere in the nearby city of Vernon was the most popular off-base housing site because of its small, relatively affordable bungalows and a convenient drive time to the base. Unfortunately, the multitude of detached garages tempted burglars. Stately pines and maples along with masses of mature shrubs in Windemere provided burglars with enough cover that garage break-ins were not that unusual in our neighborhood. I was glad we had one of the few houses with an attached garage.

I shoved the bag of espresso beans in the diaper bag, then grabbed the diaper bag and my purse before I wound my way through the quiet halls to the Scheduling Office. As I passed the squad's bulletin board, a short blond tornado, Lieutenant Georgia Lamar, one of the four females in the squadron, surged by me and entered the Scheduling Office a few steps ahead of me.

She set her steaming gourmet coffee down, tossed her gym bag under her desk, and threw a slip of paper down beside her cappuccino. "I can't believe I got a ticket. *Seventeen!* Two miles an hour over the speed limit! How anal can you get?"

"Took the shortcut through base housing?" Tommy Longfellow, chief of scheduling, swiveled his chair around and stretched out his long legs. "Hi, Ellie," he said to me.

"Yeah, but *two* miles?" Georgia ran her fingers through her short blond curls and shrugged out of her leather flight jacket.

"You gotta slow down, George. This is the military. Things change slow." Tommy's words were teasing, but there was an edge of seriousness to his tone.

Georgia snorted and whipped her hand through the air impatiently. "Things change. The Air Force has to get with it."

I set Livvy down and she waddled over to Mitch's office chair. Bundled in her thick winter coat, hat, and mittens, she looked like a small, pink-padded post as she shoved the chair and set it spinning. "Hey, don't I get a kiss?" Mitch asked as he crossed the room from a metal bookcase, carrying two thick notebooks. Livvy paused long enough to give him a distracted kiss on the cheek and then went back to spinning the chair with one mitten-covered hand. In the other, she clutched a two-inch plastic figure, a girl with short red hair in pink shirt and pants. Pink Girl, Livvy called her. Livvy didn't do anything, like eat, sleep, ride in the car, or nap, without Pink Girl.

"How was the vet?" Mitch asked me.

"Busy." My ears were still ringing from the high-pitched yaps of the poodle in the waiting room. "Rex is up to date on his shots. Ready for lunch?"

"Sure." Mitch put away the notebook and reached for his leather flight jacket.

I set the espresso beans down on the tiny table beside the coffeepot and the can of Folgers coffee (Tommy's) and the fresh-ground Kona (Georgia's). "Here's some espresso beans." It's a fact that inedible, stale food, like three-day-old donuts or hard cookies, left in any office will disappear within a day. I figured the beans would be gone in minutes, considering Georgia's love for coffee. Georgia's shriek overpowered my words. She turned from her little alcove by the file cabinet and removed a large framed poster that had been propped up out of view. "Very funny, guys."

The poster, a photo of a man in tight jeans clutching a dozen red roses behind his bare back, focused on the man's butt. Georgia twisted it around and put it against the wall. "You guys are gonna get me in trouble. Colonel Briman said I had to get it out of here."

"Then why were you so intent to get it up on the wall in the Hole?" Tommy asked with a wide grin. The Hole was the basement break room. It was adorned with plenty of posters of scantily dressed females holding beer cans.

Georgia rolled her electric-blue eyes. "Briman ordered me to get rid of it."

Mitch had Livvy in the chair now and was spinning her around. Her giggles had his full attention.

Tommy leaned back even farther in his chair. "I don't know why you're so spun up. They're just a bunch of pictures."

"They're smut. Soft-core porn. Why should I have to look at them?" Georgia turned to me, a female ally, and explained, "I wanted to take down everything, but Briman wouldn't buy that. Tradition! So I figured, fair's fair. The women in the squad should have something in there to look at, too."

"I don't know, George. McClintock doesn't seem to mind looking at those women a bit." McClintock, an angular no-nonsense sergeant, worked in Life Support. Rumors said she had a female lover, but no one knew for sure, since no one was asking and she sure wasn't telling.

Georgia looked at me for support.

I said, "I vote for smut." I wouldn't want to work in an office with photos of bikini-clad women on the break room walls. I feel guilty enough about not working out as it is.

The intercom crackled and a voice announced, "Aten-*shun!*"

As everyone in the office stood, I glanced at Mitch. "DVs," he muttered. "I forgot." Livvy made a dash for the door. Great. Distinguished Visitors were in the squadron and I'd brought our high-energy almost-two-year-old. A real career-enhancing move for Mitch. I scooped Livvy into my arms at the office's threshold and looked back at Mitch. He suppressed a smile as he and everyone else stood at attention. Oh well, if Mitch had remembered

DVs were visiting, he would've met me at the car. I stood still and hoped my quietness would transition to Livvy. She squirmed, then noticed the stillness of the office and looked around, her eyes wide.

The flight crew I'd seen earlier was caught in the hall and stood against the wall with their posture sharp and gazes fixed in middle distance, except for Rory. He adjusted his round glasses and checked his cell phone. His stance was sloppy.

They made an interesting group with the two shorter men, Rory and Aaron bracketing Zeke, who was over six feet tall. Rory and Aaron both were shorter and had blond hair, but everything about Rory was plump and robust from his barrel chest to his thick, wavy gold hair. Aaron, on the other hand, with his skinny build, beige hair, and narrow face, looked reedy and water-colored as he stood stiffly at attention. Zeke seemed poised to sprint out of there when they gave the all-clear, Rory slouched lazily, and Aaron stood so stiffly he looked like he was carved from marble.

An entourage strode down the hall with an older craggy-faced man in the lead. A group of people, their shoulders liberally sprinkled with eagles and stars, followed him. Lounging against the wall, Rory whispered something to Zeke as the DVs passed and Zeke fought to keep a straight face until the DVs entered the Orderly Room.

Someone barked, "At ease," over the intercom and everyone came to life.

"Who was that?" I asked Mitch.

"Bedford, the wing commander, giving some generals a tour."

"How did you know it was him?"

"I've seen him before. He flies with our squad sometimes." Mitch flashed me a quick smile. "Glad I wasn't on those flights. Come on, let's get out of here," he said as he shuffled some papers, cleared his desk, and logged off the computer. Mitch's philosophy on "face time," time spent in the presence of superiors, was less is better. He'd rather lie low and draw no attention to himself. "Less chance of screwing up when some colonel or general is watching," he'd said.

Tommy sat down and went right back to his argument with Georgia. "What about freedom of expression and all that? Don't photographers have a right to take those pictures? I've got a right to look at them if I want, right?"

Georgia didn't look at him. Tommy winked at me. He argued to irritate Georgia. He was one of those people who thought making someone mad was better entertainment than a movie.

"Sure, in your house," Georgia retorted as she sat down at her desk and opened a file on her computer. "Doesn't mean I have to look at them at work."

"You do here."

Georgia picked up her phone and punched numbers. "For now."

After a quick lunch with Mitch, I drove home, pushing the speed limit to reach our house before Livvy went to sleep in the Cherokee. Once she was asleep, even if it was for five minutes, that was it, no more naps for that day. I turned onto our street and crept through the scattering of pickups, vans, and cars in front of the Wilsons' house. Our neighborhood of arts and crafts bungalows from the twenties and thirties had plenty of charm and character. Gorgeous maple and pine trees towered over the homes, each with its own special touches. But modern conveniences, like dishwashers and garage door openers, were in short supply. The Wilsons had tackled a complete modernization and had a different set of contractors and work crews clogging the street every day. I edged past an oversized shiny pickup, an ancient blue van with a mountain landscape painted on the side, a van labeled BUZZARD ELECTRIC, and a dented Ford Tempo. Finally, I pulled into the driveway in front of our basement garage.

Despite the inconveniences, I loved our house. Its honey-colored brick looked cozy even on this cold day, and the graceful Tudor-inspired lines and the leaded glass gave it a uniqueness that we'd never find in modern tract housing, or in base housing, either. Our house sat on a corner lot. The lot sloped down at the rear of the property and the builder had taken advantage of the drop. He'd burrowed into the slope to create a two-car attached garage on the basement level.

With Livvy's head tucked under my chin to shelter her from the wind that made my eyes water, I crunched through the snow and ice that rimmed our driveway. Inside, I peeled her out of her snowsuit like I was peeling a banana and changed her diaper.

"Dogs. Woof, woof," she said, her face serious as I carried her to bed. She held her eyes wide open to keep them from shutting.

"Yes. There were some very loud dogs today at the vet." I snuggled her in bed, positioned Pink Girl on the night-stand, sang a lullaby, and tiptoed into the hall. I left the answering machine blinking 3 and went to get Rex, our mutt, a mix of lab and rottwiler, out of his kennel in the Cherokee. Since we didn't have another of suburbia's staples, a completely fenced backyard, I put him on his long tether in the backyard. He galloped through the powder, dug his nose into the snow, and flung it into the air while I dragged the kennel inside and put it in the kitchen.

I shut the kitchen door and stood still, trying to absorb the warmth of the kitchen. I worked my boots off and padded across the golden oak floorboards to turn up the heat another notch. Then I hit PLAY on the answering machine and scrounged in the pantry for hot chocolate packets.

A languid voice stated, "Hello, Ellie. This is Clarissa Bedford. You said to call you about a consultation. Next week, either Tuesday or Friday morning, works for me." I heard a trace of an accent on the message that I hadn't noticed in person. Southern? Or more of a Southwest drawl? I'd have to ask her where she was from. The machine stated the date and time, then beeped.

"Ellie. Jill. Call me. It's urgent." I smiled as I pulled out the cocoa and marshmallows. The staccato commands from the squadron commander's wife couldn't have been more different from Clarissa's slower, deeper voice.

I picked up the phone and dialed Jill's number, but my cell phone trilled, so I hung up the kitchen phone and dug my cell phone out from under a sippy cup in my purse.

"Ellie. Where are you?" Abby, my best friend, sounded breathless and shaken.

"I'm at home."

"I just got a busy signal," she said sharply.

"Hey, can't I listen to my messages? I was returning a phone call." The wonders of technology. Now when someone is too impatient to wait for the phone not to be busy they can call my cell phone.

"Sorry," Abby rushed on, "Jill's trying to find you. You remember that form, the one we filled out? With all the info? Penny never filled one out. They don't know who to call."

"Slow down. What's going on?" I was used to Abby's scattered conversations, but I felt a finger of cold that had nothing to do with the weather trace along my neck. Her trembling voice held a note of fear. Something was not right.

"I'm doing this all wrong." Abby took a deep breath. "Penny's dead."

An Everything In Its Place Tip for Organized Closets

Add more room to your closet with these ideas:

- Capitalize on unused space in the top of a closet with additional shelves for low-use items like extra blankets and pillows. Upper closet shelves are also a great place to stash Christmas gifts that you pick up during end-of-season sales.
- Dropped rods double your clothes space. Look for the kind that hook over the upper rod so there's no installation.
- Invest in a shoe organizer. The possibilities are as varied as your taste: Cubes, racks, and over-the-door-models come in a variety of finishes and styles.
- Multigarment hangers allow you to hang several items on one hanger.

Chapter
Two

"No, she's not," I said. "I saw her this morning. Just a few hours ago."

"Ellie. I'm sorry, but Penny is dead," Abby's voice transitioned to her firm third grade teacher voice.

I stood there staring at the cocoa box, shaking my head. Rex scratched on the door. Automatically, I opened the door, unhooked his tether, and he bounded into the kitchen, leaving wet puddles. "What?"

"Will came home for lunch and found her. She'd committed suicide."

"No. She couldn't—I mean, I saw her this morning. She looked . . . radiant." There was no other word for it. "She couldn't have done that."

Rex stopped bouncing and watched me with his ears perked up and his head cocked to one side.

"Ellie, I know it's hard to believe. I'm having trouble believing it, too. She was quiet and kind of mousy, but she didn't seem depressed. Anyway, Jill called me looking for you, since you knew her so well. Will's in shock."

Abby swallowed. "He found her in the bathtub with her wrists slit. So he's not functioning real well right now. Jill wanted to know if you knew anything about her family."

"No. Not really. I think she mentioned Michigan once. I'll call Jill." Rex came over to rub against my side, apparently deciding I needed some affection.

"I'm sure the police will sort it out, but Jill wanted to try to contact the family, too."

"Okay. Let me call her."

While I patted Rex's head I called Jill, confirmed that I didn't know enough to help her, and she hung up.

I twisted the cocoa box back and forth on the counter. I couldn't believe it. I walked back and forth across the kitchen as I reviewed my conversation with Penny this morning. She'd been happy. I was sure. I barely noticed when an icy puddle of water soaked into my sock. She'd been concerned about something, too, but only momentarily. She certainly hadn't been depressed.

I leaned against the counter and pushed PLAY on the answering machine, expecting Jill's sharp tones again.

"Ellie! I can tell you now." Penny's soft but unmistakably sunny voice came out of the little speaker. I felt that touch of cold again and shivered. "I'm so excited. I'd promised Will I wouldn't tell anyone until the test was confirmed, but now it's official. I'm pregnant! Can you believe it? I can't. It must have happened right before Will went TDY in January. I didn't even realize until last week. I thought I was late. I'm babbling, aren't I? I can't help it." She laughed, a bubbly sound. "I've waited so long. I'm going to find my baby name book. Call me when you get in. We can go shopping for baby clothes."

I put my head down on the counter and cried. The automated voice stated "Monday. Twelve thirty-four." After I wiped my eyes, I went to the little secretary desk that my dad made for me. I pulled a stack of business cards out of one of the cubbyholes and flipped through them until I found the plain white one with small black type: OLIVER THISLEWAIT, SPECIAL AGENT, OFFICE OF SPECIAL INVESTIGATIONS.

Chapter
Three

Thistlewait listened to the tape with his head bent, intently studying the countertop. I paced back and forth in the kitchen, tensing as Penny's voice, light and joyful, floated through the air again, "Ellie!"

It was too hard to listen. I hurried into the living room where I'd left Livvy with a mound of pastel blocks, her favorite doll, and *Sesame Street* on DVD. She sat in the middle of the rug with her back straight, swaying slightly from side to side as she sang along with Elmo.

I returned to the kitchen, sidestepped a stack of Livvy's miniature pots and pans, and belatedly noticed the pile of white clothes on the kitchen table waiting to be folded, the dirty dishes in the sink, and the layer of dust over everything. I got that self-conscious my-house-is-a-mess feeling and wished I'd at least picked up before I'd called Thistlewait. His tall form crouched over the answering machine, turning it in his hands.

Had I done the right thing? I could have called the police, but after last year and my contact with them during a spate of burglaries, I thought it would be too hard to convince anyone to take me seriously in the few minutes I'd have on the phone or in person.

"This thing have a tape?" Thistlewait asked.

"No. It's electronic." He hadn't changed much. Same curly brown hair, same tan overcoat, but today he'd arrived wearing a wool scarf and gloves.

"I need to take it with me."

"I thought so. Last time they took my vacuum cleaner and I still haven't gotten it back."

He shrugged. "Sorry about that. Evidence." He put the answering machine down and glanced pointedly at my mug and cocoa on the counter. "Don't let me get in your way."

I smiled and went to make hot chocolate. He'd hardly changed at all. Last time he arrived to ask me questions about the break-ins he'd mooched our leftover dinner rolls. As I punched buttons on the microwave to heat water, I considered my approach.

"There's no way Penny would commit suicide if she knew she was pregnant," I said and set a steaming mug topped with marshmallows in front of him. I leaned against the counter and sipped my own.

Thislewait sighed. "Mrs. Avery." His voice was a warning, tinged with weariness. "It is always hard to accept the death of a friend, even in the most uneventful circumstances."

I slammed my mug down on the counter. A milky brown puddle sloshed over the edge. I usually didn't know what to say when someone made me mad until about three hours later, but I had to let him know about Penny. I had to speak up. I gathered my swirling thoughts. "Penny adored kids and wanted her own. She'd had two miscarriages in two years, but she wanted a baby. Her doctor told her it was possible, but not probable." He raised his eyebrow, skeptical. "They were beginning to talk about adoption," I continued. "She would not kill herself if she knew she was pregnant."

"Calm down." Thistlewait finished his hot chocolate, rinsed out the mug, and balanced it gently in the sink brimming with dirty breakfast dishes. "I'll pass the info along to the Vernon police."

I'd learned more about law enforcement jurisdictions than I'd ever wanted to know last year. If Penny had died on base, his office, the OSI, would lead the investigation, but since she died off base the Vernon Police Department had her case.

Thistlewait continued, "There'll be an autopsy. It's just too early to make any leaps in judgment about her death. Maybe she had a spontaneous miscarriage or maybe she got some bad news about the pregnancy between her call to you and her death."

I gritted my teeth at his placating tone. "Was there a note?"

"Computers and e-mail complicate things. It'll take the Vernon PD a few days to check all the possibilities." He held up a hand to cut off my next protest. "You were right before, I'll give you that. Otherwise I wouldn't be here."

I heard frustration in his tone. He was referring to the death of a neighbor last year that had turned out not to be a natural death at all.

"Just don't jump to any conclusions before the evidence is in."

He unplugged the phone cords and twisted them around the machine. Then he wrote me a receipt. "So you'll get it back," he said with a straight face.

At the door he turned back to me, his voice laced with caution. "I'll let you know what happens. The Vernon police will probably keep me in the loop as a courtesy. In the meantime, don't get wrapped up in this."

That made me clamp my teeth together again. I didn't ask Penny to call me right before she died, did I? He thought I was a snoop and a busybody. But then he wiped the anger right out of me when he said sincerely, "I'm sorry for your loss."

With the anger gone, that empty, dark feeling flooded through me again as I closed the door. Penny was gone. I clicked the deadbolt into place and surveyed the scattered toys and the film of dust on every surface. Trivial details. Forget dusting. I'd play all afternoon with Livvy.

I'd told Mitch about Penny and he'd come home from the base as soon as he could. We'd spent the afternoon playing with Livvy and then I'd thrown together some sandwiches for dinner, but I couldn't eat mine.

I put my sandwich back down on the plate and said, "I can't believe Penny's gone. Just a few hours ago I was talking to her. And she was so happy." I felt my throat go scratchy and my eyes watered.

Mitch squeezed my hand. "I know." He didn't say much. All that military training helped him hide his emotions better than I could hide mine, but I could see the sympathy in his look.

"Where Pen go?" Livvy asked.

Mitch and I exchanged a look. We had to tell Livvy her favorite sitter was gone. I hadn't even thought about how I'd do that. Parenting is like that—a three-word question from Livvy and I'm ripped out of my grief, casting about for uncomplicated answers to one of life's most unfathomable issues.

As always, I had to parent on the fly. "Penny's gone to heaven. We won't see her anymore."

"Why she go?"

The question and her puzzled blue gaze undid me. My throat prickled again and I felt the tears I'd fought off earlier seep out of the corners of my eyes. How did I answer?

Mitch said, "We don't always know why things happen."

"Pen no go." She'd picked up on the sadness radiating from me and her eyes turned glassy.

I swallowed hard and wiped my checks. "I know. I didn't want her to go either. But heaven is a nice place." I pulled my paper napkin out of my lap and blew my nose. "There's no crying there. No sadness. No one hurts."

Livvy blinked hard and wrinkled her brow. "No boo-boos?" she asked, her tone laced with doubt.

"No. No boo-boos."

She nodded slowly. "Okay."

Mitch wiped his hand down over his face and I knew he was wiping away a tear, although he'd never admit it. "Okay. Dad's taking everyone to Cobblestone."

I shrugged into my coat, bundled up Livvy, and we headed out for a short drive to the trendy little café a few blocks over. It was the kind of place with a patio and umbrella-topped tables outside. Tonight the umbrellas were gone and the wrought-iron furniture looked stark and cold. I felt better as I stepped in the door where mingled smells of coffee and chocolate greeted me. "What do you want to eat?" Mitch asked.

I didn't care. "You pick something," I said. I found a table close to the fireplace and hooked the diaper bag over the chair. After I strapped Livvy in the high chair, I studied the watercolors and oils by local artists on the brick walls.

"Fire," Livvy informed me, then shook her head. "No, no." She understood playing by the fireplace was off-limits. Mitch returned, balancing thick white plates with a blueberry muffin, apple pie, and triple chocolate cake.

The bells over the door jingled and Oscar Marsali walked in with a newspaper tucked under his arm. Mitch raised an eyebrow at me and I said, "Yeah, invite him over. You can talk turkey."

Marsali lived down the street. A widower and a retired linguistics professor, he spent most of his time powering his riding lawn mower around his lawn in the summer, whether the grass needed to be cut or not. Mitch had stopped to chat with him one day when he took Rex out for a walk. When Marsali had found out Mitch was back from a TDY to Turkey, a place that fascinated Marsali, they had a long conversation. Now Mitch stopped to talk to Marsali every few days.

Mitch waved and Marsali collected a cup of coffee, then stepped delicately, despite his squat build, through the maze of tables to ours. He dropped his newspaper, folded open to the crossword, on the table and sat down with us. "Hello. How are you on this cold night?" He removed his cap with ear flaps and ran his hands over thinning, wiry gray hair, which grew over his collar. His glasses with large lenses were popular around 1980 and magnified the bags under his eyes. Even without the cap flapping around his face, his expression reminded me of a sad-eyed basset hound.

"Fine. How's the mall-walking?" I asked, determined not to focus on my grief. Marsali was going through hobbies as fast as he could think of them. He liked crosswords, but he'd said, "I can't do them all day. I have to find something else." So he'd run through chess and bridge, then moved on to mall-walking.

"Boring. Container gardening is next at the senior center."

I broke the muffin into pieces for Livvy, but she pointed to my plate. "Cake!" she demanded.

Marsali smiled at Livvy. "Ah, it's good to be around kids. They make you smile." He sipped his coffee. "To tell you the truth, I'm a little restless tonight. That news about Penny. It's horrible. It's got me shaken up."

I blinked. Normally silent and reclusive as he was, this was major soul-baring for Marsali. He always seemed to have an underlying sadness, kind of a lost look. He once told me he missed his wife, and I gathered that he still struggled with her death, even after two years. Although he always looked melancholy, he usually didn't mention his grief. He plowed on through his days, determined to avoid pity. "I didn't know you knew Penny," I said.

"Well, we do live on the same street. I used to say hello to her and William when we happened to see each other, but once I talked to them at the bookstore. They were looking at crossword puzzle books. So we talked after that. They had me over for dinner. I gave them tomatoes from my garden last summer." His garden had been another of his attempts to find an outlet during retirement.

"That she died is terrible, but to think she committed suicide . . ." He buried his nose in his mug.

Mitch gave me a warning look, which I interpreted to mean, "Don't say anything about the answering machine."

Ah, the joys of nonverbal marital communication. I looked back at him and conveyed silently, "Of course, I won't say anything." Instead, I said, "I knew her, too. She used to babysit for Livvy. I can't believe it either."

Marsali set down his mug. "She just didn't seem depressed at all when she called this morning."

An Everything In Its Place Tip for Organized Closets

Before you dive into organizing your closet, take a few minutes to gather some items you'll need:

- Large boxes or plastic bags (leaf bags work great) for throwaway and give-away items.
- Pad and pencil to jot notes.
- Measuring tape in case you decide you need additional shelving.

Chapter
Four

"She called this morning?" I asked.

Marsali nodded. "She wanted to come by this afternoon. She did that sometimes. Said she had a hard puzzle for me to look at, but she never came by."

"A puzzle?" Something, a filmy question, teased at the edge of my consciousness.

"A crossword," Marsali said. "Sometimes she'd come by and look things up in my books. I have several foreign language dictionaries. She'd usually bring something from here, too. A cinnamon roll or a bagel."

I swallowed hard. "That sounds just like her." Then the vague thought crystallized. I'd been so wrapped up processing the fact that Penny was dead and then focused on convincing Thistlewait to check into the message that I hadn't had time to think about why someone made her death look like a suicide. No one accidentally slashes their wrists.

"I saw her, too, this morning. She was happy." I wondered who else Penny had spoken to this morning. "It was about eleven o'clock when I saw her."

"She called me right at lunch. I was sitting down to my tomato soup and the noon news. She said she'd be by before three."

"I wonder where she went between eleven and noon."

Mitch gave me a warning look.

"Cake! Cake! *Cake!*"

I fed Livvy a sliver of my cake and then I quickly finished the last bite. "All gone," I told her.

"So Penny did crosswords. I didn't know that," Mitch said, obviously trying to steer the conversation to safe ground.

"William enjoyed them as well, but he never stopped by."

"Umm. I never would have guessed that." I had trouble picturing Will even reading a newspaper, much less filling in a crossword. Of course, I tried to spend as little time as possible around Penny's rowdy, knuckle-cracking spouse. I guess I could have missed some of his finer points.

Livvy's foot thumped me in the shin as she flutterkicked her feet. She stuck her fingers in her mouth and stared, glassy-eyed, at Marsali's mug. Then she jerked her fingers out of her mouth and grabbed for the silverware. I snatched it away. "Time for us to go. Livvy's getting tired."

"Sure. Good to see you." Marsali pulled out a silver pen and adjusted his glasses to read the clues for the Across section.

"Maybe I'll drop by some afternoon," I said as I zipped Livvy into her coat. "Cinnamon rolls in the afternoon sound great."

Marsali pushed his huge glasses up his nose and smiled. "I'll look for you."

On Wednesday the cold front moved on and glaring sunshine bounced off the snowbanks and reflected off the sheets of ice. I sat in our overstuffed chair with Livvy on my lap. Sunlight covered us like a warm quilt as I turned the pages of our picture books from the library. "Okay, pick another one," I said.

"Spot! Eed, Spot!" Livvy commanded, meaning "Read, Spot."

"Okay, for the seventh time today." I opened the book with the smallest sigh I could manage. The phone rang when we were on page 3.

"Ellie. These people won't leave me alone."

"Who is this?" I didn't recognize the low, garbled voice.

"Will Follette. Penny was always going on and on about you. How smart you are and how you always knew what to do."

I'd had a high GPA in college, but I always knew what to do? I didn't think so. "What do you need?" I asked cautiously.

"The phone's ringing all the time. They all want something. I'm going out of town to bury my wife and don't have time for this crap. My wife is dead. I don't have time to return their stupid messages." His voice wavered up and down.

"Just a minute."

I pressed the phone into my shoulder and leaned over the arm of the chair to talk to Abby, who was using my computer because hers had crashed. "This is Will, Penny's husband. He needs help sorting out some messages for Penny. He sounds pretty upset. Could you watch Livvy while I run over there and see what he needs?"

"Sure." She spun around on the chair and headed to the living room. "I haven't got to read to anyone for two days." Abby was out of seclusion after suffering through a vicious forty-eight-hour flu. She'd stayed home today from her third grade class to make sure she was completely over it and get caught up on grading papers and lesson plans.

Outside, it was bright, but it wasn't warm. The snow wasn't going to melt any time soon. I crunched through the shell of frozen ice and the puddles of dirty slush as I made my way down the street to Penny and Will's house. Perched on the tiny slab of a porch, I rang the doorbell.

Will opened the door. "Come on in." He headed back to his green leatherette recliner and collapsed. Several beer cans on a rickety end table clanked together as he bumped it with his arm.

I took a seat on a worn beige sofa. The decorating scheme was a combination of bachelor pad mismatches and garage sale finds. Black and chrome modern pieces contrasted sharply with faded brown armchairs and the sofa that was way past shabby chic. A few pictures of military jets dotted the stark, white walls. The house had a utilitarian air, like the temporary austerity of a dorm room. The only splash of color came from rugs in the living room and dining room. They looked similar to the ones on our floors, so Will probably brought them back from a trip to Kuwait, Turkey, or Iraq. Those rugs and Penny's throw her aunt had made with various shades of blue fabric had been the only bright spots in the room. I didn't see the throw. I was kind of glad it wasn't there. I swallowed. It was hard enough to know that Penny wasn't going to walk out of the kitchen any minute. Livvy loved the fringe on the throw and Penny always pulled it out when we came over.

Will listlessly sipped his Budweiser, then lifted it toward me. "Want one?"

"No, thanks," I said. "I'm sorry about Penny."

He sighed and looked up at the ceiling. "Man, she was good to me. Better than I deserved." His gaze dropped back down to me. "And you know what? I treated her like shit." His eyes watered and he wiped the corners of his eyes with the back of the hand that held the beer can.

Silently, I agreed with him. Will always seemed to be gone. He was either out of town or out drinking. And if he happened to be home he'd never been there emotionally when Penny needed him. I shifted uncomfortably on the couch, glad I hadn't brought Livvy. At least he was a sentimental drunk.

He picked up a framed snapshot and brought it over to me, then wove his unsteady way back to the recliner. "That was when we started dating. Panama City."

I studied the smiling faces. The couple stood with their arms around each other. In a wide-brimmed hat and red tank top, Penny looked almost pretty instead of plain. Will's brown hair drooped down over his eyes. He waved a greeting with his ever-present can of beer in one hand. His smile was relaxed and seemed to mesh with his casual T-shirt, shorts, and sandals. They looked tanned and happy.

I set the picture down on a bookcase at my elbow next to a snapshot of a middle-aged man wearing a cotton baseball cap with flaps pulled down to cover his ears and neck. A knotted red bandana encircled his throat. He gave a thumbs-up to the camera as a smile split his face.

"Her dad," Will said, "on a dig." The background looked pale and dusty in blazing sunlight.

"He's an archaeologist," I said, remembering Penny had talked about him quite a bit.

"At least he was nice to her," Will said, "even if he didn't have much time for her. Not like her mom."

I searched the shelves, but couldn't find a picture of a middle-aged woman to match to Penny's father.

"Man, is she a piece of work. Pushy. No wonder Penny caved on everything. I couldn't even get a word in when her mom called about the funeral. 'Of course, it will be here,'" he mimicked in a nasal voice, complete with a disdaining shake of the head. "'This is where *all* her family and friends are.'"

"So the funeral will be in Michigan?"

"Yeah." He drained the last of his beer, heaved himself out of the chair, and lumbered into the kitchen. The refrigerator door sighed open, then slammed shut. "All out."

Thank goodness. "When is the funeral? You said something about leaving town."

"Friday. I'm leaving tomorrow." He dropped back into the recliner and absently studied the ceiling again while he cracked the knuckles on his right hand. "Never thought I'd be glad to be in the vault."

"What?" Maybe I should leave. He wasn't making sense.

"Yeah. You should have seen the police when I told them I was in the vault all morning on Monday." He switched over to crack the knuckles on his left hand. "They had it all pegged on me. Otherwise, I couldn't leave town. And right now there's nothing I want more than to get out of this town."

"Wait a minute. The police are investigating her death? It wasn't suicide?"

"No." He glanced at the beer cans. He probably had started drinking when the police brought him the news.

For once, I could understand him getting sloshed. "I'm sorry, Will," I said again.

He shrugged and wiped at the corners of his eyes again. "Yeah. They think someone murdered her. They wouldn't really say anything, but, man, after a few minutes, I knew where they were going. 'Did you ever fight? Have any disagreements lately? Where were you on Monday morning?'"

And Will was in the vault, a closed nuclear procedures training class. No one could reach you when you were in the vault. All cell phones went off and no one left. He wasn't a suspect.

The phone rang and he closed his eyes. For a minute I thought he would cover his ears with both hands like Livvy having a tantrum, but the machine came on and a clipped, masculine voice with a British accent asked that Will return the call as soon as possible.

Will dropped his hands and said, "That's Victor. About the exhibit. Can't they give me a friggin' day? Why can't they give it a rest?"

"Will, I don't mind returning his calls to see what he needs. I met him once when Penny and I were having lunch."

Will nodded. "Now, her archivist stuff, that stuff." He shook his head as if he couldn't understand it. "Man, she was passionate about it."

I realized he didn't want to deal with today's phone calls. He wanted to think about Penny. My respect for him, about at zero to begin with, went up a little. He seemed genuinely grieved.

His words reminded me of when I'd asked Penny why she became an archivist when the job market was so tight. She'd said, "Artifacts are so much easier to deal with than people. They never yell. Never criticize. And they never let you down." With the husband and mother she had, it sounded like Penny had made a brilliant career choice.

Will absently pushed the floor with his toe, rocking the recliner. He stared at the ceiling.

"Umm, Will, I'll take down the messages and figure out what everyone needs."

He nodded, concentrating on the ceiling. "I think she picked up some stuff for the exhibit. Not sure where it is.

Maybe the computer room? You can find out what everyone needs and give them their stuff. Let them in while I'm gone. You've got a key?"

"Yes. Penny gave me one when she locked herself out that time. I'll take care of it."

I went to the kitchen and made notes on the fourteen calls on the machine. Most were condolence calls, but a few, like Victor Roth, were beginning to sound impatient.

A page of grid paper held on the refrigerator with magnets caught my eye. I read one of the clues written in small cursive script on plain paper beside the grid paper. *Wild Goose* _____. Squared-off letters filled the blank squares beside the number 1 on the grid with *chase*, and then commented on the side *Too easy. Give me a hard one next time.* The square handwriting continued with a clue that read *pelt.* The cursive writing spelled out *hide,* using the *h* in the word *chase.* A note in the margin read *Here's a literary one.* The next clue read *Hills Like White* _____. The blanks for this clue began with the letter *e* in *chase,* but they weren't filled in. A note printed beside it said *Another clue?* This must be some sort of crossword game Penny and Will played, leaving each other clues and notes. I was surprised that Will had any interest in it. It didn't seem his type of thing.

I checked my watch and went back to the living room. "I need to get back home. I'll follow up on these for you," I said.

He rocked and nodded some more. I made a mental note to send Mitch down here to make sure Will was packed and had a ride to the airport.

I perched on the edge of the sofa. In my mind, I'd been going over and over my last meeting with Penny.

"Will, I saw Penny on Monday morning. She seemed happy."

"Yeah. We were gonna have a baby." Another tear leaked out of his eye and he didn't bother to wipe it away. "She thought that would make everything better."

I didn't disagree out loud with him, but when Penny confided that she wanted to have a baby, I'd tried to tactfully ask her if she thought that was the best thing to do, especially since Will wasn't very supportive.

"Ellie," she'd said, "I've always wanted a baby, someone I can love. And that little baby will love me back. If there's any way I can have a baby, I'm going to do it. He'll come around when the baby's born. You'll see."

I focused on Will again. "She was ecstatic, but there was a moment when she seemed upset. It was when a crew came in from the flight line, Zeke, Rory, and Aaron."

Will laughed, a full laugh. "Yeah. She was pissed about that, but I'm not telling. Sworn to secrecy."

"But you told Penny?"

"I'm not telling," he said in a singsong voice.

"Okay, well, she mentioned her art appreciation class, too. That Clarissa Bedford had joined."

"Penny told me. Clarissa wants to be cultured. Clarissa Bedford couldn't be cultured in a million years. What a joke."

He leaned back and rocked faster. That was the end of our conversation, such as it was. No matter what I asked I couldn't get anything else out of him.

Chapter
Five

As I walked home I squinted into the bright sunlight to see who had parked in front of our house. Thistlewait climbed out of his car, a plain dark blue four-door sedan beside the ever-growing snowbank that the snowplow tossed up after each storm. Balancing a pizza box, he stepped over the three-foot snowbank. "I brought you dinner. Figured I owed you some food."

"Great." I pasted a smile on my face, but I felt my stomach sink. Thistlewait was not a casual friend who just dropped by. Either he had questions or he had bad news. Mitch pulled into the driveway and we met in the kitchen where we sorted out coats, drippy boots, and introductions. Abby tucked Livvy into her high chair and avoided Thistlewait.

Abby had issues with Thistlewait, and I could tell she wanted out of our house fast. On the way out she whispered, "Call me. I want to hear all about it."

Mitch poured drinks and dispensed plates while I cut up a piece of pizza for Livvy. "This is nice of you." I took a slice of pepperoni.

Thistlewait devoured a slice in three bites, then chugged his Dr Pepper. "No problem. The autopsy's back on Follette." He grabbed another slice, then seemed to realize he was talking about an autopsy at the dinner table. "Well, that can wait."

I'd never been squeamish, so I said, "I don't mind. I want to know what they found out."

Mitch made a go-ahead motion with his hand while he chewed.

Thistlewait shrugged. "Okay. First, she was pregnant. Around four weeks and there's evidence that her death wasn't natural. Looks like she was suffocated, then someone cut her wrists."

I managed to finish off my slice of pizza, but I knew I wouldn't eat any more. Talking about the violent death of a friend was in a whole different league than talking about dissecting frogs at lunch after biology class.

"How could you tell?" Mitch asked.

Thistlewait studied Mitch for a moment, seeming to consider how much to tell us. When Thistlewait first showed up on our doorstep a year ago, I'd had the feeling that Mitch knew him, but Mitch would never say a word about Thistlewait. Maybe he did know Mitch and that is why he told us what he did, or maybe it's hard to stay removed and uncommunicative when you're sitting around a kitchen table eating pizza in your socks. He nodded slightly at Mitch and said, "Petechial hemorrhaging in the eyes, capillaries that burst in the eye. It's a sign of asphyxiation. And there aren't any hesitation cuts." My face must have looked puzzled. He explained, "Usually a person about to commit suicide makes a few shallow cuts, getting up the courage. Ms. Follette had only two cuts, one on each wrist. And the cuts on her wrists are too exact. She was right-handed?" He looked at me.

I thought a moment. "Yes. I remember her writing a note in there by the phone one day."

"A right-handed person usually cuts the left wrist first and that's the deepest cut. The cut on the right wrist may be shorter and shallower. The cuts on her wrists were almost exactly equal in depth and length. There was also some faint bruising on one shoulder. And then there was the amount of blood."

I looked down at my plate, blinking hard. I missed the rest of what he said. Mitch reached across the table and squeezed my hand. When I looked up Thistlewait wiped his mouth, then crumpled his napkin. "This is strictly the Vernon PD's case. They only shared that with me as a courtesy, so I don't have any input on this, but it looks like they're on the right track. I shared what I know with you, Mrs. Avery, so you'd know this is serious. Stay out of it."

Normally, I'd have bristled at his fierce, commanding tone, but I was still immersed in thinking of how Penny died and what a useless waste it was. Thistlewait reached back to his overcoat that was draped over the back of his chair and pulled a folded newspaper out of the pocket. "Did you see this today?"

The headline under the fold read POLICE INVESTIGATE SUSPICIOUS DEATH. NEIGHBORHOOD STUNNED.

"No." Mitch pulled the paper to him and I leaned over to scan the article over his shoulder.

Vernon resident Penny Follette was found dead in her Black Rock Hill home, 3407 West Nineteenth Avenue, on Monday afternoon. Initial reports indicated the death was a suicide, but police are now treating the death as a homicide, a source close to the investigation reported on Tuesday.

Police are tracing the movements of Follette on Monday, but there are few leads as to why Follette, a volunteer in the arts community and an archivist, died.

The quiet neighborhood of Windermere on Black Rock Hill is stunned. "She was very nice. I just can't believe it," said one neighbor, Reginald Baker. Other local news sources report that another neighbor, who asked not to be identified, saw Follette at another home in the neighborhood, 3415 West Nineteenth Avenue, shortly before Follette died. Mitch and Ellie Avery, residents at the home Follette reportedly visited shortly before her death, were unavailable for comment.

"What?" I said.

"A neighbor?" Mitch said. We looked at each other and then spoke at the same time. "Mabel."

"Your unidentified neighbor?" Thistlewait asked.

"It has to be. She and her husband, Ed, watch everything that happens on this street," I said.

Mitch put the paper down and reached for another pizza slice. "When I saw Ed this morning on my way to the base he said Mabel was in bed with that flu that's going around."

"And he didn't ask you anything about Penny?" I felt my eyebrows shoot up to my hairline. The Parsons always wanted to talk and ask questions.

"No, I was leaving for work, so I didn't hang around to talk."

"But, still, I can't believe she'd tell a reporter that Penny was at our house. I saw Penny on base, but I wasn't supposed to meet her until that afternoon, anyway. Why would Mabel say that? And why would Penny come over early? To tell me she was pregnant?"

Thistlewait shook his head. "There you go again. Leave it to the police, Mrs. Avery."

"More pizza?" I tilted the box with the last piece toward Thistlewait. I decided I'd better check on Mabel. To make sure she was recovering from the flu, of course.

After Thistlewait left, I pulled the wrinkled list of names out of my coat pocket and returned phone calls for Will. Besides Victor Roth I also needed to call Hetty Sullivan, a chairperson for Frost Fest. I dialed the home number she had left on the message.

"Hi. I'm Ellie Avery," I said when she answered and identified herself. "I'm returning a few phone calls for Will Follette. You mentioned on your message that you need to pick up some photographs from Penny?"

"Yes." Her rough voice scratched over the phone. Then she sighed. "Such a shame about Penny. I feel awful. I wish she had come to me or that I'd realized she had problems."

"Me too." I didn't elaborate on how she died. I figured that Hetty would read about it in the paper soon enough. Talking about her death being a murder, not a suicide, over the phone to a stranger seemed too gossipy, so I stayed quiet.

"Well, we do have to move on." Hetty cleared her throat, but it didn't make her voice any smoother. "And Penny would want the exhibit to be ready for Frost Fest. She said she picked up, let me see, photographs and framed ink drawings of early military planes from General Bedford. She also had photos of Greenly from the 1940s. Do you have those?"

"Not with me, but Will said she had some things at their house. Do you want to meet me there?"

"I could be there tomorrow night after a meeting," she said. "Around seven thirty?"

"Fine. I'll see you then."

I gave her directions and then dialed Victor Roth, thinking of when I'd met him briefly a few weeks ago. I was having lunch with Penny at Caliente, a trendy Mexican restaurant in a refurbished warehouse in Vernon's downtown business district. Aqua, fuchsia, and canary murals celebrated chili peppers, parrots, and Mexican pottery. The murals fascinated Livvy. Music pulsated through the crowd of young professionals dressed in business casual, who swiveled from side to side with their phones pinned to their ears, looking for their lunch dates.

Victor Roth had spotted Penny from across the room and waved.

She said, "I think that's Victor. I haven't seen him in ages."

"Very Euro-looking," I said as a man in his twenties wearing a tight gray shirt that showed off his squared shoulders made his way through the crowd. He had longish thick brown hair and a face with sharp plains. He looked like he'd just left the country club, or at least a photo shoot trying to replicate a country club background for a luxury sports car ad. He leaned over to kiss Penny on the cheek. "Penny, how are you?" he said in his crisp British accent.

"Fine. This is my friend, Ellie. Ellie, Victor Roth. He's an art dealer. *What* are you doing here?"

"Opening a gallery. West Coast is very big right now."

Penny laughed. "This isn't exactly the West Coast. You're off by a few hundred miles."

"Ah, but rent is so much more reasonable here. A few hundred miles doesn't make a difference." His wide smile revealed startling white teeth. "You must come see my new gallery. It's on Washington, north of the river."

His cell phone rang and he waved as he returned to his table, already deep into his phone conversation.

Penny tucked a strand of hair back into her ponytail

thoughtfully. "London and New York I can see, but, Vernon? Not the usual lineup for gallery locations. I wonder what he's up to. He's always up to something."

"Really? How do you know him?" I gave Livvy a few Cheerios and glanced across the room at Victor. His height, his toned physique, and teeth as white as a fresh snowfall made him easy to spot.

"I met him at a cocktail party in London. I was there with my dad on one of his sabbaticals. Victor was actually born in New York. His mother is British, but his father is American, an international banker. Victor went to the best British schools. Then his dad set him up with a gallery."

"Sounds like a jet-set lifestyle."

"It is. He's the adventure-sport type of person—rock climbing and white-water rafting. He's got all the English charm and wit, but none of their sometimes wimpy attributes. I guess his robust American genes kicked in."

Victor's answering machine message with its elegantly precise British accent made me stand up straighter and try to speak more clearly. "Hello. This is Ellie Avery, returning calls for Will Follette. Please call me and let me know what you needed from Penny." I left my number and hung up.

An Everything In Its Place Tip for Organized Closets

The next step of a closet reorganization—or any organization project—involves the "holy trinity" of organization: keep, donate/give away, and throw away.

- Keep only the items that fit, are in good condition, and that you like.

- Donate/give away wearable clothing that doesn't fit or is out of style by a few seasons.
- Throw away anything that is broken, has stains that can't be removed, or is extremely worn or dated.
- As you sort, you might need a fourth category: things that belong somewhere else. Add things to this pile that have a place in another part of your home, but for some strange reason, the items have been put away (or left) where they don't belong. For instance, the coat that really goes in the coat closet, but has hung in your closet for ages because you forgot to put it away. Add it to the "goes to another room" pile. Don't put things away now; you'll probably get sidetracked. Instead, wait until you've finished sorting one closet or one area of your closet before putting the "goes to another room" pile away.
- After you finish your initial sorting, bag or box the donations and put them in your car. Drop them off the next time you run errands. Trash the throwaway pile and then take your "goes to another room pile" and distribute those items where they belong.

Chapter
Six

"Ellie, I feel terrible." Mabel took another sip of her Sprite. "I'd never have said a thing to that woman if I'd known she was a reporter. She showed up Tuesday around noon. She said she was from the squadron and was looking for you." Mabel's age-spotted hand quivered slightly as her grip tightened on the glass. "It makes me so angry. I called the paper and television stations to complain, but they only said they would look into it."

The age spots stood out in sharp contrast to the pale, thin skin of her hand as she transferred the glass back to the tray beside her rocking chair. The tremble of her hands, usually hardly noticeable, caused the ice cubes to clink against the glass. As I'd walked next door, I'd thought about what Mabel had done and I got angrier with each step.

I'd had it with the Parsons' snooping and spying. Taking note of the comings and goings in the neighborhood was one thing, but telling a reporter that a murder victim was on my doorstep right before she died was not good. Mabel could have put us in danger. I'd entered their house with my anger barely under control. But it died down from a rolling boil to a simmer when I saw her, wan and shaky, tucked under a quilt made entirely of squares from different types of plaids. Mabel loved plaid. Every time I'd seen her she had on something that was plaid.

"Mabel, it's all right. Don't worry about it." Normally, Mabel could stare down a tank in Tiananmen Square, but today she looked much older and frailer than her seventy-plus years.

"I wanted to call you as soon as I realized what had happened, but I was sick and Ed wouldn't let me do anything." She threw a quick smile toward the kitchen where Ed was banging pots and dishes. She lowered her voice. "Doing the dishes. Such a racket that I can hardly rest, but I'm not saying a word. He hasn't done dishes in thirty years."

My simmering anger cooled down completely. I believed her apology. Now that I'd calmed down and thought about it, I realized Mabel was nosy, but Windermere was her turf and she valued the privacy of the neighborhood. Of course, she would pump me for information, but she'd never knowingly share information with a reporter.

"I was coming down with the flu when that reporter showed up. I wasn't thinking straight."

"Really, it's okay. Don't worry about it. I'm sure it will all work out. Don't upset yourself." I didn't want to get her any more agitated than she was.

"But you need to know. In case she comes back," Mabel insisted.

"Well, I guess that's true. What did she look like?"

"She's petite with short dark hair in that messy hairdo, if you can call it that. It looks like she doesn't own a hairbrush. She was wearing red, an overcoat, and had on dark sunglasses." Mabel plucked at a blue and green plaid square on the quilt. "That should have been a red flag for me right there. It was cold and overcast that day. Why would she need sunglasses? Anyway, she wanted to know if her friend had been by and described a woman with long dark hair, plain face, droopy clothes. Said she was supposed to meet both of you at your house.

"I assumed she was talking about Penny, so I told her that I hadn't seen Penny that day. I didn't know until Tuesday night that she died."

Mabel must have been really sick with the flu to miss that bit of news. I took a sip of my own glass of watery Sprite and managed to return it, without knocking anything over, to the coaster wedged between framed pictures of Mabel's grandkids pursuing various sports.

Mabel continued, "Then she said, 'Well, maybe I got the day wrong? Did you see her yesterday?' "

Mabel's shoulders surged up and then down as she sighed, "And I said, 'Yes. I saw Penny on the porch on Monday about that same time.' Then she wanted to know if Penny went inside and I said no, she just rang the bell."

I sat on the spongy couch and chewed my lip. If Mabel saw Penny at my house Monday at noon, then she was there. "Why would she come to the front door? She always came to the back door, the kitchen door."

"Maybe she already had," Mabel said.

I hadn't realized I'd spoken my thoughts aloud.

Mabel's face was pale from the flu, but her eyes were clear and sharp as she continued, "Maybe she went around to the kitchen first. I can't see that side of your house from here." There was a tad of regret in Mabel's voice that almost made me smile. She would love to know everything about us. "Then if you didn't answer, maybe she went to the front door to ring the bell in case you were in the basement and hadn't heard her knock on your kitchen door."

"Could be. I'm sure the police will figure it out," I said to dampen her enthusiasm. "I wonder when the reporter tried to talk to us. Did she go over to my house after she left here?"

"No. She got right on her mobile phone as she walked back to her car." Mabel pronounced it "mo-bile." "Maybe she called you right then." Mabel leaned forward. She'd obviously been thinking about Penny's death. "Have you checked your caller identification?"

"No. Not in a while. In fact, not since the police took my phone with built-in caller ID and answering machine. I'm sure the police will track down the murderer, so you don't need to worry about it."

"Oh, I'm not worried about it. I'm sure you're going to figure it out like you did last time. With a little help."

"Mabel, I'm not going to do anything about Penny's death, and you should leave it alone, too." I was relieved when a crash from the kitchen interrupted me. I sounded too much like Thistlewait. This was like a twilight zone conversation with me taking the role of Thistlewait and Mabel saying my lines. Maybe I was more like Mabel than I realized.

"Don't worry, I've got Corell," Mabel said when a second clatter sounded from the kitchen. "Just come back around when you're ready to investigate. I've been keeping an eye on the neighborhood for a long time. I know quite a bit about everyone."

Except for a short, perfunctory visit from the Vernon detective investigating Penny's death, Detective Jensen, I didn't think about how or why Penny died during the next day. Jensen assumed I didn't have anything to add to his investigation and I was distracted since he interviewed me while Livvy was sick. She came down with the flu and I spent Wednesday night and most of Thursday holding her, cleaning up the bathroom, and examining every twinge of my stomach to see if I was about to start throwing up, too, which in an odd way would have been a relief because then I could postpone my Friday morning consultation with Clarissa Bedford.

But Friday morning, I ate my waffles with Livvy and downed a glass of orange juice without any strange stomach pangs or grumbling. I felt fine, so I had to rush around and grab my newly designed flyers and brochures. I kissed Livvy, waved to Mitch, and headed out the door as I jammed the papers into a folder labeled EVERYTHING IN ITS PLACE. ELLIE AVERY, PROFESSIONAL ORGANIZER.

On the drive to the base, I crept along freshly iced roads. I felt a flutter in my stomach, but I knew it was nerves. Clarissa's beauty pageant perfect looks and standoffish manner made me uncomfortable, but she was an important client and would be a good reference, so I'd better get with it. I didn't have to like someone to work for them.

In the special section of base housing for colonels and generals, I drove slowly until I found the nameplate that read BRIGADIER GENERAL JACKSON BEDFORD. I pulled into the driveway of the largest two-story house right on time. Clarissa Bedford opened the door. "Hi. Come on in." She looked like a life-size Barbie doll, tall with flowing hair, big boobs, flat tummy, and long legs. Her face with careful makeup, including a wide lipsticked smile, reinforced the image. Today she looked like Workout Barbie with her wavy brown hair caught up in a ponytail that bounced as she led the way to the kitchen. "Coffee?" she asked as she refilled her mug. A white T-shirt, navy windbreaker and sweats, and pristine white tennis shoes completed her outfit. It looked like the clothes had come straight out of the little pink plastic-sealed boxes.

"No, thanks." I sat down on a bar stool and pulled out the brochures and folders. They were wrinkled. She sat down beside me and I explained what I did, saying I would need to look over her closets and then give her an estimate of how long it would take and what I'd charge. "I can help you organize any room in your house. Garage, bedrooms, kitchen, anywhere." I tried to smooth the wrinkles from the brochures.

"Jackson cooks for us," she said shortly.

Okay, the kitchen was his territory and she wasn't messing with it.

I managed to keep from biting my nails while Clarissa skimmed the brochure. My other jobs had been for friends. This was the first time I had to sell myself.

She looked up at me with her hard brown eyes. Comparisons to Barbie seemed ludicrous after looking into her eyes. Barbie did not have cold, assessing eyes. "So is there a charge for this estimate?"

"No. Estimates are free."

"All right." She jumped off the stool. "There's just one closet."

She led the way through the dark house. The curtains were closed, lamps off. After our interview Clarissa must be leaving for the day and wouldn't be back. I couldn't see very well, but the house looked like it was furnished in a traditional style. I caught a glimpse of a cherry-wood Queen Anne table and chairs, leather couches, and wing-back chairs flanking a fireplace.

Scattered throughout the living areas were items General Bedford must have brought back from his trips. A Japanese tea set's gold trim glowed dully in the dim light. A statue of the Virgin Mary draped with rosary beads was arranged on a wooden trunk with intricate carvings, similar to the one Mitch had brought back from the Azores. Turkish rugs muffled our footsteps as we crossed the living room, climbed the stairs, and walked along the upstairs hallway.

Clarissa moved through the house without touching

anything. The furniture, sturdy, classic pieces, didn't seem to be Clarissa's style. Paintings of idealized scenes dotted the walls, girls in pigtails with ponies or kittens. I wondered if the furniture and decor were leftovers from the era of the first Mrs. Bedford. Clarissa seemed like she'd favor contemporary styles that weren't fussy or ornate.

I paused beside several black-and-white photographs lining the hall above a table budding with a dusty silk flower arrangement. The photos were of a shiny-faced young man, his military hat tilted at a cocky angle. He leaned casually on a T-38, a jet used for training. I pointed to the photos. "In case you're worried about the photos Penny picked up from your husband for Frost Fest, I called Hetty Sullivan and she's picking them up tonight."

Clarissa gripped the doorknob of one of the doors lining the hall. "I wouldn't know anything about that." Her eyes were frigid and her posture stiff. She threw the door open and crossed the room to the open closet. "This closet and these boxes," she said sharply, pointing to several boxes stacked on a queen-size bed.

I pulled out my legal pad and jotted some notes. I opened the boxes with Clarissa at my elbow. I realized I was moving slowly and watching her out of the corner of my eye. She was tense. She reminded me of Livvy's jack-in-the-box, about to explode.

"Okay, what are your goals? Do you want to weed out old items and reduce the amount of things you have stored? Sort and throw away what you don't need? Or do you want to keep everything, but make it neater and easier to get to?"

She relaxed a little. "A little of both, I guess."

I stifled a sigh. So far, of the people I'd organized for, no one could answer this question. The usual answer was "I don't want it to be such a mess."

"Most of it belongs to Jackson," Clarissa continued.

"He never wants to get rid of anything, so keep his stuff. But my things, I could get rid of some of them, I guess." She sat down on a corner of the bed that wasn't covered with cardboard boxes while I looked through the closet.

"So where are you from?" I asked. It was one of my standard conversational gap fillers that I'd developed since becoming a military spouse. Everyone had a story, and the question was a way to get them started.

"Savannah, but I've lived in the Northwest for years."

"I thought I heard a slight accent on your message. What brought you up here?" I scrawled a few figures as I talked, then tore the page from the pad.

"Medical sales. I have the Northwest region."

"Well, here's what I've got," I said and she stopped examining her red polish to look over the page I handed her. "I figure it will take me about six hours to sort everything and organize it. I'll need to buy some sort of containers, plastic bins or shelving, depending on what you want. This includes my time, but not any materials. I can get you an estimate on that after you decide what you want."

"Fine." She barely glanced at it. "I don't have time to get in here and go through things. I've got so much going on, work, the gym, base activities." She tried to hide a slight cringe when she said, "base activities," and I felt an affinity with her because she obviously didn't relish those any more than I did. "And now I've added that art class, too."

The doorbell rang. A tiny frown marred the perfection of her face. "Now, who is that? I'm leaving for the gym after we finish."

"I'm done in here. I'll go down with you." As we walked downstairs we discussed container types and I set up a return time.

I intended to slip discreetly out the front door. Two men in business casual dress stood on Clarissa's porch when she opened the door. One man said, "Mrs. Bedford, I'm with the OSI. Is there a Mrs. Avery here?"

I stopped trying to sidestep around them. "Right here."

"We need you to come with us," said Man Number Two.

"Why?"

"We have a few questions for you."

"About what?"

The men exchanged a glance; then Number One said, "Oliver Thistlewait would like to talk to you."

I didn't move. "What about?" I repeated.

Guy Number One said, "Lieutenant Georgia Lamar's been hospitalized."

Chapter
Seven

Being practically taken into police custody is not how I want to end the first meeting with a client, but I went with them. I drove myself to the OSI building. It felt less like they were arresting me that way.

I waited in a small room long enough to memorize the flecked pattern on the tabletop, the worn spots on the carpet, and the six nail holes in the walls. I'd called Mitch and gotten his voice mail on his cell phone and no answer at home. He'd probably taken Livvy to the store. I hung up without leaving a message. What was I going to say? "Honey, I'm at the OSI office and I don't know why I'm here, but I'm waiting in what looks like an interrogation room." Not a good message to leave.

Instead, I dug around in my purse, a pebbled leather Prada shoulder bag, just businesslike enough to project an efficient air, but the red color still made it fun and not too boring. I found a Hershey's Kiss in a corner and peeled the foil away, then popped it in my mouth. I concentrated on savoring the chocolate so I wouldn't think about where I was. Thistlewait walked in the door and I chomped the rest of the chocolate and swallowed quickly.

"Mrs. Avery." He sighed, his usual reaction on seeing me, and took a seat across the table. "Tell me about Monday again."

"What? Is this about Georgia or about Penny? Is Georgia okay?"

"I'll give you the details later. First, tell me about your day on Monday."

Obviously, Thistlewait wasn't going to tell me anything until I went over my day again. "All right. Monday." I summarized my day from my conversation with Penny to dessert with Marsali later that night. Thistlewait rephrased his questions and I answered them again. Finally, he said, "You've heard about Lieutenant Lamar?"

"Just that she's in the hospital."

"Since yesterday."

"Is she going to be all right?"

"She's in critical condition right now. You said you saw her on Monday?" he said, returning to my earlier statement.

"Yes. Like I told you, she came in the Scheduling Office when I went to meet Mitch for lunch. She seemed fine. Well," I amended, "she was hot. She'd just gotten a speeding ticket."

"Anything else?"

"She was mad about the posters in the Hole. She wanted them taken down. She thinks they're sleazy."

"Okay. Anything else happen?"

"No. Oh, wait. I left the chocolate-covered espresso beans there." Thistlewait stopped writing on his notepad and sat still, eyeing me like a strange creature he'd never seen before. "Penny gave them to me that morning. She said she couldn't have them anymore." Then I made the connection. "Because of the *baby*. No caffeine."

Thistlewait didn't say anything, just watched me. I shifted in my chair, uncomfortable under his intense gaze. "I'd completely forgotten about it until now. I don't like espresso beans, so I took them in and told everyone that they were there, but no one ate any right then."

"Describe the bag." Thistlewait's gaze bored into my face.

I shifted in my chair, suddenly uncomfortable with his intense scrutiny. I hadn't done anything wrong. *Relax*, I told myself.

"It was a small gold bag with a top that folds down. It had a cursive font on the front. I don't remember the brand, but Penny usually had a bag with her. She loved them." I swallowed hard. There were too many questions about food. "Was Georgia poisoned?"

Thistlewait sighed again and rubbed his hands over his eyes. "It looks like it. Vomiting and convulsions, an apparent poisoning. They're rushing the tox screens, but we don't have the final word back yet. Her stomach contents and the food in her refrigerator look all right. Most of the foods she ate Tuesday and Wednesday, she ate with her roommate or went out with friends at lunch. No one else is sick."

"I bet it was the espresso beans. Mitch doesn't like coffee, so he wouldn't eat the beans, and Tommy only drinks Folgers. He's kind of a coffee snob in reverse. He thinks the fancy brands are just a rip-off and nothing is as good as plain old grocery store coffee. He wouldn't touch gourmet coffee."

Thistlewait pulled out his cell phone and punched a few numbers. He motioned for me to stay and wandered out into the hall. "Yeah." His voice carried down the hall. "The food from the base. Especially the espresso beans." His voice faded as he paced down the hall.

I sat looking at the freckled tabletop, but not seeing it

now. Something was bothering me. My thoughts chased themselves around in my head. "Oh," I said to myself and half stood, but then I heard Thistlewait's voice growing louder as he walked back down the hall. "And you'd better send the results over to Jensen at the Vernon PD so they can compare it to the tox screen from the Follette woman. Right."

I sat back down in the chair.

He returned as he slipped the cell phone back into its carrier on his belt. "Well, Mrs. Avery, thanks for the information. I'd advise you to stay out of this mess. Since I know you and I know you've shown an interest in bringing the guilty to justice, so to speak, in the past, I doubt you'd do something as stupid as try to murder a friend and then call the police in and help them with their investigation. But"—here he paused and leaned on the back of the chair across from me, arms braced—"not everyone around here is inclined to give you the benefit of the doubt. So, I'd advise you to act like any normal citizen and mind your own business."

"Are you saying that I'm a suspect?" My heart skittered. He hadn't read me my Miranda rights, so I couldn't be an official suspect, right?

"We've had two incidents in four days, a murder and a poisoning. You're linked to both of them. You gave Lamar a bag that may contain poison; we certainly can't find it anywhere else. And you alerted us to the possibility that Follette might not have committed suicide, which was correct. We're trained to look for the unusual connection, the discrepancy. You look like a pretty glaring discrepancy right now."

My armpits felt damp and I pressed my hands down the front of my jeans to hide my trembling fingers. "But I had nothing to do with either thing. I just handed off the bag. I could have thrown it away. And I would never hurt

Penny. She was my friend. If I'd murdered her, I could have erased the answering machine message."

"But, in both cases, you didn't. There are some strange people out there who do odd things like call the police with evidence that they've committed a crime. Arsonists do it all the time. They like to watch the furor their actions create. They get a charge out of it. Murderers do it, too. They leave little clues or call tip lines."

A rush of emotions coursed though me. "But I would never—that's absurd!" I couldn't put a coherent sentence together as rage, anger, and disbelief converged.

Thistlewait pulled back and headed to the door. "All I'm saying is I'm inclined to give you the benefit of the doubt, but you better stay out of trouble. Try to be that average citizen who never notices anything and doesn't get involved."

An Everything In Its Place Tip for Organized Closets

Don't plan to organize every closet in your home in one day—an overwhelming thought. So overwhelming, in fact, that it may stop you even before you get started! Instead break your organizing task into several smaller tasks to achieve your overall goal. For instance, start with one closet, even one area of your closet, and use the "Keep, Throw Away, Give Away/Donate" model to get started. Then tackle changing the shelving or storage containers in your next organizing session.

Chapter
Eight

"**M**itch, I'm a suspect. Whether or not they read me my rights, I'm at the top of their list. I could see it. I could feel Thistlewait's attitude shift as soon as I said I took the bag from Penny and brought it to the Scheduling Office. I can't leave my future in the hands of some investigators. What if they get it wrong? What if they go with the easiest answer? That's me. Like Thistlewait said, I'm connected to both Penny and Georgia. I got the feeling Thistlewait was cutting me a little slack, but what if someone wants a quick solution to this thing? I'm it."

Mitch leaned against the kitchen counter with his arms crossed and his legs splayed out at an angle, propping him up. He looked like a mule with his tight, set jaw. He didn't want to budge. "Thousands, no, millions of people, do just that. They trust the police to get it right. They go on with their lives and don't think about getting involved."

"But millions of people only have brushes with the police, a speeding ticket or something minor. Most people are not murder suspects."

Mitch growled and marched over to the refrigerator.

He jerked open the door, which set off a clatter of clinks and thuds. My shoulders tensed as I waited for Livvy to cry. We'd just put her in bed, and any little sound could wake her up. He pulled out a Dr Pepper, shoved the door closed, and guzzled half of it. Livvy must be catching up on her sleep, because the house stayed quiet. Mitch strode to the other side of the kitchen.

I took a sip out of my water bottle and doodled circles in the margin of my notepad. I had two headings across the top, *Penny* on the left and *Georgia* on the right. Under *Georgia* I wrote *Accidental*. I said to Mitch, "If those espresso beans were poisoned, they were intended for Penny. The fact that Georgia ate them is purely coincidental. There was no way Penny knew what I'd do with them once she gave them to me. They had to be for Penny."

"Where did they come from?"

I shrugged. "You know Thistlewait is following that trail." I didn't mention Rachel, my friend who just happened to be the spouse of an OSI special agent. I made a mental note to call her later. Right now, I wanted to focus on my conversation with Penny. I'd talked to her shortly before she died. I wanted to get down on paper what I remembered. I couldn't imagine anyone being angry enough with Penny to want to kill her, but someone had murdered her and there might be a clue in our conversation or in what Penny had done during the last few days before she died. I'd start with my conversation and then try to fill in the rest of her morning.

She'd looked so happy and I'd commented on it. I wrote *Happy/News*.

Then she'd given me the espresso beans. I wrote *Beans*. Under that word I wrote *Problem/Needed Help*. I'd forgotten about that until now. I drew some more circles. No matter what Mitch thought, I couldn't let this go now. Penny had asked for my help before she died. She'd even mentioned the murder last year. She must have realized she was in danger and wanted my help. If only we'd talked right then. That dark feeling descended again. I wished we could go back and live that day over again, but this time I'd insist Penny tell me what bothered her.

Mitch tossed his empty can in the recycling bin and sighed deeply. He pulled out a chair at the table. "Okay, what have you got?"

"You'll help?" I asked guardedly, unsure if he really wanted to help or if he wanted to see my notes.

"Ellie, you are the hardest-headed person I know. I'm not about to let you get into this without knowing what you're thinking. I'll help, if I can."

"Well, you were looking pretty mulish yourself over there just a minute ago."

"Yes, but I can be flexible. I can give in. Unlike some people." He leveled a look at me and pulled the notepad toward him.

"I'm not going to give in until I know the police don't suspect me and aren't going to arrest me. I have no alibi for Penny's death. I was driving home from lunch with you."

Mitch ignored me; well, technically he acknowledged my statement with a grunt as he read over the list, which I took to mean he gave me a little on the alibi point, but he didn't want to concede that in words. "This is what you and Penny talked about?"

I explained my notes. Then I said, "She was about to tell me something, but then the door opened and a flight crew came in and she looked . . . funny." I paused, trying to remember her exact expression. "She was afraid, but there was something else there, too. Defiance?"

I wrote, *Flight crew* and listed the names as I spoke. "Zeke Peters was there. Pilot?" Mitch nodded. The squadron didn't have hard crews, so once copilots upgraded to pilot and flew in the left seat the Air Force kept them dual qualified, so they could fly as either a copilot or a pilot, depending on what the needs of the moment were. I remember Zeke's towering figure dwarfed the others as they labored up the ramp.

"Then Aaron, our new neighbor. He didn't say anything. Do you know his last name?"

"Reed. He's our newest co." Mitch meant copilot. Aaron and Bree had moved into the property left vacant when our neighbor requested a transfer after his wife died last year. A management company now rented the bungalow, and the Reeds were the first to live in it. I'd met the couple one day when I was planting ground cover in a flower bed. They seemed polar opposites; Bree had spiky tomato-red hair and was an artist, a painter. She'd chattered nonstop about the local art scene while Aaron stood mute in the background. "Is he as quiet at work as he was that day I met them?"

"Quieter. We call him 'the Stealth Co.' "

"Oh. I almost forgot. Rory was there." Barrel-chested and with a thatch of blond hair over his owlish round glasses, he'd powered up the ramp.

"Rory Tyler? Yeah, he was on it and someone else hopped on that flight." Mitch left the kitchen and then returned with a small packet of paper, the week's flying schedule. Now that everything's computerized, the hard copy should have faded away, but the wing commander liked to see it on paper, so a hard copy went out every Friday for the next week.

Mitch scanned the blocks filled with data. "No one else is on here, but I remember someone came in that morning, wanting to fly."

I wrote a question mark as Mitch said, "Willy. It was Willy. But it wasn't this flight. The same crew flew the week before, Friday, I think. He hopped on the Friday flight with Zeke, Rory, and Aaron the week before."

"Will Follette? Wasn't he just back from the deployment? Penny said something about being glad he'd be home for a few days."

Was it only last week? Things had changed so quickly. Will had been gone on the first rotation to the "sandbox," or "SWA," pronounced "sa-wah," an abbreviation for Southwest Asia. Mitch was scheduled to leave in three weeks for his turn. Usually, you had some time off when you returned from a deployment. Sometimes it took a while to get readjusted to the time zone after being halfway around the world for months.

"What was Will doing hopping on another flight right after he got back from a deployment?"

"Don't you know why we call him Willy? Because he always wants to be on the road." Mitch tossed the schedule in the recycling bin and sat back down. "No matter how much he's flown, he always wants on another flight."

"But doesn't everyone? You always want to fly. There's not enough hours to go around, is there?"

"Well, no. We'd all rather be flying. But Willy takes it to an extreme. He never has any conflicts. Most people have *some* time they don't want to fly, you know, a kid's basketball game or family reunions or something. I can't remember Willy ever blocking out any of his schedule. He even requested a trip during the weekend of that Frost thing. Penny put up flyers around the base, so I asked him if he wanted to be off and he said, 'No, it's not a problem. Penny won't mind.'"

I tossed down my pen. "And all this time Penny thought it was the schedulers who were working him to death, but he was requesting it." I picked my pen up again and scribbled Will's name, but anger distorted my handwriting so that I could hardly read it. "How could he do that to Penny?"

"There's three reasons to go TDY," he said, referring to the acronym for Temporary Duty. I'd never understood

the acronym. Why not just TD? Too easily confused with
a touchdown in football? Did some committee tack on the
y to baffle spouses and friends of military members?
Mitch ticked the reasons off on his fingers, "To travel.
You know, 'join the military, see the world.' Of course, the
only problem with that idea is that military bases are the
only part of 'the world' we usually get to see. Number
two, to party. That's Willy. For him, a few beers and everything's a party. And number three, to make money, the per
diem. That's me, by the way, I go for the per diem."

"You'd better either be in the money category or the
travel category," I said and refocused on the list. "Okay.
After the crew passed us, we talked about the exhibit and
she mentioned Clarissa Bedford was in her art appreciation class." I summarized those two items.

I skipped down a few lines and wrote *AM meeting at
the Mansion. Bedford—10:30?* Under that question I
listed *11:00—Conversation at the squadron. 12:00—
Called Marsali. Around noon—Mabel saw Penny on my
porch. 12:34—Called and left a message for me. 1:00—
Will finds Penny.* A fresh wave of grief washed over me as
I read over the list, a picture of the end of a life.

Mitch glanced at the clock. "Wow. Seven already. I've
got to read. I'm flying tomorrow with Tommy."

"Oh, Hetty Sullivan!" I tossed the pen down. "I forgot.
I've got to meet her at Penny and Will's house at seven-
thirty."

"Who?" Mitch asked. He pulled a three-inch-thick
notebook from his pubs case and sat down at the table.

"She's working on the exhibit and needs to pick up
some drawings and photographs from Penny's house. I
said I'd let her in. I'd better run down there and make sure
I can find everything. And that reminds me. Victor Roth
never returned my call." I shifted through the papers in
the cubbyholes on my small secretary until I found the

note with Hetty's and Victor's numbers. I dialed Victor's number as I walked to the closet. He answered and I explained I was following up on Penny's messages.

"That issue is taken care of," he said and hung up.

"Well, you're welcome," I said as I stabbed the OFF button. "Not even a thank-you!" Victor Roth's accent sounded a lot less appealing when he snapped at you.

Mitch hadn't heard me. He hunched over the tiny text titled *Engine Ground Operation*.

I pulled on my coat and gloves. "Don't fall asleep!" I called on my way out the door. If I had to read those monotonous pages of technical data, I'd be out in a few seconds.

Mitch looked up, waggled his eyebrows, and said, "Not without you."

I clutched the collar of my coat together and scurried down the deserted street. With darkness descending around five-thirty, most people hurried home from work and holed up in their warm houses, a mini-hibernation until dawn and work forced them outside to unplug the extension cord transferring heat to their engine block and scrape the ice off their car windows. Besides the weak streetlights, the only light came from gold squares radiating out from the edges of closed curtains. There was no wind tonight, and my steps crunching through snowmelt crystals seemed to echo in the still street.

I turned where I estimated the Follettes' narrow sidewalk would be and sank into the snow. Will hadn't shoveled snow for a while. In the darkness on the porch, I fumbled with the keys and tried several times before I got the right one in the lock. I needed to leave the porch light on when I left.

After I clicked on a table lamp, I locked the front door and swished the curtains closed. I stood in the living room, shivering, reluctant to go into the rest of the house.

The living room opened to the dining room and kitchen behind it. To the right of the dining room, a tiny hall connected two bedrooms with a bathroom between them. The house was cold and I wondered if Will had turned the thermostat down too low before he left. It was probably in the narrow hall. I took a tentative step.

A wheeze rattled through the house. I jumped as the floor vent jangled and the furnace heaved out a spurt of warm air. I paused to click on the dining room light, then worked my way around the house with floorboards screeching under my feet, turning on the rest of the lights. The bare white walls and stark lighting put an end to my uneasy feeling. In the hall, I cranked the red line on the thermostat from sixty-two degrees up to seventy-five.

I reached into the bath to turn off the light. There was no need to leave it on. I'd flicked it on during my quick circuit of the house when I turned all the lights. Now I stopped. This was where Penny was found.

My wet boots squished on the small one-inch pink tiles that covered the floor and lower two-thirds of the walls. I took in the white muslin curtain at the window and the sink with exposed leg supports. Then I sucked in a gulp of air as I looked past the clear plastic shower curtain into the pink bathtub and saw a dark red, almost brown, color in the tub. I pushed the curtain back. My stomach seemed to clench and roll at the same time. I let out a breath. It was rust. A line of it trailed from the overflow cover down to the drain.

I glanced in the bedroom and then turned the light off in there, too. A mattress and box spring covered with a mustard blanket pushed up against a wall. A pressboard nightstand and dresser crowded the room.

I turned to the second bedroom that Will had described as their study. A computer and portable CD player sat on a pressboard desk combo that dominated most of the room. A sleek swivel office chair with rollers rested on a grid of plastic over a Turkish rug. In contrast to the rest of the house, which had all the charm of a storage unit, the study felt lived in. Stacks of books covered the desk and teetered in a pile beside a soft brown leather chair. A battered floor lamp angled over the shoulder of the chair. I examined the books and magazines. Flight manuals in black binders intermingled with books on archaeology, a catalogue from Harris Museum, a book about hand-woven rugs, and *American Archaeology* magazines.

A yellow sticky note on the monitor read *Call Oscar*. Marsali? My gaze swept over the rest of the room. The far wall dominated the room. Three rows of shelves held a variety of dolls dressed in brilliant colors. They were displayed with the same precision that Penny would have used in a museum display. Evenly spaced, a card in front of each doll noted names and either purchase dates or who had given the doll to Penny. Their bright clothes gave the room a cheerful air, but their sparkling, fixed eyes and perfectly arranged shiny hair seemed a little creepy in the empty house.

The doorbell rang and I went to let Hetty inside. She stamped her high-heeled boots on the Astroturf mat and stepped inside. "Hetty Sullivan," she said as she gave me a firm, quick handshake. She had a long nose and thin lips bright with red lipstick that matched her nail polish.

"Ellie Avery." I shut the door.

"It's freezing out there. Thanks for doing this." She tossed her purse down by the door and ran her fingers through the dark cap of hair threaded with gray and said, "I don't want to take up any more of your time, so show me where everything is and I'll take care of it." She quickly scanned the room.

"Will said they were in the study, back here." I led the way. "But I haven't found anything yet." I found myself walking and talking quickly. She had an air of busy efficiency and competence.

She did another quick visual survey. When she didn't spot the photos right away, Hetty's forehead wrinkled. "They shouldn't be that hard to find." She stooped and began burrowing through a box beside the desk.

"Maybe the closet." I opened that door. "Oh. I bet this is it." I saw a box with bundles encased in bubble wrap. At the same moment I spoke, I felt a sick sensation sweep over me as I had so many times in the last few days when I realized Penny was dead. Stacks of baby toys crowded the rest of the closet. Bright boxes reached up to almost touch a row of baby clothes on miniature hangers. Clothes in pastel pink, blue, yellow, and green hung down from the rod. I touched the toe of a small, footed sleeper. I'd been shopping with Penny when she found the sleeper on sale. She bought it, saying, "I'll save it. I know we'll have a baby someday."

I jerked the box out of the closet and closed the door quickly to shelter Penny's dreams from Hetty's gaze.

Chapter
Nine

Livvy angled her body sideways, stretching to the right as she tried to grab a pack of gum. "No," I said firmly and pulled her back upright. "No reaching." I checked the shopping cart's seat belt to make sure it was still fastened and looked around for something to distract Livvy while the woman in front of me tried a different credit card. Livvy was bored with the strap of my Kate Spade satchel. Pink Girl, Livvy's toy that I could maneuver into amazing jumps, rolls, and leaps, was waiting in the Cherokee. The plastic bins in the cart were too big for Livvy to hold, so I settled for tapping the shopping cart handle with my fingers and letting her chase them back and forth.

"Excuse me." A man in a green flight suit squeezed past me. I glanced up at the sign over the cash register. MILITARY PERSONNEL HAVE PRIORITY 11:30 TO 13:30. Great. I'd managed to pick the slowest line and the one where people could legally cut in front of me. I checked my watch as my fingers danced and Livvy giggled. Eleven-thirty. I still had fifteen minutes to make it to Clarissa's house.

Apparently my run-in with the police hadn't put her off. She'd called me and said, "Pick up whatever you think will work for storage containers and add it to my bill. I really don't care what you use. How about Monday afternoon? Around twelve."

I'd replied I'd need a partial payment and could be there three hours on Monday and finish up Wednesday.

"Fine. I just want to get it done."

The man in front of me leaned on the checkout counter. "Can't you ring this up for me?" He dropped a can of shaving cream, razors, and a package of gum on the counter. Then he pulled a ten from a thick folded stack held together with a monogrammed money clip. He held out the money.

"No, sir. I'm sorry. I have to finish this first," the checker said as the woman in front of her pulled another sliver of plastic out of her wallet.

The man slapped the ten against the counter, checked the time on the diamond-studded face of his Rolex, and turned to survey the other checkout lines.

"Rory," I said. "I didn't realize that was you."

He turned to me, eyes behind his round glasses puzzled as he tried to place me. I stuck out my hand. "I'm Ellie Avery, Mitch's wife."

He nodded and gave my hand a quick clasp as he mentally measured the other lines. They were more backed-up than ours. I'd never spoken more than a few words to Rory, mostly "Hi" and "Bye" if I walked past him in the squad or saw him during a squadron function, but here he was captive and right in front of me. I had to ask about Penny and her reaction when she saw the crew on Monday. Livvy pounced on my fingers and giggled. Rory threw another angry glance at the cashier and then leaned his broad shoulders against the partial wall separating the checkouts. He looked a little mismatched with his barrel

chest and his owlish glasses, like he was part bodybuilder
and part scholar. He crossed his arms. "You'd think they
could call a few more people to the front."

Yeah, and you'd think you could wait your turn. I wondered what his hurry was. Mitch said the Safety Office
where Rory worked played more solitaire than the rest of
the squadron combined.

I murmured a noncommittal sound. "I saw you last
Monday after you landed. I was talking to Penny in the
hall when you came in from a flight." His gaze stopped
roaming the store and focused on me. "She seemed upset
about something. Something about a flight you were on?"
That last bit of information had come from Will, but Rory
didn't need to know that.

"From what Willy said, she was always upset about
something." I'd let my hands fall motionless on the handle, and Livvy was straining toward the tabloids this time.
I hauled her back in and tried to collect my thoughts as I
tapped a speedy rhythm with my fingers. The woman in
front of us finally signed her receipt and took her bag.
Rory tossed his money on the counter and grabbed his
plastic bag.

"So you don't know why she was so upset when she
saw your crew?"

"I hardly knew her." Rory jerked the dollar bills out of
the cashier's hand and strode away through the congestion
of baskets.

After I checked out, I pushed the basket loaded with
Livvy and my bags to the parking lot. I paused at the curb.
Rory didn't want to talk about his flight or Penny. Maybe
he was naturally reticent. I opened the hatchback door on
the Cherokee and set plastic bins in the back. Wouldn't it
have been more natural for Rory to shrug off Penny's attitude or simply deny anything was wrong?

I lifted Livvy out of the basket, stacked her on my hip,

and reached up to close the hatch. Out of the corner of my eye I saw the basket slowly roll away toward a black SUV across the aisle. I turned to run after it, but a lean man in blues took a few quick steps and caught it.

"Thanks," I said and shoved the hatchback door down to close it. "Here, I'll take it." I walked over. "I'll put it away."

"Don't you worry about it. I've got it. You've got your hands full there." A hooked nose dominated the man's craggy face, and a fringe of silver hair edged the rim of his hat. Unlike his bumpy face, his voice was fluid and resonant. It was trained. I noticed the star on his hat. "You're General Bedford."

I hitched Livvy up higher on my hip and introduced myself. I figured this would probably be my only chance to talk to him. After all, I didn't usually run into the wing commander, but I guess everyone has to make a trip to the BX sometime. "You talked to Penny Follette the day she died."

His face registered surprise, then settled into a serious expression as I continued, "She was a friend of mine. Could you tell me what you talked about? She told me she interviewed you."

He hesitated, so I pressed, "I just wondered . . . It was so sudden . . ."

"Well, sure." He squinted across the distance. Like a hawk perched high above a field, Bedford seemed to survey his territory, his gaze darting back and forth, looking for a scuttling mouse. I hoped no one crossing the parking lot had forgotten to put on their hat. I didn't think Bedford's reaction to seeing someone out of uniform would be pretty. "It was for her article. I'm a military brat. She wanted to know about my memories of my dad's years here at Greenly."

"Was she upset? Anxious?"

"No. Focused. She wanted quotes for that article. Now, I can tell, you're blaming yourself for her death. Don't go there. You've got enough on your plate." He patted Livvy on the head. "You don't need to add guilt to it." His smooth voice rolled on and I couldn't get a word in. "Just take care of your little one there and don't dwell on Penny." I thought he wanted to pat me on the head, too, but he seemed to think better of it. He settled for giving my shoulder a quick tap. "You take care now."

I tracked Mitch down to the Hole where he was dropping quarters in a box to pay for a Dr Pepper. A burst of laughter sounded from one of the tables across the room as I hurried in the door. "There you are. I've been looking all over for you." Livvy leaned over almost horizontal and fell from my grip into Mitch's arms. I dropped her car seat on the floor and realized the room was silent.

I looked over at the group in the corner. Rory and Aaron looked quickly away. Rory had a barely suppressed smile on his face, but Aaron's face was red, with embarrassment or anger, I couldn't tell which. "I've got to run. Don't lose Pink Girl. See you tonight," I said and gave them both a quick kiss and flew out the door. Mitch was heading home for a few hours of sleep before a night flight. He planned on sleeping while Livvy took her afternoon nap.

I zipped over to Clarissa's house, breaking every speed limit on base, especially the fifteen-mile-an-hour limit in base housing. There was definitely something going on with Rory and Aaron, but I didn't have time to think about what it could be as I wheeled into Clarissa's driveway. Only four minutes late, I rang the doorbell with my elbow and gripped the plastic bins in my arms. Clarissa grabbed the lids out of the top bin and ushered me directly upstairs. She dropped the lids on the floor and said, "I'll be across the hall. Call if you need anything."

I worked steadily for a while opening, sorting, and stacking the accumulation of stuff we all seem to attract, a sea of memories and junk lapping at our closets and attic doors, but unlike the ocean, it only seemed to swell, never retract. Most of the things in the boxes belonged to General Bedford: worn professional papers, photographs of pinning-on ceremonies, and books on management, war, and leadership.

I stopped and wiped the glaze of dust from one photo. A petite, plump woman with a bob of highlighted hair stood on one side of General Bedford fastening on his new rank, major, it looked like, on his shoulder while on the other side a colonel adjusted the new rank. Must be General Bedford's first wife, smiling up at him. Rumors said that severe asthma caused her health problems, but General Bedford took a job in Southern California, despite the poor air quality. She hadn't survived to the next assignment, Greenly. Bedford stayed single for four months, then married Clarissa, which had the rumormongers spinning so fast around base that it made some of them dizzy.

In the picture, General Bedford looked straight ahead, his craggy face set and serious, unaware of his wife's smile. I wondered what would attract a woman as young and beautiful as Clarissa to a rather crusty man like Jackson Bedford. I set the photo down beside a stack of catalogues and printouts from online auctions. A photo of a gold cross dominated one auction printout. The cross had a blue stone at the center and a loop on top so it could be suspended on a chain.

"Would you like a Coke?" Clarissa held out a Caffeine Free Diet Coke.

"Sure," I said and popped the top on the can. "I need to ask you about a few things."

She pushed up the sleeves of her white sweatshirt with *Princess* emblazed across it in sparkly letters and leaned against the door frame.

"Just check through these piles and make sure you want to keep everything." She picked at the piles, barely looking at the photos and plaques in General Bedford's pile. She pulled out a doily from another stack. "My mom made this. I'll find a place for it downstairs." She smoothed the wrinkles. "She taught me how to make them. I should try it again and see if I still remember." Her hands raked through nail polish, cosmetics, and lotions. "Trash these. God, look at that eye shadow. I hope I never wore that!" She tossed the blue eye shadow in a large garbage bag I'd left at the foot of the bed.

I opened the last box, a jumble of high-heeled, pointy-toed shoes and boots.

"Here, I'll look at that stuff." She took the box.

I asked, "Do you need any of this where it's easily accessible?"

She glanced around the room and shook her head.

"Do you want everything back in the closet or do you want to sort it and put the less used items somewhere else, like your attic?"

"The closet's fine."

"Okay, I'll group similar things together and put them in labeled bins." I might as well have been talking to the walls. Clarissa didn't seem to care what I did with her stuff. Of course, most of the heaps mushrooming around the room belonged to General Bedford. Did Clarissa have her things already unpacked somewhere else in the rest of the house, or did she travel light?

"About General Bedford's things. It would be a good idea for him to look through them," I said.

"Just pack it away," she said shortly.

"What about these catalogues and eBay printouts?

Yours?" I asked as I held up one titled *Byzantine Gold Cross, Sixth Century A.D.*

Clarissa pursed her lips. "Jackson's first wife." She paused, eyed the black trash bag, but then sighed and said, "Store it."

A little Rebecca-type anxiety going on here with Clarissa and the first Mrs. Bedford? Did Clarissa have the exquisite cross tucked away in a jewelry box? "It's beautiful," I said. "Did she buy it?"

"I'll never know. Jackson stored most of her stuff."

Maybe Clarissa's interest in art wasn't so unexplainable. She wouldn't be the first trophy wife who felt like she had to live up to or surpass her predecessor. Clarissa pulled out three pairs of boots with heels so high my toes hurt just from looking at them. "Good shoes for work," she explained and added them to the doilies.

"You said you're in sales, right?" She must have to dress up.

"Medical equipment sales."

"Do you have to travel?"

"I've got the Northwestern territory for Medivar. It covers three states, so I'm gone every other week." We were getting almost chummy so I asked, "Do you ever think about quitting?"

She gave a bitter laugh as she fished a red stiletto out of the box. "No way. I want my own money. I'll never rely on a man." She found the mate to the red shoe, looked up, and caught my expression, which must have been surprise.

"Hey, I'm not the typical commander's wife. I don't care. I don't want to be on every committee." She grabbed her small pile of things and left. I slapped a lid on the first box. I was beginning to like Clarissa Bedford.

I finished packing the boxes I'd brought, noting the contents of each bin on my inventory list. I squinted at the remaining piles, trying to estimate how many more bins I needed. Probably six. I cleaned up what I could and told Clarissa I'd be back on Wednesday to finish.

On my way home I swung into the gas station to fill up before I left the base. The price was usually a little cheaper on base. I pushed the correct buttons and got the gas pumping while I gathered my coat collar closer to my neck to keep out the chilly wind.

"Hey, girl. Haven't seen you in a while." Tessa Jones stood on the other side of the pumps replacing the gas cap on her green Volkswagen Beetle. "How are you doing? Got the little one with you?" Tessa worked in the Orderly Room at Mitch's squadron. One of Livvy's biggest fans, Tessa always wanted to hold Livvy.

"No, she's with Mitch. I've been doing one of my organizing jobs."

"That's great! Who are you working for?" Her Louisiana accent blurred the edges of her words, and the syllables rolled together in an almost musical rhythm.

"Clarissa Bedford."

Tessa pursed her lips together and shook her head. "You better watch out. That lady has a vicious temper."

"She's been fine to work for." Her physical perfection was intimidating. I could never look as good as she did, but she'd been civil, even nice.

"Yeah, well, don't get on her bad side. Keep your distance from General Bedford. I saw her one day—well, heard her—up at the Mansion. You know, the bank is right next to the Mansion and they share that parking lot?"

I nodded and removed the nozzle from the Cherokee.

Tessa continued, "I was on my way to lunch and I couldn't find a place to park by the bank. I had to park all the way over by HQ. I was sitting in my car filling out my deposit slip when I heard this woman yelling, 'I don't want you spending any more time with her.' I looked out the window and there they were, yelling across the top of the car in front of me."

"Did anyone else hear?"

"No, no one else was in the parking lot. Anyway, General Bedford laughed and said, 'It was a business meeting. Penny and I were deciding which photos should go to the exhibit.' "

"How did you hear that? Was he yelling, too?"

Tessa looked a little embarrassed. "I rolled my window down an inch so I could hear, okay? I mean, I wasn't going anywhere while they were arguing, was I? So I was stuck. And I was curious, too."

"They were arguing about Penny?"

"Yeah, timid, little Penny. I couldn't believe it," Tessa said.

I ripped the gas receipt off with red, chapped fingers. "Do you have time to grab a cup of coffee or something? I'm freezing."

"Sure. I finished at the gym early. I'll meet you at the BX."

An Everything In Its Place Tip for Organized Closets

As you empty your closet:
- Now is a good time to vacuum, dust the shelves, and clear any cobwebs from the ceiling corners.
- Throw away wire hangers and purchase hangers that don't damage the lines of your clothing. Options range from inexpensive plastic hangers to more pricey plastic and wood ones. Don't forget you'll need hangers for pants, too. Using a

single style of hanger will give your closet a neater appearance.

- Decide if you'll store all the clothes in the closet or if you'll rotate your out-of-season clothes to another area. If you don't have room in other closets, check with dry cleaners in your area. Some dry cleaners offer storage services, but make sure of the price and pickup policy.

Chapter
Ten

A few minutes later, my fingers, wrapped around my cup of hot chocolate, had returned to their normal color. "So General Bedford acted like the whole thing was a joke?"

"Yeah." Tessa picked up her brownie and said, "Good thing I did my workout today." She chewed a bite and added, "Love these things. I can't come in here without getting a cup of coffee and a brownie. Anyway, Bedford laughed, but that seemed to make Clarissa furious. She hit the roof of the car with her fist and said, 'I can't believe you can't see it. I don't want you spending time with her. Ever! I hate that woman.'

"Then Bedford said, 'You have nothing to worry about.' He sounded exasperated. Then he convinced her to get in the car and they drove off."

"Are you sure it was Clarissa he was talking to?" I asked.

"There's not that many women walking around the base who look like they left their tiara at home. It was her."

"I don't know. I just can't see Clarissa being jealous of Penny."

Tessa sipped her coffee and said, "I couldn't either, but I talked to Marilyn. She's a friend from church who's a civilian and works up on the third floor in Bedford's office. She said Penny had been to see him the week before and they talked a long time about the exhibit stuff. Marilyn said when Penny got on the subject of art it was like she came alive and they could hardly pry General Bedford out of there for his next meeting."

"I suppose that's true. Penny loved preserving finds and displaying them. She felt after all the work and money went into finding things it was just as important to take care of them." As Will had said, it was one of her passions. Could an intellectual attraction be as strong as a physical attraction? Maybe Clarissa wasn't so far off the mark after all.

Tessa ran her finger around her plate, picking up the last crumbs. "Anyway, Marilyn said Clarissa showed up the next time Penny had an appointment with General Bedford. Clarissa pitched a fit right in the hall in front of General Bedford's office." Tessa shook her head again. "That was one jealous woman. At least, she was jealous of Penny."

"What day was this?"

Tessa thought a moment, then pulled out her checkbook. "It was Monday."

"I wonder if Will knows what time she left their house. Do you think he would know what her schedule was?" Abby pulled another piece of Thai chicken pizza onto her plate and studied my timetable for Monday, the day Penny died.

I hooked my foot around an empty kitchen chair and

drew it closer, then propped my feet up on it and blew out a breath. From the time I'd walked in the door from Clarissa's house, I hadn't had a spare moment as I fed, bathed, and tucked Livvy into bed. With Mitch night flying, I'd planned to order a pizza, but Abby insisted she'd whip one up and bring it over when she realized I was by myself. "You don't have to do that. Let's just order one," I argued.

"I don't mind," she said. "I like to cook. And it'll give me something to do since Jeff is studying for his class tonight."

I sprinkled more Parmesan cheese on my second slice. Abby was right. Her pizza was better than takeout. "I doubt Will knew Penny was coming out to the base that day."

"Yeah, you're probably right."

The phone rang and I picked up the cordless handset, our only phone since Thistlewait still had our other one. "Hello." Silence. After a moment, I clicked the OFF button. "Hang-up."

"Sales call," said Abby. "I hate those."

Abby's finger traced down over the names of the flight crew. "You know, Jeff said something the other day about Zeke and Rory." She stared intently at my kitchen cabinets, then shook her head. "I can't remember exactly what it was, but it was something they were bragging about. In fact, I don't think they told Jeff what they'd done, just hinted."

I chewed slowly. The seasoning on the pizza had just the right blend of teriyaki and ginger. After swallowing, I said, "I tried to ask Rory about Penny, but he stonewalled me. Then I saw him with Aaron at the squad. It looked like Rory was giving Aaron a hard time. There's definitely something going on there, but is it related to Penny?"

The phone rang. Again, a dial tone buzzed in my ear.

"I've got to get an answering machine." I punched the OFF button. It rang again. We waited through ten rings before silence filled the kitchen. I looked at the list again, trying to focus.

"Well, maybe you can ask them about it at Jeff's party tomorrow night."

"Yeah," I said weakly. I'd completely forgotten about Jeff's birthday. Abby was throwing a party for him on Wednesday night and she'd invited the whole squadron. I retrieved the iced tea pitcher from the counter and topped off our glasses. On the way back to the fridge, I jotted a note on my pad of sticky notes to buy Jeff a gift. "How's that going?" I asked as I closed the refrigerator and returned to the table.

"I'll be cleaning tomorrow afternoon, but I made the lasagna already. I just have to heat it up and toast the garlic bread."

"I'm bringing ice and Cokes, right?"

"Um-hmm." Abby stretched her arms over her head and said, "I'd better hit the road. I still have to do laundry so I can pack tomorrow."

"I think you're crazy giving a party the day before you leave on a trip."

Rex let out a sharp bark from the backyard.

Abby shrugged as she picked up her plate and carried it to the sink. "It's just shorts and swimsuits. It won't be that hard."

A gust of freezing wind whipped into the kitchen as I opened the door a crack and let Rex inside. He pranced back and forth from one of us to the other, frisky from being in the cold air. It would be really nice to escape winter for a few days in warm Las Vegas. But then I remembered why Abby and Jeff were taking a short break.

"How's everything going?"

"Fine. I'm not going to get my hopes up. I'm going to

do what everyone keeps telling me to do. 'Take a cruise. Go on vacation. Relax. Don't worry about it. It will happen when the time is right.' What about you? Any signs of a little sibling on the way?"

"No." Things had been so crazy that I hadn't even thought about it. "We're on the Air Force family planning routine. Mitch's been out of town so much we haven't even had a chance to try and get pregnant."

"Tell me about it."

I could hear the smile in Abby's voice, but she kept her back to me as she rinsed her plate in the sink. We'd known each other long enough that I could tell she didn't want to talk about it today. After two miscarriages, Jeff and Abby were still trying to get pregnant. Because it had been ten months since her last miscarriage with no sign of a pregnancy, they were stealing away for a long weekend. "I can't take off long enough to go on a cruise, but we can go to Las Vegas," she'd informed me a few weeks ago, her face split in her wide smile that I'd missed recently.

"Call me if you need help tomorrow," I said.

"Okay." She stuck the pizza leftovers in the refrigerator and left. I watched her trudge through the snowbanks, head tucked down into the wind, until she rounded the corner and cut through the streetlight's circle of light. I let the curtain on the kitchen door fall back into place with a tiny sigh for Abby. I wouldn't trade Livvy for a whole summer of Las Vegas sunshine.

After Abby left, the phone rang. I stared at it while it rang a few times, and then I answered.

"I've thought of something," Mabel said. No "Hello" or "How are you?" but that was Mabel, straight to the point.

"About Monday, the day Penny died," Mabel continued. "I've been thinking, trying to see if I could remember anything different about the street that day."

Mabel would notice a leaf out of place, so I said, "And?"

"Well, at first all I could remember were the pickups coming and going at the Wilsons'. They're remodeling, you know. Kitchen, basement, and adding a deck. Then I remembered the white car. One of those that are so small they almost look like a toy. It was a convertible. The top was closed, of course, but I saw her back out of Penny's driveway and speed down the street. A woman with dark hair was driving."

"Really? Did you know her?"

"No. She flew by too fast for me to see her. I'm calling the police tomorrow, but I thought the information might interest you."

Before I could answer her she'd hung up.

I groped for the phone. In the dark, I patted the night-stand and jerked the phone off the stand. "Yes?"

Silence.

"Hello?"

A tiny click sounded, and then the dial tone droned in my ear. I checked the clock. Ten after twelve. It was probably Mitch calling. If he'd been cut off for some reason, he'd call back. But the numbers on the clock silently transitioned to 12:13 without another phone call.

I clicked on the light and pulled out the phone book. After a few minutes of flipping pages I found the tiny paragraph on call return. I punched star-six-nine.

"We're sorry. The service you have requested is not available for this number," an automated voice informed me. I clicked the light back off and snuggled down under the thick blankets, but I didn't sleep until Mitch returned from his flight at twelve-thirty.

* * *

"Are you almost done?" Clarissa snapped from the doorway. "I have to leave for the airport in ten minutes." She was leaving on a six-day business trip. In her power suit and with her hair up in a twist, she looked like Executive Barbie. Was there an Executive Barbie? From what I remembered, Barbie was heavy on glamorous lifestyles and the serving professions. I didn't remember a tiny pinstriped suit with a nipped-in waist.

"Yes." I clicked the top on the last storage bin and hoisted it up into the last open slot in the closet. "Let me gather up my stuff and I'll be out of here."

I grabbed my notepad, labels, scissors, and marking pens. I stuffed them into my Tommy Hilfiger tote bag and ran a hand over the comforter to smooth out the wrinkles. As I slipped on my coat, I glanced out the window. Gray clouds skimmed across the sky so low they looked like they were about to snag on the ice-coated treetops. We'd had sleet all night and awoken to a crystallized world. Every branch and twig had a glossy coat of ice.

I slid the bifold closet doors closed. *Oh no.* A small suitcase had been tucked behind the open door next to the wall. I'd seen the dark tapestry suitcase in the closet on the first day, but I'd totally forgotten to make a place for it in the rearranged and neatly organized closet. I could kick myself for not checking behind the doors for any extra items.

I jerked open the doors and scanned the neat arrangement of shelves. I might be able to fit it in a little space on the left side. Clarissa wanted me finished and out of here. She wouldn't be excited when I said I'd forgotten one item. In fact, I thought I might see the mean side of Barbie if I told her I wasn't done yet. I grabbed the suitcase and pulled it over.

It was heavy. *Aargh.* Not only had I missed the suitcase, I'd forgotten to check it to see if there was anything in it. I tossed it on the bed and unzipped it. Maybe the things in it were small and I could slide them into the appropriate bins quickly, then stow the suitcase.

I flipped the top back and blinked. Chiffon, silk, and filmy gauze frothed over the suitcase's zipped edge. Clarissa swept down the hall as fast as her pointy-toed heels would let her, but she didn't look in the room. I stuffed a red see-through nightie back into the suitcase, but the feathery trim caught on the zipper. I used sparkly sequined mules to hold down the trim and ran the zipper back around the suitcase as fast as I could, but not before my gaze snagged on a pair of lacy, black, crotchless panties. Wow. I zipped up the suitcase, set it down beside the bed, and pulled my tote onto my shoulder. I'd just have to admit I missed the suitcase and offer to return and fix my mistake.

Clarissa flew into the room, attaching her last gold earring. I squared my shoulders and cleared my throat.

"Oh, good. There it is." She adjusted the double-breasted jacket on her suit until it fell perfectly over her slim hips. Then she pulled out the extendable handle on the suitcase and wheeled it into the hall to stand beside her laptop case and another small carry-on bag.

"Finished?" she asked as she hurried back to open the closet doors and skimmed over the contents. "Looks great. You can follow me out."

With the laptop and carry-on bag slung over her shoulder, she clattered down the stairs in her heels, dragging the suitcase. I followed her into her garage, where I skirted her white BMW convertible. "Send me the bill for the balance," she called and slammed the trunk.

It was a good thing she didn't give me a chance to say anything. I couldn't have responded. I was speechless. I backed out of the driveway and drove down the street, but something bothered me. Something besides the fact that Clarissa had a lingerie department in her carry-on bag. I glanced in my rearview mirror at Clarissa riding my bumper as I obeyed the low speed limit.

A white convertible!

At the corner stop sign, I put the Cherokee in park, jumped out, and ran back to her car. She powered down the window and I leaned over.

"I don't have time—"

I interrupted, "You went to Penny's house last Monday. The day she died."

Her glossy lips formed a sulky pout. "Look, nothing happened. Sure, I was mad at her. I went to tell her to back off from Jackson."

"But you were there."

"I rang the bell. No one answered. I left. End of story. Now I've got a flight to catch." She cranked the steering wheel and I stepped back as she accelerated around the Cherokee with a sharp turn and ran the stop sign.

Chapter
Eleven

"**E**xcuse me. Excuse me." I slithered through Abby's updated kitchen, complete with a dishwasher, and stepped through the sliding glass door, another part of the remodel, onto the deck and left the crowded, overheated rooms. The brisk air cooled my face. The low clouds were gone and the ice-coated trees and bushes glittered in the setting sun.

With my elbows propped on the rail, I took a deep breath of the piney air and tried to gather my thoughts. I hadn't had a minute to myself since Clarissa trotted away with her lingerie-stuffed suitcase and I wanted to think. I hadn't mentioned it to anyone, and my instinct was to keep it to myself. Clarissa must be having an affair. Otherwise, why take sexy, lacy underwear on a business trip? A whole suitcase of it, too. But then why would she be jealous of Penny? Maybe she didn't love Bedford, but she didn't want to lose him either?

I couldn't do anything about those questions now, but I could focus on the crew that made Penny uncomfortable. They were the ones who drew the strongest reaction from

Penny that morning, and there was something going on from the hints they'd given to Jeff.

A short man with thin blond hair leaned on the other end of the rail, mirroring my posture. "Hi. Aaron, isn't it?" I asked. He was the new guy on the crew that made Penny nervous.

He walked over to shake my hand. "You're Ellie. We live across the street from you."

He returned to his leaning posture and looked back at the trees. "Interesting the way the ice catches the light from the sun. Look at how the ice magnifies the twilight."

I turned back to the trees and realized the ice-coated needles did seem to glow with the orange of the setting sun. "It's beautiful."

The silence began to stretch. I couldn't dive in and ask him about Penny out of the blue. I'd start off general and try to work the conversation around to her. "How do you like Vernon?" This was one of my stock conversation starters.

Aaron rotated and looked back to the sliding glass door. He ran a hand over the little bit of bland, blond hair he had. The color reminded me of the neutral beige paint on the exterior of every Air Force building. I'd nicknamed it "Pale Blah."

"It's fine here."

Okay, so he wasn't chatty. This might be harder than I thought. I'd cooled off. Now the air seemed frigid instead of refreshing. My hands started to ache. Aaron took a drink of his beer and I could see his hands were chapped and red with the cold, too.

I glanced back at the glass door. In contrast to the growing darkness outside, light glowed from the uncurtained window. It was like watching a movie with the sound on mute as people moved in front of the window.

Mitch walked past with Livvy on his shoulders. Her fingers clutched his hair and I smiled because I could tell she was squealing. I glanced over at Aaron to see if he'd noticed Livvy. Sometimes you can't help but smile when you're face-to-face with delight on a two-year-old's face.

But Aaron was looking at Bree, his wife. Her shocking red hair stood out in little spikes below a black beret as she tilted her head and smiled at Zeke. Against her pale skin, stark black eyeliner and rectangular glasses emphasized green eyes. She spun around to speak to another person. Her flowing multiprint skirt swirled and her long, chunky necklaces flew.

"That's Bree, your wife? She's a painter?" I asked, trying another conversational track.

Aaron's eyes narrowed and anger seemed to radiate from him. "She paints," he allowed. It didn't look like I was going to be able to subtly work Penny's name into the conversation because so far we hadn't *had* a conversation. I might as well be blunt.

"Aaron, you were on a crew with Zeke and Rory, right?"

He quickly turned back to the trees and intently studied the view, but the sun had set. There was nothing to see except a black wall of pines. I flexed my fingers and stamped my feet to stay warm. "Did something happen on that flight?"

"Nothing but flying." He ducked his head and focused on the grain in the wood railing.

Water dripped from the icicles and plinked onto the deck. "But something happened," I insisted. "Rory acted funny when I asked him about it and he's been bragging around the squadron. Did it have anything to do with Penny?"

"No. We just flew," he insisted in a tense whisper I had

to strain to hear over the swish of the sliding glass door as it opened.

"Yeah," a slurred voice came from behind us. "Aaron-boy there can really fly!" Will walked with a sailor's rolling gait and braced himself against a deck chair. He had returned from the funeral, and apparently he was still trying to drink his sorrow and guilt away. "Aaron, man! He can fly by the seat of his pants!" Will jabbed the air with his can of Bud on the last word.

I glanced at Aaron and then looked closer. He was blushing!

"Or should I say by the seat of his unther—unther—by the seat of his boxers!" Will shouted the last word and leaned over the deck chair laughing.

Will had left the glass door open. The people in the kitchen froze like someone had hit the PAUSE button on a remote control. Jeff came outside and patted Will on the shoulder. "Come on, buddy. Time to head home."

"No, you don't understand. We flew naked." Will leaned over, laughing again. Aaron pushed away from the rail and strode quickly through the crowd that parted to let him through.

Zeke said, "Will, come on in. You're confused."

"Nope. You were there, too. You did it, too. I'm not going down by myself. Did everyone hear? We flew naked." Will shouted the last line as Jeff maneuvered him inside. Voices, music, and laughter surged into the void of silence.

I found Mitch at the buffet, piling another helping of lasagna on his plate in the dining room. "Where's Livvy?"

"Downstairs watching *Winnie the Pooh*."

I grabbed a dinner roll. "Did you hear Will?"

"Yes." Mitch glanced around the room, and I could tell he didn't want to talk about it in the middle of a crowd. He picked up his plastic fork and I grabbed some napkins. We settled on the deserted steps leading to Abby and Jeff's finished basement.

"When do you think they flew naked? It couldn't have been that Monday because Will wasn't on that flight."

"No," Mitch agreed. "And he'd been gone TDY before that."

I tried to mentally reconstruct my list. "Wait. Didn't you tell me Will hopped on a flight after he got back—on the Friday the week before Penny died?"

"Yeah. That's right. He hopped on at the last minute. It must have been that flight and then he told Penny over the weekend."

"So what could happen to them for flying naked?"

Mitch took long enough between his bites to whistle softly. "Stupid thing to do. I sure wouldn't want to be in their shoes. They were out of uniform. They might get an LOR." At my puzzled look, he said, "Letter Of Reprimand, or worse. It depends on what Briman decides."

"Will said Penny was upset about one of his flights. If she knew that they flew naked, she wouldn't like it, but there wouldn't be any reason for one of the crew to kill her. An LOR is bad, but it's not the end of a career. So that lets the crew off the hook."

I broke off part of the roll. Clarissa looked like a better suspect all the time.

I hesitated a moment before I picked up the phone. Then I shook my head and reached for it. Just because someone had called and hung up a few times, I didn't need to worry about answering my phone.

"Turn on the TV," commanded Abby.

"What?" I dribbled a few Cheerios onto Livvy's high chair tray and went to get her milk.

"I know you never turn it on in the morning. Put it on channel 2, quick."

Still holding the milk, I clicked on the TV in the living room and found the channel.

A solemn brunette with short, tousled hair and a pointy chin stood beside the sign proclaiming GREENLY AIR FORCE BASE. In the background, traffic crept through the main gate. "So far officials at Greenly Air Force Base have not responded to the rumors. If a crew did fly out of uniform it would be a breach of regulations and the consequences could be grave for the pilots as well as for Greenly Air Force Base. This is Chelsea O'Mara reporting *live* from Greenly Air Force Base. Back to you, Matt."

"Thanks, Chelsea," said a fresh-faced kid from behind the desk. "There is a press conference scheduled for later today and News for You from Channel Two will keep you updated. Now on to the story of a hometown hero, a man who saved a chicken after a car struck it on a two-lane highway."

I turned off the TV. "How did it get on the news so fast?" I asked. "And how did they find out?" I returned to the kitchen.

"That reporter was there at Jeff's party. Chelsea O'Mara. Tommy introduced her to me. She's dating him, or at least that's what she said."

"What do you mean?"

"Well, I don't think they've been going out very long. Like maybe a week. I think she hooked up with Tommy to find out more about Penny and the squad. Tommy said he met her at the O Club last week. She talked to me for a long time. Actually, it was an interview. I thought she was friendly! Anyway, she wondered if I knew Penny, if I'd heard any rumors about her, stuff like that."

"Did you tell her anything?"

"Of course not. The little tidbit she overheard about

flying naked was icing on the cake. Look, I've got to get moving. We're leaving for the airport in a few minutes, but I wanted you to know she's snooping around."

"Okay. Have a great trip."

As soon as I hung up, the phone rang again in my hand. "What did you forget now?" I asked.

A laugh came over the line, but it wasn't Abby's. "To invite you to lunch. This is Irene. You were expecting someone else? Listen, I'm sooo sorry I forgot to call you. We're having a playgroup thing at McDonald's today?"

"You are?" I knew Irene from spouse coffees. I was never sure if she was making a statement or asking a question.

"Yeah, today? Can you make it?"

"Okay. I don't know if I can, but thanks for letting me know." I had a mountain of laundry waiting for me after the breakfast dishes were cleaned.

"The one on Falls Avenue? Eleven-thirty?"

I spent the morning washing and folding laundry and trying to pick up the house. Forget actual cleaning. I never got past the first step of picking up so I could clean. I tossed a toy drum, a grandparent gift—what were they thinking?—into the toy box and turned to find Livvy bent over the laundry basket, grabbing neatly folded shirts and tossing them on the floor.

"Help," she explained proudly.

I sighed. She loved to help. I picked her up and headed for the changing table. "McDonald's time!"

Livvy sat inside the ball cage with her straight back pressed against the wall, her eyebrows drawn together as she observed the other kids jumping and bouncing in the balls. She looked like an anthropologist absorbing the unknown customs of another culture.

Irene pushed her fluffy bangs off her forehead and said, "She's so cute, isn't she? Serious. Will she get in there with the other kids and play?"

"There's too much going on right now. She's taking it all in. She always does this. She's got to check everything out."

"Well, I wish my boys would slow down like that." Jill, the squadron commander's wife, sat beside me in her sweats and T-shirt. She'd just finished teaching her step-aerobics class. I'd been surprised to see her. From her attitude, I thought she held me personally responsible for the murder in the squadron last year. Never mind the fact that I didn't commit it, just revealed who did. But today she'd actually smiled and asked about Livvy.

"Bang! Bang! *Bang!* You're *dead!*" Shouts rained down from the tunnels above us. Then high-pitched screams resounded off the walls and glass enclosing the play place.

Jill tilted her head back and shouted, "Brandon! You'd better stop that right now!" I thought she'd add, "Give me fifty push-ups!" She didn't, but that voice would motivate flabby people to get moving.

Jill finished her salad and pushed the container away. I looked down at french fries scattered across the paper in front of me. I gathered the last few, dipped them in ketchup, and ate up, resisting the twinge of guilt.

"So what's the deal with the naked flight?" Irene asked. "I saw it on the news this morning . . ." Her voice trailed off and she shrugged.

Jill rolled her eyes. "I don't know anything. But if they did it, then they're in trouble." She stood and angled her tray to slide the empty food wrappers into the trash. Topic closed.

I looked across the table to the woman Irene had brought with her, Ballard Nova. She doubtfully examined her Quarter Pounder through her half glasses.

"Don't come here much, do you?" I finished off the last of my Diet Coke. She was probably in her early fifties and had a halo of frizzy gray hair, pale skin, and dark blue eyes. In her dark brown tunic and skirt, she didn't look like the usual sweatshirt-jeans-and-tennis-shoes-wearing mom that pushed through the glass door to the play place, balancing a tray stacked with Happy Meals.

"No." Her wind-catcher earrings swayed as she shook her head.

Irene pulled the band of her pink sweatshirt over her ample hips and said, "I don't know why I bother to bring the kids, you know? They don't like the food that much . . ." She gestured to the table beside us that held hamburgers and chicken nuggets abandoned with only a few bites out of them. "Next time maybe we should meet in the afternoon and get an ice cream or soda while they play? Does that sound okay?"

I liked Irene, but her tentative conversation style grated on me after a while. How did she make a decision when there wasn't a group to follow?

"Fine by me," said Jill and that settled the matter.

Irene smiled at Ballard and said, "Before everyone leaves—Ballard, will you tell them about the group? I ran into Ballard at the post office and practically dragged her here. I want everyone to know about the Pathway group. I love it and I think everyone else will, too. Won't they, Ballard?"

"They'll have to see for themselves. Anyone is welcome at our meetings on Sunday night."

"Pathway group?" asked Jill. "What is it, a support group?"

"In a sense, but we're more than that." Ballard put her hamburger down and removed her glasses. They dangled on their chain and clinked against a string of brown beads with white designs. She laced her fingers loosely together

on the table, almost like she was about to pray. She made
eye contact with each one of us and smiled gently. "Through
extensive studies of ancient texts, I've found a path to
inner joy and peace. We gather to study ancient wisdom
and encourage each other on our different journeys."

"What texts do you study?" I asked.

"Many ancient works contain great insight. One of the
greatest is the Bible. 'The unfolding of your words gives
light. It gives understanding to the simple.' Psalm 119,
verse 130. The Koran also contains valuable knowledge."
Ballard's singsong voice indicated she'd said this many
times. "If we are to come together as people and understand
each other, then we must understand each other's beliefs.
It is only in unity that there is peace."

"We meet at Ballard's orchard. It's just beautiful out
there, isn't it, Ballard?" Irene jumped back in the conversation, her voice a jarring note compared to Ballard's
even monotone. "She's got tons of great natural products.
And the best part is she grows them herself. That's how I
found her. I'm using her facial cream? Doesn't my skin
look so much smoother?"

Jill smiled for about a nanosecond and I remained
quiet. Sometimes "no" is the hardest word for me to pro-
nounce, so I decided to keep quiet instead of making a
weak half promise to go to her group.

"Penny liked her products, too." Irene sensed our re-
luctance and pressed, trying to convince us. "Penny came
to the group to babysit for us at first. She loved kids, you
know? But she ended up liking the products, too. She
swore the hand cream was the best she'd ever used."

"That's great," I said and glanced at Livvy, who had
ventured into the center of the ball cage after the other
kids left. She was tossing the balls in the air as fast and as
high as she could, her cheeks flushed with exertion. I

asked Jill, "Would you keep an eye on her? I'm going to get a refill."

"Sure." Jill didn't look any more interested in Ballard's group than I did. She pulled her coat on and yelled, "Brandon! Kyle! Time to go." She turned back to me and said, "I know it will take them five minutes just to get to the top of the slide. You've got plenty of time."

The door to the playroom shut and muffled the kids' shouts. I entered the main seating area of the restaurant and went to stand in line for a refill. I glanced back through the windows to check on Livvy. Balls were still flying and she was smiling. I took a step to the ice machine, but a construction worker in a tattered coat clomped in front of me with his heavy boots and shoved his cup under the ice dispenser. His two-way radio attached to his dirt-streaked jeans jolted out static and garbled words. He moved on to the fountain drinks and I stepped up to the ice machine shaking my head. He reached for the Coke nozzle at the same time as a woman in a long coat and heels. A small name tag clipped to her coat lapel had her name and VERNON REALTY printed on it. The construction worker stopped, stepped back, and waved her toward the drinks.

I rolled my eyes. What was I, invisible? This was not the first time this had happened to me. It seemed if you picked up an infant car seat or shepherded little kids around, you became unimportant. I'd seen the gaze of salesclerks slide over me in stores. "Just a mom, no big deal. She can wait," seemed to be their thoughts.

I jabbed my cup under the ice dispenser and filled it. As I stepped over to the drinks and filled my cup, I heard a crisp British accent behind me. I waited for the Diet Coke to fizz down and glanced over my shoulder.

"Look here, I'm telling you I don't have it." Victor

Roth leaned across a nearby table, his face tight and un-smiling. There was tension and fear on Victor's face. I turned back to the drink dispenser and heard him say, "Ellie Avery might."

What? I looked again.

"Look, I don't care who's got it. You said you'd get it and we want it," replied the man with his back to me. In my quick glance all I could see of him was the back of his head. Clumpy brown hair stuck out from under a blue baseball cap and crept over his collar.

I tilted my head and twisted my cup around. Victor said, "I said I'd try, but she died before I could get it from her. *I don't have it.* I'm telling you, I think she gave it to this Avery woman. It was in the paper. Penny went to her house before she died. Penny wouldn't leave something like that at her house. She'd find someplace else to hide it or give it to someone to keep for her."

An Everything In Its Place Tip for Organized Closets

As you replace your clothes in your closets, there are many ways to arrange items.

- Color—this is a good option if you're looking for new ways to mix and match clothing.
- Outfit—use this system if you're always running late. It will be easy to grab the whole outfit without hunting through your entire closet.
- Use—put the clothes your wear the most in the most accessible place. If you wear business suits every day, those should be front and center. Likewise, jeans and casual shirts, if your life allows a more relaxed dress code. Don't forget to make workout wear handy, too, since you'll

probably use (or intend to use!) it several times a week.

There's no "right" way to arrange your clothes. You may have to experiment a bit to find the system that works best for you.

Chapter
Twelve

My fingers trembled as I snapped the lid back on the cup. I didn't want Victor or the man in the baseball cap to see me. If I walked back through the tables to the play area, I could leave through the exit there.

"You better not be holding anything back, 'cause that would be real stupid." The baseball-capped man stood and strode out the door. I felt like my feet were glued to the floor. I couldn't have moved if I'd wanted to.

I managed to crane my neck around and look back at Victor. His head was down, bent over the table. He ran his hands through his hair and then leaned back. He looked pale, like he was about to be sick. I managed to lift my heavy feet and make it back to the play area. I followed a mom with a baby in a high chair. Victor was so absorbed in his study of the tabletop that he didn't see me.

Inside the play area, I checked on Livvy and then quickly cleared our trash off the table and grabbed my suede crescent hobo bag and Livvy's diaper bag. As I gathered Livvy's shoes from the shoe keeper, I scanned the parking lot. A dark pickup, one of the oversized kind that rumble and need two parking spaces, pulled out and swung onto the street. A person wearing a baseball cap was at the wheel.

I went through the motions of driving home, tucking Livvy in her bed for her afternoon nap, and singing her a song, but the whole time I was preoccupied with what I'd overheard. I scooped up the clothes from the floor where Livvy had tossed them and dumped them on the ottoman. With a thump, I plopped down into the overstuffed chair and contemplated the lumpy gray sky. Tiny flakes floated to the ground, but I was thinking about Victor. He'd said he didn't have "it." He'd tried to get "it" from Penny, but she died before he could get "it" from her. I picked up a black turtleneck and smoothed it out on the ottoman. I'd thought Penny's death had something to do with what we talked about the morning of the day she died, either the flight crew or her activities with the exhibit. But the flight crew was just nervous about flying naked. That's why they were so skittish when I talked to them. Penny wouldn't have liked the stunt Will participated in, but even if Penny threatened to tell, flying naked wasn't the kind of thing you killed someone over.

I folded the turtleneck into a perfect square and stared at it. If only the questions surrounding Penny's death could be squared away so neatly. There was still the question of what Clarissa Bedford was up to. She'd hated Penny and was probably having an affair, but now there was the question of Victor, too. He'd wanted something from Penny. He told the man he hadn't got it. But what if he had? What if he was just saying he hadn't to keep the man away from him? And throwing Mr. Baseball Cap my name to keep him occupied? I quickly grabbed a soft long-sleeved white shirt and folded it. I wished Mitch wasn't in a training class today or that Abby wasn't gone on her trip. I needed one of them to talk through this with me.

Then there was Ballard Nova. Penny babysat for her group. With a sigh, I stacked the shirt and grabbed another. So there was another person. How many people had Penny's life intersected with? There was her art class, too. I left the laundry and pulled out my list. I added *Victor, Ballard*, and *art class*. My mood felt as gray as the day.

"But what is 'it'?" asked Thistlewait.

"I don't know." I shifted in the thinly padded office chair. I'd called Thistlewait late that afternoon and he'd agreed to see me at three o'clock at the OSI office. I was trying to convince myself that the hard looks I'd received on my way in had nothing to do with the investigation.

"Well." He closed his small notebook and shifted gears. "Mrs. Follette ingested the same poison that put Lieutenant Lamar in the hospital."

"But Penny didn't die of poisoning," I said, puzzled. I glanced over to the corner to check on Livvy. She looked like an Olympic weight lifter as she squatted with her back perfectly straight to examine the carpet.

"No, but if she'd lived long enough, she would have. The type of poison Mrs. Follette ingested sometimes takes seventy-two hours to affect the victim."

"What was it?" I asked. Livvy tottered over, a staple pinched in her chubby fingers.

"I'm afraid I can't go into that," he said, his tone formal.

I took the staple and said good-bye, thoughtfully. Wasn't poison supposed to be a woman's choice for a murder weapon? The only women on my suspect list were Clarissa and Ballard. I needed to talk to Clarissa when she got back from her trip. Thistlewait hadn't seemed very interested when I told him about Mr. Baseball Cap. And Mr. Baseball Cap looked more like the type to use direct, hands-on violence than a removed murder weapon like poison. Besides, if Penny had something he wanted, it wouldn't make sense to kill her.

I thought I'd seen the last of Thistlewait for a while, but he showed up at my door at six that night and handed me a piece of paper. "Search warrant," he said and motioned to a group of people behind him.

"What?" A stream of people pushed past me. "Wait a minute." I flicked a glance over the paper. "You can't barge in here—"

"We can," Thistlewait said with a mixture of finality and sympathy. Mitch came in from the kitchen carrying Livvy, who was chanting, "Moe, peez," words she knew would get her more food.

"They say they've got a search warrant." I handed the papers to Mitch and took Livvy.

Mitch's face went from puzzlement to anger as he said, "What is this?"

Thistlewait said, "Sorry. We've got to do it."

"I'm calling Legal." Mitch left the room.

"There's a problem here?" asked a man on my porch. In his quilted vest over a plaid flannel shirt he looked like he'd just returned from deer hunting.

"No, I don't think so," Thistlewait said, then turned to me. "This is Detective Jensen. Vernon police. He's investigating Mrs. Follette's death."

Detective Jensen held out his hand. I looked at it, then Thistlewait. A rush of anger surged through me. How could Thistlewait perform perfect social introductions at a time like this? People were invading my home! Did he think I was going to politely shake Jensen's hand, fall into chitchat mode, and say things like "So how is homicide these days?"

I don't think so. "We've met," I said shortly. Detective Jensen pulled his hand away and smoothed his salt-and-pepper beard. I stepped back stiffly and the men came inside. I was so angry I was speechless, a common condition for me. I couldn't put the phrases flying through my mind into coherent sentences. I shoved the door, it slammed, and I retreated to the kitchen.

I put Livvy in her high chair and gave her some plastic cups and bowls to play with. At the stove, I automatically stirred the ravioli noodles. It cooked so fast, it would be done in a few minutes. What were we supposed to do? Eat it with the police poking into our closets, drawers, and papers? A strange sound bubbled up my throat, half laugh, half sob. Why was I thinking about dinner at a time like this? Through the doorway, I saw the people, crime scene technicians probably, pull on latex gloves and then spread out through the living room and back into the bedrooms, like bugs, infecting each room. How could they invade our life, our privacy like this? I heard Mitch talking to Thistlewait, and then Mitch returned to the kitchen and sat down heavily at the table. "Legal's closed."

"It figures, it's after four-thirty. How can they do this? How can they come in and search?"

Mitch tossed the paperwork on the table. "Thistlewait said they had information about the poison, and there was something else that he wouldn't tell me."

"Can't we stop them?"

Livvy banged her bowl on the high chair.

Mitch sprawled back in the chair. Anger edged his words as he said, "How? Do you know a good lawyer we can call quick?"

"No, I don't know any lawyer, much less a good one."

"We don't have anything to hide, anyway." Mitch sat up. "Let them search."

Something sizzled behind me and a scorched smell permeated the kitchen. "The ravioli!" I pushed the pan off the burner, just as the buzzer went off. I dumped the noodles in the drainer in the sink. "Agh! I forgot to warm up the sauce."

"Don't worry about it." Mitch went to the pantry and came back with a jar of spaghetti sauce. "I'll nuke it." He tipped the jar's contents into a bowl, slammed the microwave door, and pushed the number pad. By the time I had the noodles drained, the sauce was done and we sat down to our one-item supper.

"I was going to make a salad." I heard the creak of the linen closet door opening. "I hope they like my towels," I said sarcastically. Then came the faint beep of the computer starting up. "Can they do that? Search our computer, too?"

"Yeah," Mitch said with a sigh, "they can. But they're not going to find anything."

There was a shout from the back of the house and Thistlewait left the living room where he'd been looking through drawers in our end table. I glanced at Mitch and we both followed Thistlewait back to our bedroom. The room was small to begin with, but with the technician, Thistlewait, Detective Jensen, and Mitch crowding in, I could barely get in the door. I popped up on my tiptoes and looked over Mitch's shoulder.

A long beaded necklace dangled from the technician's gloved hand above my open jewelry box. Then it dribbled down into a pool of dark beads inside a plastic bag. After scribbling a note, the technician handed the bag to Thistlewait.

"You're interested in the necklace I brought back from our honeymoon cruise?" I asked.

"That's where these came from? Your honeymoon?"

"Yeah," I said as I watched the technician continue his inspection, opening our dresser drawers and shuffling the clothes around. I was going to be busy cleaning up after these people.

"Where?"

"What?" I said, drawing my gaze away from the mess of the linen closet down the hall where towels and sheets puddled on the shelves and on the floor. "Do they have to make such a mess?"

"Where on your honeymoon?"

"Cozumel. Or was it Saint Thomas?" I looked at Mitch.

He shrugged. Jewelry made his eyes glaze over, so no help there. "Well, I'm not sure, but it was on our honeymoon. We stopped at Jamaica, Saint Thomas, and Cozumel. It was in one of those places."

"And it's been in your jewelry box ever since. How many years?" Detective Jensen asked.

"It'll be four years in June. But I wore them a few weeks ago. They're really popular now. There's even a little shop in the mall that sells them." I didn't like the way Thistlewait studied the bag, then eyed me carefully, as if he was reevaluating me. "If you think that had anything to do with the poisoning, then you're going to have to look in a lot of jewelry boxes. I've seen lots of people wearing those necklaces lately."

Thistlewait's eyes narrowed. "Really?"

"Yes, really. You know something, a purse or a necklace gets 'hot.' Everyone wants one. Like that necklace in the movie *Tin Cup*. For a while everyone I knew had a floating pearl necklace." I walked over to the twisted pile of necklaces on the dresser and plucked out a necklace with pearls suspended individually along the chain about one inch apart. "Those dark beads are just as popular around here." I closed my eyes. "I saw some the other day." I opened my eyes. "Ballard Nova was wearing them at McDonald's and she knew Penny fairly well. And Bree had some at Jeff's party. They're everywhere."

"I see." Thistlewait rubbed his hands through his curly hair and didn't bother to try and hide his sigh.

Despite four hours of poking and prodding into every corner of our house, the only thing Thistlewait and Detective Jensen left with was the small bag of beads. I hurried out of the grocery store the next day and wished I'd parked under a light instead of on the murky fringes of the parking lot. Mitch was home with Livvy so I'd made a quick trip to the store. I'd been so busy cleaning up the mess the police left that I'd forgotten to buy milk.

I shivered, remembering the search and Thistlewait's assessing look when he held the necklace. That stupid necklace. I'd bought it on a whim. If only I'd admired it and put it back. I could've bought a T-shirt instead, but no, I had to have something different from the usual tourist junk.

I took a deep breath and maneuvered the cart over icy ruts in the parking lot. *Stop worrying.* Worry wasn't going to get me out of this mess. Surely there was something I could do instead of playing the same track of worries repeatedly in my mind. With my keys laced through my fingers, I gripped the basket handle tighter and splashed through the slush as huge snowflakes dropped from the darkness. The flakes had grown during the day and now floated down like large weightless quarters.

Maybe Georgia could help me out with more information. And then there was Irene's phone call earlier in the evening inviting me to the Pathway group on Sunday night. I pushed the basket into the narrow valley between

the Cherokee and the SUV parked beside it. I stepped in
the V of the open back door and heaved in my tan Coach
bag. Then I grabbed two gallons of whole milk and set
them on the floorboard. Since Livvy had transitioned to
whole milk, I couldn't seem to keep it in the fridge. Between her and Mitch, we were going through three gallons a week. I turned back to scoop up the bags with
diapers, cereal, and apples. I leaned in the Cherokee,
tucked away the last bag.

Feet pounded through the slush near me. I glanced
back and got a quick impression of a large man in a
hooded coat bearing down on me. Before I could move he
shoved the basket aside and cinched his arm roughly
around my chest from behind me and pinned my arms to
my side.

I felt his labored breathing. Gaspy white puffs of air
floated above my ear. An acrid sweaty smell enveloped me.
Move, scream, fight, I commanded myself, but I couldn't.
It was like one of those awful dreams where I strain with
all my might to move or talk, but I'm held motionless and
mute. Bits of self-defense classes and advice flickered
through my mind. Where were my keys? Probably on the
ground. Go for the eyes, I remembered. I took a deep
breath, ready to reach back and poke, but then a thin coldness touched my neck. I stayed still.

The fur trim on the coat's hood tickled my cheek. He
leaned down and whispered, "I'll give you one chance to
give it up."

I thought of my purse tossed so casually on the seat,
far out of my reach. I pulled my hand up slowly and
pointed inside the Cherokee.

His grip tightened and the knife pressed harder against
my neck. He said something, but I focused on the headlights that swept over us as a rumbling SUV pulled into
the slot directly in front of the Cherokee. The headlights

blazed as the door opened, and then a woman popped up on the running board and shouted, "Hey, are you okay over there?"

His grip lessened and I felt the cool night air on my neck where the knife blade had been. The lights and another woman's voice seemed to free me from my motionless spell. I croaked, "Help!" and stepped down hard on his instep, twisting, writhing to get away. My hip slammed against the basket and it skidded down the length of the Cherokee. "Help," I screamed again, this time louder. The blare of a horn sounded from the SUV.

My attacker let go, cursing, and then ran down the narrow aisle between the cars away from the headlights. A skinny kid in a leather jacket and a green apron was pushing a line of carts. "Get him! Get him!" screeched the woman from the SUV. The kid looked up, puzzled. The hooded figure pounded toward him. The kid stepped out from behind the line of carts. The man shoved him square in the chest and sent the kid sprawling. The man pounded across the parking lot and disappeared into the nearby residential area. I heard a car engine roar, the screech of gears, and then a muffler thumping away in the night.

The kid picked himself up and totted to the edge of the parking lot, then returned to the Cherokee where I gripped the cart and tried to get my breath back. I was drenched in sweat and my hands and legs were shaking uncontrollably. I probably looked like a possessed wind-up toy.

"He's gone," the kid said to me. The door of the SUV slammed and a woman hurried over to me, her cell phone tucked next to her expensively highlighted blond hair. "Yes," she was saying as she daintily stepped over the piles of slush, "an attempted mugging. Copeland's parking lot." She gave the address and then slid the phone into the pocket of her long double-breasted wool coat. "Are you all right, dear? Oh, look. You're bleeding, but it's not deep. Just a scratch."

She stepped carefully back to her SUV. I touched my neck and saw a thin dash of red on my gloves. The woman appeared again, a wad of tissue in her hand. "Here, put this on your neck. Come this way. You need to sit down." She opened the driver's door and guided me into the seat. This must be how my grandmother felt after she broke her hip and had to learn to walk again. I concentrated on putting one foot in front of the other.

The woman turned away and I heard her inspecting the kid for damage and fussing over him. I leaned back in the seat and focused on the snowflake mosaic frozen on the windshield.

Chapter
Thirteen

Between the three of us we were able to piece together a description of the man.

"Dark, hooded coat with fur trim around the hood," I said, then sipped at the hot coffee a store employee had brought for us.

"It was dark green," said the woman who had made the phone call. She finished her coffee, adjusted her bright scarf, and pulled out a slip of paper, her grocery list. "And he was wearing jeans," she added. I couldn't remember her name.

The kid who was bringing in baskets stood awkwardly on the other side of the grocery store manager's office, fingering the ring through his eyebrow. He shuffled his feet, slurped his coffee. "Big boots," he added suddenly. "I forgot to tell the police officer that. He was wearing those heavy boots like construction workers or hikers wear."

I fingered the tiny cut, a scratch, at the base of my ear. It had already stopped bleeding and scabbed over.

A woman in the dark blue of Vernon's police department entered the tiny room. Her radio squawked and she turned it down. "We're finished with your car, ma'am. We'll talk to the people in the neighborhood to see if they saw any unusual cars tonight."

"He was wearing heavy boots, brown. You know, like construction worker boots," said the kid, edging to the door. The police officer pulled out her small notebook, jotted in it, and nodded to the kid and the woman. "Thanks for your help," she said and stood aside to let them leave the room.

As the woman in the wool coat sailed past, she patted my shoulder and said, "Take care."

I stood up experimentally. My legs held, so I shuffled over to the desk and set down my full cup of coffee. It had done a great job warming my hands. "Does this happen a lot in this neighborhood?"

Officer Rutledge adjusted the zipper of her heavy coat and shook her head. "No. We're seeing more muggings and purse snatchings, but usually downtown. And it's tapered off since Christmas."

I led the way out of the office into the store. The fluorescent lights glared and the bright colors of magazines, candy bars, and balloons seemed to shriek at me as an ache throbbed behind my eyes. Great, a headache. As I walked past a bagger stuffing groceries in plastic bags, he shouted someone's name. I started.

"You're still in hyperaware mode," said Officer Rutledge. "I'll follow you home."

That statement did nothing to reassure me. Instead, the bar of lights in my rearview mirror made me more nervous and jumpy. I was afraid I'd do something stupid, like forget to signal or run a stop sign, but I managed to coast into my driveway without seeing the lights flash in my mirror. I got out, waved at the patrol car, and then stood there a moment, trying to remember something. Oh yeah. The groceries.

I opened the back door and stared at the gallons of milk and the bags of apples. The kitchen door opened and Mitch bounded down the steps. I'd called him from the store. He'd stayed at home because Livvy was asleep and he couldn't leave her. His arms encircled me and he said, "Are you okay? I could have woken Livvy up and come up there. I didn't think about that when you called."

I leaned into his shoulder. "Are you kidding? Never wake a sleeping baby, or a toddler, for that matter! I'm all right. A little jumpy, but I had a police escort home. Won't that drive Mabel crazy?"

Mitch released me and grabbed the groceries out of the Cherokee. "She probably won't be able to sleep tonight."

I grabbed the last bag and gallon of milk, then elbowed the door shut. "I just hope I can," I said and walked into the kitchen with a sigh of relief. What is it about being home that makes everything better? It's illogical, the feeling that I'm safe or that everything will be okay if I can get inside my kitchen door. I was probably as vulnerable in my driveway as I was in the parking lot at the grocery store, but the feeling of security enveloped me. The ache behind my eyes eased and I plopped into a chair while Mitch put the groceries away.

"Do you think it could have anything to do with that conversation you overheard? Did you tell the police about it?"

"No. I didn't think of that." I stood up to get some ibuprofen. I washed it down with a glass of water from the faucet, so cold that it made me shiver, even though I was still in my coat. I walked into the living room and curled up in our overstuffed chair. "They assumed it was an attempted purse snatching. They even told me I was lucky that I'd tossed my purse into the Cherokee first where he couldn't reach it. What good would it do Mr. Baseball Cap to attack me or try to take my purse? Even if Penny gave me something, I wouldn't carry it around in my purse."

"Maybe he wanted to scare you."

I shook my head. "I don't think so. This was one of those random crimes. He saw I was preoccupied and that he could get some cash or credit cards. All he said was, 'I'll give you a chance to give it up.' He had to mean my purse. Why do you have your suitcase out?" It was open on the couch and piles of clothes spilled out of the laundry basket on the coffee table. I ran through my mental calendar, but Mitch wasn't supposed to go on a trip until his deployment next week.

Mitch squashed the last plastic bag and walked over to lean on the door frame. "I'm on twenty-four-hour phone alert."

"What? What's going on?"

"They won't say. I'm supposed to stay near the phone, so they can put me in crew rest, if they need to."

I grabbed the remote control. I could usually guess why Mitch was on alert, if I watched the news. I folded clothes as the news anchor said, "A trade delegation from the Middle East will arrive in the Northwest next week. Delegates from Bulgaria, Turkey, and Macedonia, nations allied with the United States in the War on Terror, hope to expand cooperation with the U.S. from security issues to economic interests. Another ally in the War on Terror, the Gulf nation of Osan, has seen tensions rise over the United States' use of its airfields. Escalating violence there threatened the American embassy. There's no word from the White House on whether more U.S. troops will deploy to the region."

"What about your regular deployment?"

Mitch called from the kitchen, "Don't know. If I go, it might be a short turnaround and then we'd still go on the deployment. Or they could roll us from this into the deployment. Or they might task another unit to fill the deployment and then send us home after this, if we go."

It reminded me of the convoluted sports reporting near the end of football season when the sports anchor runs through all thirty-five variables if team A wins and team B loses.

I stacked a neatly folded T-shirt next to Mitch's pile of tan flight suits. "Well, maybe this will be like all the other times and nothing will happen." Usually, Mitch lived out of a suitcase for several days and we jumped every time the phone rang, only to have the whole thing evaporate after a few days. I picked up my jeans and put them away. I slid the drawer shut and Mitch's arm encircled me. He said, "It'll be okay. I probably won't have to go." He kissed my neck, just below my ear.

"I know. I hate the waiting, though."

"I don't like it either." He kissed the other side of my neck. "You know, we should go to bed early," he said in a lighter tone. I watched his reflection in the dresser mirror. He waggled his eyebrows at me. "I might ship out any minute."

I circled in his arms and put my arms around his neck. "Then we'd better use our time wisely."

It was later that night when I was curled up next to Mitch's warm back that I remembered the man's words before the headlights spotlighted us. When I pointed to my purse, he'd said, "Not that."

I slid out of bed and went to the kitchen. Moving blindly, I felt for the cabinet door, found a glass, and filled it with water. After a few sips I sat down at the table, trying to make sense of the thoughts racing around in my mind.

A random mugger wouldn't have turned down my purse. I forced myself to go over the words I'd heard the man say. Again, I felt the bite of the cold air and the even colder sliver of steel against my throat. He'd said I had one chance to give it to him.

"It" again. I sipped the water. I took a deep breath and reminded myself I was back in my kitchen, safe and unharmed. Was it the same "it" that Victor and Mr. Baseball Cap were talking about? Were Victor and Mr. Baseball Cap in something together? Something illegal or shady? Was it linked to Penny's death? The faster I figured out what it was and whether or not it was related, the safer we'd be. I placed the glass in the sink and rechecked the dead bolt on the back door. I snuggled into bed against Mitch, but it was a long time before I slept.

I decided to visit Georgia Lamar. I knew she'd been released from the hospital a few days ago. I wasn't sure if she'd slam the door in my face, but there was only one way to find out. After church on Sunday afternoon, I left Mitch immersed in a basketball game with Livvy snoozing in her room. I zipped down the sweeping curves of Rim Rock Road between twin ribbons of snow that the plow had pushed up. The main artery into downtown, the road itself was sanded and clear of snow. I felt like a bobsledder streaking down a course between the mounting walls of snow.

I stopped at the little gas station tucked into the residential neighborhood, picked up a newspaper, and considered the heavy gray sky. Well, it wasn't snowing at that moment and there was no wind, so I might as well fill up the Cherokee with gas now. Tomorrow's forecast was windy with snow.

After I paid for the gas, I borrowed the cashier's phone book. There were ten Lamars listed, but only one had just an initial G. Lamar on Lilly Avenue, and I bet it was Georgia. Why do single women list only an initial and their last name? Instead of camouflaging them, it shouts, "Hey, I'm a single woman, living alone." I checked the coordinates on the map and realized I was only a few blocks away from Lilly Avenue.

Back in the Cherokee with a Hershey's bar to sustain me, I continued down Rim Rock Road until I neared the interstate and the Victorian houses transitioned from single-family homes to divided apartments. I found the address and edged into a precarious park on the car-lined street. The two- and three-story gingerbread-trimmed homes had plenty of space to convert into apartments, but not a lot of parking. Studying the pale yellow Queen Anne that now sported peeling paint and two front doors, I ate half the Hershey's bar and debated whether I really wanted to talk to Georgia.

Thistlewait was definitely not going to let me in on the investigation. He'd been formal and exact during the rest of the search of our house. Georgia would at least have some details about her poisoning and maybe she'd share them with me, I hoped. Of course, if she thought I'd tried to poison her, she might be less helpful. I popped the last rectangle of chocolate into my mouth and got out of the Cherokee. Normally, I wouldn't pester someone just out of the hospital, but besides the attempted purse snatching, the OSI had searched my house. That was enough to banish any restraints I usually felt. Until Clarissa returned from her trip I could focus on Georgia and Ballard. I couldn't figure out a way to find out anything about Victor yet.

I took a giant step over the snow piled on the curb and tromped to the front door. As I contemplated the two blank cards inserted above the doorbells, wondering which one was Georgia's, a sporty CRV crunched up the narrow driveway and parked behind the house. I wished I'd brought something like a casserole or dessert. She'd just gotten out of the hospital, after all. On second thought, she probably wouldn't touch any food from me. I walked around the side of the house and caught Georgia as she inserted her key in the lock of the back door.

"Hi," I said. Georgia's vivid blue eyes narrowed as soon as she recognized me. "I'd like to ask you a few questions," I continued awkwardly. "Would you like to go get a cup of coffee with me?" Even though I didn't drink coffee, I'd choke some down, if that would get Georgia to talk to me.

She surveyed me without moving an inch. I felt like we were kids playing freeze tag and someone had shouted "Freeze." She wore aerodynamic running shoes, cherry-colored leggings, and a blue Air Force Academy sweatshirt. She'd obviously been working out. She sure looked healthy for someone recovering from an attempted poisoning. I'd expected her to be resting on the couch. With a click, she pushed the key over and said, "You might as well come in. I make better coffee than anything you can buy."

She left the door open, so I followed her inside the kitchen and shut the door. I glanced around the large kitchen. When the house was divided Georgia's side got the original kitchen. Harvest-gold appliances showed the house had been remodeled, but not recently. "Have a seat." Georgia indicated a counter that separated the kitchen from the living room. I scooped up a bundle of pink yarn bristling with knitting needles and sat down.

"Sorry," Georgia said as she shoved the knitting down

the counter to a pile of junk mail, keys, phone books, and a cordless phone. It was the typical "drop everything here" area that most people have somewhere in their house. I mentally sorted and rearranged the clutter at the end of the counter, putting the phone on a shelf with the phone books underneath and the mail in a hanging basket on the wall. But I wasn't here for an organizing consultation, so I focused on Georgia.

"Does your roommate knit?" I asked once the coffee grinder fell silent.

"No. I do. That's for my sister. She's having a baby in May. It helps pass the time, especially when I'm TDY."

Not what I would have thought of as one of her pastimes. She strode back and forth across the kitchen, grabbed milk and mugs. I frowned. She looked extremely healthy and physically fit for someone who'd recently checked out of the hospital. "You were working out?"

"Yeah. The faster I get back into my routine, the faster I'll get back where I was."

"Is that a good idea? Shouldn't you take it easy for a while? Give your body time to recover?"

She gave an impatient snort. "I'm running in White Falls. I don't have time to go slow."

I raised my eyebrows. Vernon's unofficial kickoff for spring, the White Falls Run was a demanding race that began in town, wound up through the foothills, and then twisted back to end at the historic bridge over White Falls in downtown Vernon. It was a huge event. Thousands of people turned out each year and there were several classes of participants. I'd definitely be in the "Walkers." Georgia probably got a place in the timed 10-K race.

We were both silent as Georgia started the coffee. A little question prodded its way into my mind. Could Georgia have poisoned Penny and then eaten some of the poison herself, so she wouldn't be under suspicion? She'd

made an excellent recovery if she was already training for
White Falls.

As the silence stretched I began to wish I hadn't come.
Georgia wasn't in a confiding mood. "Let's go in here,"
she said after she handed me an oversized yellow mug
and led the way into the living room at the front of the
house. The wood floors creaked under their layer of worn
shag carpeting, just like our floors did, but this house had
a different feel to it than ours. Both houses were old, but
ours, an art-and-crafts style bungalow, had a sturdy, bulky
feeling, like a stout matron. This house was even older
and it seemed more delicate, like a fragile Victorian spin-
ster.

Georgia took a Papasan chair. I sat down on the wicker
couch with floral cushions. An exercise bike angled in
front of a massive entertainment center and a drafting
table stood in the dining area. I recognized a few of the
framed snapshots on Georgia's walls. Most were from her
TDYs and deployments around the world. In one picture,
she wore her flight suit and smiled with a bare Middle
Eastern landscape in the background. I noticed the poster
of the man's backside that had caused such an uproar
propped against a far wall behind the drafting table with
some other prints.

I turned back to her, realizing she was going to let me
do the talking. I'd try the head-on approach like I had
with Aaron. "Georgia, I'm sorry about what happened. I
had no idea about the espresso beans."

She shifted in the shallow bowl of the chair, tucking
her feet up under her. "Yeah. Well. Okay."

She sipped her coffee and studied me for a moment before she spoke. "You know I was really mad at you in the
hospital. But looking at you." She scanned me up and
down and shrugged. "You don't look like you'd be able to

do anything that vicious. You look too much like . . . a mommy."

Did I look like a frumpy housewife or bland and perfect like June Cleaver? Probably frumpy.

"Hey, don't take that the wrong way. I mean it as a compliment."

"Oh. Well, thanks." *I think.* Maybe I was a tad defensive about being "just a mom," but I could sort that out later. I focused on why I was here. "Did you know Penny?"

"No. I'd seen her around the base, but never talked to her."

"What about Clarissa Bedford?" I asked.

"Who?"

"The wing commander's wife."

A spurt of laughter erupted from her lips. "Bedford's wife? Why would I know her?"

"Just asking."

This line of questioning wasn't getting anywhere, so I asked about the poisoning. "It was pretty bad?"

"You don't want to know what they did."

"What kind of poison was it?" I asked.

"Ricin." Her aloof manner dropped way. "It comes from a castor bean." She leaned over to a stack of books and papers on the floor and pulled out a set of papers stapled together. I studied the color printout of several large dark brown beans, each covered with unique white designs. I gripped the coffee mug tighter in my hand as I realized it was quivering. These looked exactly like my necklace. And the other necklaces I'd seen recently. "A tiny amount can kill an adult. I was very lucky to survive. They think I only ate one bean."

And I had that stuff in my jewelry box? Thank goodness I didn't let Livvy play with my jewelry. Scratch the idea of Georgia trying to poison herself to cover up murder. I doubted she'd be stupid enough to use something as powerful as ricin. "So not every bean in the bag was poisonous?"

"No. A few chocolate-coated castor beans were mixed in with the rest of the espresso beans."

Penny carried that little gold bag in the side pocket of her backpack all the time. It wouldn't be hard to slip a few extra beans into the bag. Anyone who'd spent time with Penny knew how much she loved chocolate-covered espresso beans. But it would take time to get the beans ready. Someone had to find the beans, coat them with melted chocolate, then mix them in with the other beans.

"When did you eat them?" I asked.

"Monday, but I didn't start feeling sick until Thursday."

"Wait. Castor beans? The caption on this photo says 'prayer beads.' "

"Well, they're made into necklaces, earrings, rosaries, bracelets, all that kind of stuff. Pretty common around here. There's a woman down at the mall, a real granola-and-Birkenstock type. She grows the plant so she can make them into necklaces and bracelets. Her whole shop is beans, seashells, and wind catchers."

"They must be pretty common," I said and felt relieved since that fact probably lessened my chances for arrest.

"I'll say. Now that I've started thinking about it, I've remembered a lot of women wearing them. You. My roommate. Bree. Irene. Of course you were the first one I thought of. Mitch has that picture of you and him on his desk. You're wearing them in the picture."

"Our honeymoon."

"Sorry to sic the police on you like that."

So that's how Thistlewait got his search warrant. I looked at the picture again and said, "But surely not many people would know they were poisonous. I didn't."

"The OSI tells me there was a report on the news about a month ago. A little girl down in Yakima died after chewing on a necklace. Of course, the newspeople had to go into detail about how poisonous it is, what plant it comes from, the whole thing."

"So anyone who watched the news could have known."

"You got it."

An Everything In Its Place Tip for Organized Closets

Once you've sorted your closet items take a look at the "Keep" pile and assess what you have and what you need in your closet. You might even draw a rough draft of where you want to put everything in your closet. Here's a few ideas to use as you put things back in your closet:

- Use shelf separators, baskets, or crates to keep sweaters and purses where they belong.
- Use an over-the-door shoe holder with clear pouches for sorting small items that tend to get lost on shelves or on the floor: belts, scarves, hose, ties, even jewelry.
- Shoe caddies are an easy way to organize shoes, but if you like to keep your shoes in shoe boxes simply write on the end which shoe is in the box or put a photo on each box.
- For belts, purchase a hanger with small hooks spaced across the bottom bar.
- If you don't have a clothes hamper make room for one in your newly organized closet. A ham-

per can be as simple as a large laundry basket. You can even get a jump on your laundry if you've got room for a three-compartment container. Some models also come with wheels.

Chapter
Fourteen

Ballard Nova looked distinctly monklike in her rough black tunic, loose pants, and sandals over thick socks. Did she really wear those outside? Surely she changed into boots before tromping out to her house located a few yards away from this building. Her reading glasses, suspended on a chain, clinked against strands of plastic beads as she shifted in the rocking chair. I checked her necklaces, but she wasn't wearing castor beans.

Her body language reinforced the religious associations. With her elbows propped up on the arms of the rocker, she placed her palms together and murmured, "I sense a turbulence, a disturbance, here. Does that speak to anyone?"

Her pose looked meditative, but it reminded me of a boss I'd had. Now it seemed like an eon ago, but it was only a few years ago at my first PR job. He'd lace his fingers together and look like he was about to pray, but then he'd ask why such-and-such client was complaining. After a few months I'd cringe when I saw that fake prayer pose because I knew "the team" was in for a royal chewing-out.

But no one else in the rough circle of folding chairs and cushions seemed to notice anything off with Ballard's pose or words. Soft classical music floated down from speakers hidden in the rafters, the only sound as the people closed their eyes or stared intently at the no-frills industrial carpet.

"There's no one with any turmoil in their lives?" Ballard asked again.

Pretty general question. In a group this big there's got to be something bothering someone. Or actually, there's probably something bothering every one of us.

"Yes, I have a disturbance," said Irene. She sat cross-legged on a pillow beside me. With her eyes closed she said, "There's tension in our house?"

"Let's all concentrate. Send soothing thoughts to Irene and her house," said Ballard.

I watched as the people, mostly young women, closed their eyes and furrowed their brows. When I'd arrived with Irene I'd been surprised to recognize another squadron spouse, Bree Reed, Aaron's wife. Her hair was still shocking red. Today she had the beret on again with a red fringed sweater and orange velvet pants belted with an orange-and-red-patterned scarf.

I watched her out of the corner of my eye to see if she'd speak up. Having the fact that your husband flew naked on a military flight broadcast on the news had to be disturbing, not to mention the punishment aspect. Mitch said the rumor was that the guys were getting an LOR, a Letter Of Reprimand, sort of a slap on the hand. I bet that would get Georgia fired up again.

"Anyone else?" asked Ballard. After a pause, she continued, "Well, does anyone want to share?"

I twisted my wrist to see my watch. I'd been here for an

hour. First Ballard read passages from the Bible and the Koran. After a meditation time, she read a poem about snow written by one of the group members. I wiggled my toes and felt pinpricks trickle across the soles of my feet. Great. My feet were asleep.

"I have news," Bree said. "I've sold two more paintings."

A chorus of congratulations greeted this announcement. I tried not to grimace as I moved my feet an inch. How much longer would we sit here? I began to compose what I'd say to Irene when the meeting was over because I knew she was trying to sign me up as a member.

"I'm leaving for Turkey next week," said the only male in the group, Rory Tyler, the boom operator, also from the notorious naked flight. He was another surprising face to see here. He pushed up his round glasses that magnified his eyes as he scanned the group.

"You're *always* off to Turkey," said Ballard with a smile. "We'll concentrate on good travel and a safe journey. Now, let's have a few moments of meditation. Empty your mind and let the stillness flow into your body."

I leaned over to Irene and whispered, "Bathroom?"

She pointed to the door we'd come in. I slipped out of the circle as unobtrusively as I could, but I probably drew some attention as I limped to the door with sharp needles piercing my legs. This had turned out to be a waste of time. Ballard was another aspect of Penny's life and I'd hoped to find out if anyone knew anything about Penny and her death, but so far all I'd gotten were pins and needles in my feet.

As my circulation returned, I left the new prefabricated aluminum building and entered a small attached store, the way we'd entered. I suspected this building, a large shed with cement floors and wood siding, had stood on the property as long as the small frame house we'd passed on our way up the ridge. Ballard's property, a cherry orchard, was located northeast of Vernon where ridges and foothills of the Rocky Mountains began. On the drive up, our headlights had picked out several faded signs that read CHERRIES. BING. RAINIER. U-PICK. Under the crude lettering, wavy arrows pointed down rutted lanes.

In the summer, SUVs packed the roads to Cherry Bluff as families with young kids arrived to pick cherries. But now in the middle of winter the lanes were empty and deep with snow. On the drive to the meeting the security lights on the homes tucked up on the bluff flickered faintly as we passed, and then we'd been plunged back in the black night with only our headlights pressing against the white kaleidoscope of falling snow.

That same feeling of isolation, the deep quiet, permeated this little shack. I walked through the long tables in the back that held cardboard boxes. Rows of flowers and herbs hung from wooden rafters. A bank of shelves near the back held stacks of lotions, creams, herbal teas, and bath soaps.

A counter cut across the front of the room, and up near the main entrance the same bottles and jars decorated with raffia bows were displayed in crates stacked on bales of hay. Rough, brown bags spotted with little dots to show it was recycled paper sat at the end of the counter near an antique cash register and a sleek calculator.

Trying to pick up a signal on my cell phone, I walked from the long tables in the work area where the beauty products were assembled and packaged to the front where they were sold to Ballard's faithful Pathway group members and any customer that might arrive mistakenly in search of u-pick cherries. If I stood in the corner of the counter between two bales of hay with my head at a forty-five-degree angle, I was able to dial.

Mitch answered. "I just got the call. I'm off alert."

I breathed a sigh of relief. I'd rather have Mitch home than halfway around the world. I'd be fine without him, but it was much nicer to have him around.

"How's it going?" he asked.

"Boring. They're not through with the meeting yet and I haven't found anything to connect Ballard with Penny. Ballard's a little out there, kind of kooky, but that's all I've found out. All Irene knew was that Penny watched the kids. I haven't seen any kids tonight. Aaron's wife, Bree, is here and Rory Tyler is here, too."

"Rory?"

"I know. I was surprised, too."

"What's he doing there? He didn't strike me as the spiritual type," Mitch said.

"I don't know. He's the only guy and there are about fifteen women here. Maybe he likes that ratio."

"No one at the squad is going to let him forget this. Is it his first time there?"

"I don't think so. He said something about leaving for Turkey, and Ballard kidded him about always going to Turkey."

"Even better."

"Mitch, you're not going to be mean, are you?"

"Are you kidding? Everything's fair game. Remember when I couldn't find my boxers on that trip last spring to Japan? Rory took them out of my suitcase before we left and stapled them to the antlers above the bar in the Hole. I owe him."

I rolled my eyes. Sometimes the squadron seemed more like a college frat house than a workplace. If there was something serious going on, a difficult mission, they were focused and all over it. And they excelled too, but when it was boring, they regressed to baser instincts. "Look, I'd better go. I'll get home as soon as I can. Love you."

We hung up. I wished I'd driven, but I hadn't so I was stuck here until the meeting broke up. I studied the calendar tacked on the wall with work schedules. I'd drawn a blank with Georgia and now I wasn't finding anything to connect Ballard with Penny. It still seemed Clarissa had the only motive to want Penny dead. I walked back to the newer building, thinking about motive. I stopped. Wasn't that the weakest thing to pursue? Motives could be hidden, but what about opportunity? I went back and checked the calendar. Ballard ran the store the Monday Penny died. Had Ballard been in the store all day?

And where was Clarissa that morning? Tessa saw her on base fighting with General Bedford. What if she'd dropped the poison into the gold foil bag earlier in the week without realizing it took several days for it to work? Or what if Clarissa was afraid Penny hadn't taken the poison? After she argued with General Bedford, Clarissa could have left the base, driven to Penny's, and killed her. Then afterward she could have tried to make the crime scene look like a suicide. I definitely needed to talk to Clarissa when she returned from her trip on Tuesday.

I paused in the doorway to the meeting room. The Pathway group sat with hunched shoulders and closed eyes. I didn't want to endure another case of pins and needles, so I slipped down a short hallway that we'd bypassed earlier. Several closed doors showed dark offices with metal desks and filing cabinets through their small windows. A shriek sounded from the end of the hall. "No! I want it," screamed a high-pitched voice. I'd found the kids.

I leaned over the lower half of the divided door that kept the kids in the room and introduced myself to the teenager in charge. My sudden appearance drew the attention of the kids.

"Thank goodness," said the teenager as she tugged her crop top down. The baby she held grabbed a fistful of fabric at her shoulder and pulled it up, revealing another few inches of her naval. "Which one is yours? I thought you guys would never get through."

"Sorry, but none of them are mine. I think the meeting's almost over, though. I didn't want to go back in after I had to leave."

"Jeez. This isn't a one-person job." She pulled her shirt back down. This time the kid grabbed a handful of her straight black hair. She disentangled it from his sticky fingers and sat him down in a bouncy chair. Immediately, his face turned red and his mouth opened in a large O as he gathered air for an extended crying bout. "Here, let me hold that one," I said. He reminded me of Livvy.

The teenager handed him over the half door and then broke up a fight over a toy truck. The boy was so startled to see a new face he forgot to cry. He stared at me. After the teenager sent the older kids off to play on the minislide in the corner she returned to the door. "Man, I need a helper."

"Did you have help before? I knew the woman who used to babysit here. Did you know Penny?" I asked her, but kept my gaze focused on the baby. He was sucking his thumb now. A dispute broke out near the slide. "Me first. I want to be *first!*" yelled a boy as he shoved another kid out of the way.

"Yeah. Well, I just helped out. Penny was a magician with these kids. She could get them to do anything. It was fun when she was here. She'd have them singing songs and playing games. Without her it's terrible. Can you believe she committed suicide?" The teenager seemed to be implying that if a roomful of babies and toddlers hadn't driven Penny to suicide, nothing could.

"Actually, the police think she was murdered," I said.

"No way," she said as she strode over to a cabinet and grabbed a box of animal crackers. "Snack time!"

The kids scrambled to small tables and sat down. She gave each one a few crackers and returned to the door. As she took the baby back I asked, "Did Penny ever say anything about anyone threatening her?"

"Are you kidding? Everyone here thought that she was an angel and wanted her to babysit their kids."

"Did she ever say anything about a big problem she had or that she was afraid?"

"Nope. She was really focused on the kids when we were here. We didn't talk much about anything else."

"Okay. Well, thanks for talking to me. I'll head back and see if they're done yet."

"Thanks," she said as she yanked her shirt back down.

There was one more door at the end of the hall past the kid room. I peeked in for a better look.

Chapter
Fifteen

Glass boxes shielded books and pottery on pedestals scattered around the room. The corners of the room were in darkness, but dim track lighting spotlighted each display. I crossed my arms to keep warm as I moved to the nearest display, a book with yellow, crinkled pages and script so ornate that I couldn't have read the words even if they'd been in English. I circled the glass case and then bent over the small card attached to one side. *Bible, Old German. C. 1650.*

"Wow," I whispered.

I moved on to the next display, a delicate aged piece of papyrus? I searched for the card. I felt my eyebrows raise as I read *Papyrus fragment*. Wasn't papyrus so fragile that few pieces of it survived? How did one end up here in a cherry orchard/New Age religious compound/alternative beauty product factory? Turning in a circle, I surveyed the other items in the room including pottery, more worn books, a rosary, and a slender statue of a woman with six arms. A thermometer and cards with a strip of colored cloth were positioned in the corners of each display case.

"I see you've found my little collection."

I turned back to the doorway and saw Ballard's squat form blocking the light from the hall. In the dim light, she looked even more like a medieval priestess in her loose clothes and sandals. I wondered if she had a rope she could use for a belt. It would be exactly the right touch for her outfit. I'd been so absorbed in the items in the room, I hadn't heard the voices down the hall as women came to collect their children.

Ballard snapped on a bank of overhead fluorescent lights, and the resemblance to an ancient holy woman disappeared. She was a middle-aged woman dressed in comfortable clothes. "What did you think of the meeting?"

"Interesting." Such a handy word, interesting. Not really a compliment, but it wouldn't offend Ballard either. "Tell me about your collection."

Ballard walked over and gently rested her hand on the case with the papyrus. "My father's collection, actually. He was a theology professor. Religious artifacts fascinated him. He traveled extensively in the Holy Land and collected many rare pieces. Toward the end of his life, he broadened his interest from Christianity to all the major world religions."

She went to a desk in the corner and pulled on the long black cardigan that was draped over the desk chair. "Sorry it's so cold in here. Better for the books." Brushes, a small vacuum, and bottles littered the desk alongside books held together with strips of linen.

She walked over to the Bible in German. "One of his students brought him this. The family was going to throw it away, but my father asked for it instead."

"Do you collect as well?" I asked.

"A little. I'm more interested in compiling his work into a format that groups or individuals can understand."

She pulled a small book from a large canvas bag dangling on the back of the desk chair.

I tilted the glossy cover to read the title. The words *Path of Three* marched across the blue sky above an oak tree. Smaller type at the bottom of the cover noted *Compiled by Ballard Nova*. I flipped through the pages, noting lots of passages and a few discussion questions. A popular e-publisher was listed on the title page. I recognized a slick product from my work in the PR office. Ballard had taken the time to put together a professional quality book from the cover to the layout of the text.

"It's so nice to have original texts when we study them in the group. That way after people read about them in the meeting they can see the actual books and papyrus the study is based on. We'd be happy to have you join the group," Ballard said as I handed the book back.

"Well, I'm actually happy with a group I go to right now through my church. I'll probably just stick with that. I was a friend of Penny Follette's. Did you know her well?"

"Our child care specialist? No, unfortunately, I didn't get to know her. I interviewed her, of course, and checked her references, but she had only worked with us for a few months. Terrible what happened."

Bree's red head leaned around the door frame. "Ballard. There you are. There's a woman with a question about the night moisturizer and I'm too new. I can't remember if it has jasmine or jonquil in it."

Ballard nodded and I followed her into the older building where I found Irene sampling a hand cream. "Here, smell this? Do you like it?"

I sniffed dutifully, but all I could smell was hay.

"Isn't it divine? You should get something. You know it all goes together. The group helps you take care of your spirit, and these creams help you take care of your body."

I murmured a noncommittal sound and wandered across the room to the counter where Ballard rang up body lotion, herbal teas, and a soothing room fragrance as Bree stuffed the purchases in brown bags. Ballard's prayerful stillness and mystical aura were gone. With her half glasses perched on her nose, her dark blue eyes were sharp and piercing as she totaled sales and counted out change.

Irene's SUV ate up the snowbank on the side of the road as she cruised down my street. I automatically checked out the neighborhood before I opened the door, an involuntary habit I'd developed since the incident in the grocery store parking lot.

"Thanks for the invitation," I said as I climbed down from Irene's SUV like a mountain climber scaling a mountain in reverse.

"Sure." Irene turned down the police scanner. She'd said it helped her avoid traffic jams. She leaned across the seat.

"I know you've got a lot going on, but let me know if you change your mind, you know? Let's get the kids together for a play date. Why don't you drop Livvy off next Tuesday afternoon around four?"

"I don't know. She's going through this separation anxiety stage."

"Oh, she'll be fine."

"You obviously haven't heard her cry at full volume before."

"Why don't we at least try? I can call you if she won't quit crying, right?"

"Well, I suppose we could try it," I said and shut the door. I'd given Irene the same reason for not attending again that I'd given Ballard. I already had a group. I made a mental note to make sure we attended our small group Bible study this week. We'd been hit-or-miss lately, but after the Pathway group, I wanted to get back.

As I opened the kitchen door, Mitch said into the phone, "Oh, here she is. I'll let you talk to her." He handed me the phone. "Hetty Sullivan."

"Ellie." Hetty's brisk but raspy voice filled the phone line. "I can't find three photographs that Penny described to me. They were from the base, photos of the first squadrons. Black-and-white. This is the first chance I've had to go through the materials and I can't find them. Could they still be at Penny's house?"

"I don't know. I can check. Or you could call Will."

"I've tried! I've left him three messages and he hasn't returned my calls. I wanted to use one for the exhibit brochure and I have to get it to the printer the day after tomorrow at the latest."

"Hang on just a minute."

I walked into the bedroom where Mitch was hunched over the computer. Multicolored shapes flew across the screen. "Is Will TDY?"

Distracted, Mitch paused. "Umm, he's at Sutton." A crescendo of music and an annoying buzzer drew Mitch back to the game.

I translated military jargon into civilian terms. "He's in Kansas. I think, if I've got the right base. How about I run down to their house and see if I can find them? If I find them, do you want to come down and pick them up?"

"No, I'm afraid I can't. I can't get away right now and I'm booked all day tomorrow with meetings about Frost Fest. I'll run by after six. Oh, I can't do that either because I'm teaching Penny's art appreciation class."

"If I find it, I can drop it off at the end of your class."

"That would be wonderful."

Even though it was another thing to do, I was almost

glad that Will was gone. It would give me an excuse to go back to his house. I'd also get to talk to Hetty Sullivan about Penny again and I could try and catch Clarissa at the class.

The phone rang again and Mitch picked it up. After a pause, he said, "Okay. This is real world, not an exercise? Warm or cold weather gear? Come on, you have to have a clue."

I sighed with a mix of exasperation and dread. I went back to our bedroom to drag Mitch's suitcase out and check the news. He was on alert again.

We didn't hear anything from the squadron all day Monday. I was beginning to think the squad had forgotten about Mitch. He shoveled the driveway and sidewalks, lined up Mabel's husband to clear them if he was deployed, and then played with Livvy in between his absent-minded wandering around the house. The situation, we jokingly called it house arrest, put an end to a Valentine's dinner out. I canceled the sitter and Mitch grilled us steaks. We ate by candlelight, which Livvy found amazing, but we were all a little jittery and that was unusual for Mitch.

The phone rang at three-thirty in the morning. Mitch answered and I stumbled down the hall to close Livvy's door, my stomach doing flip-flops. I hated this part of his job. The abrupt good-byes were awful, especially when I didn't know when he'd be back.

He took a quick shower and I put two energy bars, a juice box, and a note in his flight bag. He came down the hall carrying his boots so he wouldn't wake up Livvy. I shivered and turned up the heat while he sat at the table and laced the boots and tied them.

"Want anything to eat?" I asked, even though I knew the answer.

"Nope. I've got to go. I've got forty-five minutes to get there."

"Did they say where you're going?"

"No, again. Oh, my bag." He tiptoed down the hall and stealthily returned carrying his shaving bag. "A man's gotta look good," he joked.

I managed a small smile. His joking attitude was a defense against anxiety. I walked into his arms. After our good-byes, I watched him load his suitcase and his C bag into his car and back out of the driveway. I was ready to wave, but he didn't look back. He was already focused on the mission. I let the curtain fall back into place and walked through the dark house, absently straightening a pillow on the couch and a dining room chair. I felt sad that he was gone, but it was tinged with a bit of excitement that he was—and to some extent we were—participating in something bigger than ourselves.

I couldn't sleep, so at five-thirty I got up and switched on the television. A perky local anchor informed me, "Six crews from Greenly deployed to support Operation Shelter. They left early this morning for the Azores where the refuelers will create an air bridge for fighters and cargo jets tasked with stabilizing the situation in Osan, where militants threaten the U.S. embassy."

I rolled my eyes and turned on the shower water. Mitch didn't know where he was going, and even if he knew, he couldn't tell me. But the PA office could release the info to the local news. Give me a break.

My boots squished on the slick tiles of the long hall. I switched the box with the remaining photographs for the art show from my left arm to my right and picked up my pace. I sailed past dark classroom doors, my gaze flicking over the numbers mounted on the lintels. Occasionally, large floor-to-ceiling windows broke the monotony of the doors. The dark squares of black reflected my image back at me in their blank panes of glass. There's probably a nice view from those windows during the day, but at night the empty black voids unnerved me a bit. Finally, I heard a voice from the end of the hall, a scratchy, hoarse voice. I was almost there. I took a deep breath and slowed down, realizing that I'd been moving pretty fast down the hall and was out of breath.

When Mitch had to go on trips I tried to keep our routine as normal as possible. So I'd dropped Livvy off at her play date with Irene's kids. Actually, Irene had held Livvy while I pried Livvy's fingers off my arm and shoulder. I'd gone out to the Cherokee and waited. No need to get too far before Irene called me to come back and get Livvy. Sure enough my phone rang. "What are you doing sitting in my driveway?" Irene asked.

"Waiting for you to call me to come get Livvy." I strained to hear her cries in the background, but I didn't hear anything.

"She's fine. She's playing with Megan. They're cooking in her play kitchen."

"Oh. Okay. See you in what? An hour?"

"How about two?"

So I picked up the photographs from Penny's house, then hurried up to Vernon Community College to drop them off with Hetty.

I paused outside the door. "So what do you notice? What's different?" asked Hetty as she stood beside a large screen on the stage of the darkened theater. A photograph of a Madonna and child glowed on the screen.

A student near the door said, "It looks a little more realistic. Not so flat."

"Right. For the first time we see figures that have depth. See the curves of the faces in Giotto's *Madonna in Glory*?

And notice the posture, the position, of the child? More natural than the mosaics."

Scattered students filled the front third of the theater. Hetty clicked the remote and the slide carousel whirred and snapped to a blank screen. No PowerPoint presentations at the community college. I wondered if it was lack of funding or a resistance to technology. "That's it for this week," Hetty said as she switched on the overhead lights, which moved the light in the theater up from "dark" to "dim." Over the rustling of paper as students closed notebooks and grabbed purses and backpacks, Hetty yelled, "Perspective next week. Read the section on Masaccio and look at *The Holy Trinity*. See you then."

I set the box down and waited as the students filed out in clumps, a few planning to get a latte at the coffee shop across the street. I scanned the faces, but didn't see Clarissa Bedford.

Toting an oversized leather purse, the slide projector, and three books, Hetty arrived in the hall and spotted me. "You found them! Thanks so much for bringing them over."

"No problem. I found them in Penny's car. She hadn't unloaded it yet." I set the box down and pulled out the framed photos cushioned in bubble wrap. "Are these what you're looking for?" I folded the cushiony plastic back and showed her the black-and-white photo of a crew posed in front of a sign that read GREENLY AFB.

"Yes. You're wonderful."

"No problem. I found this, too." I held out a color snap of a cocky airman leaning on the wing of a plane. I flipped it over to show her the faded handwriting on the back. *Jack Bedford*.

"Oh, that's priceless. He'll kill me, but I have to use it."

I replaced the framed photos in the box and set the snapshot on top. "I'll carry this for you. You look like you've got your hands full."

"Thanks. Let's take it to my car. My office is on the other side of the building and it's packed to the gills right now anyway."

"Okay." I followed her down the hall and out a door that opened onto a side parking lot for faculty. "I didn't see Clarissa Bedford tonight. Is she still in the class?" I really needed to talk to her since she was the only person who was actually seen at Penny's house. Ballard seemed a little kooky, but harmless. Victor and Mr. Baseball Cap needed Penny alive to help them, and the crew was only hiding their own stupidity. Clarissa admitted being at the scene of the crime and she had a motive, jealousy.

Hetty thought for a moment. "She wasn't here tonight, but she was here last week. I remember her arguing with a man in the hallway before class."

"Was it General Bedford?"

"Good heavens, no. This man was wearing a flight suit. But he was short with blond hair. And young."

Definitely not Bedford, then, since he was bald with just a fringe of hair. And he'd be more likely to wear blues, the uniform with a light blue shirt and dark blue pants.

"I did miss her tonight. I didn't realize how much she contributed to the class." Hetty continued, "She's fairly quiet, but when she does speak up her comments are well thought out. Asks good questions, too. But as far as I know she's still enrolled." Hetty unlocked a red Volvo station wagon, placed her load in the back, and then took the box from me. "Well, thanks for your help. I really appreciate it. Here." She dug in her pocket. "I want you and your husband to have these. They're for the preview party the day before the show opens. It will be quite a gala, for Vernon. We'll even have a foreign trade delegation there. Not to mention the governor."

I took the tickets. "Thanks so much," I said. Maybe Mitch would be back and could go with me, if I could convince him. He'd jump at tickets to a basketball game, but I knew he'd frown when I told him about the preview show and then say, "And what am I going to have to wear to this thing? Are you sure we have to go?"

Hetty opened her car door and slid behind the wheel. "I'll see you there. This is definitely my last Frost Fest." She waved and shut her door.

I retraced my steps to the building and walked around the path to the parking lot for students and visitors. I bet next year Hetty would be in the thick of things when the planning committee met for Frost Fest. She had too much energy to sit back and enjoy the thing without working on it.

If I hadn't been concentrating on the ground, stepping carefully through the puddles left after snowplows scooped up the snow and deposited it in minimountains around the light poles, I probably wouldn't have noticed the shoe lying sideways on a dirty patch of melting snow.

Chapter
Sixteen

A bright red stiletto heel protruded into the light. The long, dark form attached to the shoe halted me. I could see a pale leg extending up from the shoe, a coat, and a thick mass of hair in the weak light.

I glanced around the deserted parking lot, then slowly approached the shape between the cars, remembering news reports about criminals who pretended to be hurt to entice victims near enough to mug them. Part of my mind noticed that when I stepped into a puddle and splashed water on the leg, there was no reaction, no movement. I focused on the upper part of the body, searching in the dim light for a face, but I could only see the person's back.

"Hey, are you okay?" I realized I'd whispered. No response. I wanted to back away and find my cell phone, distance myself from this scene, but I forced myself to slide carefully between the cars and squat down. I searched for an arm, a wrist to touch for a pulse, but both arms were tucked underneath the body. I gently pushed on the shoulder, but the body didn't roll over. I didn't push again because the solid coldness from the shoulder seeped against my hand. There was no way that person could be alive. I jerked up and splashed over to the light where I'd parked the Cherokee. I leaned against it and concentrated on getting my breathing under control as I dialed my cell phone. I paused before I hit SEND. I could drive away. Just back up and leave. But I couldn't do it.

Clarissa Bedford deserved more than that.

By the time police lights flooded the parking lot, I'd almost convinced myself that maybe it wasn't Clarissa. During the wait for the police, the EMTs, the forensic technicians, the medical examiner, and the countless other people that descended on the parking lot and set up shop, I'd decided the shoe and the long hair could be coincidences. Perhaps it was a tragic death unrelated to the turmoil surrounding Penny, Georgia, and the base. I could give my statement and go home. But when the harsh lights revealed soft hair that waved out, beautiful and glossy even in death, I knew it was Clarissa.

I'd retreated to the Cherokee, where I had the heater blasting, but I still couldn't stop shivering as I watched the official personnel swarm and swirl around the body. From this distance, they looked like an amoeba with rippling borders as people came and went. But always there was a dark knot, a nucleus at the center. A police detective segued away from the throng around the body and crossed the parking lot to tap on my window. Detective Wright had spoken with me earlier.

He asked through my open window, "Mrs. Avery, you think you know the victim?"

"I might," I hedged, still hoping that it wouldn't be Clarissa. "I think it might be Clarissa Bedford. She had an art appreciation class tonight, but she wasn't there."

"You're in the class?" he asked.

"No, I met the professor briefly after the class to drop some things off with her. I knew Clarissa was in the class and asked if she was there and the teacher said no."

"So you know Clarissa Bedford. How?"

"I've done some work for her. I'm a professional organizer. And she's the wing commander's wife. My husband's stationed out at Greenly."

"Okay. There's no identification—no purse or wallet—on the body. We need you to take a look at the body." His statement didn't give me much choice, and even though I knew I could probably protest and not look, I wanted to see if it was her. Then I wouldn't have to wonder all night if I was right. I knew I wasn't going to get much sleep anyway, but at least one question would be answered this way.

He rubbed his hand over his buzz cut as I contemplated his request. Then he waited with his arms hanging from his droopy shoulders. Apparently, he was used to waiting people out.

I reluctantly left the warmth of the Cherokee. On the way across the parking lot, he asked, "So what were you taking to the class?"

"Photographs. The teacher, Hetty Sullivan, is coordinating the art show for Frost Fest."

I thought I was going to have to go into the convoluted details of Penny's death and my tangled associations in her life, but thankfully, we arrived at the edge of the amoeba. Wright made his way through the crowd and I followed until I was at the edge of the spotlighted scene.

They must have finished with the photographs and the measuring, because the body had been turned over. Two men pulled a stretcher through the slush. I took a deep, unsteady breath and turned away. Now I knew why I couldn't find the wrist to search for a pulse. Clarissa had died with her hands at her neck trying to claw away the tight line that encircled her throat.

"Mrs. Avery? Are you all right?" Wright asked.

"No," I said, but turned back to the body. Once I got past the grotesque protruding tongue, I looked at her face, but it didn't look like her. Instead, it was a strange and evil caricature of what she'd looked like alive. "It's Clarissa Bedford."

The busy, clinical atmosphere continued around me, but the sounds seemed to recede as I studied her body. It was like the scariest part of a movie. I wanted to stop looking, but I couldn't. A muffled conversation flowed around the circle. I heard a sharp comment and then a bark of laughter, but I stared at the red around Clarissa's throat.

Not blood. I squinted and leaned closer. A thin line of shiny scarlet encircled the throat, and on the edge, trailing away under the mass of hair, was a bit of frothy red lace. I stepped back quickly, turned, and shouldered my way through the crowd.

Wright loped along beside me and I realized he'd asked me a question.

"Look, I'm sorry, but I can't stay here right now. I'm—I think I'm in shock. Can we do this tomorrow?"

"Wright!" someone bellowed. "Channel Two is here."

Wright sighed, his shoulders sagging lower. "Okay, Mrs. Avery. I'll be in touch with you tomorrow."

Later that night, I tried to drift off to sleep, emptying my mind as Ballard had suggested, but I kept thinking, why strangle Clarissa with lingerie?

I knew Abby watched the morning news as she got ready for school, so when she arrived at my kitchen door, breathless and sending out white puffs of breath in the cold air, I handed her a cup of coffee. Even though I don't drink it myself, I keep some for visitors. After I'd un-earthed the can of coffee from the back of the freezer, I'd scraped the ice crystals off the top layer. I hoped you couldn't taste freezer burn on coffee granules. "Thanks," Abby said and took a sip. Apparently it didn't taste too bad, because she didn't grimace or gag, just set it down on the table, stripped off her gloves and coat, and then gave Livvy a pat on the shoulder.

"I saw it on the news. Tell me about it." She plopped down in the chair across from Livvy's high chair.

"But what about your trip? I haven't seen you since you got back last night and I want to know all about it," I teased.

"It was great. And I have news, but you first. I couldn't believe it when I turned on the news and saw you running away from the scene of the crime."

"I couldn't either." I slammed the freezer door shut with my shoulder and opened the box of frozen waffles. "And I wasn't running. Wright told me I could leave, so I walked—quickly—I'll give you that, but it was cold out there. I wanted to get away from those people. It was kind of creepy with them talking and joking over a dead body. I know they see it all the time, but it bothered me." I shiv-ered and popped a waffle in the toaster for Livvy. I real-ized she was hammering her sippy cup on the tray of her high chair. I'd been blocking the noise out, but I noticed Abby winced each time Livvy brought her cup down with a thump. I scattered a few Cheerios on the tray. What would I do without Cheerios, a mom's best friend? "It was that Chelsea O'Mara who used the word 'fleeing,' " I said.

"Who's Wright?" Abby asked.

"The police detective. He asked me some questions

and then told me to leave. He'd said he'd get in touch with me today."

"So who was it?"

The police hadn't released the identity of the victim to the media yet.

"Clarissa Bedford."

"No." Abby's eyes widened. "It can't be."

"Yes, I'm sure it was her." I swallowed and removed the waffle from the toaster with two fingers. I resolved not to eat any breakfast. I was too queasy, just thinking about Clarissa's face.

"It can't be. I just saw her."

"Didn't we have this conversation before, but in reverse?" I cut the waffle and sprinkled it with powered sugar. Livvy didn't like syrup. "Icky," she'd say, meaning too sticky.

"You're right, we did." Abby took another gulp from her coffee cup and hopped up from her chair. "I saw her on our trip, though. First in the Portland airport."

"Clarissa? You saw Clarissa? I thought you had a direct flight to Vegas." I set the waffle in front of Livvy. I poured a glass of orange juice and raised the pitcher and my eyebrows toward Abby, but she shook her head.

"No, I'm too hyped already."

I leaned against the counter as Abby paced across the kitchen.

She reached the end of the kitchen and whipped around. "The travel agent forgot to tell us she booked us on the flight with a layover. So we were hanging out in the gift shop, arguing over buying a pack of gum. Two dollars! Such a rip-off. I could buy two jumbo packs for that at the Comm."

I had to smile at Abby, who pinched every penny, but you'd never know it from her clothes or her house. She

had a knack for buying cheap things and putting them together the right way. Like today, she wore a white fisher-
man's sweater that she'd picked up at Tate's winter clearance.
(I knew because I was with her that day and she tried to
get me to buy the sweater. When I wouldn't, she snatched
it up.) She'd paired it with black pants she'd bought on
sale at Target and chunky boots from the outlet mall. An
emerald scarf swirled at her neck, topping off her outfit. I
looked down at my sweats and worn house shoes stained
with Rex's muddy footprints and baby spit-up and
promised myself I'd buy anything Abby told me to next
time I went shopping with her.

"Anyway, that's when I saw Clarissa across the aisle.
She bought a copy of *Investment Today* and went to the
restaurant next door to the gift shop. We ate lunch there,
too, but she never noticed us. In fact, I don't think she
would have recognized me, if she really looked at me."

"*Investment Today*? That doesn't sound like Clarissa."

"I know. That's what caught my attention, too." Abby
made another trip up and down the kitchen. "It had something on the cover like 'Ten mutuals you need now.' And
let me tell you, she pored over that magazine during lunch
and on the flight."

"I saw her on Wednesday. She was leaving on a business trip. She must have been going to several cities. She
told me she was in sales."

"I'll say," Abby said darkly. She finally stopped pacing
the kitchen and settled down at the table. "She was on our
flight to Vegas. She read that magazine the whole way and
didn't look up except to order a Diet Coke. She's not the typical commander's wife, so I watched her. Jeff was embarrassed. He kept telling me not to stare, but I was curious."

I suppressed a yawn as best I could, but Abby noticed.
"Sorry, I didn't sleep very well last night," I explained.

"Well, this'll wake you up. When we landed, she hooked up with a man as we came out of baggage claim. We were right behind her, waiting to cross to the hotel shuttles, when she walked over to a black limo. The guy got out of the limo and kissed her on both cheeks. He was dark, kind of swarthy in a Middle Eastern sort of way. She was wearing this microminiskirted "business suit" and the man noticed Jeff and me staring. Clarissa leaned over to pick up her carry-on bag and climbed into the limo.

"Let me tell you, it was quite a sight. I don't think Jeff's seen that much leg outside our bedroom since Derrick's bachelor party. Jeff's mouth was hanging open and the man with her turned to Jeff and wagged a finger at him. 'No, no. She's all mine tonight,' he said in an accent. Then my mouth dropped open, too."

I sat down in the chair across the table. "What?"

"She's a hooker, Ellie. Or was a hooker, a high-class call girl."

"But how can you be sure? Maybe she was having an affair." I remembered the flimsy lingerie popping out of the suitcase.

"I guess I would have assumed that, too, except I turned to Jeff and said, 'Can you believe that?'

"He hadn't regained his power of speech yet. The flight attendant was standing beside us waiting for her hotel shuttle and she answered me. She said she sees it all the time when she's flying in and out of Vegas. She even recognized Clarissa. The flight attendant said, 'She's a regular. Always meeting a different man.' "

"But—" I sputtered and then stopped as Livvy's minifork slipped out of her fingers and pinged onto the floor. I tossed the dirty fork in the sink and grabbed a new one. "Are you sure it was her?"

"Not a doubt in my mind."

"But she's the wing commander's wife. Why would she do that?"

Abby shrugged. "Who knows? Asserting her independence? Maybe she had some sort of sexual addiction? An adrenaline junkie, she gets a thrill out of it? I don't know. All I know is she was doing it."

"Yeah. Well, she won't be anymore. Someone killed her last night."

The kitchen clock's tick seemed to be amplified during the silence.

"This is too much like last year," Abby said, finally.

"I know," I said, remembering the death of two spouses that no one realized were connected. "Do you think Clarissa's death is connected to Penny's? I thought Clarissa was a great suspect for Penny's murderer, but apparently I was wrong. Although I do have a hard time picturing her dipping castor beans in chocolate. Too tedious."

"Castor beans?" Abby asked.

I updated her on what Georgia had told me.

"Yeah. It would've messed up her nails," Abby said. "But it may not be connected to Penny's death at all. Maybe General Bedford found out about her real 'job.' Or maybe it was something else. Clarissa's occupation was dangerous. Organized crime's involved in prostitution. What if she made some mob boss mad?"

"If that happened, wouldn't it be easier to kill her in Vegas?" I asked.

"But look what finding her here does—it makes a 'hit' seem like an even more remote possibility. If she'd died in Vegas, it would be one of the first aspects investigated."

"I don't know." I shook my head. "Maybe those Mafia movies exaggerate things, but I think if it was a mob hit, then her body would never have been found. You'd better talk to Wright today."

"Well . . ." Abby looked reluctant. "Maybe it was a random killing and had nothing to do with her trips out of town."

"I don't think so. She was strangled with a piece of lingerie."

Chapter
Seventeen

A stack of paperwork thudded onto the table. Detective Wright took a seat next to Thistlewait and said, "She was strangled with a piece of rope. We're releasing her name, but no details about how she died." To me, Wright said, "Keep that to yourself. And don't talk about the lingerie, either. The red thong was twisted around her neck on top of the rope."

"Oh," I said. "That makes sense. It seems like lingerie would be too thin and flimsy. I'd wondered if the material would be strong enough to strangle—" I stopped abruptly. I didn't want them to think I sat around pondering which materials would provide the best support for strangling people.

"With the information your friend gave us this morning, we've been able to check on Mrs. Bedford's travel schedule. Did she mention any other travel plans or anything about her business when you worked for her?" asked Wright as he ran his hand over his short, bristly haircut.

"She said she was going out of town, but didn't tell me

where. I asked her if she thought about quitting and she laughed. Said she'd never do that. She never wanted to depend on a man. One other thing. The woman who's teaching her class, Hetty Sullivan, mentioned she saw Clarissa arguing with a man in a flight suit. She said he was young and blond."

Thistlewait and Wright exchanged a look. Thistlewait made a note and Wright stood up. "Okay. Thanks, Mrs. Avery. I'll be in touch." He loped out of the room. I wondered how many police detectives Vernon had on their force. Now that I'd talked to Jensen and Wright, I'd probably met the whole department. Not a good thing to know more than one police detective, unless it's in a social setting.

Thistlewait leaned over the table. "This is number two."

"I'm sorry?"

"Look, I'm getting tired of standing up for you around here. My gut instinct is that you're innocent, but this is body number two that you're connected with. Do you think you can avoid them in the future?"

"It's not my fault that I found Clarissa. And I could have left. I didn't have to call 911. I could have walked away and let some student find her on the way to class the next morning."

Thistlewait sighed. "I know." He stood and snatched the file. "That's what makes me think you aren't the perp. You couldn't walk away, not even from a dead body. Couldn't leave it in the cold for a few hours, so I don't see how you could actually murder anyone. But let me tell you, people around here are trying to connect the dots and your name is coming up a little too often not to include you in the picture on the criminal side. Maybe you could just go home and stay there for a few days?"

I prevented myself from rolling my eyes, but just

barely. "And what should I do? Fold laundry? Bake cookies?"

"I like chocolate chip, myself," he said blandly.

"I'm not going home to bake cookies," I snapped. Then I realized he was trying to suppress a smile and I did roll my eyes.

The smell of warm sugar, vanilla, and chocolate greeted me when I opened the door of my kitchen. "Hi, sweetie," I said as I dropped a kiss on Livvy's head and surveyed the floury mess of crusty mixing bowls covering the counters. "You've been busy helping Miss Abby, I see." I stopped to scratch Rex's ears. He wriggled and danced around my feet in awkward half leaps. He knew he would get in big trouble if he jumped on me, so he'd developed a wiggle combined with a low hop and topped it off with yaps to greet anyone who'd been gone for more than five minutes.

Livvy nodded and the chocolate ring around her mouth widened with her smile. "Brownie," she pronounced proudly. "Brownie. Fun."

"Yes, it is. A lot more than cleaning up." I grabbed a brownie off the plate. It was still warm and thin lines of icing trailed off the sides onto my fingers. I closed my eyes and relished the rich chocolate. "This is just what I need," I mumbled.

Abby cranked on the hot water in the sink and dumped the dishes into the bubbling water. "We had a blast. Of course, I don't see how you get a thing done during the day."

Abby had talked to Wright and Thistlewait as soon as school was out and then she'd come over to watch Livvy for me while I took my turn with the investigation team.

"Did Mitch call while I was gone?"

"Nope."

I mentally counted off the days since his 3:00 a.m. departure. Only two days. Sometimes I didn't hear from Mitch for several days after he left for a trip, so I wasn't really expecting a phone call, but I dreaded to think what Abby would have told him if he'd called while I was out. She wouldn't mean to tell him about me finding another corpse, but a little detail like Thistlewait asking for another interview might slip out.

"So what happened?" Abby left the bowls soaking and came over to the table.

"I went through everything again for them. About five times, in fact."

Abby said, "Rachel told me Clarissa was strangled with rope, not lingerie. The lingerie was added afterward."

Tall and skinny with lots of kinky red hair, Rachel taught art at the same school as Abby. Rachel's husband was in the OSI. Abby continued, "Rachel said if anyone finds out she told us she'll be in hot water, so we have to keep it to ourselves. Anyway, she mentioned the rope. Said it was like rope you could buy at any Home Depot or Lowes and the red thong was twisted around her neck on top of the rope. Do you think the killer was trying to make a statement?"

"Like let them know about her trips to Vegas?" I said as I wiped Livvy's mouth and retrieved her sippy cup from the floor.

Abby nodded. "Or, if the killer doesn't have anything to do with her jaunts to Vegas, maybe the lingerie is to distract them. Rachel also said they've checked her travel schedule and she was out of town every other weekend. She'd go to Boise or Seattle or, like when I saw her, Portland, and spend a day or two. Then she'd fly down to Vegas."

"I wonder if they've found her money. I'll bet she had some sort of special, separate account for her 'earnings.' "

"Probably," Abby agreed. "But get this, General Bedford's been TDY to Florida for the last two days."

"So that lets him off the hook." A perfectly good suspect, out of the running. I pushed my bangs off my forehead with a sigh, remembering the intense scrutiny of the OSI office as I left. As one of the suspect pool, I was all for having as many people in there with me as I could get. "He'd have a great motive, if he found out about her being a hooker. You know he wouldn't have wanted that to get around," Abby said.

I dumped the cup in the sink and grabbed a dishcloth. "I'm nervous. I'm on their short list." I wiped Livvy's tray as I said, "All my ideas about suspects were wrong and I'm afraid if more solid leads don't turn up they'll come back to me."

"Well, where's your list? Let's add what we know."

"Okay." I put the dishcloth down and pulled the paper out and studied the line I'd drawn through *the crew.*

"Clarissa's death changes everything." I drew a line through her name and rewrote *Crew.*

Abby had been leaning over my shoulder and asked, "Do you think one of them did it?"

"I don't know, but Hetty said Clarissa argued with a short, blond guy. The only guys that I can think of who fit that description and knew Penny are Aaron and Rory." I tossed the pen down. "I need to talk to Will again, too."

"Good luck with Rory."

"He's out of town anyway. I'll start with Aaron."

A sharp knock on the kitchen door punctuated my sentence. I shushed Rex and put him in his kennel, then opened the door.

Even in the dim light filtering through the low-slung gray clouds, Bree Reed looked unhealthy and pale. In full sunlight she'd look like a patient recovering from a round of chemo. Her red pointy hair accented the pallor of her face. "Thank God you're here. I thought I saw you drive up. I've got to talk to you. Could you come over to my studio for a few minutes?" A cold breeze pressed the thin cotton of her flowing poet shirt to her torso. She shivered and clutched her elbows, pressing several beaded necklaces to her chest. Her artistically ripped and worn jeans were probably drafty, too.

"Ah, sure. Do you want to come in for a minute and warm up? While I get Livvy in a coat?"

"No. Thanks, though. Just come over when you've got a minute." She backed down the steps and ran back across the street, her loose shirt flapping like a sail.

She obviously hadn't seen Abby inside, so I closed the door and turned to ask Abby if she wanted to go over with me.

"No, you go ahead, I'll stay here with Livvy. We'll do the dishes." Abby already had Livvy on a step stool beside her at the sink.

"Okay," I said and shrugged back into my coat. I'd have Livvy wanting to "help" me with everything now from the laundry to the dishes. I'd never get anything done.

I picked my way across the frozen sheet of ice that was our street, avoiding a few puddles and the slush near what would be the curb when the ice melted in the spring. Hopefully, that would happen before Memorial Day. Maybe before April Fools' Day? Better not to get my hopes up. Last year we didn't turn off the furnace until June.

I paused in the long driveway of the Reeds' house. Bree had said studio, so she probably meant their garage. The vintage bifold doors were locked and didn't look like they would move for anything short of an earthquake, so I walked down a well-shoveled and de-iced path to the side of the garage.

Bree opened the door after I knocked. "That was fast. Where's your daughter?"

"She's with Abby at my house."

Bree led the way to a rectangular table with folding chairs at one side of the garage. The last time I'd been in the garage was over a year ago, before the owner decided to make the house a rental. "Did you and Aaron do the work in here?" The gloomy, dirty garage had been transformed. Skylights let in some natural light, banks of overhead lights hung from the exposed rafters. A no-nonsense, low-pile carpet covered the floor, and the walls had been drywalled and painted a light cream. Since the garage, or studio, was warm, I suspected someone had put new insulation behind the drywall. I spotted a few shiny heat registers, too.

"Aaron worked for a contractor one summer and can do anything, drywall, electrical, whatever. About all I can do is paint."

And she didn't just mean the walls. Two easels contained works in progress, and paintings were propped, stacked, and hung around the room, their bold splashes of color jumping off the canvas on this dreary day.

"You did a great job, remodeling this place." I walked over to a row of paintings propped up on the wall. To my untutored eye, they looked almost abstract, but not quite. Scenes in sharp, economical strokes depicted a beach, a forest at sunset, a street crowded with people. I leaned closer to another painting. "That's my house," I said, picking out the distinct honey-colored bricks and the Tudor-influenced sweep of the roofline.

Bree studied the painting and nodded in agreement. "There's some great variety in the architecture around here." She walked back to the long table. "Want a cup?" She poured herself a cup from the small coffeepot stationed on the end of the table.

"No, thanks."

I studied the initials in the corner. "Why do you sign with 'A.R.'?"

"Bree is short for Aubree. Soda?" She gestured to a minifridge tucked under the table.

"Diet Coke?"

"Sure." She pulled out a can and handed it to me.

I sat down at the table and popped the top, noticing a phone. "You must spend a lot of time here."

"Oh, I do. Sometimes the whole day. We even remodeled the back. Added a bathroom." She pushed some brushes over to the side of the table and sat down across from me. "I didn't ask you to come over here to talk about the studio." She fiddled with the brushes, lining them up from the smallest to the largest.

Finally, she asked, "You're taking over Penny's work with Frost Fest, right?"

"Well, no. I helped the chairperson, that's Hetty Sullivan, find some artwork that was at Penny's house, but that's it."

"Oh." Bree slouched over her mug, and her necklaces clicked against the table. I counted a thin gold chain, strands of shells, small pastel beads, and a chunky turquoise.

"This is *Dilemma*," Bree said as she leaned over and picked up a painting that was propped against the table leg.

"What?" I tuned into the conversation. "I'm sorry. I'm a little distracted today."

"I imagine you are, after finding that witch dead."

"What?"

"Clarissa Bedford. I heard you found her body."

The squadron grapevine transmitted news as fast as the Internet.

Bree continued, "Anyway, I know this isn't the best time, but Frost Fest could be really important to us, to

Aaron and me." She pointed to the painting. "Penny told me to send something to display in the art show, but it took longer than I thought to finish it. I thought I'd missed the deadline, but Penny said they needed more artwork and, well"—she waved her long, red nails at the painting—"*Dilemma* is the result."

"Oh." *Dilemma* was the name of the painting. "You'd better talk to Hetty Sullivan. I'll give you her phone number."

"Could you put in a good word for me? Give her a call first?"

"Sure. I could do that." I didn't know how much clout I had since I didn't know that much about art, but I wanted to ask Hetty a few more questions about Clarissa anyway. "I'll call you when I get home with her phone number, and then I'll call her."

Bree smiled. "That would be wonderful!"

"So you didn't like Clarissa?"

Bree snorted. "She commissioned a painting and then wouldn't pay for it. She said she didn't like it and wasn't going to take it. Like we're Wal-Mart or something."

The phone rang and Bree answered. "Yeah, it was a killer, uh-huh." The chorus of "uhs" and "mmms" continued until I gave up and left. I wanted to ask Bree a few more questions, but I couldn't leave Abby babysitting all day. I'd catch up with Bree later.

Later that day, I called Hetty. "Hi. This is Ellie Avery," I said as soon as I recognized Hetty's scratchy voice. I explained Bree's request.

"I'll give her a call. What's her number?"

I read it to her, then said, "You mentioned you saw Clarissa talking to a man the last time she was at your class. Did you happen to hear what they said?"

"No, but I could tell they were fighting because of their body language."

"Was anyone else in the hall?"

"I don't think so, but you might talk to Karen Barakat. That's who I suggested the police contact, too. She sat next to Clarissa and they seemed to be friends."

"Great. Do you have her number?"

"I'm sorry, but I can't give that out. Policy, you know. Check the phone book."

"Okay. Thanks, Hetty."

I pulled out the phone book. One Karen Barakat listed on Ponderosa. I called the number and a recording informed me that the number was disconnected. I called information. No new listing for either Karen or K. Barakat in Vernon.

After I got Livvy in bed that night, I did an Internet search, but Karen Barakat didn't net any results. I pushed away from the computer and found Rachel's phone number. Her message came on, a lengthy one with each little Smith family member chiming in on the message. If you were the grandparents, those phone messages were cute, but for me—and I like kids—they were annoying. Rachel coaxed the youngest to repeat, "Leave a message at the beep." Finally!

"Hey, Rachel, this is Ellie. Call me."

I didn't think about my phone call to Hetty again until an afternoon two days later when the phone rang.

"Ellie? This is Bree." I heard a gurgle, and then Bree mumbled, "Hold on."

"App juice, peez," Livvy said, waving her sippy cup at me.

I help up one finger, indicating I'd be just a minute. Livvy interpreted this sign, as all kids did. When grown-ups had a phone pressed to their ear it meant, "Mom's distracted, so let's see what we can get away with."

Livvy dropped her cup on the floor and Rex and I dove for it. I won, swiping it up seconds before Rex could lick it. I looked around for Livvy, but she wasn't in the kitchen. I tossed the cup in the sink and found her in the living room trying to put her Cheerios in the VCR.

"Livvy!"

"Sorry," Bree said weakly in my ear. "I've got that flu that's going around and I was going to drop *Dilemma* off with Mrs. Sullivan, but Aaron's TDY and there's no way I can go farther than five feet from the bathroom, so— Oh no. Hold on." A slam sounded through the phone line and footsteps pounded away.

I grabbed Livvy's hand and guided her to her high chair. "Finish your breakfast in your chair." Wails of protest greeted this ultimatum.

I strapped Livvy in and patted her shoulder, then walked back into the living room so I could hear Bree. She came back on the line as I crouched in front of the VCR with a flashlight. I didn't see any Cheerios so I went back to the kitchen.

"Sorry," Bree said. "Could you take my painting to Mrs. Sullivan? I thought of you right away. You're close and since you stay at home, you're not doing anything."

I think I suppressed the growl I felt coming on, but my silence must have conveyed my irritation, because Bree continued, "Please, it would mean so much to me. This kind of opportunity doesn't come along every day."

Even as I eyed my grocery list and the muddy footprints and paw prints covering my kitchen floor, I knew I couldn't turn her down. How could I say no to someone in the throes of a nasty flu? I'd been in the same situation before, searching for help with no relatives or friends to call.

"Sure. I'll come by in an hour to pick it up." It would

beat mopping the floor, anyway. Bree gave me directions to the gallery.

I left Livvy in the car and opened the door to the studio with the key Bree had handed me out the front door. She'd said, "It's crated and ready to go," before she swallowed hard, slapped her hand over her mouth, and banged the door in my face.

I flicked on the lights inside the studio, but I didn't see a crate. I walked to the back of the studio and passed a bathroom. I saw another tiny, windowless workroom with a crate standing on another long table. I'd expected to see more paintings in this room, but it contained furniture.

Unpainted chests, nightstands, headboards, and armoires stood in one corner, while finished pieces done in white paint with decorative trims and accents were spaced across the floor. Some were decorated with flowers, others with race cars or footballs. Some had intricate designs of ivy, while others, especially the pieces for kids, were bright and almost cartoonish in their designs. I walked slowly over to the table to pick up the crate. The furniture was an unusual contrast to the paintings in the next room. I wondered if this was what Bree did to make money until her paintings caught on with the public.

I snagged a parking spot directly in front of the downtown gallery, White Walls. Instead of parking in the public parking garage, I'd driven by the gallery on the off-chance that there might be an open slot. I saw one and, of course, I was on the opposite side of the street. But for once in my life, there was no oncoming traffic. I whipped the Cherokee around in a U-turn and, my miracle for the day, slid into the parallel slot flawlessly. I scrambled out, thankful for the Cherokee's tight turn radius, and punched Hetty's cell phone number into my phone.

She met me out front. A guy in a thin T-shirt with bangs down to his eyelashes followed her out and reached for the crate. I hesitated to give it to him because his shirt hung on his pointy shoulders, looking like it was hanging on a wire coat hanger. I expected him to collapse under the weight of the crate, but he adjusted his grip back inside the gallery.

"Like to come inside for a quick tour of the gallery?" Hetty asked.

"Sure." I pulled Livvy out of her car seat, settled her snow hat on her thin fluffy blond hair, and fed the meter some quarters.

Paper covered the windows of the gallery, giving it a blank look, but inside lights blazed down on shiny wooden floors as a few people moved gray partitions and adjusted track lighting. Hetty walked through the small gallery pointing out where the artwork would be displayed. It didn't take us long to make a loop around the small gallery. Hetty steered us back to the door, mentioning names that I didn't recognize.

"So this is just one location where art will be displayed?"

"Yes. We're using several galleries downtown, and the Rotunda on campus will have a large portion of the artwork on display, too. But we really want to get people out of their houses and downtown to shop. Look for the red banners with snowflakes and icicles outside the galleries."

"So will Bree's artwork be displayed here?"

"No. It will go in another gallery, Riverview. I had two artists, one of them fairly prominent locally, promise to support our show with several pieces and they both backed out at the last minute. So I've reviewed Bree's work—she sent me slides—and I've made an executive decision. Normally, a panel of judges decides which works will appear in the show, but we can't have blank walls in our show. We've never had so many problems. I've called another friend and he's coming through with a few sculptures, so we should be okay."

We stopped near the door and I kept a tight grip on Livvy's hand. I could imagine her stepping on someone's canvas without realizing it. She leaned away, pulling my arm taut and forming a triangle out of our arms and legs.

Hetty considered the door with a frown. "I think I better order a bigger banner for this location," she murmured to herself and whipped out a handheld computer. "This is our only gallery that isn't connected with the skywalks, so we may have to work a little harder to get people in here." A complex system of glass-enclosed bridges connected several downtown businesses with the sh̲o̲

"You've got to take w̲

An Everything In Its Place Tip for Organized Closets

Kids' closets

- Make sure you've got rods at lower heights so kids can reach their clothes. This is a big confidence-booster when they can pick out their own clothes. And they can also put away their own clothes after the laundry is finished.
- If you're going to store toys in the closet, add shelves or use buckets or bins to control the toy area.
- Moving a dresser into a closet can open up ~~~~ the child's bedroom.
- ~~~~ baskets or bins will

_____pping district.

"_____what you can get, though," said the bony-shouldered kid from beside us. Livvy jerked my arm back and forth, pulling as hard as she could away from me and then running to my side to hug my leg.

A plump young woman with blond hair straggling down her back walked past us toward the office at the back of the gallery. She shook a sheaf of paperwork at the kid and snapped, "Yeah, it was a real sacrifice to allow us to use *this* gallery." She jerked the papers back into place like a shield over her ample cleavage. Musky perfume swirled around us in her wake, and the guy beside me grinned and said to her back, "He's just doing it out of the goodness of his heart."

Hetty's phone rang. "Just a minute," she said to me and threw a warning glance at the guy.

The woman paused and said over her shoulder, "Victor Roth has never done anything that didn't get him something in return." She stomped away, her platform heels thudding across the hardwood floor.

more play space in the ~~~~

- Shoe caddies and laundry ~~~~ ~~ bins ~~~~ help keep the closet floor clear.
- A morning time saver: Create a place to lay out a week's worth of outfits with everything from the shirts and pants down to socks and underwear. You could use hangers labeled with the day of the week, a labeled shelf, or hanging bins to prep the clothes.
- Those clear plastic over-the-door shoe organizers come in handy in kids' closets, too. Use them to store small toys like plastic blocks and action figures.

Chapter
Eighteen

At the mention of the name Victor Roth I let my attention slide from Livvy to the bony-shouldered guy. He missed Hetty's look as he crouched to toss packing materials into an empty crate. Hetty paced over to a corner of the room to conduct her conversation. A file drawer slammed in the office. When the guy paused to push his long bangs out of his eyelids he caught my glance. I asked, "Why is she so upset?" and looked at the office where the woman had gone.

He stood up and pulled off work gloves, then flicked them in the direction of the office. "Roth dumped Mary a few days ago after he had the deal set up with Hetty to use the gallery for Frost Fest." He glanced around and said, "It looks like we're going to get it ready, but it'll be close."

"So, this is a last-minute addition?"

"Yeah. The Cerulean Villa got smoke damage last week from the fire in the restaurant next to it. There was no way to get it cleaned up in time, so Victor kindly volunteered his new gallery here. Pretty convenient for him."

"Why's that?" I asked, ignoring Hetty's glare at the guy. Livvy ran in a half circle around my legs. I kept a firm grip on her hand, but my arm felt heavy from tracing the arc in the air.

"Victor Roth said he wants to help out local artists, but we all know it's a ploy to get the gallery and himself noticed. He's brand-new in town, so this is great—it gets his gallery in the paper and he gets the bonus of being the good Samaritan."

Mary emerged from the office with one arm in her coat and the other flailing around behind her as she searched for the other armhole. Her struggles tested the limits of the baby blue shirt as it stretched against her curves. Finally she found the armhole, flung her purse onto her shoulder, and snatched up a stack of files. She shoved them at the guy and said, "Give these to Hetty. I'm done." She stalked out, again leaving the imprint of her perfume on the air around us.

The door closed and Hetty snapped her phone closed, then took the stack of papers. A pink "While You Were Out" message slip flittered to the ground. "Sorry about that." She tucked the paperwork into her elbow. Hetty wasn't apologizing for the interruption, but for Mary's behavior and stormy exit. The guy grabbed the empty crate and disappeared behind the dividers.

"Everyone gets a bit edgy with the start of the show so close."

Livvy picked up the paper. I dug in my coat pocket with my free hand. My fingers closed on a small figure. I pulled it out. "Look, Livvy, I found Pink Girl."

"Oh," Livvy sighed in contentment and dropped to the floor to walk the two-inch figure around between the crates. I took the paper from Livvy, shook out my arm, and said, "So White Walls is Victor Roth's gallery?" As I handed the note to Hetty I noticed a familiar name, Ballard Nova. She'd called at 3:20 and wanted Roth to call her back.

"Yes." Hetty's lips thinned in disapproval; then she sighed. "I'm sorry about Mary. She's a friend of my daughter's. She thinks Victor used her to get to me, that's why she's so angry. She's not the only one that thinks we shouldn't use the gallery, but we have to. There's not that many options left at this late date."

"But I thought you said several artists dropped out," I said.

"They did. Not enough to drop a whole gallery from the program, just enough to leave rather large empty spots in the galleries. We're fortunate that Victor made this available. At least I don't have to tell the artists there's nowhere to display their work."

Livvy crawled across the floor, making Pink Girl jump and hop. She moved toward the door, so I edged along behind her.

"In all my time working on this, I've never had so many problems. And so much controversy." Hetty shook her head.

"Come on, Livvy. Time to go." I adjusted her hat and said, "Sometimes controversy can be good. You might have a bigger crowd this year because of it." I waved to Hetty and headed to the car.

With Livvy snapped in the backseat, I merged into the line of headlights pushing through downtown and out to the suburbs around Vernon. I checked the radio, but didn't hear anything about Osan during the top-of-the-hour newsbreak. That was good. It meant Mitch and the other crews were doing their job and the situation in Osan was too boring—that is, no death, destruction, or threats—to include in the news.

I cruised under the freeway overpass and gave the Cherokee some gas so I could make it up Black Rock

Hill. As I chugged up the incline the car behind me closed on my bumper. The Cherokee definitely wasn't in the turbo-charged category, more like a snail's pace off the starting line, so I pushed the gas pedal harder and muttered, "Back off." The traffic thinned a little and I leaned my head on the headrest. I didn't want to go home. With Mitch gone, the evenings were the worst. I needed to fix something for supper, but I never wanted to put a lot of time into a meal because Livvy had decided she only needed five foods besides Cheerios and Goldfish crackers: milk, bread, waffles, apples, and grapes. At least some of the items were fruits, but it did limit dinner choices. Maybe I could convince her to eat some scrambled eggs and I could have an omelet.

The headlights flashed in my rearview mirror again and I checked my speed. I was already doing forty-five and the speed limit was thirty because the road wound through residential areas. The road widened and I pulled over to the far right. It was really only a two-lane road, but for a few blocks the road opened up and impatient people liked to use the short stretch to whiz past slower cars. I slid right, expecting the car behind me to pass, but it lunged closer to my bumper. Blinding white light flashed into the Cherokee, then disappeared as the car behind me closed the distance. I shoved the gas pedal to the floor. My shoulders tensed for a crash. The Cherokee did its usual hesitation and then the needle inched up to forty-seven.

The road narrowed again and I pulled back into the middle of the lane, gripping the steering wheel. My gaze slid between the road and my mirrors. I swallowed hard. Livvy said, "Mommy, I drop Pink Girl. Pink Girl."

"I can't get it right now." I realized my voice sounded harsh. I took a quick breath. "In a minute, sweetie."

The car behind me backed away and the headlights reappeared. The road leveled as we came to a plateau in the hill and the Cherokee's speedometer needle jumped up to fifty-two. I loosened my fingers on the wheel and took a deep breath.

"Need Pink Girl. Pink Girl," Livvy chanted.

"Okay." I reached back to feel around the floorboard, but the headlights surged forward, then disappeared again. I jerked my hand back to the steering wheel and took the curves of Black Rock Hill at sixty.

Was this some kind of game? Some kids out for a thrill? The turn for my street was coming up fast, but I wouldn't be able to make it at this speed.

Tree trunks, dark against the snow, flicked past. I stayed in the center of the cleared and sanded lane, avoiding the white mounds of cars parked along the street. Quiet streets flew past perpendicular to Rim Rock Road. The dark houses lined unplowed roads that were too slick for me to turn onto. Their corner street lights flicked over the Cherokee quicker and quicker as I pressed the gas when we hit another flat section of the road. If I did manage to make a turn without skidding out of control, would the car behind me follow me?

I felt myself taking shallow breaths. I forced myself to focus on the steep curve of the road ahead as the march of houses on the right stopped abruptly.

"Pink Girl, Pink Girl," Livvy chanted.

The car dropped back again and I watched the headlights, ready for it to close the distance again. I flicked a glance at the road and eased the wheel to the left, following the road as it hugged the escarpment of Black Rock Hill. To the right, the ground dropped away and I could see tiny pinpoints of light in the valley and the flash of silver, the river. I took in the dark drop, then refocused on the road.

"Pink Girl, Mommy. Pink Girl," Livvy continued her refrain.

The headlights closed. I pressed the gas, but the next incline ate up any speed the Cherokee had. The skin between my shoulder blades tightened as I tensed. Suddenly the headlights glared in the driver's-side mirror. I pulled the Cherokee slightly toward the snowbank on the edge of the drop-off. The headlights inched up to the back door. I glanced over my shoulder. A pickup. The wheel jumped in my hands. I gripped it and pulled back to the left. Snow flew as my tires churned into the snowbank.

I heard the roar of the truck's engine. It floated closer. With a scrape of metal, the truck growled past. I fought the wheel and touched the brakes. "Lightly, lightly." I realized I was repeating my dad's words the day he took me out to a deserted, frozen parking lot and taught me to drive on ice.

My side mirror dangled against the car door. "He hit me!" I was incredulous. "On purpose!" The driver of the truck accelerated. I knew the driver wasn't going to stop. I maneuvered out of the snowbank. On the sanded road again, I pressed the gas and followed the truck. "White. New, with curves, fancy taillight covers," I inventoried as the mirror flapped against the door like a wounded bird.

The Cherokee inched closer. "Eight-oh-six," I said out loud, reading off the license plate as the truck pulled farther away. There was no way I was going to catch it. I slowed down and pulled over. Blood pounded in my forehead and I felt a headache coming on. I found a scrap of paper and wrote down the first three numbers on the license plate and the details about the truck. My pen jumped and wiggled over the page. I pulled my phone out of my purse and dialed 911.

"Mommy?"

"What?" I said to Livvy.

"Vernon Emergency Services. What is your emergency, please?" asked the calm voice in my ear at the same time Livvy said, "Pink Girl, now?"

"A car sideswiped me. I'm on Rim Rock Road." I leaned back and patted the floorboard with my right hand until I felt the small toy.

"You need to go by the Windemere Police Station and pick up an accident form."

"You're not going to send someone out?" I angled my arm back and Livvy grabbed the toy out of my hand. I'd spent a lot of time retrieving toys from the floorboard in the last year. My triceps were more toned than they'd ever been.

"No. Just pick up the form and fill it out."

I closed the phone and carefully navigated toward home. Since the 911 operator didn't feel it was very urgent, I'd pick up the form in the morning.

As soon as I stepped in the door at home the phone rang. Probably Mitch. I shushed Rex's barking, set Livvy down, and dropped the diaper bag on the floor. I paused before I picked up the phone. What was I going to tell him? There wasn't much he could do to help me out and he didn't need to be worried about me in the middle of his flying. I'd just wing it. Maybe he'd have news that they were coming back.

"Hello?"

"Give it up."

Not Mitch. "What?" I struggled to place the voice. It was a medium kind of voice. Nothing special about it. It wasn't distinctly male or female, soft or loud.

"Not ready to give it up yet?" The bland tone and the pronunciation sounded almost automated. "It will only get worse."

"What are you talking about? Did you try to run me off the road?"

Chapter
Nineteen

Silence.

"What? What are you talking about?" I shouted. Livvy turned from her spot in front of Rex's kennel and watched me curiously. I took a deep breath. "Listen—"

A click and then a dial tone came over the line. I leaned against the counter. The deliberate, slow voice was worse than someone yelling threats. The robotic, automatic delivery chilled me.

I hit the hang-up button and then punched in the buttons to trace the call. A recording informed me that the service I requested could not be performed. I carefully set the phone down. Then I scrambled eggs and made toast on autopilot. For once, I didn't miss adult conversation at the dinner table. I needed time to think. So Livvy pushed her eggs around on her plate and ate her toast, smearing both her cheeks with grape jelly, while I tried to decide what to do.

I could call Thistlewait or the local police, but I wasn't eager to do either one. I was already a suspect in two—
two—murders and I didn't want to draw any more atten-

tion to myself. Less contact with "authorities" seemed better for me. And figuring out who was calling wouldn't make them stop. I needed to get to the real problem: what the person wanted. I had to find out what "it" was and where "it" was.

After we ate, I stacked the dishes in the sink and got Livvy ready for bed. The bedtime routine of bath, story, and a song soothed me as much as it did Livvy.

"Good night, Livvy." I adjusted her blanket and stood up.

"Where Daddy go?" Livvy was used to Daddy being gone on trips for a few days, so his abrupt departure hadn't fazed her. But it had been several days and she missed him at bedtime.

"He went on a trip. He'll be back as soon as he can."

Livvy contemplated this for a few moments, then nodded.

"Good night." I brushed her hair off her forehead and kissed her.

"Night, Mommy. I wove you."

"I love you, too."

I dropped into the overstuffed chair and clicked on the television, then switched back and forth between the twenty-four-hour news channels. Finally, there was a brief mention that American troops and aircraft had arrived in Turkey, the base for their operation of creating an air bridge to Osan. The reporter seemed almost apologetic as he said, "Things seem calm now in the capital city." Like he was sorry he didn't have a little more action and danger to report. Calm was good for me. I skimmed channels a little bit more. Watching the news, searching for any scrap of info, could become an obsession when Mitch was deployed to a dangerous place. The phone rang and I punched the OFF button, then snagged the phone before the second ring.

"Ellie? This is Rachel."

"Hi! How are you?"

"Fine. Toby!" I pulled the phone away from my ear for a second. I could hear Rachel say, "I said get in the bathtub, now!" Rachel continued in her normal tones over the sound of a small riot in the background, "Sorry. You left me a message?"

"Yes. If you can't talk about this, it's fine. But I wondered if the OSI had been able to find Clarissa's friend Karen Barakat?"

I heard a door shut and the background noise faded. "They've looked, but from what I've heard it sounds like they can't find her."

"You're kidding. She's disappeared?"

"Yep. She skipped on her apartment in the middle of the night and she hasn't been back to her job since Clarissa died. Matt's so frustrated. Seems like everything is turning into a dead end."

"Really? Even stuff about Penny? The castor beans?"

"Yep."

"They checked out Ballard Nova and Bree Reed?"

"Sure did. Ballard was in her store when Penny died and she had the video surveillance tapes to prove it, and Bree had driven over to Seattle to try and sell some of the art galleries there on her work. She's got the receipts and witnesses to prove it, too."

"All that proves is that they didn't actually asphyxiate her or slit her wrists." I had to pause and take a deep breath; those words brought awful images to my mind. "They could still have given her the beans."

Pounding sounded down the phone line. I jerked the phone away again as Rachel shouted, "Mommy will be out in a minute. Sheesh! With four kids I can't even take a potty break alone. I've got to go."

"Okay. Thanks." I realized I'd picked up *Time to Sleep*, one of Livvy's favorite picture books. I ran my hand over the cover and put it on the coffee table on top of the tee-tering stack of picture books. I knew sleep wouldn't come easy for me tonight.

"Rex, come." Rex trotted to the back fence, his tether zinging down the string between two maple trees as he ran his favorite circuit around the barren lilac bush and down the partial chain-link fence. "Come!" He twisted his head around to look at me over his shoulder, then turned back to the fence.

"Fine. You can stay out." The snow in the back was over two feet deep. Two inches of new snow fell this morning. "I'm not ruining my shoes to drag you inside."

"Kelly." I slammed the handful of dog bones on the counter and teetered across the slick wooden floor of the kitchen into the living room. Did I really wear these shoes when I worked at the PR office? I stepped onto the Per-sian rug and felt steadier. "Kelly," I said to the round-faced, brown-eyed girl I'd hired to watch Livvy, "I can't get the dog to come inside. If he starts barking, take him off his tether and let him in. He'll go right in his kennel for a treat. I left some on the counter. If he doesn't want to come inside, just leave him out. There's an old doghouse in the back. He can use that if he gets cold." Not that he'd ever been in there since we'd owned him.

"Now, about Livvy. She's been fed and bathed. She likes a story before bed. And I always sing her 'Hush, Little Baby' after she's in bed."

I walked over and kissed her on the head. "Bye, sweetie. See you in a little while."

"Bye," Livvy murmured, immersed in her game of blocks.

"Okay." I backed reluctantly toward the door. "Oh, and change her diaper before bed."

"Sure, Mrs. Avery," Kelly said. "I've got four little brothers and sisters. We'll be fine. Have a good time."

"Oh. Okay. My cell phone number is by the phone." I picked up my vintage clutch bag with the amethyst clasp and smoothed my hand over the soft skirt of my little black dress that Abby had talked me into buying. I hadn't wanted to spend the money, but now, even after a little alteration, it still looked great. My hair was another story. I swept my bangs out of my eyes. I had to get my hair cut soon.

In the Cherokee, I checked the passenger-side mirror. I only had to squish down a little to see the reflection of the road. Bob at the gas station down the street had wired the mirror back on as best he could and ordered a replacement. I looked at the clock on the dashboard.

There was time for a quick detour. I'd arrive fashionably late, but if Abby arrived on time, she'd be stranded. I took my foot off the accelerator as I hit a patch of ice. Abby was never on time. I cleared the ice and accelerated. She'd never even know I was late.

I found the address on Ponderosa, pulled into the small parking lot, and crept along, checking numbers on the doors. The new apartment complex, the Cedars, perched on a steep hill with the apartment buildings rising three stories above the trees that gave the complex its name. I slowed as I passed building 400. Karen Barakat had lived at number 431. But the last apartment was 420. I tapped the steering wheel. I'd seen the manager's office, but it was dark. Had Karen ever lived here?

A movement in the shadows caught my eye. A girl pushed a large rolling trash can through the fresh snow into position beside a Dumpster. I drove over to her and rolled down my window an inch. "Hi," I said.

She jumped and spun around. As she turned, I realized she wasn't a girl, but a young woman with a slight build.

A thin black sweater with a low neckline clung to her spare body. Instead of looking sexy, she looked anorexic, all pointy collar bones and sharp elbows.

"I'm looking for number 431."

She studied me and the interior of the Cherokee before she said, "Down there." She pointed to a lane that I hadn't seen. It wrapped around behind the soaring buildings. "They're duplexes," she explained.

"Thanks," I said brightly. She didn't reply, just lined up the other trash can. "I'm looking for Karen Barakat. Do you know her?"

The black lace choker that encircled her throat jumped as she swallowed. "She's gone. She was next door to me, but she moved."

"Did you know her?" I asked again.

"No."

"I'd like to talk to her. Do you know where she moved?" I didn't have much hope she'd know, but I had to ask.

She snorted. "Yeah, right. Like she left a forwarding address. I'm the manager here. She took off one night and left everything. She's not coming back."

I scrambled in the console and found one of my organizing brochures. "On the chance that she does come back or call, would you give her this? And tell her I really need to talk to her about her friend Clarissa. Did you know her?"

She shoved the paper into the skintight pocket of her black jeans with some difficulty. "No." She turned and walked back down the lane to the duplexes.

I pulled alongside her. "Her stuff? Is it still here?"

"Nope. Try the Salvation Army." She picked up her pace and walked swiftly away.

Ten minutes later, I circled higher and higher in the downtown parking garage until I found an empty slot. Then I click-clacked my way through the dim garage with the heavy concrete ceilings seeming to press in on my head. I joined a small group of matrons with shiny artificially blond hair twisted up in chignons pacing beside gray-headed and bald gentlemen in suits. I trailed them to the gallery and saw Abby waiting for me at the door.

"Thanks for meeting me here." I handed over my coat and gloves. "Been here long?"

"Nope. Just got here. My parent conferences ran long. Let's circulate before the good food is gone. I didn't have time to eat."

I realized I'd forgotten to feed myself in my rush to get Livvy ready for the babysitter. "Me either."

We hit the hors d'oeuvres. "Okay. What are we trying to find out again?" Abby asked, reaching for a passing waiter's tray. "These cheese things are wonderful. Want some?"

"Umm, I'm not sure. Yeah, get me some, too." I spotted Aaron leaning against the wall with Bree a few feet away at the center of a knot of people. Tonight three inches of bracelets clattered on each wrist as she moved. Her purple dress contrasted with her spiked red hair. She threw back her head and laughed. Aaron absorbed the scene without moving and I got the feeling he didn't like what he saw even though his face didn't change expressions. His body language, crossed arms, made me hesitate. I walked over.

"Hey, Aaron. Big day for Bree. She must be thrilled."

His gaze bored into Bree's back. "Ecstatic."

Wow! "You don't seem very happy." Before he could reply Bree seemed to feel his gaze and broke away from her group to join us. I congratulated her being in the exhibit.

"Thanks. It's great. You can't imagine what it feels like." At this Aaron seemed to swell, reminding me of a puffer fish.

Bree sensed my discomfort and patted my arm. The bracelets, most of them silver or clear plastic, jangled. "Don't mind Aaron. He's the tiniest bit jealous, aren't you, honey? You see, he's an artist, too. He's striving to find his style," she said.

Aaron's face flushed. The words were innocent enough, but she emphasized the last sentence in a condescending tone. There was a nasty undercurrent between them that added tons of emotional baggage to the actual words.

Bree turned to me. "Excuse me. I see the photographer for the newspaper."

Aaron took a step to move away as well, but I put my hand on his arm. "Wait. I wanted to ask you about Mrs. Bedford. Did you know her?"

"Who?"

"Clarissa Bedford. General Bedford's wife."

"No." His face was blank and bland. He didn't seem nervous or worried at the mention of her name. Either he didn't know her or he was a great actor.

"Bree told me Clarissa wanted a painting, but then she wouldn't pay for it."

"Oh. That was Clarissa? I didn't know. Bree handles all that."

"Did it make you mad she wouldn't pay for the painting after Bree painted it for her?" I pressed.

"I told you, Bree takes care of that, the business side," he repeated.

"Did you see her the week before she died? At the community college?"

"No, why would I?"

"Someone saw her arguing with a man with blond hair who was wearing a flight suit the week before she died."

"Listen, I didn't know her and I really don't care if she wanted the painting or not." Aaron strode away through the crowd.

A broad shoulder bumped into me. "Excuse me," said the man as several heads turned toward us to check out the melodious voice. He reached out to steady me with his hand like I was a teetering figurine about to fall off a shelf.

Even without his star insignia, I recognized his hooked nose and wide shoulders. "General Bedford, hello." He left his hand on my shoulder.

"Are you all right?" he fussed. "Sorry about that."

I shifted, stepped back, and he dropped his hand. "I'm fine. I'm sorry about Mrs. Bedford."

"Yes." His craggy face stilled and he clasped both hands behind his back, reminding me of an eagle on a high perch with its wings tucked back. "Thank you. I'm still trying to figure out what to do . . ." He scanned around the room. "I thought coming here would get my mind off things."

Hetty joined us. She kissed Bedford's cheek as she greeted him. "Not quite your style, I know," she said to him. "But I'm so glad you came. It'll be good for you to get out," she said briskly.

Hetty turned to me. "Jackson has an excellent eye for Byzantine mosaics."

"Not me," Bedford amended and took a drink from a waiter. "My first wife. She managed to pick up a few nice things. I just brought back what she told me to."

"A few nice things." Hetty rolled her eyes. "Go on." She turned to me. "Enjoying yourself?"

"Yes. Lovely party. Thank you for the invitation."

Hetty saw someone and dragged Bedford away to introduce him to a friend. I watched Hetty pulling on his arm and saw his resigned look. It seemed Bedford wouldn't have to stay single long, if Hetty had anything to do with it.

I made a circuit of the room, snagged some shrimp/

cream cheese things, and followed a musky scent to a group where Mary, the disgruntled employee from the art gallery, was in an intense conversation with Victor Roth. His head poked up above most of the crowd and made him easy to spot. A fixed smile was attached to his face, but his eyes were narrow. Mary's lush body was tense as she leaned toward him, her knuckles white as she gripped her cocktail.

Victor slid away to the other side of the room.

The bony-shouldered guy from the gallery merged into our group. Even a sport coat couldn't disguise his pointy shoulder bones. He handed a small plate to Mary. She finished her drink with a gulp and set down the empty glass on a window ledge.

"Hi. I'm Ellie Avery. I talked with you at the gallery."

"Yeah, I remember. I'm Carl. This is Mary."

Mary nodded at me and picked up a cheese curl.

"So you both work at Victor's gallery?"

"No," Carl replied since Mary had bitten into her cheese curl with a snap. "We're art students at Harris. We're helping Ms. Sullivan set up the art show."

"Are you in and out of the galleries a lot?"

Carl shrugged. His shoulder blade threatened to punch through the seam in his coat. "Yeah. More, now that it's getting closer."

"I'm trying to find out a little bit about Victor Roth."

"Why?" Mary asked sharply and popped the rest of the cheese curl into her mouth.

"I'm thinking of buying something at his gallery," I improvised.

"What? The walls or the desk in the office?" Mary sneered.

"Umm, I must have misunderstood."

Carl took Mary's empty plate. "I bet Victor told you he had something 'astonishing' that would look great in that 'space' and 'make a statement.' " Carl's voice slipped in and out of a British accent.

"Well . . ." I hedged.

Mary sighed and turned to me. "Listen. You'd better really check him out. Check him out good. He's a user. Don't trust him. And don't trust his artwork either."

"Why not?"

Mary waved a hand. "Questions, whispers. No one can nail down anything solid, but I wouldn't buy anything from him."

"So he doesn't have anything in his gallery?"

"A few pieces. I've seen about three paintings and a few sculptures. But nothing stays long," Carl said. "I've heard him talk to clients. He always says he's got something in his New York or London gallery that will be perfect. He'll have it sent over, but I've never seen anything delivered from London or New York. A box just appears in the back. No labels or anything."

"If you want to know more, ask her," Mary said and nodded to a person over my shoulder. I swung around and scanned the crowd. I stared at the profile of the dark-headed woman with the intentionally messy hairdo. Chelsea O'Mara, the reporter for Channel Two. I wondered if she'd chosen her hairstyle so she'd look great standing outside some city building reporting on a committee meeting as the wind ruffled her hair.

"She's been asking a lot of questions, too," Mary said.

"Thanks," I said and moved through the crowd.

I didn't want to talk to Chelsea O'Mara since she'd been trying to track me down and had reported on the crew flying naked. I'd bet she had some new questions for me about finding Clarissa's body. But maybe I could keep an eye on her and overhear a conversation.

I edged up to her group, but kept my back turned so I'd

look like I was studying the displayed artwork; I was the only one in the room actually looking at the artwork; everyone else mingled and talked. The swell of conversation grew as more people arrived and I moved over to a picture, closer to Chelsea's group.

As the sounds swirled around me I tried to focus on Chelsea's voice. A waiter swept past on one side and caused a brief lull as people grabbed food and drinks. I heard the end of Chelsea's question, ". . . illegal goods and smuggling?"

"I can assure you, the Frost Fest planning committee has no connections with anything illegal." It was Hetty's scratchy voice, loud and angry, but it didn't rise above the general din of conversation, so only my head turned toward her. "We have the utmost confidence in everyone associated with Frost Fest. Anything you have heard is a rumor. You should treat it as a rumor, not a fact."

Hetty pushed away and Chelsea turned in my direction, so I snapped back toward the painting and focused on it, trying to appear so enthralled with it that everyone would leave me alone. Or maybe if I stood really still Chelsea wouldn't notice me. I felt like I was six again and playing hide-and-seek. I'd always been lousy at the game. I remembered standing immobile, thinking, *Don't look at them. Don't move. If I don't look and don't move, then they won't see me.* It rarely worked when I was a kid, but I couldn't get through the crowd without walking right by Chelsea, so I was stuck.

I kept my gaze on the landscape in front of me and listened until I heard her voice move away to my left. I breathed a sigh of relief. I needed to find Abby and get out of here. The last thing I wanted was another report on me showing up on the morning news. I glanced around, but didn't see Abby. I'd browse through the gallery and track Abby down. I turned back to the painting and for the first time, I really looked at it. It was the one I'd picked up from Bree's studio. Her initials showed faintly in the corner, A.R. I glanced at the card beside the painting, DILEMMA. A. REED.

I studied the painting again and tilted my head to the side. The scene of a forest at either sunset or dawn reminded me of something. I took a step back and studied the dark pines that were backlit. Sunlight glinted on the frosted branches. I felt someone watching me and glanced to the right and met Aaron's intense gaze. Then I remembered. I'd looked at this scene, not as a painting, but in real life on the deck at Abby's house.

And Aaron had commented on the colors of the sunset, the way the light sparkled off the ice on the pines. He closed the distance between us and gripped my arm above my elbow. "We need to talk," he said and yanked me through the crowd to a little alcove in the back where the servers set up their trays.

I jerked my elbow away and took a step back. He was obviously upset, but I didn't feel vulnerable with the activity of the servers bustling around me. They barely glanced at us, but their presence reassured me.

Aaron ran his hand over this thinning blond hair and I noticed again his chapped hands. I'd seen them the night of Jeff's party, but thought they were red from the cold. Tonight they stood out, workmanlike, against the fine cloth of his dark suit jacket as he smoothed his lapel and slightly loosened the knot of his tie. I remembered Bree's long red nails and perfect cuticles.

A few other odd things clicked into place: Bree saying, "Who does he think *we* are?" and Aaron's strong reaction to Bree's taunts about him being an artist.

"You're the artist, aren't you?" I asked.

An Everything In Its Place Tip for Organized Closets

Linen closet
- If you're lucky enough to have a linen closet (some modern floor plans have eliminated this storage area), label shelves so you can put away and find the right linens in a snap.
- If you don't have a linen closet you can store bedding for each room on shelves in individual rooms or store linens in trunks (except for cedar chests) or even in containers that fit under your bed.
- To prevent yellowing and streaking of your linens, don't store them in plastic bags or cardboard boxes. Also, don't let your linens come in direct contact with wood, even wooden shelves. Use acid-free tissue paper to protect linens and store in a dry, well-ventilated area.
- Lavender sachets discourage moths.

Chapter
Twenty

Behind his glasses, anger flashed in his dark brown eyes, but he quickly suppressed it. He pushed his hands down into his pockets. It should have been a relaxed pose, but his gaze skittered around behind me as he checked to see if anyone else had overheard.

"What are you talking about?" He shrugged and gave a pitiful half laugh, but it sounded more like a squeak.

"It's your hands. They're red and chapped, but Bree's always look like she just had a manicure. Washing the paint out of those brushes with, what is it, turpentine? It must be rough on the skin. And the signature. Bree said the *A* was for her full name, Aubree, but *A* is really for Aaron, isn't it? And the way Bree dresses, with the beret, the flamboyant colors, her spiked, dyed hair. It's all an act. She's playing the part of an artist."

He pinched the bridge of his nose, then pulled his hand away and scanned the crowd behind me. He seemed to have an internal debate going on. Finally, he focused back on me and sighed. "It's not like we're hurting anyone. People get their artwork. I get to paint." His matter-of-fact tone turned bitter on the last statement. "Bree's a natural at sales and people want to buy a painting from a flamboyant, beautiful woman, not a shy, conservative military guy."

"What? You tried to sell your work as your own and it didn't sell?"

"Are you kidding? I was stationed at Kemper, you know, in central California. At first it was great. I worked and flew, but when I wasn't in the squad, I painted. The location was great. An hour to San Francisco with all the art festivals and people interested in art. And they had the money to buy it. I had a few dealers interested in my stuff. But you should have seen them the minute they found out what I did. It was like a door slammed in my face."

A server bumped into me and I stepped farther away from the entrance to the alcove. "But they liked Bree?" I asked.

"No. They *loved* Bree. Bree's always dressed like that, funky, you know. A customer at an art fair assumed she was the artist once. I was TDY. Bree thought it was a riot and she played along to get the sale. I was furious, but she said she'd sold it and bet me she could sell more before I could get back home." He shrugged. "She did. Seven paintings in a weekend."

He shifted his shoulders around and breathed deeply. "To tell you the truth, it doesn't feel too bad to have it out in the open. I was ready to come clean, but Bree likes the attention."

He looked through the crowd toward Bree. Their gazes connected and silent communication flowed across the room.

"Your dilemma," I said, thinking of the painting's name.

Bree broke off her conversation and pushed her way roughly through the crowd toward us.

"Yes. But you've solved it very neatly." He smiled. "There's nothing to do now but tell the truth." He said the last sentence loudly enough so that Bree could hear us as could a few other people, including Chelsea O'Mara.

As Chelsea's sharp gaze focused on Aaron, I slipped back into the gallery and melded with another group.

"But the marbles *belong* in Greece," said a woman to my right as she leaned forward to emphasize her point, tottered for a second, and then swept upright.

I smiled, intelligently, I hoped, as I tried to figure out what they were talking about. Games? Home decorating?

A stout man across the circle said, "Like there would be anything left of them, if the Brits hadn't carted them off to England."

The woman swished a languid hand heavy with sparkly rings through the air, brushing away the argument. "You're so basic, Harry. Yes, the British preserved and cared for the Elgin Marbles, but that's all the more reason to return the antiquities to the country of origin." The woman smiled blearily, enjoying the debate.

But Harry's face turned red, reminding me of Livvy. I'd seen that exact shade right before one of her crying bouts. He said, "They'd have destroyed them!"

I hadn't noticed Victor Roth was part of the circle until he put a restraining hand on Harry's shoulder. "What Harry means, Allison, is that the local people didn't appreciate the innate beauty of the antiquities or care for them properly." His sharp white teeth flashed when he smiled. "Why should we return these works of art to states that may not appreciate them for their history or magnificence, but merely see them as a way to attract tourists to their countries? And there's the added danger that Greece would again ignore their care and protection."

Allison's droopy hand landed on Victor's arm. "You are so sure you're right, you don't even listen to me." Allison looked up into Victor's face, teetered on her spike heels, and then tightened her grip.

An older woman across the circle spoke carefully with a slight trace of an accent as she said, "On the contrary, some countries do appreciate their exquisite works of art and handle them with the greatest care." A scarf framed her light brown face. Her dark stare seemed to bore into me as she said, "Turkey appreciates her history. Anyone who would try to keep something that belongs to Turkey, to the people of Turkey, would be a thief."

I shifted uneasily. Her words were directed specifically to me. What was she talking about? Her dark gaze simmered with anger. I opened my mouth, stretching for a reply, but Victor, once again, stepped into the breach. "Elaina, you are right, of course." Allison hovered on his arm, gazing up at him with glassy eyes. While his tone had been playful with Allison, he was serious, almost respectful, to this Elaina. "Turkey has recognized the vast importance of preserving and regaining its antiquities. I hope your country realizes what an eloquent and beautiful asset you are to it."

Even Elaina's anger cooled under Victor's charming speech. "You are most kind, but I am merely a diplomat's wife, speaking for myself."

At a tap on my shoulder, I turned to find Abby standing behind me. "How's it going? Can we get out of here? My feet are killing me."

"Sure." I didn't know what else I could find out here and I wanted to think about what the diplomat's wife, Elaina, was trying to tell me in the middle of cocktail chitchat.

"Let's go by the ladies' room first so I can rest my feet for a few minutes before we head to the parking garage."

"Sounds good to me." Now that I had time to think about it, it felt like the tips of my shoes were forcing my toes to grow together. We collapsed on a padded bench in the foyer of the ladies' room and kicked off our shoes.

I rubbed my foot and described the scene with Elaina.

"Strange," she said as she put her shoes back on. "Let me go to the bathroom and then let's go. I'm beat."

She headed around the wall to the bathroom. The door whooshed open and Elaina walked in. She didn't look surprised to see me. She quickly checked her reflection in the mirror and then took a seat beside me.

"You must return to Turkey what belongs to Turkey."

"I don't know—"

She ignored me. "There will not be any questions. You simply give it to us. That will be the end."

"What? Give what to you? I don't have anything that belongs to Turkey."

This time she examined my face carefully, then tilted her head to one side, considering.

"Then you have a problem." She briskly pulled on her gloves and stood up. Small black oval-shaped beads edged the wrists of her gloves and caught the light as she fastened the top button on her coat. "I do not know you, but I believe you, looking at your face. But others, they will not."

"Not what? Not believe me?"

The door whooshed again and three women entered. Elaina quickly leaned down and pretended to adjust her shoe. She walked away. She didn't glance at me again.

The next morning I rolled over to Mitch's side of the bed and turned off the alarm. I listened for a moment, but didn't hear Livvy. For once she wasn't awake before me. Of course, the one day Livvy didn't wake me up calling, "Moommmmmyyy!" was the day I'd set the alarm to get up early. I slumped back into the pillows for a few more minutes, automatically reaching for an extra pillow to drag over to Mitch's side, but then I realized I didn't need to move any pillows. They were still stacked, like I liked them, two-deep with an angle to snuggle into. I sighed and burrowed deeper. Mitch hated my pillow pile, as he called it. He'd always toss any extra pillows off his side before he went to sleep. I punched the pillow and rolled over again. It was the little things like pillows and seeing the empty hook where his keys usually hung that reinforced the loneliness. I concentrated on deep breaths, hoping a steady, relaxing breathing rhythm would help me drift off to sleep.

But a few minutes later, I realized I was studying the pile of clothes I'd left on the closet floor. My little black dress needed to go to the cleaners and my abandoned heels rested under the collapsed spirals of my hose. Thank goodness, I didn't have to wear those every day. Being a stay-at-home mom had definite advantages, dress code being one of the best. The hours, now, that was a different story. Talk about always being on call.

As the growing light revealed more of the room, I looked around and realized I needed to clean up. I had a tendency to let things like cleaning and cooking go when Mitch was gone. Other wives had told me they did the same things. I smiled when I remembered one friend's comment about gearing up for her husband to come home. "I've got to go home and clean," she'd said. "The house is a pit right now."

Ours might not officially qualify as a pit, but dusting and doing some laundry wouldn't hurt.

The telephone rang and I lunged across the bed to grab it before a second ring.

"Hello."

"Hi, hope I didn't wake you," Mitch said. His words echoed down the phone line, sounding like he was genuinely calling from the other side of the world.

"No. I'm awake."

We both said, "How are you?" at the same time and then waited as our words traveled over the lines. Then we both paused again.

"I'm fine," I said. It came right on top of his comment: "We're here. I'm a little tired."

I hated international calls. The two-second delay made it hard not to talk on top of each other.

I paused, waiting to see if he'd say anything else, then said, "I saw on the news that you're helping with the Osan thing."

His laugh echoed down the tinny line. "I can neither confirm nor deny that," he joked.

"Yeah. I know."

After silence filled the line, he said, "How's everything going?"

"Okay. How much time do you have to talk?"

"Not long. Just wanted to let you know we made it."

"How long are you going to be there? Any idea on that?"

"Haven't heard anything. Watch the news. You'll know when we're coming home before we do."

I wanted to tell him what was going on, but a thread of restraint held me back. He was so far away. He wouldn't be able to help. He'd only feel frustrated and worried. Instead I asked, "So what have you been doing?"

"Not much. The usual—eat, sleep, fly, wait. Wait some more. Make phone calls. I tried you earlier, but the call didn't go through so I tried my parents. I wanted to check on Mom."

"What's up? Did you fill her in on your deployment?"

"Yeah, but I really wanted to see how she was doing. She was pretty upset about Summer last week."

"They're always upset about Summer. What did she do, change her major again?" Mitch's flighty sister kept his parents guessing.

"No. She dropped out. Says she's going to become a hairstylist."

"Oh. I bet that went over well."

Mitch avoided that comment. He only said, "She'll figure it out."

"I know. If anyone does what they want, it's Summer. I only hope your parents can handle it." I switched the topic back to him as I asked, "So what are you doing today?"

"They're setting up a market for us. We can't go off base, but they're bringing stuff in. Want another carpet? They've got some small prayer carpets, silk on silk, about three feet by two feet, that are nice."

"No. I don't really want another carpet. What would we do with one that small? I wouldn't want us to use it to wipe our feet on. They're expensive, I bet."

"Yeah. We could frame it, like the one in the Hole."

"I did see that one. So how much are they?"

"I'm not sure. I'll find out today. Probably a few hundred."

"Okay. Well, whatever you think. You always bring back good stuff." I glanced down at the gold, red, and brown carpet, the perfect complement to our dark bedroom furniture. The silence stretched for a few moments. Oh, who cared if Mitch couldn't do anything to help me? We always tried to be honest with each other. Well, except for that one time when I knew he wouldn't even listen to my worries about Jeff. But that was over and resolved. I needed to talk to him. "Mitch, there's been some strange things going on around here." I paused, trying to gather my thoughts. "Mitch?"

I realized my words weren't echoing back at me. "Mitch?"

When there wasn't an answer, I hung up the phone and rolled out of bed. He'd call back as soon as he could get another line, so I didn't want to get in the shower and miss his call. I slipped on sweats and padded down the hall.

Sometimes calls from Mitch were more frustrating than encouraging.

"Hi, Rex," I whispered as I entered the kitchen. "Be a good boy and keep quiet to let Livvy sleep." I leaned down and grabbed the kennel door to open it, but it swung open when I touched it.

"Rex?" The kennel was empty except for the blanket Rex slept on. I looked around the kennel, then the kitchen. No Rex. I moved quickly through the living and dining room, but didn't see him. I knew he wasn't in Livvy's room because I'd checked on her when I returned last night. I hurried to the window in my room that overlooked the backyard. I'd told the babysitter to let Rex inside, but what if she'd forgotten? And I'd forgotten him, too.

I twisted the dowel for the miniblinds and scanned the backyard. Small hollows, Rex's footprints, littered the snow, but there was no large, black dog.

Chapter
Twenty-one

"I'm sorry, Mrs. Avery," said Kelly's anguished voice. "I forgot about Rex. I was having so much fun with Livvy that I completely forgot. I'm so sorry."

"Don't feel too bad. I forgot about him myself."

When I got home the night before, I'd paid Kelly and asked her to return later in the week. I'd checked on Livvy, and then waved to Kelly's mom as she drove her daughter away, assuming Rex was tucked in his kennel, just like Livvy. I'd been so sleepy I'd dropped into bed myself without checking on Rex. Now I realized that when I walked in the door last night I hadn't heard any barking. Rex always barked.

I slipped on my boots, grabbed a coat, and stepped outside. I folded the lapels of my long wool coat across my chest to keep out the frigid wind. Cold drips from the thawing tree branches plopped on my head as I walked the perimeter of the yard. Even in the growing light, the snow's whiteness seemed to sting my eyes. In the crevices near the fence I tried to distinguish between slush, mud, and bits of dried grass in the areas where Rex's paws had pushed through to the ground. Nothing along the fence line. I reached the farthest corner by the shed and paused, scanning the ground again. A cold dollop hit the exposed skin on the back of my neck and I shivered. I took a step back to the house, but then I saw a small red drop in the snow near the shed. I walked closer. The small bright red trail spotted the snow at regular intervals around the shed and stopped at the curb. I looked back over the yard. No more drops. And where was the tether? Without the hook from the tether weighing it down, the string between the maple trees bobbed slightly in the breeze. I swallowed hard and retreated to the kitchen.

A soft rustling sound came from down the hall. I hurried into the bathroom and showered under steaming water. If I hurried, I could get out of the shower before Livvy was fully awake. I let the water pound on my neck and shoulders for a few extra seconds and allowed the awful thought to rise to the surface of my mind. Someone had unhooked the tether from the string and taken Rex. The trail of blood didn't make things look good. Surely, whoever had taken him wouldn't hurt him. But there were some sick people in this world. I felt a little nauseated as I turned the water off and focused on getting dressed.

I pulled on a blue turtleneck sweater, jeans, and thick socks. I blasted the blow-dryer over my hair for a few minutes. When I clicked it off, Livvy's voice floated down the hall, "Moooommy!"

I got Livvy dressed and fed us granola. Out of habit, I opened the plastic tub of dog food and then felt a sick sensation in the pit of my stomach. It was bad enough when Rex managed to slip off his tether and get out of the yard on his own. The thought that he might get hit by a car was terrible, but this was worse. He'd been taken intentionally. I scooped up the kibble and dumped it in the bowl, a gesture that made me feel a little better. For good measure, I filled his water bowl to the brim, too. I checked the animal control number in the phone book and dialed. Closed Sundays.

I tossed our dishes in the sink and then I did the only thing I could think of to do: I went to visit Mabel.

I knew she'd be up. During the summer, she swept her porch and driveway at five a.m., then yanked weeds out of her flower bed before breakfast. I didn't think something as minor as a change in temperature would change her routine.

"Have another," Mabel said and slid a warm cinnamon roll onto my plate. "Oh, I shouldn't. I've already had breakfast."

"Nonsense. You're going to need to keep up your energy. Eat that and then take a walk around the neighborhood and look for Rex. Leave Livvy with me." Today she wore a pale yellow wind suit with a jaunty blue and yellow plaid scarf and looked completely recovered from the flu.

"Oh, I couldn't do that."

"Sure. I'd love it." Her face crinkled as she smiled at Livvy and said, "I've got a trunk of toys for my grandkids in the bedroom yonder, but they don't get here that often. We'll be fine."

"So you didn't see anything? Hear anything?"

"No. Let me think. Last night we watched *Biography*, Cary Grant. Then the news. Didn't hear anything."

"Have you found anything around your house from Penny?" Mabel's words broke into my train of thought.

"No."

She pushed a plate with tiny bites of cut-up cinnamon rolls over to Livvy. "Maybe I was wrong, then. Maybe she didn't leave anything there. Remember, I saw her at your house right before she died. I thought she might have left you something. Maybe you should search her house."

"What?"

"If you didn't find anything at your house, maybe there might be something at her house. A clue."

"Mabel, the police searched her house and mine, too, for that matter." I said it automatically. But why would Penny come to my house when she could have called me? Had I really checked out my house for, well, clues, as Mabel called them? I felt silly even thinking like this.

"He's out of town again, you know," Mabel said.

"Who?" I asked.

"Will Follette."

I shook my head and asked, "How do you know these things?"

"The Wilsons live down the street. They clear his sidewalk for him when he's away. Not that Will arranged that. It was Penny, you know. She asked Mort's son, he's a teenager, to shovel their walk and paid him to do it when Will was out of town. I saw Mort the other day at the gas station and mentioned seeing his son shoveling Will's driveway. Mort said his son probably won't ever see another payment from Will, but it was the least they could do for Will, with Penny dying, you know." Mabel collected the empty plates and carried them to the sink. Over her shoulder, she said, "You go on. I'll keep an eye on Livvy."

I'd consumed the cinnamon roll and a tall glass of milk without realizing it. "Okay." I pulled on my coat. I left Livvy bent over a box that Mabel had placed in the middle of the floor, extracting a drum and a tambourine.

Mabel made a shooing gesture with her hand, then slowly levered herself down on the floor beside Livvy. I slipped out the door and heard Mabel's muted voice explaining, "See, here. You shake it like this."

Apparently cinnamon rolls and new toys had damp-
ened Livvy's separation anxiety. I walked down our street
before they could get started on the drum. I didn't see a
huge black dog bounding toward me and, to my relief, I
didn't see a forlorn black lump anywhere either. I even
stopped at Marsali's house to ask him if he'd seen Rex.
He'd put down his scissors and coupons on the Sunday
paper that was spread across his kitchen table before
checking his backyard for Rex. I remembered the snacks
from Cobblestone Bakery I'd promised and felt a wash of
guilt. He hadn't seen Rex, but promised to keep an eye
out for him.

I got in the Cherokee and made slow widening circles
of the neighborhood. An hour later I returned to our
street. Since it was Sunday the pickups and dilapidated
cars and vans of the work crews weren't crowding both
sides of the street in front of the Wilsons' house. The
Cherokee's tires ground over the snow and ice that fringed
our driveway. I put the Cherokee in park and climbed out.

Instead of marching right over to Mabel's to get Livvy,
I walked to the kitchen door and studied the concrete
steps. I blinked, trying to adjust my eyes to the sharp contrast between sunlight and the deep shadows around the
foundation. Experimentally, I swept a few prickly bushes
aside, but I didn't see anything except pure white mounds
of snow. I stepped back out of the bushes, glad for my coat
and gloves that had protected me from the sharp thorns. I
climbed the steps slowly, looking around me, taking in
every detail: concrete steps, iron handrail, and wooden
screen door closed securely. I never did really look at the
porch when I rushed in or out. And except for the de-
pressing fact that we'd need to scrape and paint the eaves
in the summer, I didn't see anything unusual. I ran my
gloved hand over the top of the door frame, and got a
layer of wet dirt on my glove.

I walked down the steps and methodically paced around the house, my gaze fixed on the deep shadows of the foundation. At the front porch, I climbed the steps and peered over the edge. Below me, the foundation plantings' thin, bare branches with pointy thorns splayed out like minifireworks bursting on the snow. I shook my head, frustrated. I doubted Penny had hidden anything among the thorny bushes, but even if she had we'd probably have to wait for the spring thaw to find it. When the snow melted last year, we found three of Rex's tennis balls, one of Livvy's sandals, and a rake.

Turning to the front porch, I surveyed the bare expanse. With our wicker furniture, flower pots, and wind chimes stowed in the shed, only a large clay pot that was too heavy to carry huddled off to the right side of the steps. A layer of frost iced the rich black soil. I managed to tilt it back, but there was only a dark circle staining the porch under it. I levered it back down and turned to inspect the arched front door. No place to hide anything there. I checked behind the mailbox, then flicked up the stiff welcome mat and found a few leftover pine needles. I scanned the porch, even the ceiling. Several bugs had met their end in the light fixture. I sighed and walked back down the steps. Aside from starting my spring cleaning list, I hadn't found anything.

I pulled my keys out of my pocket and fanned them out on the ring. The sliver of Will and Penny's key winked in the light. I glanced down the deserted street, but the driveways merged together as I squinted against the strong sunlight. I stood there a few moments debating, then shoved the keys back into my pocket and walked over to Mabel's. I wouldn't do it.

At Mabel's house I worked Livvy's arm into her coat, but I was still thinking of the empty street. It was so cold and icy that there weren't many joggers or walkers this time of year. And Mabel, our personal neighborhood watch, noticed everything.

"Mabel, how could anyone get into Penny's house without being noticed?"

Mabel replaced the toys in the trunk and shook her head. "I don't know. I spent all morning sitting right there in that chair. I made it out to the mailbox, but that was it. I did see the white convertible, but I didn't stay to see what happened. I was so tired after that I had to go to bed. I was coming down with that flu, so I didn't notice much, except that white convertible. It was different."

Mabel looked so depressed. I pushed and pulled Livvy's other arm into her coat sleeve and said quickly, "Don't worry about it. I'm sure the police have questioned everyone in the neighborhood. Someone had to have seen something."

"You know . . ." Mabel said slowly, dollhouse furniture dangling in her hands. She put them in the trunk and shoved herself off the floor. She went to the window. "The traffic at the Wilsons' would make it possible for someone to hide in plain sight."

I thought of the parade of vehicles and how I mentally skipped over them. "You're right. Someone could park on the curb and walk across the street to Penny's and their car would blend in. Do you think the work crews noticed anything?"

Mabel shook her head. "No. They're working inside, so they probably didn't see anything. And if they did, I think quite a few of them are illegal immigrants and wouldn't talk to the police."

I thanked Mabel and tried to entice Livvy away from the two-story dollhouse. I wouldn't have let Livvy play with it because the pieces were so small, with tiny, breakable parts that she could put in her mouth and then choke on, but Mabel had been right there on the floor with her, watching her every move. Livvy seemed to realize this was an extra-special treat that she wouldn't get if I'd been around and so she clung to the miniature lamp and lawn chair until the skin on her knuckles turned white.

I managed to pry her fingers away from the toys. Livvy immediately burst into tears and looked at me like I was a traitor. I tossed the toys in the dollhouse and we made an ungraceful, noisy exit. Standing on Mabel's porch I finished zipping Livvy's coat and handed her Pink Girl from the pocket. Livvy shook her head and batted at my hand. "No," she wailed. "Want the air," meaning she wanted the lawn chair. I felt my pulse pick up. When she threw a fit I tensed up, too, even though it was only over a dollhouse toy. I blew out a deep breath to calm down. "I know you're upset, but you can't have the chair. We have to leave it so it will be there next time."

After a few minutes, she sputtered a few times and then pointed up at the icicles hanging from the edge of the roof.

"Icicles," I said and took her hand for the walk home. During the slow trek home, I realized I didn't want to spend the day in a quiet house. With Mitch gone, it seemed lonely, but now that Rex was gone too, I *really* didn't want to go home. I checked my watch and decided we could make the late service at church, if we left right away. I buckled Livvy in her car seat and dashed inside for the diaper bag and my crocodile-embossed leather bag, glad that casual dress was standard.

Later that day, I plopped down in an armchair and looked around the circle of faces that made up our small Bible study group, as I listened for Livvy to cry. She'd done great this morning at church and they hadn't called me down to the nursery. Did I dare hope for a repeat? So far it was quiet. Maybe the separation anxiety stage was over? Abby and Jeff sat down on the couch near me. Ginny, a skinny nurse who'd started attending the group at the same time we did, perched on the fireplace hearth and said, "How are you doing? Any idea when Mitch will be back?"

"No. I haven't heard anything."

"Let me know if you need anything," she said.

I thanked her and glanced around the group again. Each person had asked about Mitch and offered to help. I'd only known these people a few weeks.

"Really," Ginny insisted. "I mean it. Bring Livvy over, if you need a break. I'm on swing-shift, so I'm home during the day this week."

I swallowed a lump in my throat and said, "Thanks. I might take you up on that."

"Okay, tonight's study is about peace. Jeff, why don't you start us off and read the passage for us?" asked Joe, the leader. "Colossians three, fifteen and sixteen."

Jeff found the page and began to read, " 'Give my greetings to the brothers at Laodicea, and to Nympha and the church in her house. After this letter has been read to you, see that it is also read in the church of the Laodiceans and that you in turn read the letter from Laodicea.' " He paused and looked around at the puzzled expressions. I heard muffled crying in the background. "I think I'm in the wrong place," Jeff said with a laugh. "That doesn't sound like it has anything to do with peace."

Abby leaned over and said, "You're in chapter four, not three."

He flipped back a page and said, "This makes more sense. 'Let the peace of Christ rule in your hearts.' " Behind him, the babysitter, Emily, leaned around the corner and looked at me.

Not quite through with the separation anxiety stage,

after all. I picked my way quietly through the living room. Jeff's voice faded as I followed the babysitter down the hall. She blew a bubble with her gum and said, "Livvy looked up and realized you weren't here. She won't stop crying."

I gathered her into my arms and sat down in the rocking chair. Livvy stuck her thumb in her mouth and snuggled into the crook of my arm and I soaked up every second of our cuddling time. Even though I'd been looking forward to adult conversation tonight, I stayed in the rocker, occasionally shoving off with my foot to keep us moving.

"No!" shouted David as Jessica ripped a fire truck out of his hand. "Mine!" His voice rose as he repeated the word in a high-pitched whine. The sitter intervened, rescued the toys, and told them they needed to share. I decided we probably needed to raise her salary. The scene reminded me of something—the kids' room at Ballard's Pathway group. Different set of kids, same actions. After a few minutes, Livvy climbed down and went to play with the toy dishes, but she kept a close eye on me to make sure I didn't sneak out. I checked my watch and decided I might as well spend the rest of the time with the kids. By the time I managed to sneak out, it would be almost over anyway.

A few minutes later, Abby showed up with the parents and walked with me back down the hall to the living room and into the kitchen where everyone was snacking on tortilla chips, salsa, and brownies.

Abby grabbed a brownie and said, "Let's go out to dinner tomorrow night. Just you and me. Jeff will watch Livvy."

I handed Livvy a bite of brownie and took a handful of chips for myself. "That sounds great." I dunked a chip in the puddle of salsa. It was nice to be good enough friends with Abby that I didn't have to go through the dance of "Oh, I really couldn't, that would be too much work." Instead, I said, "Where do you want to go?"

"Pablo's," she said instantly. "I've got to have one of their burritos."

"Sounds great."

"Okay. Meet me at my house at six?" I nodded, my mouth full of chips, and she said, "You can update me on the investigation."

An Everything In Its Place Tip for Organized Closets

Broom closet
- Mount hooks on the wall to store brooms, dustpans, and mops. Make sure mops and brooms clear the floor by a few inches.
- A crate or box on an upper shelf is handy for storing cleaning rags.
- A plastic-handled crate that holds your cleaning supplies can be moved from room to room as you clean and then tucked away on a high shelf to keep dangerous chemicals out of children's reach.

Chapter
Twenty-two

First thing Monday morning, I called the Vernon Animal Shelter. "I'm sorry, but we don't have a dog with that description. Did he have tags?" asked the receptionist at the shelter.

"Yes," I said.

"Well, you'll probably get a call from someone. And if he comes in, we'll call you."

I punched the button to turn the phone off and swept the crumbs on the kitchen table into a neat pile with my hands. It was the blood on the snow that worried me the most. I hoped Rex wasn't hurt. Should I make lost dog posters? Anything would be better than wondering where Rex could be.

Livvy's voice carried into the kitchen from the living room as she counted with the Count on *Sesame Street*. Of course, she stopped at two, but it was a start. The phone rang again and I picked it up.

"Ellie Avery?" asked a female voice.

"Yes."

"I heard you wanted to talk to me."

I tried to gather my scattered thoughts. Did I have a call out about Everything In Its Place? With my life in an uproar I'd let my part-time business slide. If I wasn't careful my clients or potential clients might slide right out of my life altogether. I vowed to spend more time on it, but I couldn't think of anyone who'd be calling me back. I had to resort to saying, "And you are?"

"Karen."

Karen? Oh, *Karen!*

"Hi. I did want to talk to you. I'm sorry about Clarissa. You were friends?"

"Yeah. We hung out."

"I was wondering about the art class you're taking," I said.

"Was."

"You're not going anymore?" I asked.

"No. I bailed."

"Why?" This was harder than getting details out of Mitch when he was on a TDY.

"I just did it because Clarissa wanted to. You know, because she asked. I don't care about art appreciation. It was kinda fun with her there, but since she died . . . I'm not going back."

"I can understand that. I heard Clarissa had an argument with a man one night before the class started. Did you see or hear them?"

After a long silence Karen said, "Why?"

"It's hard to explain. I knew her. I worked for her. Before she died another spouse from the base died. I think there's a connection."

The silence stretched again. Finally, Karen said, "Look. Clarissa was mixed up with some heavy stuff, okay? You don't want to mess with those people."

"Who? People here? Or in Vegas?"

"It doesn't matter where they are. You don't mess with them."

"Is that why you disappeared?"

"You got it. If you're smart, you'll back off, too."

It wasn't a threat. She was genuinely trying to convince me to leave everything alone. "So you know who it was, the person she argued with, and you're afraid." I took her silence for agreement. "If you know anything, you've got to go to the police."

"Yeah, right. That's the last place I'll go."

I heard the determination in her voice, but I had to try to convince her to talk to the police. "Clarissa's dead and you're hiding. I've got someone threatening me. If you can give the police any leads, you've got to do it. You could end it."

Karen laughed. "Yeah. More likely, that would be the end of me. No way."

I tried another track. "What about Clarissa? She was your friend. Does someone deserve to get away with her murder?"

"Oh, you're going with that 'I owe it to Clarissa and she'd want me to do it' crap. I'm not going there. Clarissa would want me to get out and not look back. She'd want me to *live*. Nothing I do will bring her back. She's gone." Karen's tone was adamant and angry.

"I'm sorry. I'm not trying to make you feel guilty. Could we meet somewhere and talk about this some more?"

"No." The syllable was barely out of her mouth before the dial tone sounded.

The phone rang and I answered it, hoping it was Karen.

"Mrs. Avery. This is Special Agent Thistlewait."

"Oh."

"Yes, and a good morning to you, too." Thistlewait was the last person I wanted to talk to this morning. He probably had another search warrant. On second thought, I doubted he'd call in advance if he did. He continued, "I understand you were at an art show Saturday night." I heard pages crinkling and then he said, "A preview show for Frost Fest?" His careful pronunciation made the title sound silly.

"Yes," I replied rather defensively, "apparently quite a few of Vernon's cultural supporters turned out."

"Victor Roth was there."

"Yes."

"Did you talk with him?"

"Yes." I had a bad feeling about this conversation. "He's not dead, is he?" I asked.

Thistlewait laughed. "Far from it."

"Then what's this about?"

He crinkled his papers again and said, "I want to know what you talked about. Mrs. Avery, you have a—how should I say this? A unique perspective on things. I want to know what you think of him."

"Oh. Well. Not much. I don't think he's aboveboard. He was in a group I was in for a while. We talked about the Elgin Marbles, the international squabble over which country should have them."

"And he said?" Thistlewait asked.

"That the original countries might not appreciate the antiquities." I considered telling him about the weird conversation I'd had with Elaina in the bathroom, but decided against it. And even though I'd just talked to Karen I couldn't tell him anything about her or where she was, except that she was scared. I stayed mum on both topics. I didn't want any more attention from the OSI than I'd already had. "So what do you think about him?"

"You're right on the money."

"Oh. That's all? You're not going to tell me why you're asking?"

There was a long pause and then he said, "Check out the paper this morning."

"Maybe he didn't mean the local paper?" I asked Abby as I flipped through the business pages again.

For the second time, Abby slowly turned the pages of the Front Page section of the newspaper. Our waitress exchanged our empty bowl for one full of hot, thin tortilla chips. I grabbed a chip and turned to the sports page. I didn't really think news about Victor Roth would be on the sports page, but we hadn't had any luck so far in figuring out Thistlewait's odd comment.

Abby flipped another page. "Nothing. I don't see anything about Victor."

"Me either."

We scanned the paper, including the Lifestyle section with a large picture of Bree and Aaron next to a feature entitled COUPLE KEEPS ART IN THE FAMILY. I pointed it out. "They're a collaboration, a team, now." Bree had on her beret and a tie-dyed T-shirt for the picture. Aaron wore a sweatshirt with an Atlanta Braves logo.

Abby glanced at the article, then asked, "No one's found Rex?"

"No." My spirits did a nosedive every time I thought about Rex. "I'm driving Animal Control crazy. They finally told me to stop calling. They said they'd call me if they found him."

"Oh! Wait. Maybe this is it." Abby pointed to a tiny one-paragraph item near the bottom of the page under the LOCAL NEWS banner.

" 'Local authorities investigate possible fraud,' " Abby read. " 'Two Vernon residents have complained the items they bought from a local art dealer, a painting and a pottery bowl, are fakes. The dealer, Victor Roth, could not be reached for comment. Vernon police spokesperson Ellen Mayfair said, 'Since it is an ongoing investigation we are not able to comment at this time.' " Abby folded the paper into a rectangle with the news item showing. "Fakes," she said.

"And the art students at the preview show said Victor was a shady character."

"Burrito Grande Platter?" interrupted our waitress, poised holding two thick white plates with potholders.

"That's mine," Abby said and shoved the paper aside.

"Enchilada and Taco Plate?"

I nodded and inhaled the spicy flavors as the waitress slid the plate in front of me and warned us both about burning ourselves on the plates.

I used my napkin to edge my plate to the right and ate a bite of the Spanish rice while the rest of the food cooled. Pablo's wasn't big on atmosphere. Steel gray tables topped with thin white paper napkins edging out of dispensers were the only decor. I swear the chairs weren't retro-modern, but were actually used in kitchens in the 1950s. What it lacked in atmosphere, Pablo's more than made up for in taste. The food was great.

"Before I forget," Abby said as she handed me a business card. "I made you an appointment for a haircut with Barb. Wednesday afternoon. Now, this is my treat. You need a break every once in a while. And you'll look great for the spouse coffee later that night."

"Oh. Thanks." I swallowed my protest. Why is it so much harder to receive than to give? "That's really nice of you."

Abby shrugged. "I want to."

A banner slashed across the television mounted over the bar, NEWS UPDATE. A map of Turkey filled the screen. I froze. The sounds from the restaurant seemed to recede as I strained to read the banner at the bottom of the screen.

"What?" Abby asked. "What is it?"

I pointed to the TV. I filtered the words through my fear. "Violence escalated today in the city of Adana, Turkey." Not good. "A car bomb exploded at a market . . ." Oh no. I leaned toward the TV and only caught the end of the reporter's next sentence. "Air Base, staging point for many United States forces supporting other missions in the Middle East and Europe." *Mitch.* "Three casualities were reported." Terrible. Casualities? Who? Americans? Civilians? Soldiers?

Abby gripped my hand. "Ellie. They said at a market. You know the guys aren't allowed off base. It's okay. It couldn't have been Mitch. Wait, there. They just said no Americans were among the dead."

My heart seemed to start beating again. I forced myself to tear my gaze away from the television. "You're right. Mitch said something about them bringing things to them because they couldn't leave." I leaned back against the booth. I felt like I'd suddenly run a fifty-yard dash. "You know, this is a crazy way to live. I go along with my day and sometimes I don't even think about Mitch, what he's doing. Where he is. Or where he might be. But then something like this happens and I feel like I've walked into a brick wall."

Abby shoved the basket of chips toward me. "Surreal, isn't it? I know exactly how you feel."

Okay, settle down, I told myself. Nothing had changed in the last few minutes. Mitch was fine and I'd just over-reacted to the news. I ate some more of the chips and took a tentative bite of the enchilada. The cheese burned my mouth. I slurped the rest of my Diet Coke, just as the waitress dumped two more soft drinks in tall red plastic glasses on the table and walked away with a margarita on her tray for another table. I noticed Abby watching the waitress deposit the drink at a table near us. Abby refocused on her meal. "This tastes so good." She was already halfway through her first burrito, one of three on her plate. "I've been dying for one of these burritos for days!"

I moved my straw to the new glass and said, "I'm surprised you didn't get a margarita to go with it. You could still order one. I'm driving."

"Yeah, well." Abby shrugged. "Doesn't sound good."

I felt my eyebrows draw together. Abby always had a margarita with her burritos. "What? That's your favorite."

Before we found Pablo's, last summer, we'd bemoaned the lack of a good Mexican food restaurant and Abby had said she needed to go back to Oklahoma to get a burrito and a margarita.

"Well, tonight it doesn't sound good," she insisted halfheartedly and pushed her refried beans around on her plate.

Suddenly, I put it together: a craving and no alcohol. I had a suspicion. "Abby, you're not pregnant, are you?"

She leaned eagerly over the table. "Maybe," she whispered, like it was top secret information.

"That's great!"

"No. Shh! I don't know for sure. I mean, I did the over-the-counter test and it said yes, but I have a blood test tomorrow. Then I'll know for sure. After last time I'm not telling anyone until after three months. Well, except you. But you guessed, so I didn't tell you."

"That's great!" I repeated and snagged another chip. Abby turned the conversation back to the investigation, but as I updated her on my talk with Mabel, I felt a tinge of what? Jealousy? No way. I wasn't ready to be pregnant again, was I? Even though we were trying to get pregnant, I hadn't expected anything to happen for us right away and it hadn't. And that was fine. Really. Or at least it had been. I really hadn't had time to think about it. I stuffed those thoughts down to examine later, and focused on what Abby was saying.

"So what if Victor was selling fakes and Penny found out? Would she be enough of a threat to kill her?" Abby asked.

"I don't know. Penny was very adamant about integrity in her work. I don't think she would have kept quiet about Victor selling fakes, especially if he was passing them off as antiquities. And I guess how much of a threat Penny would be would depend on how much money he was making off the fakes.

"Then there's Ballard." I'd told Abby about my visit to the Pathway group and her antiquities.

Abby said, "Maybe she was selling fakes to keep her group afloat."

"I don't know. Her business seemed to be booming, at least when I was there. She sold mostly beauty products," I said and finished off my crunchy taco.

"The problem is we don't know what links Penny to her murderer," Abby said.

I sighed and pushed my plate away. "Or if any of this is connected to Clarissa."

"So Mabel says Will is still out of town?" Abby dipped the last chip in the salsa and raised her eyebrows speculatively at me. "Maybe we should run by there. Take a look around."

"No. I'm not going to go in their house."

"Why not? You've got a key. It wouldn't be breaking and entering," Abby said and reached for the bill that the waitress had slipped on the table.

"No. It would just be entering and I think that would still be illegal."

* * *

"Hey. You missed my street," Abby said.

"Sorry. I was driving on automatic pilot, going home." I turned onto our street, and rounded the corner at our house. Abby lived only one block over from us, so it would only take a second to get there. "I'll go the long way," I joked and checked our house as we cruised past it. The floodlights Mitch had added illuminated the backyard, highlighting patches of snow.

"Stop!" Abby gripped my arm. I hit the brakes. The Cherokee fishtailed and I forced myself to pump the brakes as a black streak darted from the steps at the kitchen door toward the headlights. I felt the Cherokee hit a patch of slush, the brakes caught, and we stopped with one headlight in the snowbank and the rest of the Cherokee blocking the street. I hopped out and Rex wiggled, flinging snow as he leaped over the snowbank.

"Down!" I said. "Down!" Rex promptly sat down on my boots, a mass of wiggling fur and lolling pink tongue. I was so glad to see him, I let him lick me on the face a few times. "Okay, enough. Abby, would you take him inside while I get the Cherokee out of the street?"

A few minutes later I pulled off my gloves in the kitchen and ran my hands over every inch of Rex. "There's not a scratch on him." From the trail of blood in the snow when he disappeared, I'd thought we might need to take him to the vet.

Abby came back from locking the kitchen door that I'd left open in my hurry to get inside and checked Rex for wounds. "This was on the step beside the rail." She plunked a bottle of ketchup down on the table.

I sat down heavily on the nearest chair. "Do you think that means someone put ketchup on the snow so I'd think he was hurt?" Rex kept his brown gaze fixed on mine as he sat at my knees, tail swishing back and forth.

"I don't know, but the door was open," Abby said.

"What?" I stood up and went to the door that opened from our kitchen to the yard.

"I mean the door was closed, but it wasn't locked."

"I think I locked it. I always do. But maybe I forgot . . ." Rex had followed me to the door, his tail lazily swishing back and forth. "Rex, check the house." I hoped my tone was as commanding as Mitch's when he said the same sentence. Rex stilled, ears perked. "Check the house," I repeated and he was off, running the circuit through each room and closet that Mitch had taught him. Less than a minute later he bounded up the stairs from the basement garage, his tail beating the air, ready for a treat.

I gave him a dog bone and lavished praise, and then Abby and I completed our own tour of the house. Everything looked fine, but I felt drained, so I collapsed on the ottoman and Rex plopped down at my feet. Abby came back from the kitchen. "Door's locked now. I double-checked. And it doesn't look like it was forced open."

"Good. I'm pretty sure I locked it, but . . . Rex, what have you got?" I picked up a tiny oval black bead that Rex was pawing away from the edge of our oriental rug. I rolled it around in my hand. "This looks like the beading on Elaina's gloves."

"Who?"

I looked around the living room, but didn't see any more beads. I belatedly realized Abby had asked me a question. "What?"

"Who's Elaina?"

I leaned closer to the bookcase. "I met her at the pre-view party. These books—look, they're pushed too far back. I think Elaina got in here somehow—either she broke in or I accidentally left the door unlocked—and she looked through my bookcase.

Abby spoke slowly like she was humoring one of her

students. "Okay, why did she have your dog? And why would she leave Rex outside if she was in here?"

"I don't know."

The phone rang and I went to answer it. I expected Jeff's or possibly Mitch's voice, but didn't recognize this muffled one. "Nice dog. Great watchdog. He likes beer, in case you didn't know."

"What? You took my dog?" The tone was conversational and I thought maybe someone had called the wrong number, or that I'd picked up in the middle of someone else's phone conversation.

"Yeah. I had the pooch."

I pressed the phone harder to my ear. The words were indistinct. It sounded like they were filtering through a thick barrier. It eliminated voice nuances. I couldn't tell if it was a man or a woman, but I suspected a man. "But." There was a puff of breath, a sigh? I couldn't tell. "I'm getting tired of this little game. I want the book." The dial tone buzzed in my ear.

I punched in star-six-nine and received the same recording about the number being unavailable. I wanted to scream, "What book? What are you talking about?" Instead, I repeated the conversation to Abby as Rex gulped from the fresh bowl of water, sloshing water over the floorboards.

"I need a recorder," I said and repeated the man's words for Abby. I had an urge to throw the phone across the room, but I fought it down. Even though Livvy wasn't here I could hear my voice scolding her for throwing a fit. Having a kid does help me curb some of my baser instincts—sometimes. "I hate this. I'm angry and scared at the same time. And so confused. I wish this would all go away." I settled for slamming the phone into its holder and pacing across the kitchen.

"We'd better call the police. They can trace those calls and find out who's been in here."

"I guess they could, but I don't want a lot of contact with the police right now, okay? I'm avoiding them, you know?" I placed the bead in the basket where I put our mail.

I realized my hands were shaking and shoved them into my pockets. "That person snatched Rex right out of our backyard!"

His ears perked up at his name and he trotted over to my side, sloshing his wet muzzle across my leg. I pulled my hands out of my pockets and rubbed his back. A wave of fury washed over me, driving out my fear. "They're playing with me. Toying with me. Letting me know they have the power to get to me, to get Livvy. And what book are they talking about?"

"I don't know. Did Penny ever mention a book?"

Rex collapsed onto his back so I could rub his tummy. "Not that I can think of." My hands had stopped shaking, but now I felt wobbly. I thought of the long night that stretched out in front of me. "This is crazy. I'm not going to sit here and be scared. Actually, I can't do much about the scared part, but I can't sit here." I rubbed Rex's tummy a few times and then called him to his kennel. "You go have a nice rest. I've got a house to break into."

Chapter
Twenty-three

"Come on, let's go check out Penny's house. Mabel said Will is still out of town."

"I don't know," Abby said. "Maybe we should just call the police and let them handle it."

"Abby, you were all for this at Pablo's."

"I know. All right, but shouldn't we at least change clothes?"

"What?" Trust Abby to bring fashion into the equation. "We need to look like burglars from a sitcom? You're always the first person I call if I have a fashion emergency, but I think we're fine," I said, looking over her black turtleneck and jeans and my dark blue sweatshirt and jeans.

"Will Jeff be okay with Livvy for a few more minutes?" I asked suddenly, checking my watch. "Oh, we've only been gone forty-five minutes." In addition to having great food, Pablo's also had speedy service.

"They should be fine. They were going to decorate sugar cookies and then I gave him a *Blue's Clues* video."

"Well, we're fine, then." Livvy's favorite thing in the world was to dribble sprinkles on cookies. She'd be happy for hours, but I didn't want to see what Jeff and Abby's kitchen floor would look like when Livvy was finished. Her aim wasn't that good.

I grabbed two flashlights and headed for the door. "Don't forget your gloves."

"This is creepy," Abby said as I eased the front door shut and flicked the flashlight around Will and Penny's living room. The stark white walls seemed to magnify the light. I quickly pointed the beam down to the floor.

"No, it's not. It's just a quiet, dark house," I said and stepped through the living room, setting off mini-shrieks from the floorboards.

"It *is* creepy. Penny died here." Abby still stood by the door. "Where? Where did she die?"

"In the bathroom. Abby!" I said sharply. "Let's do this and get it over with."

"Right," she said reluctantly. "I'll check in here." Abby crossed the living room with the floorboards protesting at her every step.

I scanned the kitchen. A sticky bowl and glass sat in the sink. The unfinished crossword puzzle on grid paper still hung on the refrigerator. I returned to the hallway, then headed to the bedroom. The bedroom's one night-stand contained a phone book, a blank notepad, a few pens, paperback romances, and some crossword puzzle books. With my thick gloved hands I opened the crossword puzzle books clumsily and saw both the squared-off letters of Will's handwriting and Penny's rounded style. Nothing under the bed. Their small closet had Will's green flight suits on one side and Penny's stark wardrobe on the other side. In the dim light of the flashlight, her clothes looked especially drab, with their muddy colors and drooping lines hanging off wire hangers.

In the bath, I opened the cabinet and looked through thin towels, a tiny supply of makeup that consisted mostly of mascara, and dried-out tubes of lip gloss. Will's shaving cream and razor sat on the edge of the sink inside a brown rust stain. He probably hadn't cleaned anything since she died.

I entered the bedroom they used as a study and went to the desk. I sat down and tucked the light in the crevice of my neck between my ear and my shoulder, like I did with the phone. With only miniblinds on the windows, I didn't think it would be a good idea to turn on lights.

I flicked through the magazines and books, looked under the blotter, and opened each drawer. I was getting a serious crick in my neck.

"How's it going?" a voice whispered near my ear. I shrieked and dropped the light.

"Sorry," Abby apologized. "I haven't found anything."

I patted around and found the flashlight. "Nothing exciting here, yet."

"Let's get out of here."

"Okay, but check the closet first while I look through here." I moved over to the chair and examined the books on antiquities.

"I don't see anything," Abby said and shut the door. "Not that I know what I'm looking for anyway."

"I know." I picked up a thin volume with dust along the edge. It didn't have a title imprinted on it. I fanned through the pages and realized it was a journal with blank, lined pages. Penny had dated her entries, but they were spotty, only every few weeks. I had a spiral-bound journal like this that I used to jot down ideas for my organizing clients. A few entries of Penny's were mundane: grocery lists, notes to wash the car on Tuesday, Ladies' Day Discount. An occasional phone number. I flipped to the last page with a handwritten entry. *Monday,* I read and my heartbeat picked up. *Meeting, Mansion.* After a few blank lines, a sentence noted *Ellie's—this afternoon.* Then about halfway down the page, *You lie like a* ___ . I read the entry off to Abby.

"How did the police miss this?" she asked.

"I don't know. Maybe they didn't look inside everything? They thought it was a book, not a journal? Its spine looks like a book and it blends in with all the other books. I didn't notice it either the first time I looked around. Anyway, who cares? What does that fill-in-the-blank mean?"

"Dog?" Abby guessed as she edged to the door.

"Or rug. I wonder if it was part of their puzzle game. Did you see their notes on the fridge?" I asked.

I scanned the earlier entries. "Nothing else like it. And besides, how interesting is *dog* or *rug* as a word in a crossword puzzle? Would Penny even need a note to remember that?"

"No, but she wrote it on the day she died, after her meeting with Bedford and after she'd talked to me at the squad. It's all we've got. They don't have a dog. Let's check the rugs."

"Okay, but let's get it done and get out of here."

I slipped the journal into the pocket of my coat. It stuck out at an odd angle, but I ignored it and shoved the chair off the plastic grid and the oriental rug covering the hardwood floors. I moved the plastic; we each grabbed a side and pulled it back, like we were peeling away a label. Only a few dust motes floated in the shaft of light from the flashlight.

"I'll check the runner in the hall," Abby said as we lowered the rug back.

I shoved the chair back and headed to the living room. We struggled with each rug in the house. Will, like lots of military folks who deployed to the Middle East and Southwest Asia, had brought home several carpets.

"That's it," I said as we replaced the dining room table over the last intricately patterned brown, cream, and gold rug. "What else could she mean?"

"The bath mat?" Abby asked, questioning. "That's kind of a rug."

We headed into the tiny room and flicked back the plain mat in front of the tub. "Nothing. Maybe it had nothing to do with rugs, but it was about a liar," Abby said, rubbing her dusty glove over her forehead and leaving a dark streak.

"Well, I know she wasn't talking about me. Maybe Bedford?"

A metallic groan sounded through the house and then a small series of clicks.

I sucked in a deep breath and my heart pounded into high gear. "Someone's unlocking the door." I hurried to the bathroom door, then nearly tripped on Abby as I backpedaled.

"He's back," I hissed. I could see through the dining room into the kitchen where Will had parked his rolling suitcase and was flicking through the mail in the harsh light of the overhead kitchen lights.

"Let's run for the door," Abby whispered and nodded in the direction of the front door.

"No, he'll see us. The window." I pushed her back into the bathroom and pointed to the small window with beveled glass. It was already open an eighth of an inch, probably for air circulation since this house was older, and like our house, didn't have an exhaust fan in the bathroom.

"God. I hope my hips fit through there," Abby said and pushed the window open wider.

Me too. I heard the refrigerator door sigh open and then closed. "Is there a screen?" I whispered.

"No."

Next came the faint tinny sound of a can popping open. Trust Will to need a beer the minute he walked in the door. I cupped my hands and Abby stepped up. The sole of her boot bit into my palms. She shimmied through the window and her boots disappeared with a whoosh. As I braced one foot on the rim of the tub and grabbed the windowsill, I heard a muffled thud and a few choice words from outside.

The kitchen light went off and the dining room light blazed. *Please let him go to the bedroom first to put his suitcase in there.* For a second, I contemplated staying where I was and trying to explain that I was just dropping off mail or investigating odd lights inside the house.

The hall light flicked on. Leaning sideways, I jumped and twisted. I hoped my body remembered a few of those gymnastics moves from the class I took in third grade. The cold, sharp air struck my face and I balanced with my stomach on the windowsill for a minute, looking for a handhold. Abby brushed snow off her coat. "There's nothing to hold on to. Just fall, the snow will break your fall," she whispered. A thick line pressed into my hip. I squirmed. Something blocked me from getting out the window. I looked back and saw the journal edging out of my pocket braced on the inside of the glass. That was what was shoved into my hip.

I groaned, twisted, and managed to work one arm back inside the window frame. I wrestled the journal free and dragged my arm back out the window. "Catch." I tossed the journal to Abby. As I heaved it, I lost my balance and half slid, half tumbled down the white siding of the house. I untangled my feet from an evergreen bush. "This is the hardest snow I've ever felt," I said as I flexed my arms and legs to check for broken bones. "Hey, you're stepping on me," I said to Abby.

"Sorry. I'm trying"—she pushed—"to close the window."

I stood up cautiously. An icy trickle of melting snow raced down my spine and I shivered. The evergreen bush under the window looked like Big Foot had stomped on it. Thank goodness it wasn't prickly, like the ones around my house. "Got the journal?"

Abby nodded. The light came on inside the bath and silhouetted her hands. She jerked them away from the window. It was still open an inch, but we backed away and tried to walk casually. Just two girls out for a little exercise on a dark, freezing night through the ice-and-snow-covered neighborhood.

An Everything In Its Place Tip for Organized Closets

Prevent coat closet chaos with well-defined areas in the closet.

- Choose an organizer like hanging shelves or a set of plastic drawers. Label one compartment for each family member. Everyone will have their own area for storing gloves, hats, scarves, and keys.
- Hooks or bins are a great storage place for backpacks, sporting equipment, and umbrellas.
- Store out-of-season items on upper shelves and switch out when the season changes.

Chapter
Twenty-four

The next afternoon, Tuesday, I pulled the Cherokee into the squadron parking lot. "Okay, we're here," I said to Livvy.

"Talk. Daddy," she informed me with all the solemness of a news correspondent reporting a downturn in the economic indicators.

"Yes." I opened the back door and leaned in to unbuckle Livvy. "We're going to talk to Daddy."

After I picked up Livvy from Abby and Jeff's house last night, I'd returned home damp and still slightly giddy from our frantic escape through the bathroom window. I'd checked our e-mail and found a note from Mitch. The operations center where he was had video phones, and there was also one set up in the squadron. Mitch said he'd signed up to use the video phone during what would be the next afternoon in my time zone.

So, Livvy and I were actually going to see him. We hurried through the veil of snow. I picked up Livvy and trudged up the steep incline ramp to the squadron. Before

I reached the top, the inside set of doors clanged open and I had a sense of déjà vu, expecting to see Penny propping open the door for me like she had the day she died.

But it wasn't Penny. It was Georgia Lamar. She paused for a moment, as if she was considering brushing past me without saying anything, but then she stepped back and held the door open.

"Thanks," I said as I stepped through.

"Sure." She reached down, pulled her hat out of the leg pocket on her flight suit.

"How are you doing?"

"Fine." Her voice was curt.

I searched for a subject to prolong our conversation, if you could call it that. "How's the campaign to remove the posters going? Need a signature?"

Her lips twisted. "Right. Like a petition would help. I'm going to take care of it." She jammed her hat down on her blond curls.

A few more people meandered down the hall toward us. I realized it must be getting close to four-thirty, official quitting time for the military folks, who go to work around seven-thirty in the morning. Georgia glanced down the hall at the approaching people and bit off her next sentence. "See you."

I walked down the hall, then down the stairs to the basement break room and the little alcove across the hall. It had actually been a storage closet, but it had been converted to a minioffice so spouses could have some privacy while they chatted with their husband or wife halfway around the world. A sign taped to the wall declared WET PAINT and pointed to the door frame. Irene sat in front of the computer, talking to her husband. I saw Tommy, Mitch's boss, in the bar in the Hole. I avoided the shiny coat of paint on the door frame and dropped the diaper bag on the table beside the computer, my declaration that I was next in line. I signed the video conference log-in sheet, set Livvy on her feet, and steered her in the direction of Tommy and the bar.

"Hey, Tommy." I hopped up on a bar stool and pulled Livvy up in my lap. "Heard anything about Mitch?"

"Hi, Ellie. Nothing. That's good, though."

I watched five more people enter the break room. Some sprawled on the worn couch in front of the wide-screen TV after picking up a beer out of the fridge. Even though Irene was across the hall her voice carried into the Hole. "Then Evan made the basketball team? And now he wants to quit guitar. I told him that's not an option, right? He knew that when he tried out . . ."

I sighed and scratched my plans for bringing Mitch up to date on the murder investigation.

Tommy pulled two beers out of the fridge and held one up. "Beer?"

"No, thanks. Have you got a Diet Coke in there?"

While Tommy replaced the beer and shoved some cans around I noticed beer posters still adorned the walls. "Last one," he said and plopped a Diet Coke down in front of me.

"You guys really should expand your drink selection," I said.

"Yeah. What do you think we should get? Some wine spritzers for George?"

I knew Tommy was referring to Georgia Lamar. "You're awful. I know you take the other side of arguments just to annoy her. So how's it going with her?" Livvy grabbed at my can and I jerked it away, sloshing bubbly dark puddles onto the bar. I grabbed a roll of paper towels sitting at the end of the bar and wiped up the spill. A large silver bell sat next to the towels.

"What's that doing down on the bar?"

Tommy pushed the bell across the bar toward me. "Had it engraved with Briman's name."

With my finger, I traced the two rows with the engraved names of the squadron commanders.

"We haven't gotten around to putting it back up yet," he said and I looked over at the post at the end of the bar where the bell usually hung.

Livvy mimicked me and ran her hands over the bell. "No," I said to her, but Tommy shrugged.

"It's fine," he said. "She can't hurt it. Just don't let her ring it." He smiled and roughed up Livvy's flyaway hair.

I laughed and pushed the bell farther back on the counter. If the bell rang, it meant free drinks and everyone in the squadron showed up in the bar. Whoever rang the bell had to pick up the tab.

Tommy took a swig of his beer and said, "I don't know what's up with Georgia. She's been muttering about getting her way. With anyone else I'd think it was all talk, but with Georgia—well, she's stubborn." He crushed his can and tossed it in the trash. "I'm outta here. See you."

Will sauntered in and took Tommy's place behind the bar. He popped open a beer from the fridge.

"Hey, Will." I felt a little funny talking to him, remembering the mad dash out his bathroom window. I still had Penny's journal. I'd looked at each page after Abby and I got back to my house, but I hadn't found anything new.

"Hey." His listless response reassured me that he didn't suspect we'd been in his house.

"Do you have a few minutes to talk?"

"Sure." He dropped on to the bar stool.

"Do you remember when I came by your house after Penny died?" I wasn't sure if the alcohol had erased his memory or not.

"Sure."

"Well, you said something about Clarissa. Something about how she couldn't be cultured if she tried."

Will chugged his beer, then said, "I said that, huh?"

I nodded. "What did you mean?"

"Clarissa was kinda—" He glanced at Livvy and amended whatever he was going to say. "Easy," he concluded.

A surge of anger made my next words sharp. "You know from personal experience?" If he'd cheated on Penny—

"No." His flat, almost bored denial cut off my thoughts. "I saw her and Rory on his boat last summer at Lake Coeur d'Alene."

I waited.

"They were on his boat." Will took another drink and glanced at Livvy again. "Fooling around."

"Did you tell the OSI?"

Will shrugged, set down the beer on the bar, and began popping his knuckles. "She's dead. I didn't want to get involved. Someone killed her, you know."

"Ellie, I'm done," Irene called.

I said good-bye to Will and crossed the room. I gave Livvy a baggie of Cheerios and logged on to the messenger service we'd set up. The Cheerios would ruin her dinner, but I'd work around that for a little peace.

After a few false starts, a window opened and Mitch was smiling at us across the miles.

He looked good.

"Hey!" he said. "There's my girls! You look great. How are you, Livvy? Hi, honey. It's so good to see you."

Livvy dropped her bag and pointed to the screen. "Daddy! Daddy on TV!"

"Thanks," I said. Then I heard the catcalls behind me.

"Oh, come on, Mitch, go ahead, call her 'sweetums.' "

"Hey," Mitch said, "is that Rory I hear?"

I glanced over my shoulder and realized he'd come into

the hall, probably just returning from his TDY because he parked his rolling suitcase beside his pub bags while he joked with the guys around the TV about Mitch and me. "Yes. We have an audience," I said.

"Just ignore them. How's everything going? Anything broken yet? The Cherokee still running?"

"Don't jinx us! Nothing's broken yet."

Even though our house was in the fifty-plus age category, we'd rarely had problems with it when Mitch was home, except for a few leaky pipes. But it seemed each time he left for a deployment some major catastrophe occurred on the home front. Last time it was the washing machine. The deployment before that one, a windstorm toppled one of the pines in our yard. It had narrowly missed Mabel and Ed's roof. Another time, the alternator on the Cherokee went out.

Livvy's hands left blurry fingerprints on the monitor, so I pulled her back into my lap, but she didn't want that. She poked at the keyboard.

"Hey, Avery," Rory shouted, "how's the weather? How many times a week are you flying?"

Mitch answered their questions, while my temperature rose. How rude could you get? This was our first chance to see Mitch in a week. Couldn't Rory and the guys back off? Finally, I said to Rory, "Hey, this is supposed to be my time with Mitch. Sign up for your own fifteen minutes later." I smiled, but my tone was sharp.

"Excuse me." Rory's voice dripped sarcasm. "Ma'am." He grabbed his bags and left. I watched him leave, realizing I'd probably blown my chance to ask him if he argued with Clarissa before her art class or about Will's sighting of them boating on the lake.

Mitch and Livvy had a halting conversation about Cheerios. Then she sang the ABC song for Mitch, at least as far as the letter *k*.

I felt a hovering presence behind me and saw Sidney, another spouse, waiting.

"Mitch, I've got to go. The next person is here."

"We need to get one of these at home on our computer and we can talk all the time."

"Right," I said. But when would I have time to hook it up? Assuming I could get it hooked up? Instead of that, I said, "Maybe you'll be home before I can get one."

"I don't know. Anything else?"

"Well, there are some things going on, but I can't go into it right now. Too many people."

"I'll try to call you. It's been hard to get a phone line."

We said our good-byes and then I packed up the toys Livvy had pulled out of the diaper bag. I scooted over to make room for Sidney as I swept scattered Cheerios into a pile and then tossed them in the trash with my empty Diet Coke can. I dragged Livvy away from the monitor screen and hoisted her onto my hip.

On the way to the parking lot, I ran into Irene again. She gripped my arm, nearly toppling me over. "Have you heard about Ballard?" As usual, her sentence was a question, but it didn't have her normal tentative upswing in the tone at the end. She had news, gossip, and she wanted to share.

"No." I regained my balance and shifted to one side of the hallway as I sensed someone gaining on us from behind. Rory passed us, gripping a rolled carpet swathed in plastic that was draped over his shoulder. His round glasses reflected the light coming in the glass doors, but he twisted his head slightly and his gaze slid sideways to meet mine.

His face remained impassive. No greeting, no response to my stare. He pushed the door open with his shoulder and disappeared down the ramp. I realized I was holding my breath and let it out as I focused on what Irene was saying. She released my arm and pulled on her gloves. "Of course, I don't believe a word of it. The idea that Ballard only wants money? For a cult? She's committed to helping people find wholeness and peace in their lives. And individual peace will lead to world peace."

"So what's happened?" I asked at the door. I set Livvy down and began the process of zipping up her coat and coaxing her fingers into her mittens.

"Protesters! Ballard opened a little shop downtown, you know, in the skywalk? I went by there this morning and there were people there holding up posters saying Pathway is running a cult and that Ballard only wanted money. She never asks for money!"

She didn't have to. The night I was there, the cash register didn't stop ringing after the meeting.

"News reporters were there! I can't believe it. Ballard only wants to help. Who could be against world peace?"

I pulled up Livvy's hood and snapped it under her chin. The lights in the parking lot surged on, highlighting Rory as he dropped the carpet beside several boxes and his suitcase. Another flyer, it looked like Zeke, strode through the snow with his suitcase bumping along behind him. He must have been on the same crew with Rory.

"I don't know," I said and hooked the diaper bag over my shoulder. I leaned on the bar to push the door open, but Irene caught my arm again.

"Ballard is wonderful. She'd never hurt anyone. She only wants to help, you know?"

Irene released her grip and I opened the door. She trotted along beside me. Rory opened the tailgate of his pickup and shouted something to Zeke. He stopped and helped Rory maneuver the carpet into the pickup bed.

"Irene, you don't have to convince me."

"Oh! You're right." She turned toward me suddenly. "You already know Ballard. It's all those people who'll see the story on the news I'm worried about. After they hear the protesters, you know, they won't even give Ballard a chance? And her products were doing so well, she was talking about expanding. You think I should call the news stations?"

"Couldn't hurt. Give them your side of the story."

"Okay. Great idea, isn't it?" She scurried off to her SUV.

I got Livvy in the Cherokee and turned onto the sanded roads of the interstate. As the Cherokee swooped around the curve in the freeway a plastic grocery bag slid out from under the front seat on the passenger side and skimmed across the floor. I leaned over and shoved it back under the seat. I wasn't sure what to do with the journal I'd found at Penny's. I should probably hand it over to Thistlewait, but I dreaded the questions he'd have when I showed up with it. If I could get back in their house, I could leave it there and then call in a tip, but there was no way I was going to repeat my unauthorized entry stunt.

Maybe I could mail it to the police anonymously? I swept down the freeway exit ramp and pulled into the parking lot of the Stop 'n Shop, a convenience store. Great. All the parking places in front of the store were taken. That meant I'd have to walk through the slush and ice while carrying Livvy and then haul her and the gallon of milk back to the car. I stopped and surveyed the parking lot before I got out. I didn't like being on the end of the row in the shadow of the building next to a boarded-up grocery store where the Dumpster made a conveniently dark corner for someone to lurk in. I gripped the diaper bag and glanced around as I prepared to step out of the car. I stopped and squinted.

A pickup rolled into one of the deserted parking slots on the other side of the Dumpster. Rory stepped out of the pickup.

Chapter
Twenty-five

If I hadn't seen him just a few minutes before I probably wouldn't have noticed him, but it was definitely Rory. The Dumpster blocked my view of him for a moment, but then I could see him again as he rounded the end of the pickup and let down the tailgate. His round glasses caught and reflected the glow from the dim streetlight. I gripped the door handle and stayed in the Cherokee. A second pickup pulled in beside Rory and the driver stepped out. I sank down lower in my seat, even though the second driver only took a cursory look around. A clump of hair stuck out from under his baseball cap.

Rory and the other man heaved boxes and the rolled carpet from Rory's truck into the bed of the second man's pickup. Then the men jumped in their trucks and swept in large circles before roaring out of the parking lot.

I put the Cherokee in reverse, but a compact car pulled in behind me, blocking my exit. The woman at the wheel motioned for the driver a few slots down from me to back out. That driver had to check both directions, twice, before he took his foot off the brake, and then he moved at approximately two miles an hour. By the time the way was clear, both pickups were long gone.

I slammed out of the Cherokee, frustrated. Why hadn't I gotten the license number from the pickup that the baseball-capped man was driving?

I replayed the strange interaction between Rory and the baseball-capped man. Could Rory have been bringing a rug back for a friend? But why park behind the Dumpster? There were plenty of open slots in the empty grocery store lot just a few feet away. The interaction with the rug seemed too furtive and rushed. It was secretive and quick.

I remembered Rory checking his Rolex in line at the BX. He did drive a nice new truck and Will said he owned a boat. Quite a few expensive items for a staff sergeant. Ballard said he was always going to Turkey. What better way to make a few bucks than to bring something back and smuggle it through customs when they landed? A large rug would conceal a lot of—what? Drugs? There had been an investigative report on a news magazine show a while back about Turkey. It was a distribution point for drugs from Asia.

I decided running low on milk was the least of my worries right then, so I drove home, trying to talk myself out of calling Thistlewait. I didn't want to speak to him, but if Rory was smuggling something I *had* to call Thistlewait, and the information Will had mentioned about Rory and Clarissa was too important to keep to myself. After I got home, I parked in our driveway and used my cell phone to leave a voice mail for Thistlewait, describing Will's information and what I'd seen at the Stop 'n Shop. I closed the phone, then stepped carefully down our sloping driveway to open the doors to our basement garage. Automatic garage door openers were a luxury that were swiftly moving up on my list of things to buy for the house. I heaved and the garage door rose with a groan. I glanced inside and then did a double take. I walked inside the garage and turned on the light. The double-car garage took up half the basement, like a sunken add-on to our house. The other half of the basement, the portion directly below the house, was a traditional basement with storage shelves, a huge furnace oil tank, and washer and dryer hookups.

Tonight the light from the naked bulb on the house side of the basement reflected up from a shallow pool of water in front of the washing machine. I hadn't been doing laundry when we left, so I doubted the machine, only a year old, had suddenly sprung a leak. I crossed the basement and peered into the water. From the edge, I could make out a drain in the middle. The one I always tripped on when I carried baskets of dry clothes back to the stairs. Did we know any plumbers? No, but the Yellow Pages had plumbers. I'd just call one. And pay their per-hour rate. Yuck. I wished Mitch was home. I tromped back to the Cherokee and pulled into the garage.

The doorbell rang and I frowned. I'd found a plumber and he'd already arrived, so I didn't know who could be at my door. I tossed the last of the silverware into the draining board and wiped my hands on the back of my jeans. Hopefully, it wasn't the Jehovah's Witnesses or kids from the elementary school selling chocolate bars for a fundraiser. I couldn't resist the latter and I'd had too many visits from the former. But when I opened the door it wasn't the neighborhood kids or men in white shirts and ties. It was the skinny woman from the Cedars.

"Here." She thrust a black VHS videotape at me. I opened the screen and took it.

"I thought about what you said. I don't want the person who killed Clarissa to get away with it, but there ain't no

way I'm going to the police," she said over her shoulder
as she trotted down the steps.

"Wait. Please! You're Karen?"

She paused on the last step. "Yeah. Never been an
apartment manager in my life." She smiled quickly. "But
don't look for me at the Cedars. I won't be there. I won't
be anywhere in this town." She turned away.

"Wait. Please don't go. You knew Clarissa. Please tell
me why you think someone killed her."

She must have heard the desperation in my voice.
Karen glanced at a black Accord idling in the street, then
leaned toward me and said in a low voice, "She was mixed
up with a bunch of friggin' thieves."

"Was Rory a part of it?"

The car horn tooted and Karen stepped down into the
snow. "All I know is that one of the big shots accused
Rory of stealing from them, but he said he didn't do that."
The fleeting smile crossed her face again as she said,
"Like you can believe a thief. I don't know if he was
telling the truth or not, but Rory called in some thug to
scare the English dude." Karen shook her head and said,
"I can't believe Clarissa was stupid enough to get tight with
them. She was so smart about everything else. Watch the
tape."

This time she didn't stop. Her spike-heeled boots left
deep pockmarks in the snow as she hurried to the car. She
slipped into the passenger side, slammed the door, and
the car pulled away. Only the pale exhaust fumes lingered
in the street.

The phone rang and I hurried to lock the dead bolt and
pick up the phone.

Abby said, "Hey, Ellie. I wanted to warn you that Jeff
came down with the flu. I hope Livvy doesn't get it."

"We should be fine. Livvy's already had it."

"Oh, I'd forgotten."

"That's okay." I turned the tape over in my hands. On a yellow sticky note, *32:47* was written in black ink. "I've got to go," I said to Abby.

I pulled off the note, pushed the tape in the VCR, and hit PLAY. A dark blob resolved itself into a small room crammed with people. The date imprinted on the corner noted the video was taken February 7. A loud voice cut across the mumble of the crowd as the camera zoomed in on Clarissa. "There's the birthday girl!" said someone holding the camera. The female voice came across the tape louder than anyone else.

"Karen!" Clarissa's sparkly sleeveless top glittered as she turned her back on the camera.

"No way." The picture bobbed as Karen hurried around to keep Clarissa's face in the monitor. "Come on, Risa. It's your thirtieth birthday. We gotta get it on film!"

"It is not! I'm twenty-eight," Clarissa snapped back, then stuck her tongue out at the camera. A thick arm draped over her shoulder and she turned to smile at Rory.

"Hey," a voice shouted from my basement. "I found your clog."

I hit the PAUSE button and went to the top of the basement stairs where I secured the baby gate across the top step and said to Livvy, "Back in a minute." She crouched in front of the refrigerator, sliding the ABC letters back and forth.

"Here's your clog. Tree root," said the lanky man in a dirty coverall from Righto-Roto. He held up a chunk of root about the thickness of my wrist. Water dripped off the fine, fringelike roots emerging from the larger root.

"Oh. Thanks." I squinted at his stitched name tag and added, "Jerry." It was darker in the basement than I expected and I glanced around. I'd expected one of the garage doors to be open so he could run his tube from the truck inside, but they were closed. Instead he'd run the large tube through a hole in our wall, one that I didn't remember.

"Sure. No problem. That'll take care of it." He held the root out. "Want to keep it?"

"Ah. No."

Jerry shrugged and tossed it over by his toolbox. "I'll throw it away when I leave. You never know. Some people want to keep them. Show them to their friends, I guess. I'll write you an invoice in a minute." He picked up the tube as he spoke.

"Okay. I'll get my checkbook."

I gripped the handrail to head up the stairs as he said, "Found that in the coal chute."

I picked up a dirt-smudged zip-top plastic bag. Jerry explained, "It was folded up and stuck inside the frame."

I stepped back across the basement and examined the opening he'd indicated. The dull white glow of the snow filled the opening and let in a chilly gust of wind. "I'd never noticed we had a coal chute."

"Lots of the old houses in this neighborhood have them. Most of them are sealed up, but yours wasn't." He flipped his toolbox shut, then picked it up along with the tree root. "It keeps it a lot warmer in here, if I can keep that garage door shut while I'm working."

I hardly noticed him open the garage door. I examined the dirty bag. Inside was a tiny, dark blue square. I opened the bag and pulled out the square. It looked like a miniature computer disk. It looked familiar, but I wasn't sure what it was. My heart started pounding. Had Penny left it? Out of the corner of my eye, I caught a shadowy movement on the floor. With a whoosh, the tube slithered across the floor and disappeared up the wall and out the coal chute. I took a deep breath to calm my heartbeat.

I ran up the stairs and placed the disk at the back of the kitchen counter. Jerry returned with my bill and a salesman's spiel about how I should buy the company's Roto-Crystals to dissolve tree roots in my pipes. I brushed off his sales pitch, scribbled a check, and pushed him out the door because I'd remembered where I'd seen one of the minidisks before.

I pulled out Mitch's new handheld computer and turned it over. With a little maneuvering, I slid out the disk and compared the two. Exactly the same. I took a deep breath and plugged Penny's disk into the computer. As I went back into the kitchen to check on Livvy, I explored the documents. I heard Livvy laugh before I rounded the corner into the kitchen and saw her swatting the ABC letters into a pile on the floor.

I looked back at the screen and stopped. Black letters in another language, one I didn't recognize, filled the small screen. I scrolled up and down the document, looking for some text in English that I could read, but there wasn't anything. The document was called *Doc1*.

Livvy's voice penetrated my concentration. I realized she'd been patting my leg and saying, "Mom? Mom?" for the last few moments. As usual, she was waiting until she had my complete attention before she spoke. If I did that with her, I'd probably have better luck getting her to follow my directions.

"Yes, sweetie?"

"Snack. Snack."

"What else do you say?" I asked automatically as I set the computer down.

Her eyebrows scrunched in concentration, and then her face cleared. "Peeze."

"Very good. Yes, you may."

I filled a sippy cup with a little apple juice, topped it off with water, and sprinkled some cheesy Goldfish crackers on a plastic plate shaped like a dinosaur. I set it down on her small table. She slid into the miniature seat, shoved her crayons out of the way, and pulled the plate toward her. "Keep it on the table. I'll be in the living room," I said.

Carrying the computer, I sat down cross-legged in front of the bookcase wedged in the corner beside our overstuffed chair. I skimmed along the titles until I found my dictionary, a remnant from my college days. I flipped it open to the first page of the *A* entries. Yes, there it was. Under the large letter *A* in the center, examples of handwritten letters marched across the page. Many of the letters looked similar to English, but there were dozens of characters I didn't recognize. I glanced back and forth between the computer and flipped back and forth in the dictionary for a few moments, until I found several matches. Greek. It was in Greek.

I slowly set the dictionary back on the shelf. And gave a little half laugh. It really was all Greek to me and I didn't know how to figure out what the letters meant. This must be what it feels like to be illiterate, a mixture of frustration and expectation tinged with mystery.

I shifted around on the carpet, and the flicker of the TV screen caught my eye. I'd left the video on PAUSE, but I'd been gone so long that it had switched back to TV mode. I hit PLAY. The picture went in and out of focus as people passed in front of the camera or moved away. For a long time there was a stretch of speckled Formica in the foreground and no camera movement. Karen must have set the camera down with the record mode on and forgotten it.

Snatches of conversation sounded from the recording as people moved around the room.

"Clarissa, when does the general get back from D.C.?"

"Two more days," Clarissa replied. "And when he does he's taking me to the Aurora Mansion. He doesn't know it yet, but it's the least he can do since he won't come home . . ." Her voice faded as she and her friend moved away from the camera. I checked the status and then fast-forwarded to 0:32:00, a few seconds before the time on the note. I couldn't see General Bedford going to this party with Clarissa. In fact, I couldn't imagine them socializing together. I bet they had two sets of friends.

The picture focused on Clarissa's sparkly silver top as she leaned on the counter. "You know, all this birthday stuff reminds me of another birthday present. We've got to talk," she said to the man beside her.

"What about?" His arm looped around her hips and the diamonds on his Rolex watch face flashed as his hand traced lazy circles on Clarissa's hip. Rory had a watch like that.

"About your little sideline. I want in."

His hand froze and he said, "What?"

"You heard me. I want a cut."

"No." He pulled away.

Clarissa leaned toward him. "You can't expect me to deliver your stuff for nothing. You didn't really think I believed your story about your aunt in Salt Lake and how you forgot her birthday? You didn't think I'd check out a 'present' I'd be carrying through the airport? I want something in return."

"All right, everyone!" another voice called. "Time for the cake. In here. Rissa, where did you go? Who's got the camera?"

Clarissa and Rory moved out of the camera's range; then the picture tilted back and forth. Finally, it settled on Clarissa's smiling face, lit with candles from her cake. As the camera panned the guests singing "*Happy Birthday,*" I caught a glimpse of Rory, brows low and with a sullen expression on his face. He wasn't singing.

I hit PAUSE and wrapped my arms around my knees. I felt chilled. I thought about the day at the BX when Rory had cut in line in front of me and barely been civil. Was he a killer? I didn't know. Rude, yes. Abrasive? Yes. Could he have crossed the line between decency and barbarism to strangle Clarissa? I shivered.

Livvy appeared before me with a faint orange ring around her mouth, still crunching on a few crackers. In one hand, she held a squished tube of Berry Burst toothpaste and in the other hand, she held her toothbrush, loaded with enough toothpaste for a week, tilted toward the rug.

In one motion, I levered myself off the floor, grabbed the toothpaste and toothbrush, and guided her back to the bathroom. As I helped her brush her teeth, I tried to figure out what to do. I could take my find to Thistlewait. That was probably the best thing, but I wanted to know what it was. I'd bet that it would take a while for Thistlewait to round up an expert in Greek to read it for them. And what if it didn't have anything to do with Penny's death?

"Okay, rinse." I handed Livvy a little cup of water.

She sloshed it around in her mouth and swallowed.

"No, you spit it back out," I said. She looked at me like I was crazy.

"Okay, never mind. We'll work on it later." I considered calling Harris University and asking if I could get someone to translate a document for me, but I didn't want to show it to just anyone. I moved back into the kitchen, rinsed the juice cup, and swept the cracker crumbs off the table into my hand. As I trashed the crumbs, I said, "Marsali!" I gathered up the dictionary and Mitch's hand-held computer. I grabbed the tape out of the VCR and stuck it in my purse. I had plenty of time for an afternoon visit before my haircut appointment and the Spouse Coffee later that night.

"Mar-sal-ee?" Livvy repeated after me.

"Yes! Professor Marsali. We'll go visit him. Let's get your shoes on."

An Everything In Its Place Tip for Organized Closets

If your home has a coat closet near the front door, but everyone enters through the garage, consider creating a "coat closet" near the garage, especially if your garage entry is near a laundry room.

- Hooks for each family member—with a storage container below each hook—allow everyone to neatly drop off coats and backpacks as they arrive.

- If you've got the space, a hall tree (a bench with a tall back panel and hooks across the top of the back panel) combines seating (for pulling boots on and off), storage, and hang options into one unit.

- If you transition the coats most often worn to an area by the garage, your coat closet can take on new functions. You'll probably want to keep coats that are worn less often (dress coats) in the coat closet, but much of the space could be transformed into storage for table games, household records, or even movie or music storage.

Chapter Twenty-six

"You use this little wand," I said to Marsali.

"Yes. I'm familiar with it. My daughter gave me one for Christmas." Marsali pushed his large glasses back up the bridge of his nose and peered intently at the tiny screen.

"Oh, sorry."

"Do you have a printed copy of this?"

"No, I'm not sure how to transfer the file or print it." I leaned over to move Livvy's glass of milk—a real glass without a lid—away from her elbow. She didn't notice because she was concentrating on eating every scrap of donut on her plate.

Like a doctor during an initial exam, Marsali's face remained expressionless as he moved the image around on the screen. "I can print a copy. I'll take it back to my office, if you don't mind."

Feeling extremely computer inept since Marsali, probably in his seventies, was more computer savvy than I, I said, "Sure."

"Make yourself at home." Marsali crossed the room

with a quick step, cradling the small computer in his hands.

I cleared the dishes and rinsed them in the sink. On the ledge of the window above the sink were three pots with small green stalks pushing through the dark soil. Must be from Marsali's container gardening class. I needed to ask him how he liked it.

I cleared away the bakery box from Cobblestone and cleaned Livvy's face and fingers. With that done, I looked around for something that Livvy could play with because I'd run out of the house so fast I'd forgotten to bring the diaper bag with her toys. I'd forgotten Pink Girl, but—thankfully—Livvy hadn't noticed. Yet. I found a bowl of plastic fruit on the coffee table. I wiped the thin layer of dust off the fruit and settled Livvy in the middle of the rug.

Stepping over a pile of crossword puzzle books, I went to the bookshelves. Looking at someone's books was as good a way to find out about them as looking through their trash. On Marsali's bookshelves were a mishmash of educational tomes, reference books, photographs, and a few randomly interspersed decorative items. As I moved down the wall of shelves, I realized there was a pattern: Books were shelved in an orderly way, like all the dictionaries grouped together, until a certain point and then books were wedged in next to a photograph or a ceramic decoration. I paused in front of a snapshot of Marsali wearing his huge glasses posed next to a woman in a print dress. It was Pearl, Marsali's wife, who had died two years ago.

He looked different than he did today and I couldn't figure out why. Marsali was dressed just the same as he was today, cardigan sweater with white shirt and polyester pants. He was even wearing the same watch with a stretchy gold-plated band. Then I realized it was his face, his smile, that was different. He looked lively and content with Pearl. That contentment was missing from him now and a veneer of sorrow seemed to cover his face.

I stepped back, looked over the shelves, and realized Marsali must have kept them just as they were when Pearl was alive. She'd arranged the breaks in the books, placing photographs and knickknacks on the shelves. And Marsali hadn't moved anything, just crammed his latest purchases in the open spaces until they edged up against Pearl's decorating touches.

Marsali rushed back into the room, carrying the printout and the small computer. "Ellie! Where did you get this?"

I blinked at the look on his face. He didn't look contented as he had in the snapshot with Pearl, but there was an exuberance, a suppressed excitement in his expression as he paced across the room, deposited his load on the kitchen table, and returned to pull a book off a high shelf.

"I think it belonged to Penny," I said to Marsali's back as he bent over the book on the table, flipping pages and muttering to himself.

He found what he wanted and slowed down. I crossed the room. He stared at the lazy Susan stacked with salt and pepper shakers and paper napkins without seeing it.

"The dates, the language, the spacing, the uncial letterforms." He spoke quietly to himself. "It could be possible."

"What?"

Marsali pulled out a chair and dropped into it. "Where is the original?"

"I don't know. What do you think it is?"

"We've got to find it." Marsali took a deep breath and ran his hand over the printed version of the text. "There is a possibility. It may be a copy of a letter addressed to one of the early Christian churches."

"What?"

But he was in lecture mode and didn't seem to hear my question. "There has to be more analysis, particularly of the original document, and tests to be made to date the ink and the material it is written on. Parchment is my guess, but we need the original. The language, the phrasing, needs further study, but it is an incredible document."

"Why? Because of its age?" I sat down next to him.

Marsali focused on me and realized I wasn't one of his advanced language students. "It is addressed to the saints in Laodicea." He pointed to the text, even though I couldn't read any of it. "Are you familiar with the structure of the first lines of Greek letters in New Testament times?"

I nodded. "Yes, I remember a pastor explaining the writer began with his own name, a salutation at the beginning of the letter, right?"

Marsali shoved the paper toward me. With a shaking index finger he traced a few letters at the beginning of the document. "That translates 'Paul.' "

"Paul?" I looked from the printout to the book open near him. It was a Bible. "Paul? As in *Paul*, the author of most of the New Testament letters?"

"Yes!"

I opened my mouth, but no sound came out.

"I know!" Marsali's smile stretched his wrinkles.

I recovered enough to say, "So, this document"—I pointed to the small computer on the table between us—"this letter could be very valuable?"

"It could be. On the other hand, it might be an imitation. A forgery. Much further study is needed, but upon my initial glance at it, it appears genuine. The phrasing, the structure, the letter spacing, the subject matter. They are all what I'd expect."

"What letter is it? What book is it?"

"It is a letter to the church at Laodicea."

I certainly wasn't a Bible scholar, but even I knew there wasn't a book in the Bible called Laodiceans.

Marsali pushed the Bible across the table and pointed to a verse at the end of Colossians. I scanned the verse. "Okay. It says after the Colossian Christians read their letter, they should read the letter he sent to Laodicea."

I looked up at Marsali, questioningly.

"A letter to the church at Laodicea has never been found."

Chapter
Twenty-seven

"So this could be very valuable." I tapped the small computer.

"Yes, assuming it is genuine. A find of this magnitude, well . . ." Marsali seemed to search for words and finished with a shrug. "It would be incredible, a lost book."

"A book! That's what he called it!" I'd been thinking of traditional books like the ones that lined the walls of Marsali's living room, not a book out of the Bible. "This is what they're looking for." A tremor of relief mixed with fear ran through me. "You haven't heard anything about this as an important new find?"

"No." Marsali's smile faded to concern. He spoke slowly. "And I have a friend, an archaeologist, who would want to discuss this, if he knew about it. So, I'd say this is being kept very quiet. If there was a hint that this was out there, Derrick would have called me."

At least part of the last few weeks began to make sense. The threatening phone calls, the attempted mugging, even stealing and returning Rex were all parts of a plan to intimidate and get me to "give them the book."

"Penny knew," I said. "This was why she died. She had the training to recognize it."

Marsali nodded reluctantly. "The question is, now . . ." His voice faded.

I finished the sentence. "Where's the original?"

We looked at each other for a few moments. I stood and paced around the room restlessly. I noticed Livvy had the plastic fruit spaced across the rug and was playing some sort of game with the apples, rolling them into the other fruits. Toddler bowling, I thought.

If I could trust what Karen said, Rory had been accused of stealing something from the thieves, and I bet that something was this manuscript. Rory denied it and hired a thug, Mr. Baseball Cap, to intimidate the English dude, who had to be Victor Roth. Obviously, Rory didn't have it, if he was hiring someone to intimidate Victor. And Victor *said* he didn't have it. He'd told Mr. Baseball Cap that Penny probably hid it at my house.

I refocused on Marsali as he pored over the paper. "I need to use your phone."

He grunted, which I interpreted as "okay."

I found the phone and after calling base information I was connected to Thistlewait's voicemail. "Umm, this is Ellie Avery." I paused, reluctant to go into detail on a phone message, but I needed him to call me, so I said, "I've found something that Penny left for me. I think you need to see it." I finished with a disjointed conversation as Marsali gave me his phone number and I repeated it into the phone.

I dropped into Marsali's recliner to think. I couldn't go off and leave the letter with Marsali. It was too valuable and I couldn't think of a good hiding place. Better to wait here for Thistlewait to come and pick it up. I glanced down at the table. A notepad beside the phone had *white-headed woodpecker* jotted at the top. A pair of binoculars rested beside the notepad and a copy of *Birds of North America*. I surveyed the room, checking on Livvy, and noticed the recliner was placed so that Marsali had a great view of his spacious backyard. Several empty bird feeders dotted the lower limbs of the majestic pines in his backyard.

"You've taken up bird-watching?" I guessed.

Marsali looked up at me blankly; then he seemed to process what I'd said. His smile lines deepened. "Yes. It is fascinating. I haven't seen many yet, but with spring on the way, I'm hoping that will change."

"Another class through the senior center?"

"No. A private tutor. Dorothy MacMill. She's spotted a hermit warbler, quite a feat, I gather, and has promised to give me a few tips."

"That's great." It was the first time I'd seen Marsali looking genuinely happy since I'd met him. The phone rang and he flapped his hand at me, meaning go ahead and answer it.

Thistlewait sounded, well, happy. It took me a moment to place his tone of voice. I'd never heard him sound pleased.

"How did those cookies turn out?" he asked. "I assume you've been busy turning out dozens of cookies and you're calling me to see if I want some, right?"

Did he have a sense of humor? Obviously, he hadn't listened to either of my messages yet. "Hardly. I have something I think you need to see. It belonged to Penny."

I briefly described Marsali's theory. Silence followed.

"I'm at Professor Marsali's house." More silence.

Finally, he said, "I'm on my way over. Address?"

I gave him directions and hung up, knowing he'd have more questions than either Marsali or I could answer.

* * *

"You got this how?" Thistlewait asked again, pointing to Marsali's television with the tableau of the birthday party frozen on the screen. His good humor had evaporated. I described Karen's pit stop at my house.

Detective Jensen asked, "Where's she now?" Thistlewait had called Jensen, and the Vernon arm of the law didn't waste time getting to Marsali's house. In his quilted vest, jeans, and Bass Pro Shop baseball cap, Jensen gave new meaning to business casual.

"I don't know," I said. We retraced that same path of questioning for awhile until both men exchanged glances.

Jensen said, "Unusual for an ordinary military spouse to keep turning up like this in murder investigations." He motioned for Thistlewait to join him at the side of the room. I caught a few snatches of Jensen's part of the low conversation, ". . . take her in . . . little pressure . . ."

Jensen wasn't going to read me my rights, was he? I felt like all the air had been sucked out of my lungs. It was like the time I fell off the metal bars in second grade. I'd landed on my back and lay there staring at the vibrant blue sky unable to breathe. In. Out. Breathe in. Breathe out.

I hadn't done anything wrong, just given them the tape and the info I'd found. I swallowed and glanced at Livvy. Marsali held her up so she could look out the window to his backyard. He pointed something out and Livvy leaned closer to the window. I tuned back into the low conversation and heard Thistlewait say, "You go ahead. I'll handle things here."

Jensen stalked over and stood a few inches from me. "I'm going to check you out good. Every move you've made since the Follette woman died. Every conversation you've had. Every bank transaction. Every phone call. Everything." He paused, like he expected me to suddenly break down and confess to Penny's murder. Words warred inside me but I couldn't untie my tongue.

After a second he strode out. Thistlewait retrieved the tape from the VCR and said, "Thanks for your help, Mrs. Avery. Don't leave town."

I took Livvy from Marsali. As I zipped Livvy into her winter coat, I could hear Jensen in the hall on his cell phone as he called in a renewed search of Penny's house. *Penny's journal.* I got out of there fast. Part of me wanted to go home and burrow under my quilt and ignore everything, but that instinct warred with the sheer panic I felt creeping through me. Jensen wanted to take me in. I *had* to figure this out before I ended up in the Vernon jail.

I clicked Livvy's car seat straps into place and hopped in the Cherokee. Thistlewait hurried out the door and over to my window. He pulled out a small notebook. I cranked the window down, my palm slippery on the knob. I had to get that notebook back to Penny's house. "Yes?"

He picked up on my impatient tone. "One more question."

"Okay, but I've really got to go."

"Why did Victor Roth call you?"

"What?" I'd been expecting another question about the manuscript I'd just given him. "He didn't call me. I called him when I returned Penny's phone messages for Will. He never bothered to call me back. I had to call him."

Thistlewait studied his notes for a moment, then said, "His phone records show he called your house four times in the last few weeks."

"I never talked to him." But those hang-ups. Could it have been Victor? But why would he call and then hang up?

I glanced at the clock. I could think about this later; minutes were trickling away. I didn't know how long it would take the crime scene people to get back to Penny's, but I didn't want to be there when they did. "He must have been trying to catch me at home to return my call." I cranked the window up a few inches. Thistlewait got the message. He replaced his notebook and went back inside Marsali's house. I started the Cherokee and drove to Penny's house, halfway down the block.

I didn't see Will's car. I pulled in the driveway. I'd rather have parked several blocks away in case Jensen's team showed up, but I couldn't go off and leave Livvy buckled in the car, and if I brought her it would take twice as long. I pulled on my gloves and fished the plastic bag out from under the passenger seat, locked the Cherokee, and scurried down the ruts to the detached one-car garage. I checked the side door to the garage. It wasn't locked. The warped door frame opened when I pulled hard. Penny's car, a battered gray Saturn, sat inside. I tried the handles on the passenger side. Still locked, just like when I found the photographs for Hetty in it. I sidestepped my way around the car, to the driver's door, and tried it. It opened. I leaned down and shoved the bag under the front seat. I shut the door and sidestepped my way back, then pushed the garage door back into its frame. I stepped back into the snow-grooved driveway and hurried back to the Cherokee.

I slammed my door and backed out while I buckled my seat belt. At the corner stop sign, I took a deep breath. I felt a little foolish for my mad dash through the snow. Obviously, I could have taken my time because there was no rush to search Penny's house again.

Just as I put on my turn signal, a dark four-door car that I recognized as Thistlewait's appeared in my rearview mirror and pulled into Penny's driveway. I executed my turn and only spun a little on the ice. I reminded myself that I was in the clear.

I concentrated on the traffic and the patches of ice as I drove downtown. I had one more stop to make.

An Everything In Its Place Tip for Organized Closets

Assess the function and use of each closet with these questions:

- Is the closet meeting the needs you have for that area of your home?
- How can you increase the storage and accessibility? Do you need more shelves? Would labeling help you find what you need easier?
- Are the items in the closet located in the most logical place in your home?

Chapter
Twenty-eight

I was so busy maneuvering the Cherokee into the parallel parking spot in front of Victor Roth's gallery that I didn't notice the small sign stuck in the lower corner of the window until I pushed on the glass door and it wouldn't budge. The sign read AVAILABLE. I tightened my grip on Livvy's gloved hand and stepped back to get a better look. The windows were still covered in white paper, but there wasn't any light or movement behind them.

I returned to the Cherokee, buckled Livvy in, and then dropped into my seat. I dialed the number painted on the glass under WHITE WALLS GALLERY.

"We're sorry. The number you dialed has been disconnected."

I closed the phone, disappointed. A missing and possibly valuable ancient manuscript and an art dealer accused of fraud seemed to go together like two pieces of a puzzle, but it looked like I wasn't going to get to talk to Victor.

The heater warmed my feet as I considered what to do

next. Victor claimed he didn't have it, but that could have been a lie to get Mr. Baseball Cap off his back. Maybe Victor did have it and he'd slipped out of town. Possible. But who was his buyer? I'd seen Ballard's name on the phone message slip at the White Walls Gallery. Did she have the money to purchase it? Who else would want the book?

Livvy talked in the backseat, but I focused on my thoughts, blocking out her murmurs, an essential mommy skill. Ballard had said her father was a college professor, hadn't she? Livvy continued to chant. Didn't sound like she came from money, but Irene said Ballard's business was booming. Enough that she could make an offer on a valuable manuscript? Livvy's words finally penetrated my thoughts. "Li-beary. Li-beary."

I glanced across the street in the direction Livvy pointed. "Yes, sweetie, the library sounds good to me, too." What better place than the downtown library to check Ballard out? And they had the added bonus of story time coming up in thirty minutes.

I parked Livvy's stroller beside the computer and handed her a book from my stack. We'd attended story time and now with her focused on *Brown Bear, Brown Bear* I could give my attention to a computer search.

Maybe Ballard wanted the manuscript, but I had a hard time picturing her dognapping Rex with her sensitive attitude about balance and peace. And a man had called me. But I kept thinking about the glass displays in her little museum.

I figured she had a Web site and she did. The Total Body Wellness site had lots of white, lots of quotes, and no prices. Photos of her antiquities dominated the Who

We Are page with phrases like "ancient secrets," "old knowledge rediscovered," and "unknown beauty secrets gathered from the ancients."

Next, I typed her name in a search engine. A few related genealogical links popped up. I handed Livvy an ABC book and swished the mouse around. Where else should I look? Newspapers.

With the help of the librarian I logged in to a database with news articles and tried "Pathway group." No hits. "Ballard Nova" brought up a list. A few PR-type pieces were from her time in California. Apparently she'd called her business Body Life in California. I clicked on another article and read the headline FTC INVESTIGATES FRAUD CHARGES.

"Wow."

I skimmed the article. Body Life was one of three California companies that had restraining orders placed on them. I printed the article plus a few others, then headed for the checkout.

Thirty minutes later, I parked in front of Ballard's store. Livvy slept in her car seat, occasionally emitting a petite snore. I didn't want to wake her because this would be her nap for the day.

Just then Ballard came out the door, locked the dead bolt, and crossed the porch with snow-dusted rocking chairs. I rolled my window halfway down. She saw me and came over. "I'm sorry. Closing early today."

"That's okay. I wanted to ask you a few questions."

Her shopkeeper smile went down a notch, but she remained polite. "Sure. I remember you from the Pathway group. You were with Irene, right?"

"Yes. I'm Ellie Avery. Did you know Victor Roth?"

She fumbled and dropped her gloves. "Yes." She retrieved them and flicked them back and forth against her leg. "He acquired an Etruscan deity for me."

"Did you know he's under investigation for fraud?"

Her eyes narrowed. "No."

"His gallery is closed and his number's disconnected."

She stamped her feet back and forth. This info didn't seem to bother her. "Really? Well, since I have the artifact I paid for, that doesn't concern me. Now, what's this about?"

"Another antiquity, a manuscript, has been found. Did you want the manuscript?"

"It would depend on the manuscript, wouldn't it? He did mention something was coming in that might interest me, but it didn't arrive. Now I've got to be going."

Apparently, she'd answered my first questions in an effort not to offend a potential customer, but now her patience was gone. "Why did you move here from California?" I asked.

"I was led here. This"—she turned and swept her arm across the snow-covered cherry trees—"is part of my journey."

"I bet the feds would have a different opinion."

Her head snapped back to me. "What are you talking about?"

I handed her one of the articles. She scanned the headline with her mouth pinched together, then said, "Nothing but trumped-up charges from narrow-minded right-wingers. I've done nothing wrong."

"You're making claims about your products that aren't true."

She crumpled the paper. "There's nothing wrong with what I do. I give those pathetic young women what they want. They *want* to believe they can look younger. I give them confidence and peace of mind. There's no law against that." She shoved the paper in her pocket. "I knew you wouldn't understand when Irene told me you went to one of those churches in town." She gripped the window and leaned in. The venom in her voice shocked me and it took me a few seconds to react. "You're so wrapped up in tradition that it's going to choke you." Her dangly earrings slapped against her coat collar as she shook her head. "You can't abide the idea of someone finding happiness, if it's not in your confining definition of Sunday morning religion. You're a hypocrite."

I put the Cherokee in reverse.

"Now get off—" I gunned the engine and her gloved hands slipped off the window as I backed up. I took the turn to the icy, rutted road too quickly, but I got the Cherokee under control and glanced in the rearview mirror to check on Livvy.

She still slept, hands splayed and head tilted to the side. Her hood covered her left eye. I concentrated on getting my breathing under control. I pulled at my turtleneck as it seemed to close in around my throat. I reached the light at the end of the twisty country road and stopped. I peeled off my gloves and used them to pat my forehead.

I checked the rearview mirror again. Livvy slept and the road was empty. I yanked on my turtleneck collar again. The light changed and I accelerated. Was I narrow-minded? Sure, I had my beliefs about spirituality, just like Ballard did. We both felt passionately about our beliefs. Didn't I have as much right to my beliefs as she had to hers? She wanted me to respect her beliefs, but she'd only had contempt for mine. I hadn't tried to stop her from practicing her beliefs, only pointed out that the FTC thought she was defrauding people.

Okay. Forget her viciousness, her intolerance. Concentrate on what she'd said. She'd *said* she hadn't bought a manuscript from Victor. She could be lying. Her business was definitely a moneymaking machine based on secrets from ancient texts. She could use another text to validate her products, and I could only imagine what new claims she could come up with, using a letter from Paul. It would be a huge draw.

I glanced in the mirror at Livvy. Her hood had slipped lower and now only her mouth was visible.

As I drove I turned the suspects over in my mind. Like a mental puzzle, I picked each one up and tried to fit it in the picture. But none of them worked. There were still too many missing pieces. I slunk down in the seat. I needed a break. I switched lanes and headed for Sonic. A carhop bundled up in a thick coat brought my Diet Coke and scurried away. I rooted around in the console and found some Hershey's Kisses. They were rock hard from the cold, but I put one in my mouth to thaw it out. Just what I needed, a caffeine and chocolate fix. I smiled. Just like Penny and her chocolate and espresso fix.

I sat up straighter. Clarissa's death and the discovery of the manuscript had overshadowed one player in these events, Penny. Just like she'd faded into the background while she was alive, more sensational events drew the attention away from her in death, too. I needed to refocus on the questions I'd had about Penny. I opened my cell phone to call Kelly, the babysitter I'd had the night of the Preview Show. She hadn't done such a good job keeping up with Rex, but she had taken great care of Livvy. I could leave Rex in his kennel and he'd be fine for a few hours.

"Sure, Mrs. Avery. I can come over early. You still want me to watch Livvy while you get your haircut at four-thirty, right?"

"Haircut? Oh. Right. I'd completely forgotten. Things have been a little crazy."

* * *

"Ma'am, you can't walk on this floor with those shoes."
I felt about sixty years old. On base I was "ma'am," but
when someone called me ma'am I had to fight the urge to
look over my shoulder for an elderly lady behind me. I
slipped off my boots and crossed to the bleachers in
socks. I'd tracked Will to the gym. I hadn't expected him
to be at work. Technically, the gym isn't "work," but the
Air Force wants everyone healthy; there's a physical fit-
ness test to pass, after all.

I spotted Will playing three-on-three basketball. I settled on the wooden bench to watch. He was better than I
expected, quick on the court. From his lounging, lazy
ways I'd never have pictured him playing basketball. As
their shoes squeaked and yells echoed up to the caged
lights, I thought about Penny. I knew some of her movements and actions on Monday. She interviewed Bedford.
Then I talked to her at the squadron. Around noon she
called Marsali, then went to my house and hid the miniature disk in the old coal chute. Will found her body at
home around twelve-thirty.

Why was she at the squadron? What made her go to
my house and leave the disk? I shifted on the bench and
checked my watch. Maybe Will could answer my questions. And what about the week before? Tessa had said
Penny had a meeting with Bedford. I closed my eyes and
tried to restructure the week before Penny died. It seemed
so long ago. Had Penny babysat for me? No. It was the
week Will came home from the deployment. I'd wanted
her to stay with Livvy while I got my teeth cleaned, but
Penny had a video conference at the squadron right before Will returned.

I needed to look at a flight schedule. Maybe Tommy
could pull it up for me. Or Tessa. I'd never heard back
from Tessa about her friend Marilyn, who worked with

Bedford. I pulled out my cell phone and dialed the squadron. I got Tessa's voicemail and left her a message, asking if she'd put me in touch with Marilyn.

The players moved off the court and I stood and waved. Will grabbed a towel and came over. I said, "Hey. Good game. Can I ask you a question?" He nodded and wiped his face and neck. "Do you know what Penny did the morning she died?"

His mouth turned down and he shook his head. "She had that interview with General Bedford at the Mansion. Then she went home for lunch."

"Did you see her notes from the interview?"

Will shrugged. "Nah. They're probably in her notebook. Last time we went to the BX she bought a notebook, a new one, to take notes in." He tossed the towel on his shoulder and cracked the knuckles on his hands. To complete the routine, he put his hand under his chin and pushed it up first to the right and then to the left until his neck popped.

There weren't any notes in her journal about the meeting. "Was she going to tape the interview?"

"Nah. She tried that another time and didn't like having to type it out afterward."

So where were her notes?

"I wonder why she went to the squadron," I said.

I didn't expect Will to answer, but he did. "I left my hat at home. She brought it to me."

"Did you talk to her?"

"No, I was in the vault. She just left it on my desk."

"What about the week before? You'd just gotten back from Turkey, right? On Wednesday?"

"No. It was Thursday," Will corrected.

"What did Penny do that week? You had a video conference?"

He nodded. "I think that was Monday, her time. I'm not sure what else she had going on." He wiped the towel across his forehead. "I've got to go back to the squadron."

"Sure. See you later." I checked my watch. As long as I was on base I might as well go see Tessa.

As soon I walked into the Orderly Room, Tessa saw me and said, "Marilyn hasn't called me back."

"That's okay." I glanced into Briman's office. The squadron commander's office was empty, like the rest of the cubes around Tessa. "Where is everybody?"

"Briman's in a meeting, Kinsy's sick, and DeLane and Notas are on a smoke break."

I pulled up a chair to her computer. "Can you get into scheduling?"

"Sure." She pointed and clicked with her mouse. "What's going on?"

"I'm running errands."

"Running errands. Ahem. Like I believe that. Okay, here you go. I'm guessing you don't want this week's schedule. Back a few?"

I ignored her sarcastic tone. "About four weeks ago."

"Um-hmm." Tessa scrolled and then swiveled the monitor to me. "The week before Penny died. You being careful? Who knows you're poking around in this?"

I smiled at her. "Only people I trust completely, like you." I went back to the list of sorties and crews. "Wait. Rory flew that Monday."

"Not a local," said Tessa. "He was coming back from Turkey that day."

"Really? Can you bring up only his schedule for the last few weeks?"

"Sure. There. See, he's been doing the out-and-backs, rotating the crews in and out for the deployments and dragging fighters over to England and back."

The Air Force was multitasking, refueling jets as well as moving people.

"Cushy. He goes, gets the tax break, but he doesn't have to stay," I said. "A regular route for the last month. Do you have a log or sign-in sheet for the video conference?" I asked suddenly.

"Sure." She pulled a notebook out of a stack and handed it to me. I flipped back and checked the dates and times. Penny signed in for her video conference at three Monday afternoon. Rory landed at noon. Calculating time for a debrief for Rory, I thought it was possible that they had crossed paths. Did Penny see what I saw the last time Rory landed, what looked suspiciously like a drop?

"You okay?" Tessa asked. "You look a little pale."

"Sure. I'm fine," I said, but I wasn't.

Tessa's phone rang. "Orderly Room. Marilyn! Oh, jeez." Tessa swung to check the clock. "I forgot. I totally forgot. Okay. Yeah." Tessa's gaze cut to me. "I'm bringing a friend, okay? Five minutes, I'll be there."

Tessa hung up, grabbed a red duffel bag. "I completely spaced out. Marilyn's waiting for me at the gym. We walk three times a week. Come on, you can meet her and ask her anything you want."

Marilyn, a heavyset woman in a green jacket and skirt with a sparkly frog pen on her lapel, already had on her tennis shoes and was striding around the indoor track when we arrived. We caught up with her. Tessa introduced me and vouched for me, then scooted off to change clothes. Marilyn tilted her chin up and studied me through the bifocals of her glasses. "So you want to know about Penny?"

"Yes."

Marilyn gazed at me for a moment more, then gave a

small nod. "Okay. Might as well walk while we talk. Some people can take their sweet time at the gym." She threw a glance at the women's locker room door. "But I have to get back."

"Sure." I kicked off my boots again and we walked. "Penny met with General Bedford on Monday, the morning of the day she died," I said to get the conversation going.

Marilyn nodded. "Ten-thirty. Right on time. So nice when people are on time." We took the first turn.

"What was she like? Her mood?"

Marilyn considered, then spoke. "Polite. Distant. Just like she was the week before. But she was completely different back in the fall, the first time she had an appointment with him. I remember because I had to give all the information to the police."

"How was she different?"

"She was nervous, I could tell, but she was nice. She and the general hit it off right away. I heard her telling him a recipe for some kind of foreign dumpling rice dish." She saw my disbelief and laughed. "You don't think that fancy young wife of his did any cooking, do you? I'd say unpacking the containers from a restaurant was about as far as her cooking skills went."

"Really?" Secretaries always have the dirt on their employers and their employers' families, too.

"It started when his first wife died. He was strictly a grilled steak and potato man. One day, he came in with a cookbook from the BX. 'Marilyn,' he said, 'if I have to eat one more steak, I'm gonna become a vegetarian.' He tried new things, noodles and such. Every once in a while he'd bring me a recipe. Got my rib recipe that way. They're so tender, fall off the bone—but you don't want to know about that.

"Let's see, back to Penny. The last two times she was

there, she was worried. I don't know about what, but I could see it in her face."

"Did you hear her interview?"

"No. She asked General Bedford to close the door. Hadn't done that before."

"What happened when she left? Clarissa was there?"

"Yes." Marilyn shook her head in disapproval. "There was no call for a scene like that. Mrs. Bedford was a real beauty, bless her heart, but not too smart about General Bedford. Any fool could see there was nothing romantic between Penny and General Bedford. Only business."

As we took the next turn, I asked, "What was he like after Penny left? Or did you notice with the fit Clarissa threw?"

"Oh, I noticed." Marilyn's pace slowed. "He was a little different. General Bedford's one of those people who has a long fuse. He'll go a long time and then just blow up. Sometimes I know he's furious, but you'd never tell it on the outside."

"But you could tell he was angry?"

"Not angry, exactly. Worried?" Marilyn tried out the thought, then rejected it with a shake of her head. "No. Maybe anxious is a better description."

"And she was in the week before?"

"Yes," Marilyn said. "I'm not sure what day. Wednesday? Now, I didn't hear much of that conversation, just the general telling Penny to come back next week because he needed time to get things in order. Those photos she wanted, you know."

"And you said something about her appointment with him in the fall?"

"Yes. Now, *that* was about the World War II exhibit."

Penny did a bunch of volunteer work at the museum, mostly behind the scenes.

Tessa fell into step with us. Marilyn harrumphed. "Next

time, I'm not going to call you. You'll just miss your workout."

"Thanks for talking to me, Marilyn," I said.

Some of the starch went out of her posture. "Glad to. It's a shame what happened to Penny."

I almost didn't go inside Cuts and Curls. It was the lingerie displayed in the window. Two teddies, one black and one red, and a bra and panties in zebra stripes. It made me wonder what kind of salon it was, but I hadn't found anyone to cut my hair and Barbara cut Abby's hair. Abby always looked great. I pulled my key out of the ignition. I'd try it.

I stepped under the awning that ran the length of Clairmont's only strip mall. Cuts and Curls was sandwiched between a video rental store and Domino's Pizza. The strip mall, plus a grocery store, a gas station, and a small branch of the county library, made up Clairmont. Of course, things would change when the massive Super Wal-Mart that was under construction down the highway finally opened.

I pushed through the door and smelled permanent solution. "Hi. I've got an appointment with Barbara," I said to the woman who was jerking towels through the air and folding them into neat piles.

"Hi, come on in." She had short blond hair, flawless makeup, and shiny long nails. Her bangs were pressed down on her forehead, but the rest of her hair was teased straight out. She looked like she'd stuck her finger in an outlet. She wore a red leather vest, a black belt with thick silver studs, and jeans. "That's me. Call me Barb. Have a seat." She unfurled a black cape. I settled in the chair near the window and had visions of me with an electrocuted-style hairdo. "I just need it trimmed."

"Oh, honey." Barb's red nails flicked through the ends of my hair. "You need more than a trim. You need shape. Style. I'll take care of you."

"Nothing too radical, okay?"

"Sure. No problem. I won't take more than an inch or two off the length."

Abby's hair always looks great, I told myself.

"Three at the most."

Fifteen minutes later, I focused on a sign over Barb's station that read GAELIC PUNK RULES instead of the cascade of falling hair.

"All right," she pronounced and spun me toward the mirror.

Wet hair hung in hunks on each side of my face, ending at my chin. Great. I looked like Morticia Adams, the bobbed version.

"Don't worry. I thinned it. It's gonna be spectacular."

It will grow. No matter how bad it looks, it will grow. I glanced around for something to distract me. "Why the lingerie?"

"I've got a little side business, Pamper Yourself. I do Pamper Yourself Parties. You know, like Tupperware, but silk and lace are so much more entertaining than plastic, don't you think? Here's my card. Call me, if you want to host a party."

"Umm, I'll see."

Barb swiveled the chair again and snapped on the blow-dryer. Outside, a car parked next to the Cherokee, probably Barb's next appointment. But instead of coming inside, the person, a man, got out and walked to a pickup parked in front of the video store. Something about that man. I shifted to get a better look.

"Too hot?" Barb yelled.

"No. It's fine." The man had on a baggy wind suit with the hood up. He slid into the seat, pushed back the hood, and smiled, revealing teeth so brightly white that I could see them even from this distance. It was Victor.

"Hey. Are you okay?"

I'd hopped up from the chair and run to the window. Yes. It was Victor and he was talking to Rory. Rory put the pickup in gear and backed out of the parking space.

"Barb, I've got to go." I ripped the cape off, pulled some cash out of my purse, and grabbed my coat. "Sorry. There's an emergency."

"What about your change?"

"Keep it. It's a tip. It looks great." The cold air outside seemed to instantly freeze my wet hair. I felt like a Popsicle. I jumped in the Cherokee and pulled out into the parking lot. Rory's black pickup slid out of the exit and into traffic going to the base.

As I drove, I did a little mental sorting and reorganizing, just like when I organized closets and cabinets. Sometimes I put something away and it didn't fit quite right and I had to dump everything out and start again. I dumped what I knew about Rory: strange exchanges of a carpet, regular trips to Turkey, and expensive tastes, and he'd been on the receiving end of demands from Clarissa. What did I know about Victor? Shady business deals and accusations of fraud. He said he didn't have "it," the manuscript.

It looked like Rory was smuggling something from Turkey. I doubted he was doing a land office business in smuggling religious manuscripts. After seeing how often and how regularly he flew in and out of Turkey, I figured the manuscript was an anomaly and drugs were the staple of his smuggled cargo. If Rory was smuggling drugs, maybe Victor was his distributor. It would explain why there wasn't a lot of art in his gallery; it was a front.

I cranked the heater while I waited for an opening in the traffic flow, then gunned it, which made the heater give off an extra spurt of warm air. We were out of Clairmont in a few seconds. I eased off the accelerator as we zipped through the deserted flat plain around the base. Scrub bushes alternated with clusters of pine trees, which sent long shadows across brown patches of dry grass as the sun sank in the sky. I put my visor down to block the direct sun as it hovered on the edge of the horizon.

After five minutes, the chain-link fence that enclosed Greenly Air Force Base began. Rory slid into the turn lane and I let two cars get between us.

I should call Thistlewait and tell him I'd seen Victor. Victor with Rory. I drove slowly and pulled out my ID card to show at the gate. The light changed. I hit the gas and sent my purse sprawling. My cell phone bounced across the passenger seat and slid down the gap by the door. Rory pulled through the ID checkpoint. I stopped, and a security police officer glanced at my ID and waved me through. I'd have to call Thistlewait when Rory stopped.

But he didn't stop. Most of the traffic was on the other side of the street as everyone headed home for the day. Rory sped through the streets and I dropped farther back. He turned left at the next light and I knew he was going to the squadron. I hung back until the truck disappeared around a curve. The road to the squadron was long, windy, and empty because the squadron was situated on the flight line in the old alert facility, one of the most remote buildings. I pulled into the squadron's parking lot as Rory went inside the building.

Where was Victor? I couldn't see him in the truck, but it had tinted windows. Either Rory had dropped him off or Victor was still in the pickup.

I parked on the far side and fished the phone out of the crevice, pulled up my hood, and headed for the squadron. Despite my hood, my wet hair clung to my head.

I trudged up the incline ramp and opened the inner door. It was quiet until someone shouted, "See you tomorrow," and a bank of lights down the hall went off. Where would Rory go? His office?

I pushed back my hood and slipped down the hall. The low pile carpet silenced my steps. The door to the Safety Office was closed. A faint silhouette of me showed in the door's glass panel. I'd gotten the electrocution look after all. My hair was still wet at the scalp, but the ends were dry and stuck out at odd curving angles. Sort of drowned rat meets electric outlet look. I shoved my hands deep into my pockets and tucked my arms into my sides because I felt cold all over.

Now what? Then I heard a faint thud. I went to the stairs and peered down. The lights were on in the Hole, the basement break room. I went down the stairs on tiptoe, but didn't hear anything else. When I got to the last tier, I squatted down and looked into the doorway. Nothing.

I moved down to the next step, crouched again. I could see Rory behind the bar, pushing and pulling at something. I felt as frozen as the hair on my scalp. I had to move. He was going to come up these stairs. If I didn't move he might see me before he got to the stairs. He bent down below the bar and I moved before I realized I'd started. I scuttled as quietly as I could down the rest of the stairs and slipped into the alcove under the stairs. Rory crossed the room and didn't even glance at the doorway. I'd been so cold a few moments ago, but now my heart thumped. I was burning up inside my coat and I felt a sheen of sweat cling to my skin. My head still felt cold. The contrast in temperatures made my head ache.

I edged over to see what Rory was doing. He opened a storage closet at the far end of the room, went inside, and emerged with a rolling suitcase. He came straight toward me. I merged back into the recess below the stairs. Rory pushed down the extendable handle on the suitcase, gripped the other handle attached to the top, then trotted up the stairs. I leaned my head against the chilly cinder block wall. Thank goodness the stairs were solid and not the kind with spaces between the treads. His feet pounded up the steps, sending off echoes that reverberated up and down the stairwell and provided a counterpoint to the banging of my heartbeat.

I waited a little bit to make sure Victor wasn't going to follow him; then I stood up after the echoes faded. There could be a logical explanation. Maybe Rory had forgotten a suitcase after his last trip? I doubted it. In fact, I'd seen him return from a trip a few days ago and he'd had his suitcase with him. That was the day I'd seen him give Mr. Baseball Cap the rug. Maybe Rory was on his way to another drop.

I sprinted up the stairs, then moved more sedately through the squadron. At the base of the incline to the outer doors, I watched Rory heave the suitcase into his truck and drive away. The parking lot lights had come on in the twilight and highlighted his movements. After the truck disappeared behind another building, I hurried to the Cherokee.

I pushed the heater to high again and followed Rory's taillights in the growing darkness. I didn't get close until Rory exited the freeway in Vernon. I dropped back as far as I could, but I didn't know the residential area in the North Valley and I had to stay fairly close.

Finally, Rory turned a corner and pulled into a driveway next to a tiny yellow frame house, a box on a rock, as Mitch would say. I parked on the street several houses back and waited. Rory pulled the suitcase out as the passenger door opened and Victor stepped out. They walked to the front door and Rory unlocked it. I let out a sigh of relief. They didn't act like they suspected anyone had followed them. I opened and closed my phone a few times.

What about the suitcase? I wanted to know what was in it. What if I was wrong? What if there was nothing in that suitcase but clothes? I couldn't give Jensen another reason to suspect me. I could picture it now. Thistlewait would call him and Jensen would wonder why I "happened" to run across Victor and Rory. Nope, I couldn't call Thistlewait yet.

I slipped out of the Cherokee. Literally. My foot hit ice and half my body slid under the Cherokee. Great. Now my jeans were soaked, just like my hair. At least I matched.

I scrambled up. At the end of the driveway stood a mailbox with the name Tyler on it. So this was where Rory lived. I followed a hedge that separated the yellow house from its neighbor. Darkness had descended quickly once the sun was completely down and I was glad for the blackness. At the end of the hedge, I scooted across the backyard to the rear of the house. I inched up to a window with miniblinds. Wow! You really can see through them if they aren't completely closed. I could see a portion of a wooden table scattered with mail and a set of keys. A jacket hung over the back of a chair.

I eased down the yellow siding to the next window. This one had curtains, but they were open an inch. Light illuminated a narrow strip of window between the panels. I shoved myself between some bushes and felt snow seep through the fabric of my jeans. I was going to need a hot bath after this.

Inside, I could see the corner of a bed. The bed bounced and I shifted around until I saw Rory lean over to unzip the suitcase he'd tossed on the bed. He flipped the top open and pulled out paper-wrapped bundles about the size of his fist. Then he stacked the bundles on the bed and said something. I could hear a muted rumble. Rory nodded his head toward the window. I shrank down just as the chink of light went black, then reilluminated. I watched the strip of light from the window that fell on the snow. After a few seconds, I inched up.

I strained on my tiptoes, but I couldn't see what was in the bundles. Now Victor had a cardboard box. He opened the bundles and examined them. Then he rewrapped them and placed them in the box. He filled one box, dumped Styrofoam peanuts from a trash bag on the top of the bundles, taped the box closed, then came toward the window again. This time I was ready and ducked for a few beats, then popped up again. Rory must keep the empty boxes near the window. Victor walked back to the suitcase with another empty box.

Rory emptied the suitcase, zipped it closed, and stashed it in the closet on his way out of the room. Victor put the last bundle in the box and upended the peanuts over them, but only three plastic peanuts fell out. Victor crumpled the empty bag and tossed it on the floor, then went to the closet and pulled down a stack of blankets. He tossed a thick electric blanket back on the shelf and kept a blue throw.

I pressed against the yellow siding. That throw! An intricate patchwork of different blue fabrics. And fringe. A one-of-a-kind throw. I watched Victor stuff Penny's throw in the box, close the flaps, and tape the box shut.

Oh. My. God. Rory had Penny's throw. I hadn't seen it at her house since she died. A wave of revulsion washed over me. Thistlewait said Penny had been asphyxiated. Had she been killed with the beautiful throw she loved? But why else would Rory have it? If he wanted to make the crime scene look like an accident and there was something on the throw, like blood or fluid, he'd take it. Will got so drunk after she died he probably didn't notice it was gone. In fact, I bet he didn't pay much attention to what was around their house anyway, especially the blankets and throws. I clamped my teeth together and swallowed hard on the awful taste in my throat. I forced myself to move slowly as I backed away from the window. I trotted along the shadow of the hedge, but I hit the sidewalk sprinting.

"I know it was Penny's."

"How?" Thistlewait was skeptical.

I switched the cell phone to my other ear and pushed the Cherokee's heater up to high.

"I recognized it. Her grandmother made it for her. It was her favorite color, blue. It's handmade with squares in different shades of blue. And Victor is there. You've got to get out here. They were packing those boxes to move them somewhere. I don't think they'll be here for long and I can't stay much longer." I checked the dashboard clock. "In fact, I've got a spouse coffee to go to."

"I'm on my way. Stay put. Don't—*do not*—get out of your car again."

"I'm getting another call." I punched the button and heard screaming.

"Mrs. Avery. This is Kelly. Livvy fell and she's bleeding."

"I'll be right there."

A few hours later, I contemplated the spread of food. I usually dreaded the monthly spouse coffees because they seemed outdated, a leftover from a stilted fifties family show. The wives of the squadron gathered once a month to—well, I still wasn't sure what the purpose was, something along the lines of a city junior league. I guess the spouses of each squadron were supposed to make worthy contributions to the base and the community through fundraising and service projects. I'm sure it began, too, as a way to make connections and friendships.

I ran my hand through my hair self-consciously. I'd arrived home to find Livvy had busted her lip, lots of blood, but no serious injury. In fact, she'd been happily coloring by the time I arrived. There had only been time to run a brush through my hair and change into new jeans for the coffee.

"It is hard to decide, isn't it?" a woman asked as she leaned around me to pick up a brownie off the buffet.

"Sorry." I grabbed a plate and started moving down the line. I'd pretty much missed the business portion of the coffee because my thoughts were on different things, like whether or not Thistlewait had made it to the yellow house before the boxes disappeared. And had they found Penny's journal?

I transferred a slice of dessert pizza, cookie dough topped with cream cheese and fruit, onto my plate next to an enormous chocolate chip cookie. I heard Jill Briman say the spouse fund-raiser, Muffin Monday, needed muffin donations and volunteers to collect money at the squadron bright and early at seven on Monday mornings. I didn't look up. I have a bad habit of saying yes when people ask for my help, but I draw the line at causes that require me to show up at seven in the morning.

I caught a wisp of the conversation in the group around the craft table where they were making something with picture frames, paper doilies, and paint. I'd skipped on the craft. Get me around a glue gun and the results are scary. One woman paused, her scissors in midair, and leaned toward the center of the table. "Rory Tyler's been arrested!"

I stepped toward the table and another woman said, "No! Rory? What happened?"

"Yes. I saw it on the news right before I left—"

I missed the rest of the conversation when I realized Jill was bearing down on us with one of her sign-up clipboards. I immediately began rehearsing my excuses: Livvy didn't wake up until seven-thirty. Who would expect someone to wake up a sleeping child to make change for men who had college degrees? Jill would. She'd want that table manned, or womaned, to encourage sales.

I was trying to think of another excuse when Jill cut me away from the craft table. "I need to talk to you. Let's go over here." She steered me to a corner of her dining room that was unoccupied and tucked her clipboard away in the corner of her arm. "I need your advice."

That blew me away. Competent, commanding, in-control Jill needed my advice?

"It's Lieutenant Lamar. Georgia," she continued. "She's raising the issue about the posters in the break room again. I don't know why she can't leave it alone. It isn't that big a deal."

"Maybe because it *is* a big deal to her?"

Jill sighed. "Or because it gets her attention? I don't understand why she's making such a fuss. A few pictures don't hurt anyone."

"No, but I think, for Georgia, it's more the principle of the thing. Is it right to have those pictures in the squadron? Would they be on the walls of a break room at a bank?"

Jill ignored my question and said, "She's taking it way too personally. Did you know she thinks someone poisoned her because she wanted the posters down?" Jill's eyebrows were wrinkled together and lowered over her sunburnt nose. She shook her head. "Can you believe that?"

"I think that poisoning had more to do with Penny than Georgia. It was an accident."

Jill sighed. "Penny. Now, she was great. Completely different from Georgia. Penny volunteered for everything and she took initiative, too. One morning after Muffin Monday, I even found her in the Hole cleaning up, dusting and straightening up the shelves. I didn't ask her to, but she was like that—helpful in a quiet way. Too bad we don't have more spouses like Penny."

I managed to keep my mouth closed. *I'm not trying to get the Best Spouse award*, I reminded myself.

"Well, back to Georgia. It's getting to Daniel," Jill said, referring to her husband. "She's really putting pressure on him to do something and you know most of the guys in the squadron don't want anything to change. I tried to talk to her the other day, but she wouldn't listen. She even said *she's* getting frustrated. She isn't the only one who's frustrated." Jill's tone was sarcastic. Then she switched the clipboard to the other arm and lowered her voice. "But I am worried. She said she's going to do something drastic." Now Jill's tone was serious, all traces of irony gone. "We only have a few more months here and Daniel needs to finish out his stint as squadron commander on the right note. So, I want you to talk to her," she wound up.

I nearly choked on the bite of dessert pizza. After I swallowed, I asked, "Why?"

"Because I think she'll listen to you. Convince her to put her campaign on hold for a few months and then approach the new squadron commander."

"Jill, I don't think she's going to listen to me." I didn't think my arguments would be very convincing, especially since I was pretty much in Georgia's camp to begin with. Instead of tasting delicious, my next bite of dessert pizza tasted overpoweringly sweet and clogged in my throat. I managed to swallow the bite, but set my plate down. The thought of another bite made my stomach lurch.

"Just do your best." Coming from Jill, that phrase wasn't an encouragement, it was an order. Jill twisted the clipboard around facing me.

I knew she was about to make a pitch for me to volunteer, so I said, "I think I hear Livvy crying," and escaped to the basement stairs where the kids were watching videos. If the other sounds echoing up the stairs were any indication, they were also flinging toys at the walls. I peeked around the door frame and saw Livvy engrossed in building a wall from plastic interlocking parts, unaware of the other kids playing a rambunctious game of football on the other side of the room. As I tiptoed back up the stairs, I heard the babysitter order the kids to use the foam football.

When I reached the top of the stairs, I slipped through the kitchen where Jill was passing the clipboard around for signatures and went to sit by Abby and Irene. If anyone would know what rumors were floating around, it would be Irene. She'd once described herself as a news junkie, but I think it went a little further than that; probably a better description would be a gossip junkie. Irene scooted her ample hips over to make room for me. She pushed her fluffy blond hair out of her eyes and said, "So, what do you know about Rory? Have you heard he's been arrested?"

"Uh, yes," I said and realized that Irene probably thought I was a gossip junkie, too. I smiled faintly and said, "Not much. Just that he's been arrested. What do you know?" Perhaps I wasn't that different from Irene. I shoved that thought away to contemplate later and concentrated on her words. I wondered about Victor. "Did they arrest anyone else?"

"No. I did hear they took anything with a blade. All his razors, scissors, knives, anything like that," Irene continued. "And they pulled up all his rugs."

"How do you know all this?" I asked. "Was it on the news?"

"Of course not. I stopped by there on the way over

here. I mean, he doesn't have family here and we were his sponsor when he PCS'd here. I had to see if he needed anything."

"So you saw them collecting evidence."

"No." Irene shifted and shrugged. "I heard someone say they'd bagged anything with a sharp edge and then the guy in charge, the detective, I guess, said to check all the carpets." Irene's forehead wrinkled. "I didn't understand that part."

So they'd found the note in the journal and they'd drawn the same conclusion Abby and I had. I realized Irene was studying my face intently, so I tried to rearrange my features into an expression of puzzlement. "How strange," I said. I'm a terrible actress, but she must have been so focused on her connection to Rory that she glossed over my expression.

"I'd never have imagined he had the, well, the gumption to murder anyone. When he stayed with us while he was looking for a place to live, all he talked about was his nutrition supplements and weight lifting."

I looked at my watch and said, "I'd better head home. Are you ready?" I asked Abby. We'd driven over together. I carried Livvy across the snowy yard and buckled her into her car seat. Then I plopped into the passenger seat of Abby's sports car. I leaned my head back against the headrest. Livvy got heavier every day. My shoulders and arms felt like I was carrying around twenty-pound weights. I rotated my shoulders and tried to let the tension drain out of me.

"You look beat." Abby buckled her seat belt and revved the engine.

"I am." I was physically tired and there were too many bits of information swirling around in my mind. And it was a bath night. I heaved another sigh. How did single parents manage? One of the worst things about Mitch being gone was that the responsibility of everything descended on me: Livvy, Rex, the house, the bills, everything.

"Why don't I come in and help you get Livvy ready for bed?"

Normally, I'd have shrugged off her offer, but as much as I didn't like to admit it, I could use some help.

"It's bath night," I warned.

"Great! I can practice."

After Abby pulled into my driveway, I had to nearly get on my knees to reach across the folded-down seat and unbuckle Livvy's car seat. "You know this isn't exactly a mom-type car."

"I know, but I'm thinking I'll buck the minivan, SUV trend."

"I give you a year." I wrestled the car seat away from the seat belt strap. "You'll probably have the biggest bus of any mom in the squadron."

Abby took the car seat from me. "We'll see." Once inside, she turned to Livvy. "You'll help me give you a bath, won't you? Tell me where all your things are and what to do?"

Livvy studied her, then nodded. They went down the hall hand in hand. I petted Rex, let him out, and then collapsed on the couch. I stayed that way as the sounds of splashing and giggles receded.

The phone woke me. After answering it, I met Abby in the hall. "It's Jeff." I handed her the phone.

"Thanks. Livvy's tucked in bed, waiting for you."

We performed our bedtime ritual, which was becoming more elaborate as Livvy got older. Now we worked our way through a story, song, prayer, hugs, and kisses.

I turned on the night-light in the bathroom and met Abby in the kitchen.

"Thanks. You have no idea how much better I feel. That

was a great break." I went to the cabinet and pulled out glasses.

"Sure. It was good for me. I was getting cold feet about the baby. I mean, I don't know anything! Nothing. Not even how to change a diaper."

I dropped ice in the glasses and popped the tops on two Diet Cokes. "Don't worry. You pick it up pretty quick. It's like Mitch being gone. I have to cope, so I do." I handed one glass to Abby and sat down at the table across from her with the other.

"Before I forget, Jeff had a phone call from Mitch. You better get an answering machine soon. Mitch tried to call here during the coffee, but when you didn't answer, he called Jeff. Mitch's got a time slot scheduled for a video conference. Tomorrow night at ten-thirty. He cleared it with the Orderly Room, and Tommy Longfellow will be there night flying. Mitch called Tommy and he's going to leave the door by the side parking lot unlocked for you."

"That should work. Last time I tried to talk to him, there were about thirty people listening to us. The squadron should be pretty dead that late."

"I'll come over and stay with Livvy." She gave me a warning look. She must use it a lot with her third graders, because my protest, "You don't have to do that," never popped out of my mouth.

"I don't mind helping you out. You've got to learn to let someone give you a hand once in a while. You don't have to do it all by yourself. I'll come over tomorrow night about nine. So . . ." With that topic closed she raised an eyebrow. "You knew about Rory?"

I recounted everything from finding the letter to my spying on Rory and Victor.

"Wow. No wonder you were exhausted tonight."

I took another sip of my Diet Coke. My stomach grumbled and I felt that uneasy flutter, like I was about to come down with the flu. I found some crackers in the pantry and spread them on a plate with some cheese. "The throw would fit if Rory attacked her, but what about the poison? Thistlewait said it would have killed her, probably in another day or two. Did Rory poison her, get impatient, and then use a more direct method to make sure she died?"

"I don't know." Abby made little cheese and cracker sandwiches as she spoke. "Rory just doesn't seem like the kind of guy to use poison. I wonder what happened to Victor."

"He must have left Rory's before Thistlewait got there." I couldn't imagine that Thistlewait would let Victor avoid questioning.

Abby chewed slowly, swallowed, and said, "Do you think Victor poisoned Penny and later Rory slit her wrists? Then Rory had to take out Clarissa because she wanted a percentage of the profits?"

"Okay," I said slowly, "that's possible, but it doesn't feel right. How does Ballard fit in? She wasn't involved at all."

Abby snagged the last cracker. "It doesn't fit together in a neat little package, does it?"

"No." And I liked things neat and tidy. Everything put away where it belonged. "I suppose most crimes don't get wrapped up in neat packages with all the loose ends tied up."

Chapter
Twenty-nine

The next morning Thistlewait called me on my cell phone. It is not a good thing when the OSI has your cell phone number. Thistlewait wanted me to drop by the OSI office that morning. I didn't want to go, but since Rory had been arrested, I figured *I* could stop worrying about being arrested. I settled Livvy on the carpet with three of her favorite toys that make minimal noise, and I perched on the edge of the chair. "I heard about Rory—"

Thistlewait held up his hand. "Later. We've got something else to focus on."

"Well, you could at least say, 'Thanks for the tip.'"

He shook his head, but there was a hint of a grin on his mouth. "You're right. Thank you."

"You sure moved fast. He was on the news before I made it to the spouse coffee that night."

"Keeping a murder victim's credit cards and ID in your glove compartment tends to do that."

"He had Clarissa's ID in his glove compartment? Why would he leave them there, if he'd killed her?" I asked.

"Don't know." Thistlewait shrugged. "We found them

after we got the search warrant. Then we found a rope on his boat like the one used to strangle Mrs. Bedford. The cut matched."

"What happened with Victor?"

"Not there when we arrived. No sign of him around town. Fortunately, he'd only had time to take one box."

"And the throw?" I gripped the edge of the table.

"We found it. It's at the lab right now. Along with fifteen artifacts. Coins, jewelry, glass, tiles, and seals, I think they're called."

I sagged back against the back of the chair. It was over. And I wasn't in jail. I hadn't realized how much the stress and worry had weighed me down. I felt ten pounds lighter. Of course, Victor was still out there, but I'd bet my favorite Kate Spade Sam bag that he wouldn't be back in town. His gallery had been a front, but not for drugs. I sat back up from my slouchy position and asked, "Have you found the original manuscript?"

"No." Obviously, a sore spot with him because he didn't elaborate. Instead, he put several pictures on the table in front of me and sat back in his chair. I leaned over the pictures. They were mug shots. "You want me to look at these?"

Thistlewait nodded, balancing his chair on the back two legs.

"Okay," I said, feeling like I was on *Law & Order*. "Don't know number one or two, but I wouldn't want to, by the looks of them. They're kind of scary. Umm. Three, nope. I haven't seen him. Four, I don't think," I said briskly as my gaze slid across the line of faces. "Wait." I went back to number four. "That's Mr. Baseball Cap."

Thistlewait continued to balance the back legs of the chair. "Mr. Baseball Cap?"

"Yes. Remember, I told you about him. He and Victor had that weird conversation about me. Victor said he didn't have 'it' and Penny had probably given 'it' to me for safe-keeping. And I think Rory met him at the Stop 'n Shop for a drop."

"A drop?" Thistlewait had a funny look on his face, like he needed to sneeze or something.

"What?" I asked. I suspected Thistlewait was trying not to laugh at me.

The front legs of the chair slammed down and he was all business. "Nothing. What about the others?"

I stared at each one. "No. I don't know them."

"Okay." Thistlewait made a few notes, then gathered up the photos.

"Who are they?"

A tiny sigh came from Thistlewait.

"Well, I've got to ask, don't I? You ask me to come in, the least you can do is tell me what it's about."

Thistlewait tapped the photo of Mr. Baseball Cap. "Sam Jason Fields. Vernon police picked him up in a drug bust. He's not talking." I took the next photo Thistlewait handed me. "Brandon 'Doom' Henry Fields, Sam's cousin, who was also taken in during the drug bust. He's talking faster than we can record it."

The second man was younger, a teenager probably, with pasty skin, freckles, and a thin nose. He must use the same barber as his cousin because his long black hair hung in stringy clumps around his face. "Doom likes to hang out with his cousin Sam. He worked with Sam last summer at Green Lawn Yard Service. Since the weather turned colder, they've been making meth in Sam's base-ment and doing odd jobs, like attacking a woman in the parking lot of Copeland's, trying to run a woman off the road, and 'borrowing' her dog. That's Doom's term, not mine."

"What? These two did those things? Why? I don't even know this kid."

"I don't know. Doom claims a friend of Sam's paid them to hassle you, shake you up, but Doom doesn't know why or who paid."

Later that night, I stifled a yawn as I opened the heavy door to the squadron and trudged up the slope. I just couldn't seem to get rested, even though I'd gone to bed right after Abby left last night. It certainly wouldn't be an early night for me tonight, especially after my conversation with Thistlewait earlier today. The relief I'd felt when I'd been in the OSI office had faded during the day. Penny's and Clarissa's killer had been caught and the guys who'd been hired to scare me were in custody. It was over, but somehow I couldn't make myself believe those words. Something, I couldn't quite figure out what, felt wrong. I felt like I did after I'd sorted and thinned a closet or a drawer and I put everything back, but things didn't fit right.

I checked my watch. Ten-fifteen. I pulled on the inner door to the squadron experimentally, not sure if Tommy remembered to unlock it for me. But the door opened smoothly and I walked down the dark hallway.

On my way to the basement, I noticed a new photo of Abby and Jeff on the hall bulletin board. It was stuck between a reminder about bird migration patterns and a notice about Muffin Monday.

I pushed the Muffin Monday flyer aside and studied the picture of Jeff and Abby. They leaned together, smiling for the camera at the squad's luau-themed Christmas party. Abby had a pink flower tucked behind her ear. Jeff wore a Hawaiian-print shirt and a choker necklace made of thin white shells.

I turned to the stairs, thinking about the photo. My

steps thudded down to the basement, sounding loud to me. Unlike the rest of the squadron, the lights were already on in the Hole. I went to the alcove room across the hall with the computer and closed the door in case the night flight crew returned. I wanted privacy for this discussion with Mitch. A note stuck to the monitor read *Hey, Ellie! I left the computer all set up for you. Call me for coffee soon. Tessa.*

I signed in, then pulled the note off as I swept the mouse around to bring the screen to life. I pointed and clicked, then sat back and waited, swiveling my chair back and forth with my foot. After a few moments, I planted both feet firmly on the floor and took a deep breath because I was starting to feel seasick.

Mitch smiled at me from the window on the screen. "Hey. You look great! How's everything going?"

"I think I'm coming down with the flu."

Mitch looked concerned. "If you don't feel good, we can do this later."

"No. I'm all right. You know how it hits people different ways. This is pretty mild. I'll be fine. And I need to talk to you." I told him about Rory's arrest and then caught him up to date on everything. The news on Marsali's interpretation of the manuscript drew a whistle from Mitch. I glossed over the dognapping incident and didn't mention the pickup that had tried to run me off the road. No use worrying Mitch about those things. But despite my editing, I could see he was worried and angry, a combination of emotions I didn't usually see on his face.

He shook his head. "If I wasn't scheduled to come home in a few days, I'd be complaining to every colonel I could find until I got a jet back."

"You're coming back?" I knew he must be really shaken up to let that detail slip out.

He winced. "You didn't hear anything from me. Watch the news. Looks like things here are winding down. The squadron'll call you tomorrow, but it could change."

"Oh, I know. I'll believe it when I see you." I'd learned never to believe Mitch was on his way home until I actually saw him jogging down the air stairs. "But still, that's great!"

"Let's not get sidetracked from everything you just told me. Ellie, you've got to be careful." He opened and closed his mouth a few times, then ran his fingers through his hair. "I'm not going to say anything else because I know how you are, stubborn. But, please, *please* be careful. There's some rumors going around here about smuggling."

"Really?" I swiveled the chair again and then stopped abruptly as the nausea swept over me. I clenched my teeth together and swallowed hard. The seasick feeling passed and I refocused on our conversation. I heard more noise from the Hole and turned down the volume on the speakers. I didn't want anyone to overhear this conversation.

"Thistlewait is still looking into it?"

"Yes. They're doing a huge search for the original of the letter. They were ripping up carpets at Rory's." I yawned again and rubbed my hand over my face.

"I can see this thrilling conversation is getting to you. Why don't you head home, get some rest? Try to hold off on this for a few days until I get home, okay?"

"All right, but you be careful, too. Don't ask too many strange questions over there. Don't make it too obvious that you're interested in the smuggling, okay?"

Mitch smiled. "Now the shoe's on the other foot. It's not a good feeling, is it?"

I laughed weakly. "No. I'll watch out."

We wrapped up our conversation with our usual "Love you's" and I logged off the computer. I took the note that

Tessa had left for me and scribbled *How about ten o'clock at the BX Friday?* When I opened the door a flicker of movement in the Hole caught my eye. Georgia Lamar grabbed a poster of two women in bikinis lounging on a sports car and jerked it off the wall. She ripped it into small pieces and fed them into a paper shredder.

"Georgia," I said, but the snarl of the shredder drowned out my words. As the shredder's roar died away, I repeated her name. She paused for a moment, then reached down to pick up another poster from a small pile on the floor. "Hi, Ellie."

"Hey, Georgia. Um, I don't think this is such a good idea."

She ripped a jagged tear down the center of the poster, splitting the picture of a brunette holding a beer can and drooling over a small dog. Her voice was matter-of-fact. "I'm doing it myself. You know, 'If you want a job done right, do it yourself.' I went through the channels. Did it all the right way. When that didn't work I sent a letter to the base newspaper. They wouldn't even print it!"

I hadn't wanted to talk to Georgia at all, but it seemed it was now or never. Jill would hit the roof when she heard about this. And I didn't even want to think about what the guys in the squadron would think. Mitch would shrug it off, but other guys weren't so easygoing. "Is this—"

Georgia fed the scraps of the brunette and the dog poster into the shredder, and its racket cut off my words. When the machine stopped I began again. "Georgia, is this really that important?" I waved my hands at the posters that remained on the walls.

She fed in the next glossy sheets instead of answering my question.

I shouted over the noise of the shredder. "Georgia, I'm on your side. I don't like these posters any more than you do, but are you sure this is going to help? I mean you've got the job, you're a pilot. You do the same work, for the same pay. Does the atmosphere really matter?"

Georgia clicked the shredder off, leaving strips of paper dangling down into the trash can. Her gaze flickered with anger and she said, "Yes. Yes, it does matter to me. I work here. This is a professional office. It shouldn't look like some muscle magazine. Do you really think things will change? They won't. Not unless someone makes some noise. And I'm going to make some noise."

Georgia picked up a discarded newspaper from one of the tables. She crumpled the pages and stuffed them in the bottom of a metal trash can. "I don't have time to talk. I want to be finished with this before the night flight crew lands." She looked around the room. Her gaze stopped at a small prayer carpet displayed in a framed glass case. She pulled it off the wall and dumped it into a trash can. I cringed as the glass shattered. "It'll make a nice surprise for Tommy."

She grinned as she dragged the trash can over to the set of doors that opened onto the flight line. She propped the door open and set the trash can outside. Then she dumped the shredded posters into the metal trash can. She grabbed a bottle from the bar, swished it over the shredded paper a few times, then struck a match and dropped it in the trash can.

I hoped she didn't burn the place down. Of course, she might think that situation wasn't so bad, if it got rid of the posters.

I walked back to the door. I wasn't going to physically try and stop her. "I hope you're not falling on your career sword," I said as I walked out the door to put the note on Tessa's computer.

I passed the bulletin board with the photo of Abby and Jeff again. Vague snippets of thoughts as fragile as mist stirred in my mind, but the shredder growled and I gave up and went to stick the note on Tessa's computer in the Orderly Room.

I hurried back down the steps and didn't bother to glance in the Hole as I returned to the computer alcove. The paper shredder rumbled. I shrugged into my coat. The faint smell of smoke drifted into the small room. I shut down the computer and grabbed my purse. I didn't want to hang out in the squadron with Georgia burning stuff, but I couldn't leave either. I'd get in the Cherokee and drive to the far side of the parking lot where I could see the door to the flight line. If anything looked like it was getting out of hand, then I'd call the fire department.

I clicked off the light in the alcove and headed for the stairs as the shredder fell silent. The scent of smoke tinged the air. That picture of Jeff and Abby still bothered me. I walked slowly, analyzing the different parts of the photo. It wasn't the people. Not the flower, either. The necklace of shells. I stopped walking. I'd been associating beads with women and jewelry. What if I reversed it and associated the beads with men? Just because they were made into necklaces didn't mean men couldn't buy them, too.

A memory clicked into place. I compared my thoughts with what I'd learned over the last few days. The necklace. Rory sitting in jail, not saying a word. The absence of Penny's notes. It fit together. I realized I had a death grip on my purse strap and I forced my fingers to relax. I took a few steps down the hall, then pulled out my cell phone and left a message for Thistlewait.

I paused with my foot on the first step. Was that a shout? The squadron was quiet except for the buzz of the fluorescent lights in the stairwell. Even the shredder was silent. Then I heard a muffled thump.

I walked slowly back to the Hole and looked around the door frame, expecting to see Georgia efficiently stripping the posters off the walls. I didn't see her. The smoke smell was stronger, but it was cooler with the outside door propped open. I almost called her name, but something stopped me.

A grunt and another thump made the hair along my arms stand up and pulled me into the room. I moved a few feet and saw a man holding Georgia down on the floor with his hands locked around her throat. Georgia was hitting him, her arms and her legs flailing back and forth. Her face was pale, and her eyes bulged with fear.

My mind registered that the man was wearing blues, the uniform of pale blue shirt and navy pants. It wasn't his uniform I was worried about, it was his build. He wasn't huge, but I didn't think I could do much to help Georgia. I backed a step away and stuck my hand down in my purse, searching for my cell phone. But if I called 911, would they make it in time to help Georgia? I scanned the room. The ratty couch and a few folding chairs looked like the only possible weapons in sight.

The man kept up a steady, low monologue, but I couldn't hear the words. The grunts and belabored breathing of the man revived my nausea, but I forced it back down and scanned the walls for a weapon from the "souvenirs" that crews brought back from around the world. Of course, there wasn't a gun or sword in sight. Only beer mugs, bar signs, and a few framed photographs.

Georgia's legs were barely moving. My fingers connected with my cell phone at the same moment I saw the bell on the bar.

I knew I didn't have time to get out to the hall, call 911, and wait for them to arrive.

Without consciously deciding to do it, I set down my purse, then dropped to the floor and crawled down the length of the couch and over to the bar, trying to keep a few tables and chairs between me and the man. A faint haze hung below the lights, but then a sharp breeze whipped through the open door and blew smoke in my eyes.

I reached the far side of the bar and slithered a hand up and patted around until the cool, solid metal of the bell brushed my fingertips. I pulled it to me and slid it off the counter. It made my arms sag beautifully.

I risked a peek over the top of the bar. The man still had Georgia pinned. He hadn't noticed me. Georgia's hands clutched at his arms, but her feet lolled out, toes pointing in opposite directions, like a doll dropped and forgotten.

Her limp legs made me hurry. The fire in the trash can popped, probably the wooden frame burning. Why didn't the smoke detectors go off? Another blast of fresh cool air streamed into the room, and I realized the fresh air was probably dispersing the small amount of smoke. The fire alarm wasn't going to go off.

I didn't try to low-crawl back. I didn't think I could because the bell was so heavy. I cradled it like a football against my side with one hand over the outside and the other around the clapper to keep it from ringing. I did a crouchlike run until I was behind the man. I gripped the lower edges of the bell and raised it over my head. Then I wavered.

I didn't know if I could do it.

Over the top of the man's head, my gaze locked with Georgia's. He must have realized Georgia was looking at something because he half turned to look over his shoulder.

Georgia let out a raspy gasp and I brought the bell down on the man's head with a loud clang as my mind processed the face and matched it to a name: General Bedford, wing commander.

Chapter
Thirty

I clasped my hand over my mouth as the bell rolled against my foot. I'd knocked the wing commander unconscious. Or at least, I *hoped* he was unconscious. He wasn't moving. Georgia shoved Bedford off her and then lay motionless. She made another raspy noise.

"Hold on. I'll get you some water." I grabbed my purse on the way to the bar, found my phone. My hands were shaking so hard it took me three tries to dial 911. I told the dispatcher we needed an ambulance and the police. I snapped the phone shut and grabbed a plastic cup, filled it with water, and went back to Georgia.

As I helped her take a small sip, I heard noises behind me. "That was fast," I said, but when I looked around it wasn't the police. A woman with tousled hair and perfect makeup walked into the Hole followed by a young man toting a huge camera.

Chelsea O'Mara. She took one look around and motioned with her hand for him to start rolling, but he already had the camera up on his shoulder and a light blazing.

Chelsea knelt down beside Georgia and asked if she was okay.

Georgia pointed toward Bedford and rasped, "Tried to kill me."

When it was apparent that was all Georgia could say, Chelsea swooped to me. "Did you see it?"

I asked a question of my own to avoid answering. "What are you doing here? Don't you work for Channel Two?"

She smiled. "I signed a new contract last week. Chelsea O'Mara with *24/7*."

Great. That was a national news magazine program that supposedly did investigative reports, but they tended toward sensationalism and trashy TV. "Georgia invited me here to document something big," Chelsea continued. "What's your part in this?"

"No comment," I said as several flight-suited guys appeared in the doorway, lugging pub bags.

Tommy Longfellow dropped his pub bag and smiled. "We heard the bell. Who's buying?"

The base fire department arrived next and efficiently put out the fire smoldering in the trash can. From the way they swarmed around General Bedford, I assumed he was still alive. The security police arrived, evicted Chelsea and her photographer, secured the area, and called Thistlewait and his colleagues.

Thistlewait shook his head and sighed when he arrived and saw me. After consulting with various groups working around the room, Thistlewait sat down beside me. The EMT had checked me over and pronounced me good to go. The security police had seated me at one of the tables on the far side of the room and told me to wait.

"Why am I not surprised to see you here?" Thistlewait asked as he pulled out a small notepad and pen.

I explained the video conference and he made a note. "Okay," he said. "Tell me what happened."

I recounted my talk with Mitch, the conversation with Georgia, my trip to Tessa's desk, and the scene on my return to the Hole. "He was strangling her, trying to kill her." I looked down at my hands firmly clasped together. I thought they had stopped shaking a few minutes ago, but I felt a tremor run through them again, so I held on tighter.

"I could only see his back. I hoped it wasn't—I mean, I wished the whole thing wasn't happening, but it was and—" I broke off, realizing I was shaking again. I took a deep breath. "I got the bell and hit him on the head." It sounded so simple phrased that way. Cut-and-dry, this is what I saw, this is what I did. None of the panic and fear in Georgia's face and in mine too, I'm sure.

Thistlewait flipped back a page in his notebook. "Georgia wasn't able to say much before the EMTs took her to the hospital, but she said Bedford walked in and he asked where the prayer carpet was." Thistlewait looked at me. "Know anything about that?"

Prayer carpet! Not an area rug or wall-to-wall carpet, but a prayer carpet.

I had to skate carefully here because I wasn't supposed to know about the phrase Penny had written in her journal. I said, "Georgia ripped a framed carpet off the wall to start the fire in the trash can. It looked like a prayer rug. She dumped it in the trash can, tossed the shredded posters on top, and lit it."

Thistlewait stood and consulted with a few people in a clump around the metal trash can. I moved to the edge of the circle.

A bald man wearing gloves extracted the poster shreds, then the blackened wooden frame. A woman photographed his every move and each object he removed.

She photographed the rug at the bottom of the trash can several times. The man reached in and pulled out the rug. It was blackened and the fringe was gone on one side, but the general shape was still there. He laid it down on a tarp beside the other ashes and blackened poster strips. More photographs. I was practically hopping from one foot to another. "Turn it over," I muttered. "We're not on the red carpet."

Thistlewait frowned, realized I was watching, and opened his mouth to order me back to the table, but the bald man turned the rug over. I let out a whoosh of breath. A bubble-wrapped bundle was secured to the back with tape. The man slit the plastic and delicately removed a book with a worn leather cover. They had to take more photos before he used a thin tool to gently inch the thick cover open. I saw faded strokes like the ones I'd shown to Marsali. "Send it to the lab," snapped Thistlewait.

"That's it. That's the letter," I said, stunned it had been hidden in the squadron. "That's why Bedford was here. He must have come to either check on the manuscript or retrieve it, so he could move it. When he saw the prayer carpet burning, he must have lost it and attacked Georgia."

I wondered if Penny had written *lie like a rug* during her "interview" with Bedford. It gave the phrase a kind of double meaning, a clue to the hiding place of the manuscript and her opinion of Bedford. She must have realized by that second interview that he was a liar.

Thistlewait escorted me back to the table and said, "Okay, explain that message you left on my voicemail."

"It's long and convoluted," I warned. "There's a picture on the squadron's bulletin board of a guy wearing a shell necklace, and it got me thinking about the jewelry, necklaces, stuff like that, and men. I remembered I'd seen a rosary made of castor beans at the Bedfords' house when

I was there organizing the closet. That fact clicked with a few other things like Clarissa said Bedford did all the cooking. He could have taken a few castor beans from the rosary, dipped them in chocolate, and slipped them into the gold foil bag Penny had in her backpack.

"Her car was broken into the week before she died. I bet that's when Bedford slipped the poison into the bag. She was glad the thief hadn't noticed her backpack in the trunk, but I bet that's what they were after, not her radio. Bedford may even have delegated that job to Rory. But what bothered me the most was Sam and Rory, sitting in jail, not talking. It would seem like one would rat out the other to get a deal. So I wondered, were they taking the fall for someone else?

"And I'd wondered where Penny's notes were from her interview with Bedford. You didn't find any, did you?"

Thistlewait stopped writing and shook his head. I leaned back in my chair, unclasping my hands. I felt better, steadier.

"She didn't take any," I said. "It wasn't an interview. I think she found the manuscript the week before she died. Jill Briman said Penny cleaned in here after Muffin Monday. She must have found the manuscript, but left it where it was. Maybe it was too delicate to move. She photographed it, then hung around the squadron to see what would happen. That was the day she had a video conference with Will. If Rory came in from his flight, stored some artifacts in the squadron, and dropped some off with Mr. Baseball Cap or Victor, Penny would have assumed Rory was the person who'd hidden the manuscript behind the carpet.

"She'd have gone to someone to turn him in because she was so passionate about artifacts. I don't think she'd have tackled Rory directly. It wasn't her way. She wasn't confrontational. She could have gone to Briman, but he's on his way to a new assignment and it's pretty much known that he's coasting along until it's time to PCS. Jill told me herself he doesn't want anyone or anything to rock the boat during the time he's got left. That left either the police or Bedford. She had a rapport with Bedford back in the fall, so she must have decided to go to him, thinking he'd handle it. But she was actually going to the head of the smuggling ring.

"She met with him in the middle of the week. His secretary said probably Wednesday. Bedford asked for a few days and Penny gave them to him. Marilyn thought Bedford was asking for a few days to find photos for the exhibit, but he probably convinced Penny he needed a few days to contact the right people. He may even have held her off by saying that the investigators wanted to let the operation go on to give them a chance to catch everyone involved.

"Instead of contacting anyone, Bedford got the ricin in Penny's chocolate-covered espresso beans and waited for her to die, but she didn't die. At least, not fast enough for Bedford. Maybe he didn't realize it could take several days for the poison to kill her. By then it was Monday and she was back for their second 'interview,' which wasn't really an interview. By then she must have suspected Bedford was in on it. That's why she downloaded the photos to her disk and hid it at my house. That's why she asked for my help, too. I'd dealt with you before."

I swallowed hard and said, "Since the castor beans hadn't worked, Bedford sent Rory to kill her Monday and make it look like a suicide. Neither of them, Rory or Bedford, would have known she was pregnant, and that fact, for Penny, would make a suicide attempt out of the question. Then just when Rory and Bedford thought they had their operation running smoothly again, Clarissa demanded a cut of the profits."

Thistlewait put his notebook away. "All right, Mrs. Avery. You were about fifteen minutes ahead of the undercover team tonight. Bedford and Victor Roth had been under surveillance since yesterday. Victor Roth gave them the slip, but they weren't about to let Bedford get away, too."

"So he's it? He's the top man in the smuggling ring?"

Thistlewait nodded and looked at his watch. "Yep. In the U.S., anyway. On the other side of the world, the net is closing on the other end of the smuggling operation right about now."

Relief, undiluted relief, flooded through me. It was over. Really.

As I grabbed the mail out of the mailbox a flash of movement caught my eye. Great. I stepped back inside and pulled on the screen, but Chelsea O'Mara was fast. She pounded up the steps and clamped her manicured hand around the screen door's frame so I couldn't close it. "Chelsea O'Mara with—"

"I know who you are. No comment." I pulled the screen almost closed, just sparing her pale pink nails. She yanked back and tilted a microphone toward the screen. "What do you think about the scandal at Greenly Air Force Base? How does it make you feel to know military officers were breaking the law and using taxpayer-funded equipment to smuggle goods and line their own pockets? Was your husband involved in the smuggling?"

I pulled hard on the screen. She yelped and jerked her hand away, then asked, "Did you know Senior Airman Rory Tyler personally?"

"No comment." I locked the screen and grabbed the heavy front door. The photographer was only a step behind her and zeroed in on me, flooding me with a spotlight.

"Did you know an anonymous source within the investigation says that Senior Airman Tyler and General Bedford flew together on several sorties and General Bedford caught Senior Airman Tyler trying to smuggle artifacts into the United States on military aircraft? Instead of turning him in, General Bedford took over the operation, expanded it? What do you think? Can you confirm that he was the mastermind of the scheme? Has your husband ever flown with Senior Airman Tyler or General Bedford?"

Did she want an answer? And to which part?

"What about our source's information that Bedford also masterminded the murder of Penny and recruited Senior Airman Tyler for that?"

"No comment." My phone rang and I closed the door. Her shrill voice continued, "Can you tell us how you felt when you found General Bedford strangling Lieutenant Lamar?"

I rolled my eyes and snapped the dead bolt into place. I hurried back inside to pick up the phone. Maybe it was the squadron with the details about when Mitch would be home.

"Mrs. Avery. Marsali here."

"Oh. Hi," I said, trying, but not succeeding in masking the disappointment in my voice.

"I thought you'd want to know the results of my examination of the codex," Marsali said, polite despite my lukewarm greeting.

"Yes, of course." Marsali had been called in for his expertise. "But codex? What is that?"

"It is what we call the earliest books," Marsali explained. "This codex contained the letters of Paul. Few codices contained the whole Bible, as we know it today. The early church grouped similar books together. For instance, the gospels were grouped and put into one codex and the

Pauline letters would be grouped and put into another. The thick cover protected the parchment pages from the fire. The parchment dates from the sixth century. Unfortunately, the ink on portions of the Laodicean letter is different from the ink on the rest of the document."

After a few seconds, I found my voice. "You mean it *was* a forgery?"

Marsali sighed. "Yes. It appears someone tampered with one of the letters to 'create' a lost letter from Paul. The modern ink coupled with the fact that there are no other known copies of this letter bring its authenticity into question. There are actually so many copies of the New Testament that date from the first century that it makes a 'new' letter suspect. The New Testament canon as we know it today was essentially agreed upon by the fourth century."

"So why would someone change the manuscript?"

"It is quite common for forgers to take genuine antiquities and 'make them famous.' Recently, the market for antiquities with a biblical connection has boomed. Do you remember the James Ossuary?"

"Um. No."

"A chalk box with an inscription indicating it had once held the bones of James, the brother of Jesus, caused quite an uproar. It was authenticated and sent off to Canada for an exhibit. Further examination concluded the box itself was an authentic artifact. However, the inscription was recent. The wonders of software. Scan genuine ancient texts, carve them onto ancient artifact, age the carving. Instant international sensation. Some experts still claim the box and carving are legitimate, but they are mostly the ones who authenticated it in the first place."

"But why would someone go to all that trouble to forge something so easily detected?" I asked.

"The excitement of a collector may override his caution. Perhaps the forger hoped for a quick sale and few questions."

So much death over something that wasn't even real.

Marsali continued, "Yesterday, I heard from a friend who is an archaeologist."

"I remember you mentioned him before. You said he would have called, if he'd heard about the manuscript."

Marsali chuckled. "He heard. That's why he called. And, for once, *I* was able to give *him* some news. That it was not authentic. He'd picked up on an interesting rumor, a lost manuscript from the first century had been found and smuggled out of Turkey. The current owner wanted to return it to Turkey. For the right price, of course."

"And I bet the price was high," I said.

"Astronomical. Apparently, General Bedford had dealings with, shall we say, disreputable elements in Turkey, people who accumulated artifacts and sent them here."

"Could those people who got the artifacts have tampered with the manuscript, to 'make it famous'?"

"Yes, or it could be he had someone who specialized in forging documents change it. After all, he would have to provide credentials, provenance, for the pieces he sold in the United States to prove their authenticity as well as make it appear they had been removed from Turkey in a legitimate way. But, back to the most interesting thing, Derrick heard that the Turkish government attempted to negotiate with the owner, but couldn't bring the price down. It was all very hush-hush. He's in contact with antiquities authorities in several countries and he says Turkey used a diplomatic trade delegation to try and reach the owner."

Diplomatic delegation. My thoughts flew back to the strange conversation I'd had with Elaina at the preview party. She was trying to track down the manuscript and thought that I had it. That was what she meant about "re-

turning to Turkey what belonged to Turkey." And I was sure
she'd been in my house and had lost a black bead as she
searched for the manuscript. I'd assumed Elaina and the
man who called and said he'd taken Rex were connected.
They weren't.

Marsali's words broke into my thoughts. "Ellie, are you
still there?"

"Yes. I'm sorry. It is just a lot to take in." I promised to
bring Mitch by to see Marsali as soon as Mitch got adjusted to our time zone. Then I hung up and flicked
through the mail. Credit card offers or bills. Except for
the last one, a glossy postcard with a crescent of clear
blue water rimmed in sand, palm trees, and hotels.

I flipped it over. COTE D'AZUR, stated the preprinted
caption on the back.

A scribbled line in the section opposite my address
said *Lovely here. Perhaps our paths will cross again. V.*

"How many minutes until Mitch's ETA?" Abby asked
with a smile.

"Okay, I'll stop checking my watch," I said. "Ninety-
four minutes." We strolled a few more paces down the
skywalk, which was lined with displays of student artwork. We were moseying through Frost Fest, working our
way back to the parking garage. We'd decided to burn
some time while we waited to go to the squadron and
meet Mitch's plane. Abby stooped to look at a portrait. I
ate another bite of one of Livvy's Goldfish crackers to
keep my stomach calm.

"Let's get a chicken salad sandwich at Lenny's on the
way to the squadron. I'm starving and I've been wanting
one of those."

"Okay. Oh, look." Abby leaned down to examine the

marker and crayon picture. "Jamie Planket. He's one of my students."

I studied it. "A city scene. It's good. I think I like looking at the kid's artwork better than the adult artwork. At least I don't feel bad if I don't understand it."

"Yeah, I know what you mean. And this is a great way to display their work."

I slipped my hand inside the pocket of my red fleece vest and pulled out my keys. I'd actually taken the time to coordinate my outfit and purse. I wore the vest over a white turtleneck with dark jeans and black boots. My purse was one of my favorites, a Coach bag weathered and softened almost to the texture of suede. I needed the comfort of something familiar today. I fingered my earrings and told my stomach to settle down. I was wearing earrings. I *was* nervous. Mitch and I hadn't seen each other in a while. It felt a bit like a date, that frisson of excitement mixed with edgy nerves. You'd think I'd just be happy he was coming back, but there was a hint of apprehension, too.

I swallowed a few more Goldfish and focused on the crowd around us. Frost Fest was in full swing. Drawn by the lure of little Johnny's picture or the art from the more mature artists, people had emerged from the warm burrows of their homes and offices. Crowds of people wandered through the skywalks, drifted into galleries, spun on the ice rink, or snapped up bargains.

We moved around one of the displays about Greenly Air Force Base and I recognized some of the photos I'd found for Hetty. DREAMS TAKE FLIGHT, read the banner on one side. GREENLY AFB—THE EARLY YEARS. Grainy black-and-white photos showed clean scrubbed faces, tailored uniforms, and a few buildings alongside a runway. I told Abby I'd catch up with her. I pushed the stroller through the next displays until the photos switched to color and the buildings mushroomed into Greenly's current military-industrial conglomeration. I stopped at a photo of a young man with a smirk on his face as he leaned on the wing of an airplane. The caption read FIRST LIEUTENANT JACKSON BEDFORD.

"I couldn't take it down. It would have left a blank spot."

I recognized the scratchy voice behind me. "Hello, Hetty," I said as I turned around. "Everything looks wonderful."

"Thanks. It's going really well. Good turnout. No major hitches. I was even able to reshuffle all the artwork we'd scheduled to show at Victor Roth's gallery." Hetty's gaze fixed on Bedford's photo. "It's just such a shame about Bedford. I can't quite believe it. You're acquainted with someone for years and think you know him." She shrugged. "But you don't."

"You've known him for years?" I asked.

"He and his first wife, Catherine, were acquaintances, not close friends. My husband retired from the Air Force ten years ago. We were stationed in Hawaii with Catherine and Jackson about fifteen years ago. Of course, I knew Catherine liked to collect mosaics."

Why hadn't I asked Hetty more questions about Bedford? I'd assumed that she didn't know him that well because she wasn't military. Hetty continued, "Now I know he was a good actor. I never realized it was him collecting, not Catherine. He always told me it was for Catherine and I just assumed he'd want nothing to do with it, except for her." Hetty shook her head. "Catherine told me he was an actor in high school. In the drama club. And his voice, so smooth and rich. Why didn't I remember that? He'd trained to be a sports reporter, but then he learned to fly and loved it. That was the end of reporting. Or that was the story Catherine told me. I think it was probably true. I don't trust anything Jackson told me."

A young man edged up to the group and said, "Excuse me, Mrs. Sullivan, the newspaper would like a few quotes."

Hetty left and I went to find Abby, but I turned a corner and found Thistlewait instead. He was crouched down beside a boy of about three, who was pointing to a photo of a B-2 Bomber. A woman with dark hair and eyes pushed a stroller up to them and stopped. "Honey, did you leave the diaper bag in the car?"

Thistlewait had a family? A wife and a kid? I felt like a kid who'd unexpectedly met a teacher in the grocery store and was shocked that teachers existed outside school grounds. Thistlewait noticed me and introduced his wife and son, Amy and Joshua.

"Glad I ran into you here. I've got something to give you," he said. "I'll get it from the car and be right back." He turned to Amy. "I'll get the diaper bag, too."

"Okay, we'll be down at the sandwich shop on the first floor. Nice to meet you," she said to me.

Amy led their son away and I said, "Well, Abby and I are leaving. If you're in the same parking garage we are, we'll go with you."

It was a fairly silent trip to the cars. Abby had a few issues with Thistlewait left over from our first encounter with him. Suspecting people of murder must really put a damper on Thistlewait's socializing. When we reached the parking garage, Abby said she'd see me at the squadron and headed to her car. We'd driven in separate cars because I knew Mitch would want to go home as soon as he landed and Abby had promised to stay and help clean up the spread of finger foods and drinks that the spouses were providing for the returning crews and their families.

Thistlewait returned with a diaper bag and a brown paper bag. "Thought you might like this back."

I opened the brown bag and pulled out my answering machine. Thistlewait continued, "We got the recording transferred, so I can release this to you."

"Thanks."

"And you'll be glad to know that Rory and Sam are talking."

"Really? What are they saying?"

"Basically, they're laying out the hierarchy of the smuggling ring. Bedford was in charge. He delegated to Rory and Rory hired Sam to harass you. Sam took Doom along with him."

"Hmm. An org chart for criminals."

"And we found Bedford's stash of artifacts. He's got a house in Arizona. Flagstaff. Rory told us Bedford had him and Victor sell most everything, but occasionally he'd pull something out of the shipment for himself. There's a third garage out back of his house down there, climate controlled and filled with medieval and Renaissance artifacts."

"Wow. Even though he'd pulled the manuscript, the rumors were already out there. That's why Victor told Ballard he might have a manuscript for her," I said. And why the Turkish government was trying to track it down, too.

"Well, I've got to go."

"Thanks. Enjoy Frost Fest," I said.

I was about to step into the Cherokee when I swung around and yelled, "Hey, I'd like my vacuum back, too!"

"I'm working on it," he shouted over the roofs of the cars.

I watched the huge gray plane glide down the runway. I felt the familiar clench of my stomach and I steeled myself. *Don't throw up. You don't have time.* What did I have? A seventy-two-hour flu? Maybe nerves. That was probably it.

"Daddy's almost home," I said to Livvy as the plane began its slow journey down the taxiway. "Daddy flies that plane. He's inside it, right now." Livvy's forehead wrinkled, like she wasn't sure if she could trust what I said.

"I know, sweetie. I'll believe it when I see him, too."

The gigantic aircraft lumbered along. Tiny figures waved from the windows. It was hard to believe Mitch, my Mitch, flew that monstrosity. It was a part of his life remote from me. The first plane had already taxied. The spouses around me shouted, some waved small flags.

Livvy squirmed and I held her closer. "Just a few more minutes." The wind bit into my eyes as Mitch's plane stopped.

"We're waiting for the air stairs," Jeff informed the spouses and kids.

"Where are they? Why don't they have them ready? It always takes forever for the air stairs," I snapped, but Jeff smiled back at me. Maybe he understood the tension I felt, even though he was usually on the other side of the situation.

After five minutes Tommy shouted, "They're almost done with customs."

I tightened Livvy's hat and tucked Pink Girl down in her pocket. I exchanged glances with Abby and Jeff.

He said, "It really was a good system they had set up. Customs never looks at anything when we land. I never have to open a bag."

Abby squinted at the last plane as it touched down at the far end of the runway. "So how was Rory involved? I still didn't get the whole story."

"Rory brought back antiquities and had his courier,

Sam Fields—I still think of him as Mr. Baseball Cap—transfer them to Victor Roth's gallery, until it closed. Victor would sell them himself or, at least once, Rory had Clarissa deliver the items to buyers. Victor must have felt investigators were getting too close, so he shut down the gallery. But he still had to meet Rory to pick up the last shipment since his go-between, Mr. Baseball Cap, was in jail. That was the time I saw Rory at the squadron and followed them back to Rory's house where Victor and Rory checked the shipment and then Victor took part of it with him."

"I still can't believe—"

"Okay!" Colonel Briman's shout interrupted Abby. "Red line is down!"

We surged out across the red boundary line and onto the flight line as the crews trotted down the stairs. We pushed through the crowd of women, kids, and flyers who looked oddly out of place in their desert flight suits of light brown. Mitch and I finally, literally, bumped into each other.

"Welcome home." We kissed and Mitch took Livvy into his arms. Her brow furrowed for a few seconds. Mitch took off his hat and she grinned.

Mitch hugged me again. "It's so good to be back. Let me get my bags."

Mitch disappeared into the throng of people and emerged a few minutes later, pulling his bag. We trudged up the incline to the squadron and entered the Hole.

Jeff clapped Mitch on the back. "Good to see you, man."

"You too. Hey, what happened to the posters?" Mitch asked, nodding at the stripped wall, now decorated only with pin holes and scuff marks.

"Georgia. It's a long story. I'll tell you on the way home."

"Took matters into her own hands, did she?" Mitch guessed.

"Something like that," I said. What would happen to the decorations? Would the guys get their bikini babes back? I had no idea, but it probably depended on the next squadron commander.

Abby waved at the spread of cookies, sandwiches, and drinks on the bar. "Are you hungry? Want some food?"

"Are you kidding? I want to go home," Mitch said.

"All right, but first, we've got something to tell you," Abby said. "We're pregnant!"

Congratulations went on around me. A few things snapped into place with Abby's words: the flu going around, being tired, and my craving for a chicken salad sandwich from Lenny's. I hadn't wanted one of those in forever.

"What's wrong? You look kind of dazed," Mitch said.

I dropped down on the couch as the realization hit me. "I don't have the flu. I'm pregnant!"

An Everything In Its Place Tip for Organized Closets

Organizing products that multifunction in closets:

- Over-the-door clear plastic shoe organizers—great for everything from shoes to gloves to scarves and belts.
- Garden/Garage Organizer—originally designed to hold rakes and shovels, these waist-high rectangular organizers with a grid of openings are also great for storing sporting equipment like bats, hockey sticks, and tennis rackets.
- Wall hook sets—usually designed for rakes and

shovels, these sets of hooks come in various lengths and can be mounted in coat closets and used for storing sporting equipment. Use wall hooks in broom closets for mops, brooms, and vacuum cleaner hose storage.

- Belt hangers—use the hooks spaced along the bottom crossbar to hold belts, ties, or necklaces.
- Turntable or lazy Susan—these are staples of kitchen corner cabinets, but they work equally as well in closets where they make finding less frequently used items easy.

Glossary

AFB—Air Force Base
AR—Air Refueling
BX—Base Exchange, small department store on base
Blues—uniform of light blue shirt, dark blue pants
BDU—Battle Dress Uniform, camouflage
C bag—bag with chemical defense gear, sometimes called mobility bag
DV—Distinguished Visitor
ETA—Estimated Time of Arrival
HQ—Headquarters
O Club—Officers' Club
OSI—Office of Special Investigations
PA—Public Affairs
PCS—Permanent Change of Station, moving
Pubs—Air Force publications about aircraft, flight manuals
SWA—Southwest Asia
Sortie—A flight
Squad—squadron
Regs—regulations, rules
TDY—Temporary Duty, a short trip

Acknowledgments

I really don't know where to begin. I'll start with my agent, Faith Hamlin, because she helped me launch this journey as an author. I appreciate her vision and persistence more than I can say. My editor, Michaela Hamilton, has made the Mom Zone series a reality and made the publishing process understandable and truly enjoyable. Monica Premo of Practically Perfect gave me insight into the life of a professional organizer and some great ideas. A thank-you just doesn't seem adequate to my family and friends, who have encouraged me in my writing for years. To my extended family, the Honderichs, the Rosetts, and the Suttons—you rock! Thanks for celebrating Ellie's adventures with me. Glenn, Lauren, and Jonathan have endured weekends away, significantly lower housecleaning standards, and a wife and mom often lost in the fog of plotting. Thanks for putting up with me. And thanks and gratitude to military spouses who know firsthand that staying home is a killer, but handle deployments with aplomb.

Turn the page for a sneak preview of
Sara Rosett's new Mom Zone mystery,
GETTING AWAY IS DEADLY,
available in Kensington hardcover in
April 2008!

Chapter
One

66 **N**ow, if you'll follow me, we'll go down to the crypt," the tour guide said.

I let our small group flow past me as I waited for my best friend, Abby Dovonowski, to catch up with me. "You know, if everything had gone according to my plan, right now Mitch and I would be lounging on a private beach on Saint John, working on our tans. But instead, I'm about to tour a crypt. Kind of ironic, isn't it?"

Abby pawed through her huge purse and didn't look up as she said, "Why did you think things would go according to your plan?"

"You're right. I forgot about Murphy's Law as it applies to military spouses, 'If you plan it, they will ruin it.' "

"Well, at lease we've got FROT," Abby said as she unzipped a compartment inside her purse and dug around it.

"Yeah, where would we be without FROT?" I asked.

"At home in Vernon, Washington, where it's raining.

Again. For the record-breaking thirty-fifth day in a row. I checked the weather this morning."

"I guess you're right. I'll take Washington D.C.'s humidity and sun along with FROT over rain and being at home."

We shared a smile over the acronym of the class our husbands were taking. The military has to have an acronym for everything, so Foreign Reciprocity Officer Training was shortened to FROT. Originally, Mitch and I had planned to go on a Caribbean vacation after he returned from his Middle East deployment. I had the airline tickets, a room reserved at a secluded beachfront cottage, the grandparents lined up to watch our daughter Livvy, and a reservation at a kennel for our dog, Rex, where he'd be so fawned over and catered to that he probably wouldn't even miss us.

Then Mitch returned from his deployment and learned in his absence he'd been "volunteered" to attend a week-long training school. Mitch could have begged and pleaded and tried to get out of it, but since his squadron commander had handpicked Mitch to attend the school he felt like he had to go. The fact that he'd forgotten to turn in his leave paperwork had an impact on the decision, too.

So what was I going to do? Cancel each carefully planned detail? Nope. I exchanged my airline tickets and mentally kissed my days at the beach good-bye. The only redeeming thing about the whole vacation switch—besides the fact the military was picking up the tab for the hotel room—was that Abby's husband Jeff had been picked to be the alternate to the FROT program and he had to attend as well. Since the trip fell during Abby's spring break from teaching third grade, she'd promptly made airline reservations, too.

Abby repositioned her purse on her shoulder. "Do you have anything to eat? You've always got chocolate. I'm starving."

"Of course, I've got chocolate, but we can't eat in the Capitol!" I whispered back as we navigated around another clump of people with their heads tilted back to gaze at the dome mural. I always had Hershey's Kisses. I was addicted to them.

"Why not?"

"Abby, this is the *Rotunda*. We can't eat in here." The chamber echoed with the voices of the guides and the shuffle of feet as tourists made their way around the circular room, studying the oil paintings.

"I'm starving," Abby repeated. "I have to eat. I'm pregnant. It's my right."

After struggling for months, Abby was finally pregnant and she was playing it for all it was worth. It was a bit different for me, even though I was pregnant, too. Life with a preschooler tended to make everything else fade into the background. Sometimes I'd gotten so wrapped up in parenting Livvy, our almost-two-year-old, that I'd actually forgotten I was pregnant again. Well, except for the nausea. That's hard to ignore, but, thankfully, that stage seemed to be over. I rubbed my slightly protruding belly. I hoped this mini-vacation would help me tune into my pregnancy. I felt a tad guilty that I didn't think about our little Nathan more. Abby looked at my purse with a longing expression. "Come on. Why can't we eat in here?"

"The sense of history. The artwork." I nodded at the center of the Rotunda as we walked. "Presidents lay in state here. It would be disrespectful."

"Yeah, you're right," Abby conceded.

As we reached the lower level of the Capitol, Abby and I merged back with our sight-seeing group made up of several Air Force wives from different bases whose husbands were also in Washington, D.C. for FROT training.

Our guide said, "Forty Doric columns of brown sandstone support the Rotunda directly above this room. Does anyone know what the star at the center of the floor represents?"

The gaze of our Capitol tour guide, a young woman in her early twenties, roved over our group, trying to avoid making eye contact with the petite, dark-headed woman planted directly in front of her. The rest of us were clueless, so our guide said, "Nadia, I bet you know. You've known everything else."

"Oh, I do." Nadia bounced with excitement and her dark hair bobbed against her cheekbones. "It's the exact center of Washington, D.C." Her Capitol brochure crumpled as she squeezed it. "The very heart of Pierre L'Enfant's grand plan. The diagonals that divide the city into quadrants originate from *right here*."

Our guide gave a perfunctory smile. "That's correct. As you can see, there aren't any tombs in this crypt and it has never been used as a burial chamber. It was intended to be the final resting place for George Washington, but his family buried him at Mount Vernon instead. Today, the space is used for exhibits. Feel free to take your time looking around. This concludes the tour. I'll leave you to explore." She gave us directions on how to exit the Capitol and we dispersed around the room.

Nadia headed to the gift shop, which was really just a few glass display cabinets stocked with postcards and touristy items set up on one side of the room. Abby and I set off on a slow circuit of the room. I loved reading the small print inside the exhibit cases. Abby indulged me until another member of our group, Irene, joined us. She pushed her subtly highlighted blond bangs off her forehead and checked her watch. "Shouldn't we be going? Where is everyone?" Irene had taken on the role of den mother. Abby and I knew Irene because she and her husband, Grant, been stationed at the same base as Abby and

I, Greenly in Washington state, until a few months ago when Grant got a new assignment to Alaska.

Irene shoved a plastic bag of postcards and souvenir books into her massive tote bag, which was emblazoned with a flag and the words, "Military spouse: the toughest job you'll ever love." She pulled the lapels of her black wash-and-wear travel blazer together over her busty figure and looked around the room. "Nadia's in line to check out and there's Gina, leaning on a pillar." Irene checked her watch again. "I'll go round everyone up. Don't you think Wellesley will be waiting for us outside by the reflecting pool by now?"

Wellesley Warner was our tour guide for the D.C. area. She'd handed us off at the Capitol to their expert guides and told us where to meet her when the tour was over. Some companies had tour programs for spouses who accompanied their significant other to conferences and training programs. Not the military. An expense like that would be an easy target for complaints about waste, fraud, and abuse. Can't have our tax dollars going to entertain the wives, so our group had pooled our money and hired Wellesley, the owner of Inside Look Tours, a "boutique" tour company, which specialized in small tour groups for people who didn't want to spend their time on a bus, lumbering from one site to another.

Irene bustled everyone together and we emerged from the Capitol on the West side. We paused at the balustrade to take in the view down the Mall, the grassy open space lined on each side with the Smithsonian museums. Straight ahead, the Washington Monument rose vibrantly white against the blue sky. I knew from studying the map earlier in the day that the Lincoln Memorial was directly beyond the Washington Monument. "I love the symmetry of this place," I said.

Abby snorted. "You would. You like everything lined up in a row. Neat and squared away."

Gina Trovato was on the other side of me. Abby noticed her puzzled look and leaned over to explain. "Ellie's a professional organizer. She helps people get things in order. Her business is called Everything In Its Place."

Gina smiled. "Too bad we aren't at the same base. You could experiment on me since I'm chronically unorganized. If you could help me, you could help anyone." She turned back to the view and said, "It is awesome, though. Even someone as messy as I am can appreciate good lines when I see them."

"What do you do? You're in Oregon, right?" I asked.

"I'm a social worker at a hospital in Portland." Gina leaned her bony arms on the balustrade. She looked a bit like she'd been run through a wringer and had all the color and contour squeezed out of her body. She was tall and flat-chested with gray eyes, pale skin, and long straight hair that was somewhere between a washed-out blond and a dingy brown. The only exception to the linear lines of her body was her slightly upturned nose.

"We're not that far away from you. We're at Vernon in Eastern Washington state. At least for now," I said.

Gina turned towards me. "Due for a move?"

"Yes. Well, not for the next six months or so, but we should be hearing pretty soon. We've turned in the dream sheet and now we're waiting."

"Dream sheet. That's an accurate name, if there ever was one," Gina said with a laugh. A dream sheet was a form that Mitch listed the bases where he'd like to be stationed. It was called a dream sheet because that was what it was: basically, a dream. The Air Force pretty much sent you where they wanted you. If it happened to coincide with your dream sheet, you were lucky.

Gina continued, "Not that you're going to get it, but what did you put down as your first choice?"

"Hawaii. We know it's a long shot, but after the winters

in Washington state we're ready for sunshine. Of course, we'll probably get one of the other bases down the list, perhaps one in Kansas or Georgia. Abby and her husband are up, too. We're hoping we'll get the same base again."

"Okay, everyone." A loud, perky voice rang out. "Time for a snappy."

"Not another picture," Gina muttered. "She's got to have taken at least fifty already."

Nadia must have sensed a mutiny brewing because she said, "Come on, just one more. Last group picture of the day, I promise. I just have to have this for my scrapbook."

"All right, then let's get it over with," Gina said. We all swung around with our backs to the view and Nadia recruited another tourist to take our picture. We squished together and grimaced.

"Now, that wasn't so bad, was it?" Nadia asked as we went down the steps to the Mall.

I heard Gina mutter, "Not if it shuts you up."

We made our way down to the Capitol Reflecting Pool through the beautifully landscaped grounds. I wondered how much money was spent on maintaining the grounds. Did it rival the defense budget?

"Where is Wellesley?" Irene asked, scanning the clumps of people gathered around the pool. Abby plopped down on a low wall and I joined her. I pulled some energy bars and several Hershey's Kisses out of my Coach backpack purse and handed them to Abby.

"Ah. Nourishment." She ripped open the bar and downed it in three bites. I offered a bar to Gina, but she shook her head. Abby crumpled the wrapper and said, "You have to teach me all this mom stuff, like carrying food in your purse. I'm going to be so toast as a mom."

"You're going to do fine," I said and pulled out my cell phone. I'd turned it off during the tour.

Two messages. The first one was from my parents'

phone number. They were taking care of Livvy during my
week away with Mitch. I punched the numbers for voicemail and I tensed, waiting to hear Livvy crying. To put it
mildly, she'd had some issues with separation anxiety. I'd
even debated canceling my trip several times. My mom's
voice came on the line. "Hi, honey."

No sounds of screaming in the background. I relaxed a
little.

My mom said, "Sorry we missed your call. We were in
the backyard. Livvy loves the sandbox. She's doing great.
We're having a wonderful time. Don't try to call us back
for awhile. We're going to the mall and the toy store.
Bye." Okay. No crying. That was good. Wasn't it? I had a
hard time believing Livvy wasn't in the throws of separation anxiety, but my mom wouldn't lie to me. *Would she?
No. Of course not.* I just hoped all Livvy's new toys and
clothes would fit in our suitcases for out flight back to
Vernon.

I checked our little group. Irene paced to the edge of
the reflecting pool and scanned the Mall for Wellesley.
Abby and Gina were talking, and Nadia was busy snap-
ping pictures of the Capitol dome. A noisy group of teenagers swarmed around the pool. Their matching green
T-shirts proclaimed they were from Crocket Middle
School. We were engulfed in a chattering, giggling, hor-
mone-energized crowd.

My next voicemail message came on the line and I
heard my sister-in-law's breezy voice. "Hi, Ellie! Great to
hear you guys are in town. Give me a call back and we'll
get together. I know you said you had a free afternoon
today, but I can't get away. I'm babysitting the Little Terror. She's sleeping now, thank goodness, but call me
later."

Abby saw me close my phone. "So did you hear from

your sister-in-law? Are you getting together with her this afternoon?"

"Yes. That was Summer, but she's babysitting for her landlady."

Abby's eyebrows crinkled down into a frown. "Isn't she a little old to be babysitting?"

I smiled. "Not if you're babysitting for your landlord, who happens to be a high-powered Washington lobbyist. Summer figures it can't hurt her chances of getting a job once she graduates in May." Of course, that was assuming that Summer actually graduated.

Mitch's youngest sister was as flighty as a hummingbird and changed majors as fast as some teens changed their shoes. I was amazed that her hodgepodge of college credits were going to add up to a degree in political science. Even with her short-lived detour to beauty school a few months ago, she'd pulled everything together this spring and was about to get her degree.

The green mass of teenagers departed and I recognized Wellesley striding across the Mall, her black skirt rippling around her legs. The name Wellesley conjured images of headbands and preppy plaid. Wellesley had a headband, but it was a long white scarf that held back an explosion of dark corkscrew curls. Definitely no plaid for her. She went for the minimalist look. Today she wore a white sleeveless shirt and black flared skirt with tiny white embroidered dots. The ends of the scarf fluttered behind her.

"And what about Debbie? Has she checked in again?" Abby asked.

"No. And she only called to make sure I made it to town."

Abby leveled a look at me. "And to make sure you had his phone number. And again to make sure you didn't lose it. And a third time to make sure you didn't forget to call him."

I sighed and pulled out another Hershey's Kiss for me. "I know she's being kind of annoying, but this is really important to her. She's always wanted to know what happened to her dad in Korea. It's a taboo subject. Her mom won't talk about it. No one else in the family will either, so this guy, MacInally, might be her only chance to find out about her dad. The whole situation is kind of sad. Since she couldn't get any details out of anyone in the family she used to make up stories about what happened to him, like that he died rescuing a family from a fire, stuff like that. Once, she told me that she used to pretend that he wasn't really dead, that he'd somehow escaped death and was a spy and it was too dangerous for him to return home."

"That *is* sad, but I still don't see why this guy who knew her dad doesn't just e-mail her or call her," Abby said.

"I know. I don't understand it either, but I'm doing it as a favor for Debbie. She used to babysit me when I was a kid. I idolized her. She was my cool older cousin. She was nice to me at family get-togethers. She didn't make a big deal about me following her around and asking her a thousand questions. She even sat at the little kids table with me and my brother when she could have sat with the grown-ups." I popped the Hershey's Kiss in my mouth.

"Okay. Okay. But don't you think you're taking on too much? This is supposed to be a vacation, remember? Well, a vacation for us, even if Jeff and Mitch are working during the day," Abby said.

I swallowed the chocolate and said, "No. I have to see Summer. It would be rude not to stop in and see her while we're so close. And the thing with Debbie—that won't take long—a couple of hours. Just a quick meeting. Besides, it means a lot to her. It's the least I can do for some-one who endured the rickety card table with me at Thanksgiving when she didn't have to."

My phone rang in my hand. It was the same Texas area code as my parents' house, but not their number.

"Ellie! It's Debbie. Did you meet him yet?" A mixture of expectation and fear mingled in my cousin's voice.

"No. It's tomorrow," I said as I watched Wellesley's ap-proach. I raised my hand to wave at her. She'd almost reached the reflecting pool when a man joined her. He was shorter than her and had black hair and heavy dark eyebrows. I lowered my arm and said to Debbie, "I'm going to meet MacInally in the hotel lobby tomorrow for breakfast. I promise I'll call you as soon as I talk to him."

"Okay." Debbie's voice was strained. "I've waited thirty-plus years to find out what happened. I guess I can wait one more day."

"How's Morgan?" I asked as I watched the man and Wellesley. He pulled at the neck of his thin white T-shirt, which distorted the logo of a tree and the outline of the Capitol above the words Capitol Landscaping. His dark green pants were paint-splattered and had muddy patches on the knees. He shifted his weight from one heavy work boot to the other as he talked rapidly to Wellesley. She shook her head and stepped away. He caught her arm and spun her back towards him.

Debbie said, "Itchy and mortified. Thirteen is a diffi-cult age without the chicken pox. I still can't believe she got it even after she'd had the shot. I'm so—ugh—so dis-appointed I can't be there, but I can't leave Morgan right now and I can't wait any longer. I *have* to know what MacInally has to say," Debbie said.

I divided my attention between Debbie's voice and Wellesley's encounter with the man. The rough way he'd jerked her arm worried me a bit, but she didn't seem to be bothered by the manhandling. She tugged her arm away, said a few terse words, and strode away from him.

I tuned into the silence on the phone line and said cautiously, "Debbie, MacInally may not know anything." Debbie had such high hopes for this meeting, but I was afraid I might not bring much more back than photos of her dad's war buddy.

The dark-headed man on the other side of the reflecting pool watched Wellesley walk away, his face under his heavy eyebrows expressionless. After a long moment, he turned and walked in the other direction. I expected him to join a landscape crew that was trimming bushes, but he passed them and continued on towards the Washington Monument. "Debbie, I've got to go. Our tour guide is here. I'll call you as soon as I talk to him, I promise."

Wellesley spotted Irene and they walked over together. Wellesley didn't seem shaken by the encounter with the man. She asked, "How's my band of mothers doing?" When she'd found out that morning that both Abby and I were pregnant and that everyone else in the group either had kids or step-kids, she'd dubbed our group the band of mothers. It was a cute designation, but I thought she might not think we were so endearing after a few more days of constant pit stops for bathroom breaks since one of the less exciting parts of being pregnant was the need to keep within sight of a restroom at all times.

She asked about our tour of the Capitol and then said, "Your afternoon is on your own. There's a nice exhibit at the natural history museum." She handed out brochures. "But we're going there tomorrow, so you might want to wait. If you want to see more of our founding documents, visit the National Archives, across the Mall."

"I'm ready for a nap and room service," Abby said.

"Okay, I'll head back, too," I said. Maybe Abby was right and I was trying to squeeze too much into my vacation itinerary. Lounging around the pool or even lounging around my hotel room for a few hours completely alone sounded pretty good. It might not be the Caribbean, but at least it was a four-star hotel.

"I think I'll go to the Library of Congress," Irene said as she studied the map.

Gina and Nadia agreed they were ready for a break, so Wellesley gave Irene directions to the Library of Congress and then walked with the rest of us back to the Metro stop.

The day had started out a little on the cool side, but now Washington's famous humidity was creeping in. By the time we reached the escalators and descended into the cave-like darkness of the Metro stop I was glad to get out of the sun. We inserted our Metro cards into the machines connected to the turnstiles and pushed through them. Then we took the second escalator down to the platform. It was quiet, almost peaceful, under the barrel-vaulted ceiling, except for the occasional shrieks coming from two kids running in tight circles at the far end of the platform. They were so close to the edge it made me a little nervous. Nadia had her camera poised in front of her as she took more "snappies," but she didn't ask us to pose for her, which was a good thing since I thought Gina might yell at her if Nadia told her she wanted another snappy.

Wellesley stood beside me as we waited for the train, so I asked, "Do you have another tour this afternoon?"

"No. I'm heading back to my office to work on my other business."

"You run two businesses?" I asked.

"With the cost of living in this place, you've got to have two incomes to live here. Unfortunately, I'm not married so I have to bring in both of them," she said with a smile.

"What's your other business?"

"Household Helper. It's more of a resource for people looking for a gardener or a housecleaner. We've got some handymen, too, for small remodeling jobs. If someone wants to update their bathroom—and believe me, there's a lot of that going on around here with people buying older homes for the inside the beltway location and fixing them up—but they don't want to pay a contractor I've got tile guys, plumbers, and someone who can hang cabinets. All with references and a record of actually showing up for work."

"Wow. Your clients must love that," I said.

A new group of people arrived on the platform, led by two women, both in suits and heels, a marked contrast to the usual tourist uniform of T-shirts and shorts. The shorter woman in a navy suit lugged a load of equipment, including a video camera with the name of a local news station on the side. She extended the legs of a tripod and said nervously, "This look okay? I'll set up as close to the tracks as I can, all right?" The other taller woman wore a cream suit that complemented her blond hair twisted up in a chignon. She stalked over to the edge of the platform and positioned herself in front of the camera while dialing her cell phone. She pressed the phone to her ear, then barked, "Speak up. The connection's bad." After a few seconds she said, "You're cutting in and out. Call me back in fifteen minutes. We should be done here by then." Frowning, she ended the call, pulled off a lanyard with an ID tag dangling from it, and tossed the lanyard and the phone at a man standing off to the side.

It's funny how group dynamics play out, even in impromptu groups, like random people waiting for a train. I realized the news camera had the attention of everyone on the platform, including the kids at the far end. Since I'd just had some less than pleasant encounters with the media, I was glad the camera wasn't focused on me.

The reporter threaded a small microphone under the blond woman's collar and stepped back. "Okay, we're ready." A bright light attached to the camera clicked on and, just as quickly, a smile lit the woman's face, replacing her frown. The reporter said, "Ms. Archer, tell us why the Women's Safety Initiative is so crucial."

"We're all concerned about safety. Our nation's security as been our top priority recently, but we can't overlook individual safety, especially for women. Women must be safe in their homes, at work, and on public transportation, like the Metro. That's why the Women's Advancement Center has worked closely with Senators McKay and—"

There was a burst of noise from the top of the escalator and we all turned to look. Another group of teenagers, this time wearing dark blue shirts, flooded down the escalator in a gush of chatter and the flutter of miniskirts.

I noticed the lights in the floor of the platform near the edge of the track flicker on and off, a signal the train was arriving.

Ms. Archer snapped at the man holding her phone, "Tell them to keep it down. We're recording," but her voice was overpowered by a high-pitched shout from a girl in a blue T-shirt. "Here comes one. We can make it, if we hurry!"

The train sped into the station and a whoosh of air swept across the platform, stirring my hair as a scream rang out. I thought it was one of the teenagers horsing around, but then little waves of panic rippled across the platform.

People started shouting. Someone yelled, "Call 911." Suddenly, we were pushed forward. "What happened? What's wrong?" A few people pushed back, fighting against the surging tide. The noise level on the platform swelled. "An accident."

I heard someone crying.

". . . horrible . . ."

"Can you believe—"

The reporter disconnected the camera from the tripod, yanked the microphone off the other woman, and pushed into the fray.

A woman behind me said, "Oh, God. I hope it's not terrorism. Is there a bomb?"

The whole platform descended into chaos as the word "terrorism" was repeated. We all turned and ran for the escalators. Hands pushed at my back. I looked around for Abby, but didn't see her. I was caught in the horde of people in the bottleneck at the foot of the escalator. The tide of people shoved forward and smashed me against the wall of the escalator. *Trampled. I'm going to be trampled.* The crowd surged again. The sense of fear permeated the air like the heavy stench of sweat. *I'm going to be crushed.*

"Wait! Calm down!" A man had jumped up on one of the benches. "Someone fell off the platform." The crowd swirling around him slowed. The pressure against my back eased. "It's okay," he repeated. "Slow down. No terrorism. Someone fell. It was just an accident."

An Everything In Its Place Tip for an Organized Trip

Travel planning

The Internet is a great place to start your research for a trip. Major cities usually have websites with extensive information. Some sites like TripAdvisor.com and IgoUgo.com have firsthand traveler reviews of hotels, restaurants, and tourist sights.

Get More Mysteries by
Leslie Meier